M000275354

Pride and Persistence

By Jeanna Ellsworth

Copyright 2014 by Jeanna Ellsworth and Hey Lady Publications
www.heyladypublications.com
Cover Design by Kara Watkins, Idio Designs
Cover Illustration by Rebecca Watkins
Cover Copyright 2014 Jeanna Ellsworth and Hey Lady
Publications

All rights reserved. No part of this book may be reproduced or
transmitted in any form either by mechanical or electronic
means including information storage and retrieval systems—
except in case of brief quotations embedded in critical articles or
reviews—without the permission in writing from the author.

Check out Jeanna Ellsworth's blog and other books by Hey Lady
Publications: https://www.heyladypublications.com
Follow Jeanna Ellsworth on Twitter: @ellsworthjeanna
Like her on Facebook:
https://www.facebook.com/Jeanna.Ellsworth
Or like the book's Facebook page:
www.facebook.com/PrideandPersistence
Or connect by email:
Jeanna.ellsworth@yahoo.com

This book is a work of fiction and any resemblances to actual
events or persons, living or dead, are purely coincidental
because this work is a product of the author's imagination. The
opinions expressed in this manuscript are solely the opinions of
the author.

Acknowledgements

A special thanks to my daughters, Paige, Madison, and Avery, who giggled with me at the funny parts, cried with me at the sad parts, and swooned with me when the moment was just right. I can never fully express the love I have for you. You are my inspiration.

Thank you to my editor, Katrina Beckstrand, whose patience and gentle guidance made this work possible. As the editing progressed, I learned to value her incredible talent to help me say exactly what I wanted in just the right way. She made my favorite scenes perfect, and her hours of devotion did not go unnoticed.

I also want to thank my betas, Beth Cochran and Colleen Lane, who saw my writing in its raw form but loved it anyway.

Thank you to my sisters, who have inspired and motivated me in this particular work of fiction. To Betsy, who loved me enough to laugh with me and helped me find humor when I needed it most. To Donna, whose loyalty has no boundaries and whose enthusiasm for each chapter kept my muse strong. To KaraLynne, who brightened my day when she deemed this book her favorite. Thank you all for everything.

To my parents, Ron and Patsy, who just celebrated their 50th wedding anniversary. They held me when I cried, had faith in me when I felt I did not deserve it, and taught me what a healthy romance should look like. Examples like them are what made this work more than just a figment of my imagination. I can never thank them enough for standing by me through my storms.

And finally, to Jane Austen and to all the JAFF community and authors who feed my addiction to 200-year-old characters, thank you. Without your friendship and the hours of entertainment available with a simple click of the button, I may very well have been out of debt by now. But, as my fellow JAFF addicts will agree, debt is acceptable for three things: a modest house, a working vehicle, and an overflowing nightstand.

Dedication

To the patients, families, and staff of all Neurological ICUs: may you find healing and laughter as you bravely face impossible situations. You are always in my prayers.

I dedicate this book to Madison. I love your spark, your spirit, your devotion, and your heart. You are more beautiful inside than out; I hope you realize what a compliment that is.

I also dedicate this book to all the single mothers out there who struggle to find time to fit romance into their lives (apart from the pile of novels on their nightstands and their overloaded Kindles). Writing a romance novel as a single lady is very much like letting someone read your journal. So kick up your heels, procure a good deal of chocolate, and fall in love again with my version of the perfect, yet charmingly-imperfect, gentleman.

CHAPTER 1

"She said no. Quite an emphatic no, I might add." Mr. Darcy put his hand up to stop Colonel Fitzwilliam from interrupting. "Cousin, be merciful. I do not wish to relive her words. Suffice it to say I was refused, and her words are ringing loudly in my head." He started to leave but then turned back to speak to his cousin. "You know, I never once thought she would say no." He spoke in the most crestfallen tone imaginable. Darcy's shoulders slumped as he headed upstairs to his chambers. Everything in his body language spoke of his disappointment, from his dragging feet to the furrowed crease in his brow.

Colonel Fitzwilliam watched his cousin walk away brokenhearted. When he had learned that Darcy was in love and that he would get a chance to meet this special lady, he was elated. At least one of them would not be a terminal bachelor. Darcy was eight and twenty and had put off many young, wealthy ladies over the years; to finally see him let his heart go was indeed an event to celebrate. However, the colonel's excitement for meeting this young lady, who was visiting her best friend, Mrs. Charlotte Collins, was soon stifled. He watched Darcy repeatedly lurk in the corner or ask about her family three times in a row whenever they were in her presence. He was expecting to see his cousin court the young lady. Instead, Darcy turned into a silent fool. Colonel Fitzwilliam was left to carry the conversation during these daily calls, calls Darcy insisted upon.

Elizabeth Bennet was truly everything Darcy had said she was. She was funny, kind, intelligent, and quite attractive. It was intriguing to watch her speak because her facial expressions revealed exactly

1

what she was really thinking. Although, one didn't really need to study her face to know what she was thinking because she usually spoke her mind. He let out a laugh. She spoke her mind but not like their Aunt Catherine; Elizabeth did it tactfully and kindly, without the haughty, prideful, condescending, expectant, and demanding tones their aunt favored.

Nevertheless, this lady had actually refused Fitzwilliam Darcy of Pemberley, one of the most sought-after bachelors in England. He came from money, he was the biggest landowner in Derbyshire, and he was known for his impeccable manners. So, how could Elizabeth refuse him? Because Darcy had acted like a silent fool, that is why.

The colonel recalled one time when Darcy was particularly anxious to speak with Elizabeth. He departed to the parsonage, leaving the colonel alone with Aunt Catherine and her officious ways— something that Darcy and Colonel Fitzwilliam had vowed to never do to one another. Colonel Fitzwilliam had to run to catch up and barely arrived at the parsonage door before Darcy rang the bell. After all that trouble, Darcy spoke less than ten words the whole time. He simply sat there, listening to the others converse. It was so odd to see him behave so ineptly.

The colonel and Darcy called at the parsonage every day, something that should have clued in Elizabeth to his cousin's intentions. But from what he could tell, Elizabeth knew nothing of Darcy's feelings—feelings that were held back even further whenever the parsonage party was invited to Rosings. He understood why Darcy held back in Aunt Catherine's presence, but he didn't know why he was so quiet and brooding on their daily visits to see Mrs. Collins, Elizabeth, and, of course, Miss Maria Lucas; the latter, only sixteen and shy, spoke even less than Darcy. He understood her to be the sister to Mrs. Collins, but he did not see any resemblance in personality.

Aunt Catherine was constantly correcting everything Colonel Fitzwilliam did, while praising everything Darcy did, making it very difficult for either one of the cousins to enjoy their annual visit to

Rosings. In previous visits, Darcy would entrench himself in her estate books with her steward from dawn until dusk, avoiding all the unwanted attention—but not this time. Darcy would get up at dawn and go walking, come back and work hard on the estate books, and then insist that they pay a visit to the parsonage where that ridiculous parson, Mr. Collins, lived with his new wife. Of course the visit had nothing to do with either Mr. or Mrs. Collins; instead, it was all about Elizabeth. Darcy would act like a fool and just stare at her from across the room and occasionally give short comments.

Yes, Elizabeth must have been quite surprised at Darcy's addresses, but to refuse him? Why would she turn down such a good match? She was a smart woman, and any woman in her right mind would have seen the many reasons to accept his cousin. He could hardly imagine her refusing Darcy, but from the sound of it, she had been quite adamant. He would have to make an attempt to talk to her about it. He didn't want her to slip away; the chance to see Darcy happy was too important. Surely she would see reason. He would prepare his arguments and have all his points ready on what a good match this would be. The colonel was a very good negotiator; if Darcy wouldn't talk about it, then he would seek out Elizabeth.

*****

Darcy paced like a caged animal in his chambers, tugging at his cravat. *Why? Why would she refuse me?* He sat down devastated, confused, hurt, and, more importantly, angry! He didn't know where to start with these emotions.

He was devastated because in his heart he was already engaged to her, had already seen her as mistress of Pemberley, and had already imagined holding her in his arms as she cried for joy at his proposal. Yet her refusal had been harsh—so harsh it was still difficult to take in breath, as if she had just spoken those hurtful, angry words.

Next, he was confused. Surely she had encouraged him and welcomed him graciously when he called on her at the parsonage or met her on their many walks. And those flirtatious, impertinent looks surely meant she desired more from him. But yet he was refused!

The hurt came when he remembered her most heated words, "*. . . had you behaved in a more gentleman-like manner*". His manners were described by everyone he knew as impeccable. How could he be accused of such behavior? If she were a man, he would have been tempted to call her out on that accusation alone, but the hurt didn't end there. "*I had not known you a month before I felt that you were the last man in the world whom I could ever be prevailed on to marry.*" He cringed. Yes, those words hurt, more than anything else she had said. It meant there was no hope left. She would never accept him. There was nothing he could have said that would have changed her mind.

The anger came when he thought of her reasons and the accusations she sent flying his way. Wickham! Wickham was a cheat and a rake of the worst form. He should have been flogged for all he had done over the years, but his charms always got him out of trouble. First, he charmed his sister, Georgiana, and now Miss Elizabeth Bennet. What exactly did Wickham tell her that turned her so against him? Knowing Wickham, it was half-truths laced with just enough plausibility that Elizabeth fell for it. How could such an intelligent woman be taken in by his charms? How could she not see through him?

He was so angry at Wickham that he kicked the chair by the writing desk. The chair bumped the desk, knocking a piece of paper off and jiggling the ink a little, making the bottle tip and nearly topple over. His quick reflexes caught the bottle before it fell, but he got ink on his hand. He paused for a moment, holding the bottle and watching the splashes of ink seep along the creases of his palm, and then looked at the paper on the floor. Ink and paper. Could it work? Could he change her mind? Could he convince her of Wickham's lies? Was there a sliver of hope that she might accept him?

He carefully put the ink down on a piece of paper and stared at it. He looked at the ink on his hand and knew he had to try. Where should he start? She would think he was only trying to renew his addresses. How would he get a letter to her? It wasn't proper to write her a letter. After their heated, uncivil conversation, he didn't think she even would accept it, let alone read it. But he had five years of being master of Pemberley, five years of negotiating business deals, and five years of detailing facts and dealing with problems. He had the skills on paper. He was good at running Pemberley. He was good at handling issues with the tenants. He may not have the colonel's conversation skills, but on paper, he was much better.

He quickly washed the ink from his hand. His heart was racing. Could there still be an element of hope to secure her? She was smart enough that if given the truth, she would and should recognize it as opposed to the half-truths Wickham had probably fed her. He dried his hands on the towel. There was only one thing to do. He got down on his knees and bowed his head.

"Dear Lord, I beg of you to guide my hand. I beg of you to help me know what she needs to read. She is my future. I can feel it. She is everything I need and want, and I cannot let her go without an explanation. I am just a man, and I need your help as I put pen to paper. She belongs with me. I must convince her that I am a man worthy of her. I beg of your forgiveness for losing my temper in front of her. I beg of you to move her heart, even just a little bit. She is so decided against me that I fear she will not even take this letter. I beg of you to help her see who I am.

"I will do anything, go through anything, or pay whatever price you ask, but help her to love me. I am begging, begging from my broken heart. I cannot see a happy life without her, only one of drudgery and misery. She has influenced my life in such a permanent way that I cannot go back. I will never be the same. I beg of you to guide my hand to write what it is she needs to read." He wiped away the tears in his eyes and whispered, "Amen".

*****

Dawn broke and Elizabeth was relieved. All night long she had mentally reviewed Mr. Darcy's proposal. One minute she felt all the same emotions as she did then—anger, embarrassment, indignation, offense—and then the next she was chastising herself for her willfully hurtful comments. Did she have to be so forward with her opinions of him? Why couldn't she have stopped after attempting to express her gratitude? Why did she have to keep going, one rude comment after another?

Never before had she seen such emotion in his face. Usually he was so reserved and controlled that his true feelings remained a mystery. Not last night. Last night his heart had been on his sleeve, and she had seen every emotion that danced unrestrained on his face. He had been surprised that she refused him. That was evident and supported her views of his prideful nature. He had expected her acceptance of his hand, even after a proposal like that!

After the surprise came confusion. His eyes had searched hers for answers, and she then informed him that she knew of his involvement in separating her dear sister, Jane, from his friend, Mr. Bingley. When Mr. Darcy was presented with this fact, his face showed surprise again as the knowledge was revealed, but one thing it did not show was remorse. She remembered his lack of remorse and his statement, *"I have no wish of denying that I did everything in my power to separate my friend from your sister, or that I rejoice in my success. Toward him I have been kinder than toward myself"*. It still made her angry. Why couldn't he see that he had deprived two wonderful people of a happy life! And he rejoiced in it, congratulated himself for it! In his words, he was being "kind" to Bingley. How dare he? What made him think he could make decisions for others?

After the confusion, she saw the hurt. That was what had haunted her all night—that pained expression and the hand that literally went to his chest, as if to hold his broken heart. That gesture in itself filled her with so much guilt at her hurtful words. She had called him ungentlemanly. She had said he had a selfish disdain for others. She had said so many hurtful things. She remembered the guilt she felt in seeing his face turn pink, then pale, and then pink again until he finally said, *"You have said quite enough, madam".*

Yes, she had said quite enough. She had watched him square his shoulders and pull himself together and put on a cold, indifferent face before he turned to leave. But as she watched him leave, she saw his shoulders drop. He ran his hand through his hair nervously. She knew she had hurt him; if he truly admired her, she had been cruel. With her own words ringing in her head, she didn't know what to do about it.

It was one thing to refuse him, but to be so verbally insulting in her response was unforgiveable. He had claimed that he ardently admired and loved her, and she had abused him. All night she had avoided Charlotte and claimed a headache to her ridiculous cousin, Mr. Collins, and all night she had berated herself for her behavior. She needed to talk to someone, and at the moment there was only one person she wanted to see: Mr. Darcy.

Nevertheless, it was too early to go out walking; the sun was just peeking over the hills. She doubted Mr. Darcy would be walking this early anyway; it was not when they usually seemed to meet. Perhaps if she walked closer to Rosings, she would run into him. The chance was slim. She would just have to wait and see if he came to call.

Elizabeth wandered into the hallway, hoping to get some tea and delay her walk until it was a little warmer. She stepped quietly, trying to avoid the squeaky boards by the stairs. Even more earnestly, she hoped to avoid Mr. Collins. His room was located at the top of the stairs, and he didn't approve of her unescorted walks so early in the morning. Unfortunately, she was not quiet enough.

The door flung open, and there stood her cousin in his nightshirt, his apelike chest hair overflowing out of the opening of his nightshirt. How could someone have so much fur on his chest and yet so little hair on his head? His long hair was usually combed over the bald top of his head, plastered from one side to the other with sweat. But now it was standing straight up, making his short stature look disproportionately tall. The hair was thin and usually so greasy that by ten in the morning, it nearly dripped with sweat.

However, that wasn't the most disturbing thing about her cousin. It was his mouth that bothered her. His tongue seemed to be too big for his jaw, so he used it in every syllable. And when he wasn't actually talking, which was a rarity, his mouth hung open, causing saliva to collect in the corners of his lips. He often used his handkerchief to wipe away the drops of drool that formed every few minutes. Sometimes the handkerchief went unused, and the drops launched onto innocent bystanders. Once he offered his wet, saliva-soaked handkerchief to her, and she literally gagged at the thought of using it on her own face. She was never without her own after that.

"Cousin Elizabeth, what are you doing awake this early?"

"I was hoping for some tea, Mr. Collins." She saw him look at her incredulously and knew he was working himself up for a speech. He stood there staring with his mouth open, causing the tongue to hang off to the right in a dumb-dog-like expression. *How can I be related to this anomaly?*

"Cousin Elizabeth, it is too early to go out walking. Even though I have full faith in the safety of Lady Catherine de Bourgh's grounds at Rosings Park, I must insist that you wait until you are properly escorted by a maid. Your country manners are offensive to those of a higher station. You must accept your lot in life and respect it, even if it means altering the unrefined behaviors that are so ingrained in your character. No matter how you were raised, you must endeavor to remember that my benefactress and her nephews must not be placed in a situation where they view the manners of my relations with contempt. Surely you would not wish to harm Charlotte and me by prancing about the estate unescorted or unchaperoned simply because you are a lowly, country-raised lady? I must insist that you take a maid with you. I simply must insist! If you—"

"Thank you, Mr. Collins," she interrupted. When he made long lectures like this on her behavior, which she had heard many times, his spittle would fling from his mouth in rivers. She stepped back as far as possible, but could still feel the onslaught of moisture on her person. "I shall endeavor to remember that. Perhaps I will heed your advice and secure a maid to go with me this morning." She quickly turned and ended the conversation. She used the back of her sleeve to wipe her brow which had an especially large drop of spittle on it. Her stomach curdled to be so drenched this early, and so disgustingly, especially after having seen the fur on his open chest.

She no longer had any desire for tea. She went to the kitchen where the cook was busy making bread for the day. "Good morning, Mrs. Wilkinson. May I wash my face?"

"Oh honey, you poor thing! He cornered you already?" Mrs. Wilkinson said with a look of empathy.

Elizabeth liked the Collins' cook—certainly not for the cooking, for that was at best, tolerable and some days, inedible—but because she was like the mother Elizabeth had always wanted. Mrs. Wilkinson was down-to-earth and well-read. She had been born a gentleman's daughter, but sometime in her early childhood, her mother was widowed and they were both forced to work. Unlike some servants who put their lives on hold to serve their masters, Mrs. Wilkinson married and had children while working. She was very loyal to Mrs. Collins, but because of her humorous nature, she couldn't take Mr. Collins seriously. She and Elizabeth had many conversations about him.

Making her way to the sink and reaching for a washcloth, Elizabeth said, "Yes, this time I was privileged to see just how primitive he is. He did not even have the decency to close his nightshirt."

Mrs. Wilkinson laughed out loud and then tried to stifle it, realizing she had been loud enough to be heard outside of the kitchen. "So, you got to see the animal that found its way onto his chest? Oh dear, you might need to wash your eyes as well! That image is not a pretty one. At least you did not see his shoulders. He used to make the stable man shave him every once in a while; it was like shearing sheep of their wool."

Elizabeth giggled and finished washing her face. "Now, that is something I never wish to see. I fear my maiden eyes have been scarred already by the six inches I saw on his chest. Do all men have that much hair? If so, I may never marry."

"No, dear, just the ones with mouths that do not close right. That should be your clue. If one asks to court you and his mouth hangs open, just say no, and you should be safe."

Elizabeth felt her spirits lighten. This was exactly why she liked Mrs. Wilkinson so much. She dried her face and hands on the towel. "Do you want some help with that dough? I could use a little exertion at something that will not be damaged by my energetic expression."

"Oh dear, that sounds like there is a gentleman involved."

"Yes, you are astute. But this particular man is very confusing and seems to elicit strong emotions from me—so strong that emotion-filled words fly unchecked from my mouth."

"So, you said something you wish you had not?" Mrs. Wilkinson handed half the dough to Elizabeth who took it and slammed it on the floured surface. She pounded her fist into the dough three times.

"Yes and no." She hit it hard again.

"Let us start with the 'no'. That might be a little easier to describe."

Elizabeth pushed the dough forward and folded it over again and repeated the motion, using all her arm strength to knead the dough. "I was proposed to." She heard Mrs. Wilkinson suck in a breath in surprise, but she didn't dare look at her face. "I refused him . . . and I do not regret doing so. However, I am disturbed by the manner in which I did it."

Mrs. Wilkinson had heard talk of the frequent visitors to the parsonage, but she wasn't sure which gentleman had proposed. It had to be either the colonel or Mr. Darcy. "If I may ask, and you know that my tongue does not speak all it hears, but which of the gentleman callers was it? I know you admire Colonel Fitzwilliam and have said that he is amiable which leads me to believe that you might not have refused him if he had asked. That leaves only Mr. Darcy. Am I right?"

Elizabeth groaned. "Yes. I had no idea he admired me."

"Truly? No idea? Come now, you have had them both calling on you daily, and he has somehow found your favorite walking spots nearly every morning. I imagine all those looks you say you so detest, was him doing exactly that—admiring you."

"You are wiser than I am, apparently." She pounded the dough hard, folded it over, and pounded it again.

"You mentioned you said some things that you regret. What exactly did you say?"

Elizabeth paused her kneading and looked at Mrs. Wilkinson. She had dark hair that was naturally curly and was really quite beautiful. Elizabeth had never asked her age, but she guessed Mrs. Wilkinson wasn't more than ten years older than her. "I suppose what I said is of little consequence now. I cannot take the words back, but I do wish to apologize for them. I could have refused him in a much kinder way."

"So, apologize. What is so hard about that?"

Elizabeth couldn't quite think of it so lightly. "It may not be as simple as that. He is leaving tomorrow. I imagine he is hurt and will not seek out my company, and even if he did, how would I speak to him in private?"

"I see. It is a little complicated, but it might be easier than you think. You said he walks daily? Why not take an extended walk and try to find him?"

"Well, the more I think about it, I wonder if we only met while walking because he was trying to court me and sought me out. Maybe they were not accidental meetings. I do not believe that it is his habit to go walking." She felt a new surge of frustration at the situation and pressed the dough. It was getting softer and more elastic, and she knew her method of relief was almost ready to be placed to the side to rise.

Mrs. Wilkinson placed her floured hand on Elizabeth's. "Dear, I think it is time for your walk. I will hope for the best, but you need to be open and honest with him. Do not let the moment slip by without apologizing."

"I promised Mr. Collins I would take a maid with me this morning."

"Well, as soon as I form these bread loaves, I would love to get some fresh air."

Elizabeth's face lit up. "Truly? That would be wonderful! With you there, I know my courage will not falter!"

"Darling, I would do anything to get out of this kitchen. It is not my favorite place to be, but from the half-eaten plates that come returned, I am sure you guessed that already." Mrs. Wilkinson let out a laugh and Elizabeth followed with one of her own.

*****

Mr. Darcy retied the knot on his cravat for the third time. *How does Abbott do it so easily?* His valet was probably still sleeping at this hour, so he would have to make himself presentable unassisted. He looked at himself in the mirror. *Considering she already refused him,*

12

maybe the state of his cravat didn't really matter. There was only the slightest hope that she would accept the letter.

He had stayed up all night and wrote several versions. The first was far too angry, and the second was almost begging her to believe him. Neither would work for his purposes. He needed to sound calm, but not pitiable. He intended to change her mind with his letter; it had to be just right. It had to be honest and revealing, and he had to disclose several deeply personal experiences for her to understand.

He buttoned up the waistcoat and looked once more at the letter on the table. It was too late to change it now. It would have to do. He grabbed the letter and walked toward the stables. He intended to ride this morning rather than walk. If he walked, then he might feel obligated to escort her back to the parsonage, and he was fairly sure she did not desire his company. All he had to do was find her and give her the letter.

The spring air was a little chilly this morning, with a bit of a bite to it. His ears could hear the brisk, angry, morning wind fighting against the trees. Anyone but Elizabeth would stay indoors during this kind of weather. But he knew Elizabeth. If their conversation yesterday left her in any way troubled, she would find a way to walk out her emotions.

She seemed to be the most at peace while walking. He had seen her in a number of environments: at the Netherfield Ball, in small social gatherings, and in her own home. Never did she seem to be more at ease than here on the paths at Rosings. It was one of the things he loved about her. And, with sadness, he admitted it was one of the things that led him to believe she would welcome his proposal. She seemed to enjoy the intimacy and quiet conversation that they shared during their walks.

He worked hard not to relive the emotions he felt yesterday. Today was all about composure and delivering the letter. The task should be simple enough. He focused on what he would say as he finished saddling his horse. The horse seemed a little anxious this morning. Mr. Darcy went and got some alfalfa to offer it, but it flung its head back in obvious refusal. He reached for the reins and stroked its mane. "Shh, now, it is not you who should be anxious, is it?"

Hearing its master's voice seemed to help, so Darcy continued talking to the horse. "Your job will be simple—just get me to her and I will do the rest. Whatever it takes to make her accept this letter, I am entirely committed to doing. Yes, beg even. I know, you have not had to see your master beg before, and I am afraid I am not all that practiced at it, but my very happiness depends on her accepting and reading this letter. So you see? This is one task I cannot fail at. She may have refused my hand, but she just simply cannot refuse my letter." Mr. Darcy was startled as he heard a voice behind him.

"Cousin, what do you think you are doing? Are you mad!?" Colonel Fitzwilliam normally stood slightly shorter than Darcy, but today his stature towered over Darcy's slumped shoulders.

"You really should not sneak up on people like that. My horse is anxious enough." As if on cue, the horse stomped its feet and pranced a little in the stall. "He feels the weather coming, I think."

"Darcy, she refused you. What makes you think she will break propriety to accept a letter from a suitor she refused? Come on now. Let it go, or at least let me talk to her. You know how persuasive I am with my regiment. Maybe I could help to change her mind."

Darcy shook his head and tightened the last buckle. He placed his foot on the stirrup and pulled himself on top of his horse. "No, Richard, I do not think even you could break her. In fact, I would probably shoot you if you tried. She is just like this horse—spirited, strong, and intelligent—and eventually, she will be just as loyal. Give me a chance to change her mind on my own. In breaking a horse, one must not break the spirit, just give the right guidance and let the horse find its own path. I just need to correct a few misunderstandings. Once she reads my letter, she will understand me better, and she will not be so decided against me."

"Miss Elizabeth is not some horse in need of a master. I think you are doing this all wrong. If you think you can change the mind of a lady like her, then you do not know her as well as you think. You will just be bucked off again."

"I know, but I must keep trying. I cannot picture Pemberley without her there. You know as well as I that when one breaks a horse, the horse is not the one being trained. Usually it is the master learning the needs of the horse. I do not want to master Elizabeth; I just need her to give me a chance, so I can learn what she needs from me. We would be a perfect match . . . she just does not know it yet." He tipped his hat and kicked the horse. Calling over his shoulder he yelled, "It will work out. Maybe not the way I originally planned, but it will work out."

Darcy looked up at the sky one more time and hoped he would find her before the rain started. The skies were quite dark directly above him, but the eastern horizon was letting the sun shine on him. It would be one of those rare occasions where it would be sunny, yet raining.

He roamed through the beech grove, but she was not there. He led the horse toward the river path, but she was not there. He headed toward the gazebo, but she was not there either. He checked a few other places, but soon his mind started wondering what he would do if he didn't find her walking. He was getting nervous that he would actually have to call on her to give her the letter. If he had to call on her, how would he deliver the letter privately? His horse reared its head, expressing the anxiety its rider was feeling.

He would look at one last place: the gravel path that wound through the forest east of the parsonage. He had found her there once before—the first time in fact, the only time that they had met by chance. He headed in that direction.

The forest was on the opposite side of the parsonage from Rosings and a few of the trees shaded the house. He had been out looking for her for over an hour, well past the usual time they "found" each other on these walks. The wind was whipping through the trees especially hard. He could sense the horse fidgeting under him, but he sensed something else too. She would come; he could feel it. Maybe it was false hope, but it was hope nonetheless. Elizabeth would come.

He waited. From where he was, he could almost make out the door to the parsonage. If he moved just a little closer, he would at least catch her coming back from her walk. She would come.

*****

"Dear, I do not know what to tell you. I was sure he would be out there. Perhaps I will make a batch of biscuits and you can deliver them to Rosings. Then you will have a chance to see him," Mrs. Wilkinson said.

Elizabeth laughed. "I do not intend to drive him off sooner! No, keep your biscuits to yourself. I realize you need to get back to put the bread in the oven. Thank you for walking with me. The conversation itself was helpful."

"I still cannot believe, even though I heard it from you, that you said those things to him. If you had told me what you said to him before I suggested a walk to find him, I may have counseled you differently. He very well may not even take his leave of you before he departs tomorrow. But you are right; I need to get back. Otherwise we will have mountains of bread, full of so much air that there will be pockets of nothing to hold your meat in place. The bread is well on its way to needing to be cooked. And from the look of this weather you had best come in as well."

Elizabeth looked up at the sky. Yes, it would start to rain any moment and she was beginning to get quite chilled. "Thank you. I truly appreciate having someone to talk to like this. I would say you are the best part of my trip to Kent. Thank you for just listening. Your empathetic ear has done me great service, and I feel better already."

They walked back to the parsonage in silence. When they heard the first thunder, neither one needed to tell the other that it was time to pick up the pace. The first drops of rain started just as they were entering the gardens, but that was not what startled Elizabeth. Behind her she could hear her name being called out. She reached for Mrs. Wilkinson's arm because she recognized the voice. "It is him. He came."

Mrs. Wilkinson lowered her voice and said, "I will watch from inside. Do exactly as you intended to, and just tell him you apologize." She quickened her pace and left Elizabeth at the gate.

Elizabeth took a deep breath and turned around. Darcy was getting off his horse, tying it to the post, and heading her direction.

"Miss Elizabeth, I must speak with you." She must listen to him. "Please, just give me a moment of your time."

"Mr. Darcy, after yesterday, there are things I need to tell you as well."

"No, I insist, please." Mr. Darcy said looking down at his feet. Then, finally realizing she hadn't totally dismissed him, he said, "Wait, what did you say?" The rain started coming down harder.

Elizabeth stood there as the rain pelted her. She had to say something, but at the moment she didn't know where to start. If she apologized, would he think she wanted him to renew his addresses? Would she be forced to refuse him once again? She tried to answer him, to give him some sort of response, but she couldn't. She looked at him and saw confusion in his eyes like the night before. The memories of his pained expressions were fresh. She told herself to respond, but minutes were passing as the rain soaked through their clothes. He seemed to be having just as much difficulty talking as she was.

Darcy was looking at the drops dripping from her curls on the side of her face. Never had he wanted so badly to touch her face as he did right then. He took ahold of his senses and took a deep breath, exhaling completely, causing the chilly air to show his breath. He

17

watched as it dissipated into the air. He felt embarrassed for just watching her and reminded himself why he was here.

He reached into his vest and pulled out the letter. He took a moment to look at it. It was his last hope. Before the letter there was no hope. As she had stated, he was the last man she could be prevailed upon to marry. But he wanted her. He had to have her. And that meant giving her a chance to see who he really was. She had to see that Wickham was inherently bad. She had to understand what his motives were for separating her sister and Bingley. He stretched forth his hand and offered it to her. "It is imperative that you read this. I implore you, beg of you, and plead with you to read this. I insist."

Elizabeth looked at the letter with her name written on it. She had no idea why he had even have come looking for her, let alone why he had written a letter to her. Her refusal last night had made it perfectly clear that there was no understanding between them. Accepting the letter would not be proper. All of these thoughts came flooding into her mind in mere seconds as he offered the letter to her.

Then she remembered that Mrs. Wilkinson was watching from the house. Although she knew Mrs. Wilkinson wouldn't judge her for taking the letter, she wondered who else might be able to see from the house. She knew if Mr. Collins noticed what was happening, he would not be happy to see Mr. Darcy presenting a letter to Elizabeth. With that thought, she quickly took the letter and tucked it into her pelisse.

Mr. Darcy was relieved. She had taken the letter. "Thank you. I will leave you now. I am sorry I held you up in the rain." He bowed and instantly turned back to his horse, which seemed to be dancing in place in the rain. He quickly untied the reins, and in his hurry to be gone, put his foot in the stirrup to mount from the off side. Just as he was halfway on the horse, loud thunder cracked, making the animal rear up on its hind legs.

Elizabeth watched with horror as Mr. Darcy tried to get control of his horse while not being completely mounted. But his

18

strength did not match that of the beast. The animal took off with Darcy's foot still in the stirrup. Elizabeth heard Darcy give the command to stop and saw him struggle with his own balance. Darcy had almost pulled himself up to the saddle when another crack of thunder scared the horse again. The weight of Darcy mounting from the wrong side sent the animal into a panic. Darcy had nearly managed to mount when he heard a third crack. This time the animal took off running and jumped the garden fence. The unbalanced animal came down wrong, stumbled, and then finally fell down on its right side, where Darcy had been trying to mount.

Elizabeth could not believe what she had witnessed. The animal had rolled right onto him. She ran to Darcy, screaming for help, and saw that his foot was still stuck in the stirrup. The animal was getting ready to take off again, and it was nearly to its feet. She hated horses but had seen many farmhands and groomsmen reach for the bridle to calm an anxious beast, so she grabbed the reins and held them fast. The animal jerked and snorted but did not bolt.

Mrs. Wilkinson was running as fast as she could, yelling the whole way. Elizabeth could see that Mr. Darcy was still attached to the stirrup, but he made no attempt to free his foot. It was then that she realized that he wasn't moving at all. She called out to Mrs. Wilkinson, "Take the horse! I will help Mr. Darcy!" Mrs. Wilkinson did as she was told.

First, Elizabeth pulled Darcy away, because the horse was stomping and its hooves were coming very near to his body. Then her wet hands worked furiously at the foot in the stirrup. She finally unhooked the foot, which was badly misshapen. Even in his sturdy boot, she could tell it was probably broken.

"Take the horse away! I have got him free!" Elizabeth then had the courage to evaluate the rest of him. He was unconscious and had a large gash across his forehead and a lump was becoming visible on the left side of it. She had nothing other than her handkerchief on her, so she used it. Soon Mrs. Wilkinson was by her side.

"I tied up the horse." Mrs. Wilkinson started untying the cravat around Mr. Darcy's neck. "He is bleeding quite a bit. Hold pressure."

"I am. It has already soaked through my handkerchief." Elizabeth watched as Mrs. Wilkinson untied the last knot and pulled it out from around his neck.

"I know. The cravat will have to do for now." She took the cravat and held it firmly against his head. The rain was pelting them from all sides and a few pellets of hail started falling. The storm had really taken on a life of its own.

Elizabeth said, "Go get help! We have to get him inside now! And bring a quilt to carry him on!" Elizabeth took the cravat from Mrs. Wilkinson and held it firmly. She heard Mrs. Wilkinson leave and evaluated the rest of him. He was breathing; that was good. She looked at his hands and arms while still holding pressure. They looked intact, but he had been rolled on by the horse. Who knew what kind of internal damage had occurred? The hail was getting bigger and was beginning to hurt terribly. She leaned over his face to protect him from being pelted, but that meant her back was taking the brunt of the storm.

Soon she heard Mr. Collins, Charlotte, and a few of the servants behind her. She instructed them as they neared, "We have to get him inside! But watch out for the right foot. I think it is broken. Fold the blanket in half and we can roll him onto it." The entire group was working furiously, trying to do as she instructed. Once they got him on the quilt, she said, "Now everyone take a corner or side and lift on the count of three."

She had seen her father and some farmhands once move a dead cow this way, and it was the only way she could think of to get him inside. Mr. Darcy was a tall man, and she knew none of them could move him on their own, certainly not Mr. Collins, who was the only man in the group. She counted to three, and they all struggled with the weight of his very limp body. They managed to get him into the sitting room, and Elizabeth heard the heavy breathing of her lifting companions.

"Good, now put him down right here on the floor." Her mind was trying to figure out what to do next. "Mr. Collins, go to town and fetch the doctor. Charlotte, send a servant to Rosings to notify Lady Catherine and Colonel Fitzwilliam."

"You want me to go out in that storm again?" Mr. Collins whined.

Elizabeth whipped her head in his direction and gave him a look that could have killed. "Yes, Mr. Collins, unless you feel Lady Catherine de Bourgh would appreciate her favorite nephew dying on your sitting room floor! Now go!" He was the only man in the group, and he was being the most cowardly of them all. She saw his face recognize the truth of what she said, and he turned to get his greatcoat. He seemed to take an enormous amount of time putting it on, but Elizabeth didn't take her eyes off her sniveling cousin until he left. *What an idiot!* Once again she wondered how in the world she could be related to that man.

With Mr. Collins gone, Elizabeth pushed aside her disgust for her cousin and re-evaluated what needed to be done. He couldn't stay on the floor, and his clothes were saturated with rain and blood. She motioned with her hands to Mrs. Wilkinson to hold pressure on the head wound. The unspoken command was acted upon immediately. Elizabeth's hands started removing his jacket, and she saw Charlotte start to assist her. Neither spoke of the inappropriateness of undressing him, but both were acutely aware of the necessity of it.

With the wet jacket off, she could see his arms were indeed not injured, but she had no idea about any of the rest of him. She took a deep breath and started unbuttoning his waistcoat, glancing briefly up at Charlotte, who hesitated only slightly before assisting her. Elizabeth kept stealing glances at his face, hoping without hope, that he would open his eyes and awaken.

21

With the help of Charlotte, she was able to get the waistcoat off which left him in his white shirt and breeches. His shirt was not as covered in blood nor as wet, but she untucked it anyway to make sure there was nothing obviously wrong with his chest. A memory of seeing the hairy chest of her cousin that morning flashed before her eyes and she hesitated, her hand holding the base of the shirt. She took half a second more and decided the situation called for it and, after all, surely Mr. Darcy was not as furry as her cousin.

She lifted it up and didn't realize she took in a sharp breath until she heard it with her own ears. His chest was sculpted and tight, his abdomen flat and toned, and to her relief, the hair was hardly noticeable. She realized she was staring and admiring the chest instead of evaluating his state of health. She redirected her eyes to look for bruising or bulges. She scanned for symmetry. From what she could tell, his chest was not injured.

She lowered the shirt and looked up at Charlotte, who had a small grin on her face. Elizabeth was struck with a deep blush, fully caught by her friend in the situation. Elizabeth gave her the subtlest glare back. Charlotte adjusted her grin into an appropriately serious expression. Elizabeth was suddenly drawing a blank and not thinking clearly. She unconsciously shook her head to clear it. There were more pressing matters at hand than thinking about his handsome chest.

"We need to get him to the chaise. Mrs. Wilkinson, how is the head wound doing? Is it still bleeding?" Elizabeth's mind was back, engaged with the crisis at hand, and her blush had finally disappeared.

Mrs. Wilkinson lifted the soiled cravat slightly and then immediately held pressure again. "It is better, but still bleeding."

"Well then, you hold pressure while we move him." She gave instructions to lift him the way they had before. The five women lifted his body and walked him to the chaise using the blanket to carry him. He was just as heavy as before, without Mr. Collins helping this time, which made her wonder if the revolting man had really been helping at all.

The chaise was not long enough to let him lay down completely, so Elizabeth once again made split-second decisions. "Prop him up with pillows, and keep his head elevated. That should help with the bleeding, anyway. While we are at it we should probably elevate the broken foot. It will swell, but I am too afraid to remove the boot." She evaluated his face, which still showed no evidence of awakening. She knew head wounds bled more than usual, so she was not as worried about the bleeding as she was about him still being unconscious.

Elizabeth heard the chime of the clock and noted what time it was because surely the doctor would ask when the accident happened. She tried to calculate how long ago the accident happened, and she reasoned it wasn't more than fifteen or twenty minutes, ten of which Mr. Collins had been gone. She started to pace. What else could she do? Her mind was replaying the accident over in her head, and she tried to figure out how he hit his head. She hadn't actually seen him fall, because the fence had blocked her view. He had been on the other side of it when he hit the ground.

She walked to the front door and opened it, looking across the garden hoping to see where he had fallen. The hail had stopped, but the rain was coming down in sheets. The wind was blowing it one way and then the other. Traveling on these roads would be very difficult if it didn't let up soon.

She watched as the other servants busied themselves adjusting and repositioning Mr. Darcy as she had suggested. "Let us stoke the fire and get him covered with a blanket as well." She brought a chair closer to the chaise to be near him when he woke up. A blanket was quickly retrieved, and she assisted the servant in spreading it over him. She noticed his foot again and gasped at the change.

"Oh no, the swelling is going to be significant. Look how tight the boot is! We have to get the boot off."

Charlotte asked, "Are you sure we should move him? I think the doctor should be consulted."

Elizabeth was already trying to carefully pull the boot off, but it was not budging. "I read in a medical journal about limbs turning black and blue simply from swelling. If the swelling has nowhere to go because the boot is too tight, then he may lose his foot."

"Medical journals? Truly, Elizabeth? I knew you liked to read, but medical journals?" Charlotte asked.

Elizabeth rolled her eyes. "It may not be a London fashion magazine, but it is something to read on rainy days like this. My father orders them. Did you know he once thought about becoming a doctor, but he inherited Longbourn before he could finish?"

"No, I had no idea. Is that why you are not upset at the sight of blood?" Charlotte asked. "You seem to be handling this situation remarkably."

"I do not know about that. I just cannot believe it happened! I need a razor. We have to cut the boot off. Charlotte, does your husband have a razor he has not used yet? It needs to be sharp."

"Yes, I think so. I will go get it."

Elizabeth waited and adjusted the blanket a little, as the room was getting quite hot with the fire. She took off her pelisse, realizing for the first time that she still had it on. She walked to the window and saw that it was still raining something fierce. She walked back to Mr. Darcy and took the cravat from Mrs. Wilkinson and peeked under it. The bleeding had stopped. She put the cravat aside on the table and rubbed her forehead.

She had missed her chance to apologize! What if he never woke up? She would be stuck with this guilt forever. She worried that he would die right in front of her, and there was nothing she could do about it. She returned to evaluating his foot and heard Charlotte coming down the stairs quickly.

"Here is a razor. I brought two in case one goes dull."

Elizabeth carefully took the two razors and started to slip her fingers between the boot and his shin. The last thing she needed was to cut his leg. Ever so carefully she made tiny slits all the way down as far as she could go. As she neared the ankle it was harder to separate the leather from the skin. She motioned to Maria Lucas and a servant, "Each of you pull hard up and out as I continue cutting it off. Do not let go for any reason. If your hand is slipping, just tell me, and I will stop cutting while you readjust. This will be tricky."

Maria and the servant did as she told them, and she braced herself for the next part. She was only a few inches away from the misshaped area. Everyone was huddled around her, watching her cut. Slowly the skin turned purple underneath, and she continued cutting. She got past the misshapen area and saw that his ankle was definitely broken; the bone was jutting out in a very ugly way.

She was almost done when Maria's hand let go, and the boot slipped. Elizabeth looked up just in time to see her swaying, pale as a ghost. "Catch her!" she called out. She would have done it herself, but her hand held an exposed blade. Mrs. Wilkinson had been at Darcy's head and ran to get Maria. She led her, stumbling, to the nearest chair. Fortunately, Maria hadn't totally passed out. The last thing Elizabeth needed was two patients. She made sure Mrs. Wilkinson was handling Maria and asked Charlotte to take Maria's place.

Charlotte said, "If it is all right, I am not going to look, but I can certainly hold the boot."

Elizabeth looked and nodded her appreciation. She was nearly down to the toes anyway. After a few more cuts, she slipped off the boot. "Oh dear, he must be in a great deal of pain," Elizabeth said. She readjusted the foot, holding it at the calf and toes, to be more elevated on the pillow. The foot was probably twice its size already, but the bone was still noticeable. For the first time she noticed that the leg was shorter than the other as well. Charlotte scooted the chair over to her a little more, and Elizabeth sat down.

The ever-rational Charlotte said, "I think it will be a while until the doctor can get here. We might as well make ourselves comfortable."

Elizabeth looked up at her and smiled. "Thank you, all of you; he will ever be in your debt for your help today."

Charlotte smiled and put her hand on Elizabeth's shoulder. "No, Mr. Darcy will ever be in *your* debt. I am afraid we cannot take any of the credit. You seemed to know what to do and we just followed your directions. I will sit with him while you go get cleaned up. Your dress has blood all over it, and you are soaked through."

"You are right. I should probably put myself back together before he wakes up." *If he wakes up.*

CHAPTER 2

Colonel Fitzwilliam arrived just a few minutes after the boot was removed, totally drenched from the storm. Elizabeth didn't have a chance to change her gown or even wash her hands.

"Where is that fool?"

"Mr. Collins? I sent him to town to fetch the doctor," Elizabeth said.

Colonel Fitzwilliam answered, "No, Darcy!" He charged in without even stopping to remove his outerwear.

Elizabeth stepped out of the way and pointed to the sitting room. "I believe his only injuries are his head wound—he must have hit his head on something—and a broken right foot. But the horse did roll on him, so he could have broken ribs. From what I could tell, there was no obvious damage to his chest." She blushed slightly at remembering how sculpted his chest was. She suddenly realized she needn't have told Darcy's cousin that she looked at his chest; it was quite improper.

The colonel raised an eyebrow at her but followed her blushing face into the sitting room where he found the object of his concern. "He has not regained consciousness?"

Elizabeth shook her head. "Not even when we moved his broken foot and cut off the boot. It must have been terribly painful, but he has not responded at all." She watched as he checked Mr. Darcy from head to toe. He lifted the shirt as well to inspect his chest, but he also ran his fingers around each side to check the ribs, something Elizabeth hadn't done. He studied the ankle and grimaced.

Elizabeth noticed the frown on his face and said, "I know it looks bad, but if the doctor can set it soon, it should heal."

"You seem to have known what you were doing. Another ten minutes in his boot and you may not have gotten it off. How long has he been unconscious?"

"Almost half an hour. I still do not know what he hit his head on, but I was going to go out and check," Elizabeth explained.

"I will go with you."

Elizabeth went to get her pelisse and realized it was all bloody. She decided that she would just go without it because she couldn't get any wetter. The doctor would need to know what happened, and the sooner they figured it out, the better. Elizabeth picked up her skirts and ran to the scene. Colonel Fitzwilliam followed her closely.

She had to raise her voice slightly to be heard over the sound of the rain. "The horse got spooked from the thunder and jumped over the fence right here." Elizabeth quickly scanned the area and was suddenly horrified: there on the muddy ground was Mr. Darcy's letter with her name on it.

Colonel Fitzwilliam bent down and picked up the letter. He wiped it off on his coat. "I believe this is yours. He very much wanted you to have it."

"Thank you. It must have fallen out of my pelisse. Did he tell you about the letter?"

"More or less. I overheard him talking to his horse. I am afraid my cousin was quite determined to get that in your hands."

"Yes, I hope it is still readable. The paper is saturated and very dirty."

"So, you accepted it then?"

She blushed slightly. "I suppose I did. I am sure you are thinking I probably should not have done so."

"Not at all. I trust Darcy completely. He would never do anything improper and certainly would not have involved you in such behavior. Nevertheless, I know of a certain relative at Rosings who would not be so amiable if she learned of that letter's existence. Please be careful with it."

The warning was heeded by Elizabeth. She understood the secrecy of the matter. Lady Catherine de Bourgh was convinced that Darcy would marry her only daughter, Anne. She wondered what his aunt would think about his proposal, let alone the letter. The rain had let up some, but they were still getting quite wet. However, the temporary privacy was invaluable to Elizabeth. "Colonel? May I ask if you know that Mr. Darcy called on me yesterday?"

"You mean, do I know that he proposed?" Elizabeth face revealed a gentle blush. "I knew it was his plan to do so, and when he disappeared I assumed he went to propose. I did speak to him afterwards, although briefly, and I understand you refused him. Is that correct?"

The blush got deeper and Elizabeth looked away. She bowed her head and said, "Yes."

Colonel Fitzwilliam interpreted the softer tone and blush as regret. "So, you regret refusing him?"

Elizabeth looked up at him. "Oh no!" she explained. "Not at all, it is just . . . well, I was not very kind in my refusal. I do regret that." She shivered in the chill of the air and the wind.

"Well, I am sure we will have plenty of time to talk about that. Let us get you inside before you take a chill."

Colonel Fitzwilliam knew when to retreat and find another tactic. At least now he knew a little more about what had happened. Elizabeth had told him more than his cousin had. He knew that there was still hope for changing her mind since she had admitted regret. She may not have realized it yet, but one does not feel sorry for hurting someone that one does not care for. Elizabeth may have had her reasons for refusing him, but the fact that she cared how she treated him was a good sign.

Fall back and attack another day on a different battlefield, he mused. *Elizabeth will soon see the situation differently. When, not if,*

Darcy renews his addresses, she will be more aware of what is best for her.

She looked once more at the ground. "I still do not see what he hit his head on. Do you?" she asked.

The colonel had almost forgotten why they were talking in the rain. He started kicking the ground a little. His boot hit something hard. He leaned down and moved the leaves and revealed a flat stone about a foot wide. "I think we just discovered it."

*****

It was another two hours before the rain stopped, and shortly thereafter came a flood of visitors. First was her cousin returning home, followed immediately by Lady Catherine de Bourgh, succeeded ten minutes later by Mr. Cummings, the doctor from town.

Elizabeth had escaped her vigil on the unconscious patient long enough to change her dress and stash the letter. She had opened it and set the two sheets out to dry. It appeared that the writing was not smeared too badly, but she did not want to read it just yet. That would have to wait until she had some time and until she knew Mr. Darcy would recover. This was the excuse she gave herself; if she admitted that she actually feared what it said, then she wouldn't be able to focus on anything else.

Nevertheless, the doctor had finally arrived. Elizabeth retold the story to him and explained all they did to help him. In retelling it, Elizabeth left out that she checked his chest. Instead, she said Colonel Fitzwilliam did. Aunt Catherine was oddly silent. Elizabeth kept glancing in her direction to gauge what her reaction was, but her face showed only real concern.

Everyone was asked to step out while Mr. Cummings evaluated the patient. Colonel Fitzwilliam insisted he stay and assist. Twenty minutes passed before the doctor came out rubbing his chin.

"I must admit, it does not look good. But there is little more I can do besides stitch up the head and set the foot. I believe Miss Elizabeth did a fine job of nursing Mr. Darcy. If setting the foot does not make him wake up, I do not know what will. Sometimes when the head is hit very hard, it protects itself, and the patient stays unconscious until the time is right. I have to warn you, however, that sometimes they do not recover. Even if he regains consciousness, he may have permanent damage.

"I do not know how to say it gently, but the most we can do is pray and hope. He will need a good deal of liquids, mainly water and broth to keep hydrated. If given in small enough quantities, his body will swallow it. And he will need twenty-four hour care. I know just the right nurse who will do wonderfully; I will send for her when I am done here."

Lady Catherine broke her silence, "Then we should settle him at Rosings before you set the foot. I will see to getting a carriage and enough footmen to move him."

Mr. Cummings looked down his glasses at the officious woman. "Lady Catherine de Bourgh, I am sorry, but he cannot be moved. I do not even recommend taking him into a room upstairs. There is too much at risk. We have no idea whether he injured his back or neck."

"Are you presuming to tell me what to do with my own nephew? Surely he cannot stay here when my home will make him so much more comfortable."

"My lady, moving him would be terribly dangerous. It could cause permanent injury. It could leave him totally dependent on others for his basic needs."

"What you are suggesting is completely unsatisfactory. I cannot possibly leave him here! Do you imagine I would leave the master of Pemberley on a chaise in my parson's sitting room? Indefinitely? With only one maid and no valet? No, he needs care appropriate to his station. He will be moved to Rosings immediately."

"Madam, I will prescribe the appropriate care needed, and I say he will not be moved!" Mr. Cummings was usually a gentle, caring man, but when his instructions for proper medical care were disregarded, he became angry very quickly.

Once he had cared for Sir Lewis de Bourgh and prescribed an elixir for his heart. If taken twice daily, it would have saved his life. But his wife, Lady Catherine de Bourgh, refused to buy it and insisted Mr. Cummings change the prescription to something less costly. Her demands had cost her husband his life. Remembering this incident made him so angry. Lady Catherine wouldn't put out the money to save her husband then, and now she was ready to defy his instruction once again.

"How dare you presume to tell me what to do with my own nephew! Do you realize he is nearly engaged to my only daughter? He was planning to propose before he left tomorrow. I could tell it in his demeanor. He was going to propose which makes me very nearly his mother! I will not stand here having you tell me how to care for my son!"

"Your son, if it is as you say, will not live long enough to propose if we move him. I have seen it before. I have served as physician for nearly forty years, everywhere from small, country towns to the largest most prestigious families in London. You, madam, would do well to heed my advice! If you still desire my experience and attention for Mr. Darcy, then I suggest you abide by my prescribed care to the strictest of measures, or you will find yourself at the unwelcome side of a handsome lawsuit for causing the death of Mr. Fitzwilliam Darcy! I would have plenty of evidence to call it murder!" Mr. Cummings bellowed.

Colonel Fitzwilliam stepped between the two people. "There now, Doctor. My aunt will absolutely abide by your suggestions. And there is no reason we cannot employ all the necessary means to meet his needs here at the parsonage, Aunt. Darcy's life is certainly worth following the doctor's advice."

Aunt Catherine's chest was puffed out, and her nostrils were flaring. She tried to find something to challenge him back. "Richard, I insist we move him as soon as he is able," she said. And heavy on the sarcasm she added, "But I will wait for the ever-knowledgeable doctor to let us know when that is." She stepped around Richard to make eye contact with the doctor. "Do I have your word, Doctor? Or should we argue about that as well? Do I have to endure more accusations against my character?"

Mr. Cummings bowed slightly. "You have my word. As soon as he is able and desires to move, we will move him. But not until then." He turned to the colonel and said, "I need some help setting the foot. I understand you have battlefield experience. Would you mind helping? I could use another, but we might be able to manage with just two of us."

Elizabeth spoke up, "I can help. I do not mind. I know I can do it."

Mr. Cummings quickly evaluated her. "Well, you have already shown how helpful you can be. I would appreciate your assistance." He motioned with his hands for the two of them to follow him back to the patient.

*****

The doctor was able to set the foot fairly easily with a bit of pulling. Mr. Darcy let out a loud moan when the bones were realigned. All three looked at the patient expecting to see him open his eyes or speak, but he remained silent after that. He didn't move when the doctor stitched up the head wound. Each hour, Elizabeth and Charlotte took turns spooning fluids into his mouth.

The nurse arrived that night. Elizabeth again found herself reporting on his status. "Besides the moan with the foot being set, he has not moved. Nor have his eyes fluttered. He seems to be breathing normally and to be swallowing a spoonful of fluid at a time without coughing."

The nurse stood by the patient and examined the black-and-blue foot. "I have heard from Mr. Cummings of his injuries, Miss . . ."

"Elizabeth. Elizabeth Bennet."

"Miss Elizabeth, you may call me Madeline. I suspect I will be in need of some assistance now and again, and it seems like you have already invested quite a bit in his care. The first day or two is the most critical. For now I will take over, but you can come and go as you please. Do you mind me asking your relationship to Mr. Darcy?"

Elizabeth blushed. She could have been his intended by now, but she had refused him. "He is no more than a friend. We have known each other less than seven months." It was the first time she had thought of him as a friend, let alone acknowledged it to a stranger. There was something more intimate between them now than before; she could feel it.

Just then Mr. Darcy moaned and turned his head to the right.

Madeline asked, "Is that the first time he has moved?"

Elizabeth rushed over to Mr. Darcy and touched his hand, "Yes! Is he going to wake up now?" Very faintly, Mr. Darcy moved the hand Elizabeth was touching.

"Say something else," Madeline suggested.

"Like what?" Once again Mr. Darcy moaned. Elizabeth looked up startled, eyes wide with anticipation. "You think he likes my voice?" As if to prove the point, Mr. Darcy's eyes fluttered but stayed closed.

"Well, let us see if he does anything when I talk." Madeline said a few lines of a poem. They watched him closely, but nothing happened. "I think he does like your voice. Sometimes patients respond to familiar people."

"But his cousin, Colonel Fitzwilliam, has been here with him all day, and he is much closer to him than I am. Mr. Darcy did not do anything while he was here." Elizabeth didn't know why she felt uncomfortable with this new revelation. If he should be responding to anyone, it should be to his closest cousin. "I suppose it is good that he is starting to respond. Perhaps I should send word to Aunt Catherine and his cousins."

Madeline's eyebrow rose, and she looked at Elizabeth, trying to evaluate where her loyalties lay. She was under strict orders to keep Lady Catherine away from the patient as much as possible. Mr. Cummings hadn't said why exactly, but he had hinted at ulterior motives that were not in exact compliance with the health of the patient. "Miss Elizabeth, they have had a long day. Why do we not wait it out a little and see how he does through the night? They will have, at minimum, several emotional weeks as they handle the care of Mr. Darcy; and at worst, they may have to prepare for the death of a loved one."

"Maybe you are correct, they need their rest. It is encouraging to see him start to move and respond to things around him." She looked at him and saw that his eyes were starting to twitch. "If he likes my voice, maybe I should read to him."

Madeline already knew she liked Elizabeth. She could see she had good sense. She wasn't pretentious, she was open to suggestions, and she seemed committed to doing what was right for the patient. These were all good beginnings in her mind. In all of her three and thirty years, fifteen spent taking care of invalids and injured patients, Madeline had learned how to read people and what assets they had. She trusted Mr. Cummings explicitly and could see the value of his advice about Mr. Darcy's visitors. It was clear that visits from Lady Catherine should be avoided. Visits from Elizabeth, on the other hand, would be quite beneficial. "Do you know what kind of books he likes?"

Elizabeth was a little surprised that she did. "Actually, yes. We have discussed books. He is quite an avid reader. I will go get a few that I know he would like." Elizabeth went to her chambers and retrieved two books: a collection of Wordsworth poetry, and *Much Ado About Nothing* by William Shakespeare.

She came back down into the sitting room and saw Madeline examining him. "Should I come back? Do you need some privacy?"

Mr. Darcy moaned and turned his head toward the door where Elizabeth was standing. Madeline said, "No, I think you will be very good for him. That was the first response he made since you left. Come in. What did you bring? I enjoy reading too. I should like to listen."

Elizabeth entered the room and pulled up a chair closer to Mr. Darcy. "I think I will read Wordsworth first. Mr. Darcy is from Derbyshire, near the Lake District where Wordsworth grew up. He once told me that Wordsworth's poems remind him of home. Not only that, but I have always thought Wordsworth was somewhat like Mr. Darcy himself. He did not like large groups or high society either. Mr. Darcy keeps to his own small circle of friends, and he lives frugally and simply. He does not dress to impress even though he has the means to do so. Do not misunderstand, one can tell he is a man of means, but Mr. Darcy does not adorn himself with frivolous, passing fashions."

Elizabeth was surprised again that she was voicing such personal thoughts. More importantly, she was surprised that her thoughts toward Mr. Darcy were so kind, considering how angry she had been less than twenty-four hours earlier. "I am sorry. I should not have gone on and on about him. You did not know him before his accident, and yet I feel like you should."

"I always like to know the real person I am working with. Brain injuries like this one often alter the personality a little, even after a full recovery. I would love to hear more about Mr. Darcy," Madeline said.

"It changes their personality? Why would it do that?"

"I do not know. It is just an observation. Families I work with will attest to the fact that their once sweet and kind daughter becomes nearly impossible to manage. Or their responsible, thoughtful uncle becomes a womanizing rake."

Elizabeth raised her eyebrows. "Truly? That does not sound good. Is it always for the worse?"

Madeline laughed. "No. Once there was a drunkard who found himself holding a pistol at dawn. He took a gunshot wound to the head in a duel and became blind. The man changed his ways and did more charity work in collecting funds for the church and clothes for the poor than ten men in their lifetimes. It not only changed his perspective and behavior, but he became less selfish and more kind-hearted."

Elizabeth stifled a giggle. *Perhaps Mr. Darcy will be less prideful*, she thought. "Well, Mr. Darcy, let us see if your tastes still favor Wordsworth."

She then read to him for two hours straight. Each time her voice stopped, he would start thrashing about. Once she started reading again, he would make only little movements or moan. Madeline gave her a glass of water when it was obvious that her voice was getting scratchy.

After the third hour, she looked at the clock and realized it was well past her time to go to bed. Charlotte had come in several times to look in on them. Mrs. Wilkinson had come in and asked how the patient was doing before she went home. Mr. Collins had come in and offered *Fordyce's Sermons* as something more appropriate for a lady to read. Elizabeth reminded him that she was reading according to Mr. Darcy's tastes, not her own, although she didn't point out that it was a book from her personal library. Mr. Collins rubbed his mouth with the saturated handkerchief and looked on disapprovingly. At least he kept himself spitting distance away.

After a pause, when it looked like Elizabeth was going to continue reading, Madeline said, "I will take it from here. Thank you. Now, you go get some rest."

"He seems to have fallen asleep again. It is interesting that three hours ago my voice would elicit a more alert behavior. When I started reading, it seemed he did not want me to stop. And now it seems he is resting peacefully. Is that normal?" Elizabeth was getting tired, but she was also cognizant of how much better he did when she was talking. She had a feeling of dread that if she left, he would worsen, and she would never get a chance to apologize for being so uncivil and rude in her refusal. She didn't know if she could live with the fact that she had taken the silent, cowardly way out before the accident. He had waited for her to speak. She had tried to speak. She just couldn't.

"Normal? What is normal recovery for a head injury? If you are asking if I have seen it before, then yes, I suppose it is normal. If you are asking if he himself will be normal . . . well, it is far too early to tell. But bodies heal rapidly. Do not give up hope."

It was obvious that Elizabeth cared for Mr. Darcy, but to what extent Madeline did not know. No "friend" would read for three hours straight to an unconscious patient unless there were feelings of some sort. Madeline, for the third time that night, wondered what exactly was the relationship between Mr. Darcy and Miss Elizabeth. It was certainly more than friends.

The only other explanations were either Elizabeth was extremely empathetic or she felt some sort of guilt for the accident. She had seen enough reactions from family and friends during a crisis to know it was usually one or the other. Either Elizabeth felt responsible and was acting out of guilt or she had some strong feelings for the man.

Madeline was smart enough not to take everything people said at face value, but it didn't help that Madeline had an especially tender heart herself. Her heart ached to see her patients suffer, but it was even worse to see their loved ones suffer. She understood very clearly that when she took on a new patient, she took on the whole family as patients. From what Madeline could tell, Elizabeth seemed to fit in the "family" category, even though she said they were just friends.

"I was not really asking if he was going to be normal. It is just that the wide range of behavior is a little unexpected. I do not know if I should wish him to wake up or sleep comfortably," Elizabeth said wistfully.

"I understand. For now, he needs his rest as do you. Come see him in the morning. I understand you are a guest here?" It was more than a little curious that the nephew of the great Lady Catherine de Bourgh would be "friends" with someone visiting her ladyship's rector.

"Yes. Mr. Collins is my cousin and his wife, Charlotte, is my very dear friend. Her younger sister, Maria Lucas, you saw briefly when you came in. She and I came to visit for six weeks. We are due to return next Monday to Hertfordshire. I am afraid you will not see much of Maria. She nearly passed out when we cut off the boot."

Elizabeth looked at Madeline. She was a beautiful woman. She looked to be in her thirties but wore no ring on her finger. Elizabeth rather liked her. She wasn't nosy and had praised Elizabeth's efforts profusely, so much so that Elizabeth felt self-conscious. Madeline had an expressive face. Elizabeth had been told she had one too. She had always felt it was only because of her impertinent, honest nature. Once again, Elizabeth was reminded just how impertinent she had been to Mr. Darcy. She reached out and placed her hand on his briefly. She promised herself that if he woke up, she would not be cowardly again. She would apologize next time.

"Well, that explains a lot."

Elizabeth looked at her confused, "What does it explain?"

"It is not anything really. I just noticed that you were quite irritated with Mr. Collins when he suggested you read something else. Your body language seemed disrespectful, not at all how a lady would behave toward her host. But I see now that he is family, and one does not choose family—they kind of come as a package deal. You have to deal with them, no matter how they are." Madeline gave her a half smile. "Do not worry, honey, I read people very well. It was not anything you did that was reproachful. I just see more than most people. It comes with the job description. My entire job is to assess, notice, and report to the doctor. Usually I try to keep my judgments restricted to the patient, but I do not always have the control to rein it in when the subject is not my patient. Forgive me."

Elizabeth let out a laugh. "It was that obvious then? I think he is a buffoon! A drooling, spitting, hairy buffoon! And I am related to him!"

Madeline giggled into her hand. "Hairy?"

"You would not believe me if I told you! He must have three inches of fur on his chest! It had to grow somewhere and apparently his head rejected it!"

Madeline decided right then that she did like Elizabeth. "Has anyone ever told you that you are a little impertinent?"

"My mother—all the time. She says I will never get a husband with my impertinent ways. I just like to see humor in the things people do, and with my honest nature, I often get myself in trouble when I really should hold my tongue." Elizabeth looked at Mr. Darcy. His condition was proof of how her ways could cause more trouble than she realized.

Madeline noted the faraway look in Elizabeth's eyes. She looked awfully tired. "Well, husband-seeking mothers would counsel you to get some rest, something I wholeheartedly agree with. Now, no more worrying for the patient. That is my job. Good night."

"You can certainly come get me if you need help."

"Again, that is my job, not yours. I can handle him. Besides, he is resting quite comfortably, and for now that is exactly what we want."

CHAPTER 3

Elizabeth was woken by loud male voices downstairs. She scrambled out of bed and tried to get dressed as quickly as possible. The voices were too distant to recognize, but the noise began escalating as she speedily put on her gown. She splashed cold water on her face, tied her hair into a simple bun, and simply threw two pins in it—the minimum effort required in order to be presentable.

As she opened the door, she saw Maria in the hallway, very anxiously wringing her hands. "What is going on?" Elizabeth asked.

"I am not sure, but I think Colonel Fitzwilliam and Mr. Darcy are shouting at each other. I cannot tell what they are saying. Mr. Darcy is quite agitated. From the sound of it, the colonel is trying to get him to do something he does not want to do."

"Oh! Well, at least he is awake and conscious! I will go see if I can assist." Elizabeth nearly ran downstairs to the sitting room.

She stopped at the door and overheard a little of what was going on.

Colonel Fitzwilliam said in a very firm voice, "I am sorry, Darcy, you cannot stand up. Your foot is broken. The doctor said you cannot stand up, no matter what the reason."

Darcy spat back at him, "And would *you* prefer to do it sitting down?"

Colonel Fitzwilliam responded, "It does not matter what *I* prefer, *you* cannot stand up."

Darcy nearly yelled, "I cannot keep having this argument! What is the matter with doing it the way I always do? My foot if fine!

Here, I will prove it. MOVE! Cousin, if you do not lift your hands off my shoulders, I swear to you I will break your arm!"

"Sorry, Darcy—doctor's orders. You must do it sitting down."

"I will not!" Darcy bellowed.

Elizabeth was very confused. What were they talking about and why was Darcy so agitated? She heard someone behind her, and she turned to see Mrs. Wilkinson. "What is going on?"

Mrs. Wilkinson let out a laugh. "I am afraid you do not want to know. But I would love to see you try to figure it out!" Elizabeth raised her eyebrow in curiosity and then gave her a pleading look. Mrs. Wilkinson laughed again and said, "There will be little peace until he does what the colonel tells him. I am afraid you will eventually figure it out with Mr. Darcy being as loud as he is. Let us just say it has been a long time since Mr. Darcy used the chamber pot."

Awareness graced Elizabeth's features. "Ah, and he wants to stand up to do it?" Mrs. Wilkinson nodded and walked away laughing. Now Elizabeth didn't know whether she should enter the room or not. With something so personal, she decided she probably should not, but then she heard her name mentioned by Madeline.

"Perhaps we should get Miss Elizabeth. She was very helpful last night."

Mr. Darcy's voice calmed down some. "Miss Elizabeth is here?" he asked. "Why did not someone tell me? I should pay a call on her. Cousin, let us go see her. I swear I can walk. Just let me see her."

"No, Darcy, your foot is broken. You cannot walk at the moment. Trust me, Miss Elizabeth will call on you soon. Now that you have lowered your voice, I suggest you do as we talked about before she arrives." Elizabeth could tell that the colonel was trying to placate him into being less combative. Clearly, he would use any available tactic to keep Darcy calm. It was evident that Mr. Darcy was not entirely aware of what was going on. *He may be awake, but he is not back to normal.*

She waited a few minutes more as they debated the issue of standing up or sitting down. When Darcy started raising his voice again and making threats of physical harm to his cousin, she decided she had eavesdropped long enough. She opened the door and saw that the colonel was restraining Darcy's arms, and Madeline had a hand on the broken leg, trying to keep it still.

"Unhand me, man! And who is this awful woman holding my leg? Let me up! You know what I must do, and you cannot make me do it sitting down! My foot is not broken!" A struggle ensued. Darcy nearly knocked over the colonel, and his good foot came close to kicking Madeline in the head.

Elizabeth hurried into the room and put her hand on Darcy's hand. She very firmly said, "Mr. Darcy, stop that this minute! You nearly kicked a lady in the head! Now behave yourself!"

Darcy's foot dropped back on the chaise, and he looked at Elizabeth with wide eyes. He stopped struggling and tried instead to readjust himself on the chaise. "Miss Bennet, I am afraid you came at a most inconvenient time. My cousin and I were just leaving, but you may accompany us on a walk if you would like. What I mean is, I would greatly appreciate your company." He turned to the colonel, who had lightened his grip on Darcy, and said to him, "Would you not like to accompany Miss Elizabeth to see the gardens?"

"Certainly, Cousin, but not right now, all right? At the moment, your foot is broken, and you are unable to walk." Colonel Fitzwilliam released Darcy's arms and put a firm hold on his shoulders.

Elizabeth could see that Darcy had calmed a great deal when she entered the room. She glanced at Madeline, who still had a good grip on the broken leg. Madeline was smiling, and Elizabeth could sense she was trying to tell her something with her eyes. Elizabeth tried to make out what she wanted her to understand. Finally, Madeline motioned to the pot at the foot of the chaise.

Elizabeth understood now. Madeline wanted Elizabeth to get Darcy to cooperate with urinating sitting down. Certainly Madeline wasn't suggesting Elizabeth help him use the pot! She was an unmarried lady and of no relation at all! She looked frantically to the colonel, and he too seemed to be pleading with her to help. Darcy was fidgeting on the chaise and running his hand through his hair nervously. He was obviously uncomfortable. She took a deep breath.

"Mr. Darcy, I understand you need to do something, and that you will continue to be uncomfortable until you do it. Might I make a suggestion?"

Mr. Darcy looked at her in surprise. He then looked at his cousin and raised his voice, "How dare you! You told her I need to urinate? She is a lady!"

Elizabeth saw her opportunity. "Exactly, Mr. Darcy, I am a lady. And since you are well aware that we do not discuss such topics in front of a lady, will you listen to my suggestion? I promise that after you comply, you will feel much better, and I will read to you as I did last night. Wordsworth, remember?" She could tell Darcy was not thinking logically. She felt a little bad taking advantage of him like this, but playing on his desire to be with her was the only option she had. She looked at the colonel, who appeared relieved and took one hand off Darcy.

"You read to me last night?"

"Yes, sir. You were very cooperative and seemed to enjoy it. Would you like to hear more?"

Darcy smiled briefly, little dimples forming at the corners of his mouth. "Yes, indeed I would. What are you suggesting?"

Elizabeth took courage from the look Madeline gave her. "Nurse Madeline, right there, and your cousin are going to help you. I am afraid your foot really is broken, so you will not be able to stand up. You must do as you are told. Do you understand? It will not take long, and when you are done, I will come back in."

Darcy evaluated Madeline. "You are a nurse?" Madeline nodded. Darcy looked back at Elizabeth. "And you will come back in and read to me?" Elizabeth nodded. He shifted his weight a little and looked deep in thought. "And my foot truly is broken?" All three nodded at the same time. "Well, that explains a lot. I thought someone was using sewing needles on me for amusement. Very well, I will try it." Elizabeth turned to leave, but Darcy's panicked voice called out, "You will come back?"

Elizabeth smiled and said, "Yes, I must get my book anyway." She couldn't believe it was working! "I believe the nurse has some medicine for the pain as well."

"No, no medicine just now. Maybe when you get back. You are coming back?"

"Mr. Darcy, I have assured you twice already that I will come back. Do you doubt me?" She waited for his response, but all he did was shake his head like a little two-year-old refusing to eat his vegetables. "Well then, I will give you fifteen minutes. Should I bring in tea and some ham and eggs? Are you hungry?"

Darcy smiled. "Will you eat with me?"

"Certainly, Mr. Darcy. Now do what you need to, and I will have the cook make something special."

*****

Elizabeth had waited more than fifteen minutes, just in case it took longer to do what he needed to do. She couldn't believe it had worked. She listened outside of the door. It appeared the two cousins were talking quietly. The colonel was explaining about the accident and his injuries. Darcy spoke in normal tones and responded appropriately, yet she heard anxiety in his voice. She took the opportunity to enter.

"Good morning, Mr. Darcy." Elizabeth waved her book. "Feeling like a little Wordsworth?"

Mr. Darcy smiled and tried to sit up straighter. "Miss Elizabeth, how good it is to see you. I absolutely love Wordsworth. Did you know he grew up in the North? His words often remind me of my home at

Pemberley. The way he expresses himself and his love of country life make me think of Derbyshire."

Elizabeth was a little confused. He had shared this exact opinion about Wordsworth on one of their walks two days before the accident. She made a mental note to ask Madeline about it later. "I did know he was from the Lake District. I believe he loved the land very much, and he tried to live in harmony with nature as much as possible." Colonel Fitzwilliam pulled up another chair next to his own, by Darcy's side.

"Exactly! He was a man who loved everything deeply, and his poetry expressed those passions most beautifully!" He turned to the colonel and raised an eyebrow at him, smiling. The colonel grinned back knowingly as if they were co-conspirators with a secret plan. Elizabeth didn't know what to make of the exchange. There was certainly nothing clandestine in their discussion of Wordsworth.

Colonel Fitzwilliam said, "Please, sit down, Miss Elizabeth."

Madeline was quietly reading in the corner. She looked up at Elizabeth and smiled. It appeared the earlier crisis had ended. Elizabeth took her seat. The maid brought in breakfast, and Elizabeth was pleased to see Mr. Darcy eat, even though the eggs were overcooked and rubbery. The colonel finished his account of the accident, and she blushed a little when he repeatedly referenced how vital she had been.

"So, I owe you a great deal, Miss Elizabeth," Mr. Darcy said between bites.

"No, sir, anyone would have done the same thing."

Colonel Fitzwilliam chuckled. "*Would have* is different than *could have*. Do not let her fool you, Darcy; she saved your life. I have seen seasoned soldiers who could not have done what she did. Very few would have been able to keep their wits about them."

"If everyone keeps praising me, I might just die of embarrassment! It was truly nothing!" And as if on cue, a deep blush appeared.

Mr. Darcy smiled and said, "Miss Elizabeth, that blush is very becoming of you. I will have to think up other ways to see you blush. Speaking of which, it looks like I have already succeeded. Now, I believe you promised me something?"

Was Mr. Darcy trying to be charming? Elizabeth had already finished her food, and she contemplated the changes she was seeing. Last night he had responded well to her voice. When she had stopped reading for any amount of time, such as when Mr. Collins came in, he thrashed around on the chaise until she started reading again. After a long time, resting calmly when she read and appearing uneasy when she stopped, he finally slipped into a peaceful silence. He must have regained consciousness sometime this morning in a very agitated state. Colonel Fitzwilliam had to bodily restrain him before Elizabeth entered the room. Not only did he refuse to accept that he had a broken foot, but he had threatened and struggled against his cousin.

Now, after he had relieved himself, he seemed to be making sense and had insightful understanding. But more importantly, he was reasonable and less childlike in his behavior. She was relieved that he was awake, but his mood swings worried her.

For example, when she left, he was anxious and needed reassurance on the most trivial things. Now, he seemed to retain what was told of him. He was even being somewhat charming. She didn't quite understand. Madeline had said it can alter personalities—was Elizabeth seeing a more charming and happier Darcy? One who was not brooding and aloof? She realized she still hadn't answered him. "Yes, I believe I promised to read to you." *Only time will tell,* she thought.

*****

Elizabeth picked up where she left off last night. Darcy was enthralled. After an hour or so, Colonel Fitzwilliam asked Darcy if he needed anything from Rosings. Darcy looked to his cousin with a perturbed look as if to say, "How rude of you to interrupt!" Elizabeth made a suggestion for a fresh change of clothes.

Darcy looked down and saw the state of his attire for the first time. He was still in his white shirt and breeches, nothing else. He looked at Elizabeth in a panic, suddenly realizing that she had seen him in so little clothing. "Yes, please bring me a change of clothes," he said. "Abbott will know what I like. In fact, bring Abbott and my shaving equipment." He rubbed the stubble on his chin.

Colonel Fitzwilliam then asked Madeline if she needed anything. Madeline responded, "If Miss Elizabeth is comfortable, I could use a little fresh air. I should not be long. Is that acceptable? Also, what is the best way to send a letter to the doctor? I need to update him on Mr. Darcy's improvements."

Elizabeth realized she should have suggested contacting the doctor sooner. "Absolutely! I am sure Mr. Collins has a servant who could deliver the letter. I think Mr. Cummings will be pleased to know how well Mr. Darcy is doing."

Madeline stood and put down her embroidery. "Well then, as long as you behave yourself, Mr. Darcy, I will leave you to your poetry." She gave him a smile which he returned in the somewhat-childlike manner Elizabeth had seen earlier. Once again, there was a strange nonverbal exchange that Elizabeth did not understand. First it was between Colonel Fitzwilliam and Darcy, and now between Madeline and Darcy. It seemed everyone but her was involved in some covert scheme.

Elizabeth watched Colonel Fitzwilliam and Madeline leave, and then she started reading again, but was interrupted after a few lines.

"Miss Elizabeth, I have been meaning to speak with you for some time now," Darcy said quietly.

The look on Darcy's face was familiar. It was anxious and excited at the same time. She opened her mouth to respond but heard someone enter the room. She turned to look at the door and heard Darcy groan behind her and mutter something like, "Not now".

Mr. and Mrs. Collins came in, the former earnestly rushing to his side. "Mr. Darcy! It is wonderful to see such a grand recovery in such a short amount of time. I am humbled to offer my house and services to you, the beloved nephew of her ladyship, Lady Catherine de Bourgh. I assure you that if Cousin Elizabeth or any of the caregivers do not meet your standards, I would be happy to send them away and attend to you myself. We will do anything necessary to secure your comfort. It is such a delight to be of service to you in a time of such need. I always say—"

By now, the man was standing directly over Mr. Darcy, who was left dodging the droplets of spittle spewing out of his mouth. Elizabeth froze in panic, unable to think of a way to assist.

Darcy interrupted him, "Mr. Collins, might I ask a favor of you?" He sat up a little, and Elizabeth immediately stood to help adjust the pillows. "I feel so indebted already that I am nearly afraid to ask. Your kindness and generosity is noted indeed."

"Absolutely anything, Mr. Darcy. I will do anything you ask of me."

"I am deeply fond of the lemon tarts from the bakery in town. Might I request you and your lovely wife fetch me some? I have a deep craving for something of that sweet and sour nature."

"I will send a servant for some immediately!"

"Oh no, I would not trust a servant with this task because, as you well know, only those with refined taste can pick out the best tarts," Mr. Darcy said with a straight face.

Elizabeth snickered into her hand. Mr. Darcy wasn't all that creative in his attempts to make Mr. Collins leave. She watched him discreetly wipe his cheek.

Mrs. Collins joined her husband and took his arm. "Come dear, I am in the mood for something sweet as well, and we both could use the time together. Perhaps you and I could share a chocolate truffle; I know how you like them."

Elizabeth watched Mr. Collins reluctantly leave. As soon as he was gone, she pulled out her handkerchief and handed it to Mr. Darcy. "I am so sorry. I will get you a wet cloth."

Darcy took the handkerchief but then said, "No. Please, Miss Elizabeth, I need to speak with you. Please sit down again." He waited until she did as he had requested. "For some time now I have wanted a private audience with you, and I must use this opportunity I have been given. I must tell you how ardently I admire and love you. Almost from the time I first met you, I have been captivated by your beauty and intelligence. I have never come across someone as intriguing as you. In vain, I have struggled to repress these feelings. They cannot be repressed anymore. I love you and care little for what society might think of such an imprudent match.

"I am fully aware that you have no fortune, no connections, and little dowry to speak of, but I have plenty for the both of us. We do not have to visit your mother and younger sisters but once a year, and I would not mind to see your father more often. Certainly, Miss Bennet is welcome anytime. Will you consent to be my wife?"

Elizabeth felt her anger rising and struggled to keep her composure. "Is this some kind of joke?"

Darcy's face was surprised. "Joke? Of course not. I would never trifle with your feelings. I just proposed! Will you make me the happiest of men?"

Elizabeth stood up and nearly knocked the chair over. Her face was red. She tried to control her breathing, but found herself unequal to the task. She turned from him and walked a few paces away. "Happiest of men?" she began. "Do you realize you just told me, again, how unsuitable I am? Do you realize you have belittled me and my family, again, in your proposal? Do you realize, once again, you said you struggled in vain to repress your feelings of love and admiration? Again you are choosing to offer me your hand in such a manner?"

Darcy's surprised look changed to confusion. "Again?"

"And I do not find the repetition humorous! It hurts just as badly the second time! My family may be less refined than those you usually associate with, but they are my family! You cannot belittle them and expect me to accept such an offer of marriage!"

Darcy's confused look turned to hurt. "Is this a refusal? How can you refuse me? And what is this about doing it again? What do you mean the first time?" he asked, his voice faltering toward the end of the sentence.

Elizabeth let out a slow breath and said, "You already proposed! Do you not remember?"

Darcy's hurt look went blank, and he paused. "Already proposed? Surely you must be wrong. I certainly have not! And might I ask why you have refused me with such little attempt at civility? Might I ask you why a woman with little but her mind and body to offer in marriage would refuse a match with me, the Master of Pemberley?" His voice was raised in anger, and he ran his hand through his hair. He shifted his position, grimaced, and reached for his leg.

Elizabeth couldn't believe her ears! They were having the exact conversation from two days ago! She was fuming at his comments. "Little to offer?" she retorted. "Allow me to offer my reasons for refusing you. And, I might add, these are the same reasons I gave two days ago! You interfered with the happiness of my dearest sister, Jane. You convinced your friend, Mr. Bingley, of her unsuitability, the very unsuitability that you, yourself, just told me that I possess! If a marriage with my family is so unsuitable for Bingley, why then is it appropriate for you? Is Mr. Bingley not worthy of happiness as well?

"And what of my sister, Jane?" she continued. "Is she not worthy of happiness? You cannot find a more genuine, kindhearted, and loyal lady in all of London's so-called *ton*! If you think I could accept the hand of one who rejoiced in separating two wonderfully matched people, you are indeed mistaken! And might I remind you of my other reason? Your despicable manners toward the son of your father's steward are unpardonable!"

"Wickham? You are refusing me because of Wickham? What exactly did he say to you? And, might I add, my manners are impeccable! How dare you accuse me of such a thing!" His face was red, and he reached for his foot again.

"Did you really think playing on my sensitivities toward your current situation would change my mind? Did you really think I would change my mind in two days' time?"

Finally, Darcy yelled out, "What are you talking about! I never proposed two days ago! A man would remember that!"

At that moment, it hit Elizabeth; he didn't remember the proposal. She looked at his face and saw beads of sweat forming on his brow. He was obviously quite irate. She was dumbfounded. She didn't know what to do. Not only had she agitated him, but she had hurt him once again. Once again, he had his hand at his chest. Once again, she had not held her tongue. Once again, she had been rude and unforgivable in her refusal. Not only had she not apologized, she had repeated the same mistake.

Colonel Fitzwilliam and Madeline came in and saw Elizabeth looking pale. They looked to Mr. Darcy and saw that he was quite agitated again. Madeline immediately went to the patient. "Are you in pain, sir?" she asked.

"Pain? You could say that."

Colonel Fitzwilliam was trying to figure out what was wrong. Was it a repeat of the incident this morning? *Surely it is too soon to need the chamber pot already,* he thought. He went over to Darcy and said quietly, "What is wrong, man? You look like you have been through war."

"War? You could say that." Darcy couldn't take his eyes off Elizabeth, who was backing away slightly. "Wait! Do not go, Miss Elizabeth. Please. I beg of you. I do not know what just happened, but I do not want you to go. Stay."

Elizabeth said sheepishly, "You look tired, Mr. Darcy."

"Tired? You could say that."

Madeline spoke up after checking his pulse, "I must tell you, sir, that you are very agitated."

"Agitated? You could say that."

Colonel Fitzwilliam looked at Madeline, who looked somewhat concerned. Madeline went to her table of medicine and returned quickly with three vials. "Here, Mr. Darcy, this one is for the pain." Darcy kept his eyes on Elizabeth, but he opened his mouth and drank the sweet syrup. "And this one is to help with your anxiety." He again opened his mouth and swallowed the bitter liquid. "And this one is to help you sleep." Darcy opened his mouth and swallowed the thick tea-like substance.

Darcy again made his request. "Stay."

Elizabeth felt terrible for repeating the same mistake from two days ago. She had seen all the same emotions played out on Darcy's face. Surprise, confusion, hurt, and then anger. After all these emotions, he still wanted her to stay. She nodded. Relief. That was the final emotion. She had seen the same look on his face when she had accepted the letter. She could stay for him. No matter how prideful and hurtful his second proposal was, she would stay.

"Until you fall asleep," she said. She sat down across the room, afraid of giving him the wrong idea. She felt regret for making the same mistake, but she did not regret refusing him. Besides, he would fall asleep soon with that much medicine.

Sure enough, Darcy struggled to stay awake and watch Elizabeth. Every time his eyes blinked, they flashed open in fear and found Elizabeth again. He was fighting the medicine, and it wouldn't be long until the medicine won. Elizabeth watched his efforts. Finally, she stood up and moved across the room. She took a seat by his side, next to the colonel. "I will be here when you wake up. Just rest now." She watched him take a deep breath. Finally, he laid his head down and closed his eyes. His breathing slowed, and in minutes, she could tell he was sleeping.

Madeline checked his pulse. She crossed the room and motioned to Elizabeth and the colonel. They quietly left Darcy's side to join her.

"Why did he keep saying the same kind of thing? Why the repetition?" whispered Colonel Fitzwilliam. "I was beginning to think that if I asked him if he felt ladylike, he would respond 'Ladylike? You could say that!'"

Madeline shook her head and then looked at Elizabeth. "He was perseverating. I think it was somewhat of a setback. He looked to be under a great deal of stress. I noticed he returned to somewhat childlike behavior as well." She again looked at Elizabeth for information, but Elizabeth remained mute. Madeline would have to ask her directly. "Miss Elizabeth, what exactly happened to make him agitated? What did you talk about?"

Everyone was looking at Elizabeth. She felt the weight of responsibility for his current condition, and it didn't help to have two sets of eyes on her.

"I am afraid I need to inform you of something. I believe your patient has memory problems."

"I do not understand. He seems to recall who we all are and was doing wonderfully when I left. What makes you think he has memory problems?"

Finally, Elizabeth looked up from her hands. "He did not remember a certain very important conversation the two of us had two days ago, before the accident."

Colonel Fitzwilliam groaned. "And you felt now was a good time to remind him of your refusal?" he asked. "Could you not wait until he had been awake for twelve hours?"

"It was not like that. As soon as you left, Mr. and Mrs. Collins came in, but he managed to dismiss them, and then when everyone was gone, and well, he proposed again, almost verbatim to the first time. I thought it was a poor attempt at a joke. I had no idea he was in earnest. I truly thought he was using his accident to make me pity him and accept him. We were well into an argument before I realized that he had no recollection of the first proposal. He took the second refusal just as hard, I am afraid. He showed the same emotions again. I am so sorry. I do not know what to say. I did not mean to cause a setback." Elizabeth looked to Madeline. "Will he be well?"

Madeline put a calming hand on Elizabeth's arm. "Dear, he is most likely going to be fine. But we need a plan on how to deal with this memory problem. I assume you told him he already proposed?"

"Yes, but he did not believe me, no matter how many times I kept referencing it."

"Well, my experience with memory loss is that it does no good to argue with the patient. It only makes it worse. We have to remember that their reality is literally that: a reality. It is like me trying to convince you my blue dress is really brown. No matter how hard I tell you my dress is brown, all you know is that it is blue. Arguing with him will only cause further agitation and setbacks. One or two careful attempts to reorient him are acceptable, but no more than that. If we are gentle, he may learn to accept the truth. But if we are at all insistent or forceful in trying to correct him, then he may get worse."

The colonel rubbed his chin. "So, you are saying that we should not tell him that he has already proposed and that Elizabeth has already refused him, twice?"

Nurse Madeline nodded. "Exactly," she said. "If he wakes up again with no memory of the proposals, we should not tell him. It is my professional opinion that if he experiences another setback like this again, it could cause permanent damage. We saw what it did to him today. Imagine it happening repeatedly. To him, Miss Elizabeth is someone he wishes to propose to, not someone who has broken his heart. I am sorry, Miss Elizabeth. I did not mean to be so frank. We have all seen how helpful you are in assisting Mr. Darcy. For the time being, I think we should try to keep it that way and not let him know what has happened."

She had heard enough. Elizabeth tears began to flow. "So, you think I should play along with these proposals? You are suggesting I accept him just to make him happy? I do not see how dishonest answers would help him get back to normal." She sniffled and realized Darcy still had her handkerchief.

Colonel Fitzwilliam handed her his own handkerchief and spoke up, "No. I think I see what Nurse Madeline is saying. If he does have memory problems, then he will not remember what you tell him in your answer. Let us just keep the answer away from a definite refusal. What do you think, Madeline? If Miss Elizabeth delays her answer the next time he asks, then would he be spared another setback? Am I correct?"

"Yes, exactly. I think we should avoid telling him he has already proposed and Miss Elizabeth should avoid answering 'yes' or 'no'. Could you do that, Miss Elizabeth?"

"I do not know. I still think I should be honest with him. What if one day his memory comes back? He will undoubtedly feel that we have been dishonest with him, that we have played with his emotions." Lady Catherine's voice bellowed from the vestibule, and Elizabeth realized their private conversation was over. Quickly, in hushed tones she offered, "I will do what I can to avoid a complete refusal."

She had barely finished the sentence before her ladyship entered the room. Elizabeth still hadn't taken control of her emotions, so she kept her back to Lady Catherine.

Colonel Fitzwilliam hailed his aunt and motioned with his finger to his lips for her to be quiet. He whispered, "He just fell asleep. It has been a difficult morning."

"Why was I not notified he had awoken? I demand to know the reason for this!" She turned her imposing frame toward Madeline and growled, "You should have sent for the doctor and notified me at once! I had to hear it from Mr. Collins!"

The colonel whispered as forcefully as possible, "Aunt Catherine, please, lower your voice. He really needs to rest. And you are being quite disrespectful to Nurse Madeline."

"Respect? You think she deserves my respect? She is nothing but a hired hand! And I will most certainly speak my mind. Why do you think Rosings has been so successful all these years? It certainly was not because I sat back and let others tell me what to do!" The feather in her hat shook in anger at each syllable.

Colonel Fitzwilliam decided not to correct her; Rosings's success was thanks to a good steward and Darcy's assistance. Her intrusions in estate matters often caused headaches. Darcy handled their aunt better than most people, certainly better than the colonel, but he knew it was still hard for Darcy. Broody by nature, Darcy would stew about a problem for days before addressing it with his aunt. But in issues related to the running of the estate, Darcy handled everything beautifully, often without even consulting her. It was the one area in which Aunt Catherine permitted a little respite from her arrogant ways.

Darcy avoided confrontation altogether about his supposed "marriage planned since infancy" to her sickly daughter, Anne. He didn't like to confront their aunt unless absolutely necessary. And, so far, enlightening her that Darcy would never marry her daughter was, as he put it, "not necessary". This, of course, posed a problem when they were in society. Occasionally, Darcy would be congratulated on his engagement to Anne de Bourgh, and Darcy would politely state that his aunt presumed too much. He would never outright deny the engagement, which didn't help the rumors and only encouraged their aunt in her scheming ways.

The colonel, on the other hand, usually shrugged off the constant belittling comments aimed at him. He knew he was not the favorite nephew, but his personality was such that the opinion of a bitter, old woman—family or not—did not matter. He was already the second son, heir to nothing but a meager country home outside of London. What did it matter if he was in second place as favorite nephew? The problem with his usual nonchalant, dismissive methods of dealing with his aunt was that when he really needed to make her listen, he did not have the skills to battle her. This was one of those times.

He took his aunt's arm and gently escorted her out of the room. "You know as well as I that sleep is important to healing," he said. "Darcy is in a great deal of pain right now, and the fact that he is resting is a good thing. You do not want him to suffer any setbacks, do you? You want him to return to Rosings whole and healed, no?"

"Do not be ludicrous! Of course I want him to heal! And he will, if I have anything to do with it. I have looked into Nurse Madeline, and I am not sure she has enough experience to attend him. He should be cared for by someone who is accustomed to dealing with men in his station. She has been employed by farmers and butchers!" Aunt Catherine spat out the professions as if they were foul words.

"Well, I, for one, respect her and from what I can tell, she is very knowledgeable and insightful. I spoke with the doctor while we were setting his foot and she comes highly recommended. Some people do not see rank and station like you do."

"That is my point! What if she puts Darcy in an inappropriate situation? Who knows what nurses like her are exposed to? She certainly has no respectable maiden eyes."

Colonel Fitzwilliam laughed, remembering how much more professional Madeline had been in helping Darcy use the chamber pot; the colonel had been completely inept. Between snickers he added, "I do not think you need to worry about her professionalism. She has more experience than you realize. She has accomplished more than I could have done. Now, Aunt Catherine, I suggest you go take care of Anne, for surely she is taking the news hard."

Suddenly, the colonel realized that his skills at manipulating the enemy transferred over from the battlefield; he *did* know how to handle his aunt! Treat her like a prisoner of war! Limit her freedoms! Cut off her resources! Restrict her access! Make her dependent on him for information! Of course! Why couldn't he see it before? He smiled wider and set his plan in motion.

"What is so humorous? I demand to know what could be so humorous. You must know I am very displeased!" she huffed.

"Now, I am going to have to put my foot down and ask you to let me take care of Darcy. You need not worry yourself over things. We know how delicate your heart is. And if you have contact with him, you could transfer something back to Anne. The last thing we need is two very special people in our lives critically ill. He is very unstable at present and could have any number of complications. In fact, just this morning he was extremely agitated, and you would not believe me if I told you why." He waited for her response, knowing she would be unable to resist.

"Why?"

It worked. She was his to reel in. "Darcy needed to use the chamber pot, and I had to physically restrain him to keep him from injuring himself. He is not thinking clearly, and his emotions are unstable. His complex thought process is hindered. Do you realize the critical nature of his injuries? He could die if added stress were to be placed upon him. I assure you that the smallest stimulation has already caused a setback. Now, he seems to respond well to me, Madeline, and Miss Elizabeth. And I intend to keep it that way. I have already seen the effect of Mr. Collins's interference—right before the setback."

"What setback? Was Mr. Collins involved?"

Colonel Fitzwilliam knew he was bending the truth a little in implying that it was Mr. Collins who caused the setback, but if he could kill two birds with one stone, he would do it. "The rector, as you know, can be very—how should we put this?—verbally tenacious, and

Darcy did not respond well to it. I think it would be wise for you to limit his contact with Darcy. Too much stimulation, regardless of good intention, could push him overboard.

"Nurse Madeline has already sent for the doctor," he assured her, "and I will be here when he arrives. I will report back anything he says directly to you. But you need to control your staff. You need to make sure that these three familiar faces are the only faces he sees unless absolutely necessary, and I am afraid that restriction includes you. You must keep yourself and Anne strong and healthy. Let us who are younger and who have more endurance handle the situation."

"I did have an attack of my heart yesterday while we were waiting out the storm to come see him, and my feet have begun to swell again. It has not been this bad for several months. But why in the world should Miss Bennet be involved? Surely Mr. Darcy would prefer my company to hers. What is she to him?"

"Now, Aunt Catherine, do not forget that she was the one who saved his life. We owe her a great deal. She has a very level head on her, and, for some reason, Darcy is calmer and less confused when she is around. You, however, get lightheaded at the sight of blood, do you not?" Lady Catherine's face paled, and she reluctantly nodded.

The colonel continued, "Miss Bennet has shown herself to be very useful, and for some reason, she seems to bring out the best in him. We must use anything or anyone we can to ensure only the best of care for Darcy. And do we not want the best?" Now he knew he was bending the truth. If his aunt knew what the real cause of the setback was, then Elizabeth would be sent home directly; she would permit no one to secure Darcy's heart except Anne. "Do you trust me?" This was the final ingredient to his plan. He had restricted her access, limited her freedom, and now he needed to make her depend on him for the basic needs, like information.

"Richard, obviously, I trust you. I do admit I did not respond well seeing him unconscious yesterday. I did not know what to do! It brought back memories of his mother on her deathbed with that same blank expression. I remember it clearly; only two days later she passed. Do you really think you can handle it? I would never have considered you as one well-suited to handle problems. But perhaps your war experience has better prepared for this unfortunate situation."

Colonel Fitzwilliam hadn't thought she would fold so easily. He had a nagging suspicion that she had ulterior motives. Either that or she truly couldn't handle seeing her favorite nephew in this state. He knew his aunt well enough to know it was probably the former. He would have to be on his guard and watch for her real underhanded scheme. The colonel was a good negotiator, but when it came to manipulating the enemy, he didn't hold a candle to his aunt. "Do not worry, dear Aunt. You may depend on me to watch things here at the parsonage and report to you any changes. And I will depend on you to remain at Rosings, for Darcy's sake, so that you and Anne will be safe, correct?"

"Are you trying to ensure my cooperation or my oppression? I do not like being told what to do, Richard. Now, notify me immediately of any updates," said Lady Catherine.

Richard knew when the battle was won and knew when to retreat for better positioning to win the war. He had won all he needed from Aunt Catherine; pushing her for a promise of cooperation might be the wrong maneuver if he wanted to win the war. "I assure you I will," he promised, "and if I need to, I will write down the doctor's assessment and prognosis and report it directly. Now, go attend to Anne and put your swollen feet up." He leaned down and kissed her on the cheek, something he hadn't done in years.

"Now, what brought that on? I have asked for your kisses for years now, but you have refused. Are you trying to make me leave? Because if I understood you correctly, I need to speak with Mr. Collins." Aunt Catherine gave one of her rare smiles.

As soon as he saw her grin, he knew she was up to something. He masked his concern and said, "I just feel families need to pull together during difficult times. Illness makes one revaluate one's priorities."

"Indeed."

CHAPTER 4

Mr. Cummings was surprised. "So, I missed Lady Catherine?" he whispered, trying not to wake Darcy. "Amazing. My timing could not have been better."

Madeline nodded. "Yes. She was very upset that I did not notify her when Mr. Darcy regained consciousness. The other nephew, Colonel Fitzwilliam, handled Lady Catherine and convinced her to stay away. Do not ask me how he did it. All I know is now Lady Catherine has agreed to get all her information from the colonel."

"Interesting. I would not have thought delegation was within her capabilities. It is very strange indeed. But never mind Lady Catherine, tell me more about the patient. You mentioned he was awake and talking, but was emotional and irrational." Mr. Cummings took out his pocket book, sat down at the desk, and started taking notes.

"Yes, one minute he could not be convinced that there had been an accident or that his foot was broken, and then the next, he seemed perfectly reasonable. Two things happened that could have prompted his change of behavior. To be honest, I do not know which of the two it was, or if it was a combination of them both." Madeline was used to reporting events and conditions of the patient, but she was still at a loss to explain the sudden change she had seen in Mr. Darcy.

"First, Miss Elizabeth came in and simply told him to behave, do as he was told, and use the chamber pot," Madeline continued. "The second thing was the actual fact that he was able to relieve himself. After that, he was more physically comfortable. I am not sure if it was Miss Elizabeth's presence or voiding that prompted the change. Either way, he became more rational and a little less emotional. He was still somewhat needy, needing reassurances and things like that—specifically from Miss Elizabeth—but nevertheless, it was a drastic change."

"Very interesting. May I talk to Miss Elizabeth?"

"Yes. She is anxious to talk to you too, but there is one more thing that you need to know. He has memory problems. Not all memories, but at least two days of memories before the accident are simply not there. I did not have enough time to evaluate to what extent or how far back the memory problems persist. But once again, Miss Elizabeth may be more helpful in this area because she was the one who first realized the problem."

Mr. Cummings decided he definitely needed to speak with Elizabeth. But first he wanted to see the patient. "How long has he been sleeping?"

"Four hours."

"Then I think I shall wake him and see how he is. Go ahead and have the colonel come in, but not Miss Elizabeth. I want to see for myself the kind of influence she has on him." He watched as Madeline left to get the colonel and, in the meantime, he checked Mr. Darcy's pulse. It was slow and steady. Without touching the foot, he examined it closer. The swelling was much the same, but the coloring was a deeper purple and went a little higher up the leg. The area that was broken seemed to still be set correctly.

"You wanted to speak with me, sir?" Colonel Fitzwilliam asked.

"Yes, I just wanted a familiar face for him when he wakes up. I have not seen him since he was a boy of sixteen or seventeen, and so, I doubt he would recognize me." He patted his abdomen. "I have grown too, you know," he said chuckling. When the colonel politely didn't laugh, Mr. Cummings continued, "Never mind. I would like to have you wake him up gently, so I can see how he responds to you. It seems he is stirring a little anyway. Go ahead. I will just stand over here in the corner."

*****

Elizabeth didn't know what to do with herself. It felt strange to be free, walking around, after sitting for so many hours. She hadn't dared leave Darcy's side until the doctor came in to examine him. Now, the colonel had been asked to come back in, and she found herself alone in the hallway. She realized she hadn't eaten since breakfast. It didn't take long to realize where her feet were taking her, but she knew her stomach wasn't the reason.

"Well, well, well, it appears the patient has allowed you a moment to yourself, and so, you come to visit the kitchen." Mrs. Wilkinson laughed. "How is he doing? It has been quiet for some time now."

"He has been sleeping, but the doctor is here evaluating him. I feel badly for leaving because I promised him I would be there when he woke up." It wasn't until that moment that the stress of the last two days hit her. Elizabeth's shoulders started to shake, and she covered her face with her hands as the tears flowed. Soon, she felt motherly arms around her. The comforting arms didn't help her regain control of her emotions much, but they did feel nice.

"Oh darling, tell me about it. Is he not doing well?"

She reached for the colonel's handkerchief that she had yet to return and wiped at her eyes. "I truly do not know. I have heard some people falter and hesitate around the ill because they are afraid that they will make things worse. I finally understand that perspective. I am so afraid I have made things worse."

"Nonsense! That is impossible. Do not allow yourself to think that way." Mrs. Wilkinson went back to scrubbing the dishes. Nodding toward the table, she said, "There is some cold meat I have not yet put away, if you like. And a batch of scones, too." Elizabeth wrinkled her nose. "What? My scones are not that bad, are they? I tried not to overcook them this time. Give me a little credit. I have eaten my own cooking for the last fifteen years, and I am as healthy as a horse!"

Elizabeth smiled through her tears; she couldn't help herself. "Perhaps, then, your cooking is fit for horses! No, thank you. I will pass on your scones."

"You know, one of these days I might get offended at your little comments about my cooking. Good thing I like you. Now, tell me why you think you made things worse." She took the pan she had cooked the ham in and started scrubbing. The juices had burned so badly that it would take some effort to clean it.

Elizabeth sliced off a piece of ham larger than she would normally eat because she knew half of it would be too tough to chew. She started telling the story of the second proposal, and her identical refusal, and his identical reaction. She explained how Nurse Madeline and Colonel Fitzwilliam both thought she should play along with his memory problems. She didn't get far into that explanation when she was interrupted.

"But who is to say the situation will arise again? I would assume that that worst is over now. You have told him that he already proposed, and you refused him . . . again. At first, he didn't accept that his foot was broken, but now he does, right? So, he will accept that you have refused him. There is no reason to think he will propose again."

"I had not thought about it that way. Perhaps you have a point. He did retain information about the accident once we told him. If what you say is true, then the worst is over; that is, he will not propose a third time. Then the real question I need to ask is, now what? Will he wish to never see me again, now that he knows?" She tried to chew the meat, but it had been overcooked and was quite tough. She swallowed anyway to be polite. She stood to get herself a glass of water, knowing from experience that fluids would help her stomach Mrs. Wilkinson's cooking.

"Good question," Mrs. Wilkinson said. "Have you read the letter he gave you yet? He certainly sought out your company after the first refusal, enough to write you a letter." She worked furiously at the dirty pan.

Elizabeth took a large swallow of water. "No," she answered. "I laid it out to dry yesterday, and last night was so late I could not read it . . . And you know how this morning has gone."

"And?"

Elizabeth hated this part of Mrs. Wilkinson. She always knew when there was a deeper conversation to have. It was a trait that was both helpful and annoying. "And . . . I am a little afraid of what it will say. What if the letter was an attempt to change my mind and he renews his addresses? What if he tells me how badly I hurt him? What if it is a hateful letter?"

Mrs. Wilkinson put down the pan and scrub brush. She wiped her hands on the towel, turned to Elizabeth, and said quite firmly, "What if nothing!"

"Excuse me?"

"I would bet my life that it is none of those things. Think about what you know about Mr. Darcy. Would he grovel and ask for your hand again? Well, apart from the head injury." Elizabeth shook her head. "No. Would he attempt to be civil, as he was that morning, all the while knowing that he was giving a hateful, angry letter?" Elizabeth shook her head. "No. Would he expose himself emotionally and show you how deeply you hurt him?" Elizabeth shook her head. "No. So, it is none of those things. Personally, I think you are wasting time trying to eat that ham when you really should be upstairs reading that letter."

"You are right, as you well know."

"I usually am."

With a smile, she put down her plate. "But you are right about two things: I should read the letter, and I cannot stomach this ham any longer." Mrs. Wilkinson flicked her hand towel at her but flashed a brilliant smile, which Elizabeth returned.

*****

Elizabeth left the kitchen with a piece of bread and jam, having eaten only a bite or two of the ham. She overheard voices in the sitting room again, and she could decipher Mr. Darcy's voice among them. It was filled with emotion. The others voices were hushed and obviously trying to soothe his anxiety. She wondered what the problem was this time. But she didn't have to wonder long.

The door to the sitting room opened to a breathless Madeline. "Ah, Miss Elizabeth, would you be so kind and work your magic again?"

"What is it this time?" Elizabeth asked.

"I am afraid it is the same thing. He does not remember the accident, and he will not cooperate with the doctor. He is asking for you."

"He is asking for me? Why? Does he not remember that I refused him?"

"It appears he does not."

Elizabeth put down her half-eaten bread and took a deep breath. Though not surprised, she was more than a little disappointed. The thought of having to turn down a third proposal was almost more than she could bear. But, she realized, if he didn't remember his proposals, then he didn't remember her uncivil refusals, either. A tiny part of her was relieved, knowing she might still have an opportunity to behave better. Perhaps his memory problems could do a bit of good.

She walked straight to the door and entered the room. The doctor was in Madeline's position, holding the broken foot in place, but other than that, the scene was identical to this morning's. "Good afternoon, Mr. Darcy. How are you today? I understand you wanted to see me."

Mr. Darcy stopped fighting his cousin and smiled at Elizabeth. "Miss Elizabeth, how good of you to come. Would you mind assisting me? I need to return to Rosings and am being told the most ridiculous lies to keep me here. Fitzwilliam insists that you know what happened, and I am afraid you are the only one I can trust. You have never held back your honest opinion. I beg of you to tell me why I am in my aunt's parsonage, wearing nothing but a shirt and breeches."

Elizabeth braced herself. He seemed calmer already since her entrance, but she was still wary. "May I ask a few questions, sir?"

Darcy looked perplexed. "Certainly. Would you like the others to step out?"

"No. But I am sure your cousin will take his hands off your shoulders if you agree to cooperate." Darcy looked up at his cousin; the colonel nodded in agreement and relaxed his grip.

Darcy said, "Very well. What are your questions?"

"How do you feel? I mean, think about how your body feels. Is there anything bothering you?" Darcy looked around the room and then back to Elizabeth. "Well?" she asked patiently.

He squirmed a little in his seat, but did not try to stand up. Colonel Fitzwilliam let go of Darcy's shoulders. "I have a cramp in my right leg, and I admit this chaise is somewhat uncomfortable. One other thing, I have a raging headache. I was trying to explain that to these people, but they insist I stay here. They said you would agree with their opinion."

"Well, I must say I do agree. You cannot be moved at this time. You have been in an accident. I saw it with my own eyes. Your horse was spooked by a storm while you were trying to mount, and it took off. It jumped over a fence, stumbled, and rolled onto you. You hit your head quite hard and broke your foot." Darcy looked down at the foot that the doctor was holding. "Yes, that same foot that you think has a cramp in it—it is actually broken. Does that make sense?" She was careful not to ask whether he remembered, because obviously he did not.

"Is that so? I truly broke my foot?"

Elizabeth let out a giggle because his speech and expression were almost verbatim to their conversation a few hours ago. She saw him raise an eyebrow at her. "Forgive me for laughing. There is nothing funny about your accident. Yes, you truly broke your foot. If you look at it, you can see the bruising." He looked at his ankle as if for the first time, and she saw him take a deep breath and lean back against the chaise.

"That explains a lot." Darcy said. This time Madeline and Colonel Fitzwilliam laughed as well. "What? What is so funny?"

Colonel Fitzwilliam chuckled again. "I may have played one too many tricks on you growing up, Cousin, but I promise I am not tricking you now. You really cannot be moved. Now, about my suggestion earlier—can we do what needs to be done?"

A panicked look came over Darcy's face. Elizabeth recognized it immediately. She said, "I have a few things I need to do, but would you like me to read to you when you are finished doing what the colonel suggests? Shall I return in fifteen minutes?"

"I would like that very much."

"Any book in particular, Mr. Darcy?"

"I am in the mood for Wordsworth. Do you have any of his poems?"

Elizabeth giggled. "I am sure I do."

*****

Elizabeth simply finished her bread outside the door and waited until Madeline came out to empty the chamber pot a few minutes later. "Is he ready for me?"

"Darling, I am afraid to tell you, but I think he will always be ready for you. But yes, he is decent and did his business."

"Thank you." Elizabeth knocked and entered the room. Darcy looked at her expectantly and then looked at his cousin who was sitting next to him. The colonel stood up and brought another chair to the side of the chaise and motioned for Elizabeth to sit down.

"Did you bring Wordsworth?" Darcy asked.

"I was reading it earlier, so it is already in the room. Right here on the table, in fact." She picked up the book and sat down.

"I regret I was not here to enjoy it with you."

Elizabeth was about to tell him he *was* here and *did* enjoy it, but the colonel put a hand on her arm to stop her. She remembered she shouldn't correct him too much. To him, this whole situation was new, and the pleasure of it showed on his face. "Indeed, I think you would have enjoyed it. Is there a particular place you want me to start, or should I go from where I left off?"

"Let us see how well you know one of my favorites. 'Oft in my waking dream do I / Live o'er again that happy hour, / When midway on the Mount I lay / Beside the Ruin'd Tower.'"[1]

Elizabeth smiled at the irony of his quotation; little did Mr. Darcy know that he was living *this* hour over and over again. "Ah, yes," she replied, "I remember what comes next." She quoted a few lines from a different stanza, curious whether he would notice the error: "'Few sorrows hath she of her own, / My Hope! my Joy! my Genevieve! / She loves me best, whene'er I sing / The Songs, that make her grieve.'"

Darcy looked at her with puzzled face. "Are you certain that is what comes next?" he asked. "I remember it differently."

"Yes. I am quite sure," she insisted. After a few seconds, she could keep up the rouse no longer and began giggling.

"That is definitely not what comes next, and you know it," Darcy smiled at her. "You would tease an injured man so mercilessly?"

---

[1] "Love", Samuel Taylor Coleridge, from *Lyrical Ballads* by William Wordsworth

"Very good catch, sir. It seems most of your memory is still perfect. Do you sing, Mr. Darcy?"

He chuckled. "When pressed I do."

Elizabeth smiled back. "Then I am pressing you. Sing me a song." Elizabeth didn't really want to spend any more hours of the day reading. She knew he would certainly enjoy it, but she was tired of replaying the same moment over and over again.

Darcy looked at her suspiciously. "I will sing, but I usually only sing for Georgiana." He looked to the colonel. "By the way, did you notify her of my accident?"

Colonel Fitzwilliam nodded. "I notified her immediately. Would she ever have forgiven me for even an hour's delay? She may be as shy as a Darcy, but she has a Fitzwilliam temper. I certainly do not want it unleashed on me. I suspect she got the letter late yesterday or early this morning, and she is probably already on her way. At the time I wrote it, you were still unconscious, but if I write again to update her, I am afraid my letter will pass her on the road." Colonel Fitzwilliam patted Darcy on the shoulder and stood up to confer with the doctor and Madeline, who were talking quietly in the corner.

"Well then, what shall I sing? How about one by Monk Lewis?" Elizabeth nodded and leaned back into the chair. He took this as his sign that he was to begin. He cleared his throat and began to sing:

Why, fair maid, in every feature,
Are such signs of fear express'd?
Can a wandering wretched creature,
With such terror fill thy breast?
Does my frenzied look alarm thee?
Trust me, sweet, thy fears are vain;
Not for kingdoms would I harm thee,
Shun not then poor Crazy Jane.

Does thou weep to see my anguish?
Mark me, and avoid my woe,
When men flatter, sigh, and languish,
Think them false – I found them so.
For I lov'd – Oh, so sincerely
None could ever love again,
But the youth I lov'd so dearly,
Stole the wits of Crazy Jane.

Elizabeth was perplexed by Mr. Darcy's choice. The ballad of Crazy Jane told the story of a woman driven to insanity when abandoned by her lover. Although a popular song, it seemed an odd choice for his refined temperament. She wondered if it was a favorite of Georgiana's.

Suddenly a very different thought came to her: *Does he worry he is crazy, like Crazy Jane?* For the first time that day, she wondered what it would be like to wake up in someone else's house, with barely enough clothes for decency, with no memory of the past two days, and in a great deal of pain. She had been so focused on how his memory problems were making her own life difficult; she had forgotten how difficult this must be for him. She felt a great rush of sympathy for Darcy and was fighting to keep tears from welling in her eyes as he continued singing:

Fondly my young heart receiv'd him,
Which was doom'd to love but one,
He sigh'd – he vow'd – and I believed him,
He was false – and I undone,
From that hour has reason never
Held her empire o'er my brain:
Henry fled – With him for ever
Fled the wits of Crazy Jane.

73

Now forlorn and broken-hearted,
And with frenzied thoughts beset,
On that spot where we last parted,
On that spot where first we met,
Still I sing my love-lorn ditty,
Still I slowly pace the plain,
Whilst each passerby, in pity,
Cries, 'God help ye, Crazy Jane!'"[2]

While Elizabeth was enjoying the smooth, deep baritone of Mr. Darcy's voice, the other three in the room were discussing some very important observations.

Mr. Cummings said, "I have never seen this before. It is amazing what her presence does for him! We tried for nearly twenty minutes to help him understand why he could not leave the chaise. And less than thirty seconds after her entrance, he was rational and less agitated. Madeline, I too wonder if there is something more to this injury than we suspect. We need to be very careful in the next few weeks not to cause any additional stress. Tell me about his setback."

Colonel Fitzwilliam explained the repetitive nature of Darcy's comments and how he refused to fall asleep until Elizabeth promised to be there when he woke up. Mr. Cummings went on, "But she was not there when he woke up. It seems he does not remember her promise. Interesting. I have to agree with you both on the plan to placate him until we know more. He seems to retain whatever Miss Elizabeth tells him—"

"Except he has forgotten that she refused his proposal. When she told him no, he seemed incapable of accepting it. That is what caused the setback," Madeline pointed out.

"I wonder why he accepts everything else she tells him, but not that," Mr. Cummings said. "I still stand by my assessment that he

---

[2] "Crazy Jane", attributed to Matthew Gregory Lewis

is very fragile right now. We must do everything we can do to keep him calm. Would Miss Elizabeth be able to spend a great deal of time with him until he recovers? She is obviously good for his recovery."

The colonel cleared his throat. "I believe she was planning on leaving in less than a week's time."

Mr. Cummings's face showed his displeasure. "Well, perhaps I can do something about that. I owe your aunt a visit. Madeline tells me her feet are swollen again. What good is an interfering and obnoxious aunt if not to get Miss Elizabeth to stay longer? Meddling in Miss Elizabeth's plans will be the perfect task for her." Just then the singing stopped, and all three looked at Darcy. He was smiling and staring blissfully at Elizabeth. When she started clapping, they joined in and walked over to the patient.

Darcy looked startled for a moment, as if he had forgotten the others were in the room. "I do not usually sing in public. I fear you have heard a rare thing indeed. Mr. Cummings, what is your prognosis? How am I?"

Mr. Cummings cleared his throat and looked at Elizabeth. Her face showed her curiosity and anticipation for his assessment. "Considering how hard you hit your head, I am pleased you are awake at all. I think we should be careful over the next few weeks and keep you comfortable. Is the pain back in your foot?"

"A little, but my head hurts worse than my foot. Doctor, I was wondering if I could ask you a few questions in private." Darcy turned toward Elizabeth and said, "It will only take a few minutes."

Colonel Fitzwilliam asked, "Do you want me to step out as well, Cousin?"

Darcy looked thoughtful. "No, you are welcome to stay. You already know most of what I need to ask the doctor anyway. Miss Elizabeth, will you come back in and read to me?"

Elizabeth tried not to giggle. It would be a long week if they were to have the same conversations over and over again. "Certainly, Mr. Darcy. I always do."

Darcy watched her leave and then asked, "What does she mean—'I always do'?"

Colonel Fitzwilliam smiled. "She has done little *but* read to you for two days, Darcy. You were unconscious for the first time and seem to have forgotten the second time."

Darcy was quiet for a moment as he contemplated that piece of information. After a few minutes, he looked up and asked the doctor, "So, I have memory problems?"

Mr. Cummings had been quietly observing everything Mr. Darcy did and said. "It appears so," he replied. "Do you mind if I ask you a few questions as a test?"

"Not at all. I would like to know what my limitations are, so please proceed."

"I am going to ask you to remember three words and have you repeat them to me in five minutes. Are you ready? The three words are apple, book, and tree. Can you repeat them?"

"Apple, book, tree."

"Good. Now, what was the last thing you remember?"

"I remember having a difficult discussion with my aunt. She asked me to come into her study to review something in the estate books, but then she engaged me in another one of her tirades about how Pemberley and Rosings should be united. She tried to convince me to make it official, once and for all. She was hoping that I would make an offer to Anne before I left, but the only thing she accomplished was convincing me that Anne was not who I wanted. I wanted someone else. I wanted Miss Elizabeth. It was right there in her study that I made the decision to offer my hand to Miss Elizabeth, and that is what I intend to do." Darcy smiled at Colonel Fitzwilliam knowingly.

"I should have listened to you earlier, Cousin," Darcy continued. "You asked me when I planned to make her an offer before I knew it myself. At the time of our conversation, I was still undecided." He turned to the doctor and explained, "I did not have

76

any objections to Miss Elizabeth; it was her family that caused me to delay my offer. But it was not until my aunt pushed her opinions on me about my future that I realized Miss Elizabeth is everything I want and need. She will make a perfect mistress of Pemberley. And it was not until that moment that I realized that I could not be happy without her."

Mr. Cummings continued his assessment, asking, "And when was that? Do you remember the day?"

"It was Saturday, before dinner. I remember because she wanted to be able to announce the engagement at church on Sunday. Wait, what day is it now?"

"Wednesday," they both said in unison.

"How long was I unconscious?"

"Just one day. The accident was on Tuesday and you awoke this morning," Colonel Fitzwilliam explained.

"Then, why can I not remember anything after Saturday?"

Mr. Cummings took his spectacles off and cleaned them. He took an enormous amount of time cleaning them.

"Doctor? What are you not telling me?" Darcy adjusted his position a little and sat up straighter. "Cousin?"

Mr. Cummings cleared his throat. "Emotional trauma can lead to memory loss," he said. "Can you trust us a little if we say you are not ready to hear what happened to you before the accident?"

Darcy raised his eyebrow. "Are you telling me that I had an emotional trauma? And that I should simply trust you? Why? Cousin, do you agree with not telling me?" His breathing started increasing, and it was obvious he was getting agitated. "Is Georgiana all right? Has something happened at Pemberley?"

"No, Cousin, nothing like that," the colonel assured him. "Everyone is safe and your home is fine. You don't remember, but we told you the news this morning, and you took it very poorly. You suffered a setback, and we had to sedate you. No one wants to keep secrets from you, but you are not ready to hear the truth. The doctor is just suggesting we let your mind remember what happened in its own time, naturally. Mr. Cummings was telling me that memories can come back all at once, or slowly, or not at all. Am I correct, Mr. Cummings?"

"Correct. I read a new theory about memory loss and emotional trauma which said the mind has its own way of protecting itself from reliving the trauma until it is ready to understand it. You are not ready to hear about what happened yet, but I do believe in time that you will remember it."

"I see. And everyone else knows what happened but me? I do not see how that is fair. For all I know, you are laughing at me."

"No one is laughing, Darcy," reassured Colonel Fitzwilliam. "I promise. The only thing that is funny is seeing how similar you are in speech and behavior every time you wake up. It is always the same routine. I already knew you were a creature of habit, but now it is quite evident." He smiled at the look on Darcy's face, equal parts worry and frustration. "Teasing aside, it is a good thing. It makes taking care of you easier, since we can predict your needs."

"He is right," Mr. Cummings agreed, nodding. "These first few days are simply trial and error in figuring out what you need, so you must be patient with us as we try to help you. Now, did you have any other questions?"

"Yes. I plan on proposing to Elizabeth and need to know if my foot will heal. I do not want her to be married to an invalid." Darcy's face showed just how serious he was.

"I believe the foot will heal properly if you stay off it. As of right now, there is nothing to prevent it from being re-broken should you try to stand. When the swelling goes down, I can put on a brace. Until then, there is nothing I can do but treat the pain. If you are cooperative and do not attempt to stand on it, then you should make a full recovery. But I warn you, a break this severe could take six, maybe eight, weeks to heal. In the meantime, it cannot bear any weight at all."

"And I must stay in this room the whole time?"

"I am afraid so. Until the bone has healed, we cannot risk any movement that could jar it out of place. Simply getting into the carriage would be nearly impossible. I have informed your aunt of this, and she has agreed to let you stay here." Darcy raised a suspicious eye at him, and he continued, "She and I came to a truce that as soon as you are able, and *want* to move, you will be moved to Rosings. But between you and me, I will be quite forceful on delaying that date. I hope this is agreeable to you."

Darcy nodded. "It is. But Miss Elizabeth is planning on leaving soon, and I doubt Mr. Collins's company will be as agreeable. It will be a very long six weeks."

Colonel Fitzwilliam spoke, "I think we have solved both those problems. I sort of implied to Aunt Catherine that Mr. Collins caused your setback, so he has been told to avoid you. And the doctor here thinks, well, how shall I put this . . . he thinks Miss Elizabeth will be good for you. Because of this, he is going to enlist our aunt's help in convincing her to stay longer. Would you like that, Darcy?"

Darcy smiled widely. "I think I have two very good advocates in my corner. I will have to think of a way to repay you both. I could not have thought of better suggestions myself."

Mr. Cummings smiled too. "Do you have any other questions?"

"Yes. I have a question for Miss Elizabeth that simply cannot wait another day. I would like to speak with her alone now."

Colonel Fitzwilliam and the doctor exchanged looks between themselves. The doctor shrugged his shoulders, apparently giving his approval. The colonel turned back to Darcy and said, "Of course, Cousin, whatever you would like."

They both turned to leave, and then Darcy called out, "Doctor? Book. Tree. Apple."

Mr. Cummings adjusted his spectacles. "Well, his short-term memory seems to be normal, whereas mine is lacking. I forgot to ask for the three words." Darcy proudly smiled back at them.

*****

Elizabeth knew she didn't have enough time to go upstairs and read the letter, but her mind kept returning to it. What did he want to tell her that was so important? She remembered he was quite insistent that she take the letter. Colonel Fitzwilliam had also said that Mr. Darcy really wanted her to have it. She was beginning to feel some guilt that she had waited this long to read it, and she wondered if it would give her some insight into his current condition.

"You appear deep in thought," Charlotte said.

"Yes, I suppose you could say that."

"Are you well? You have been spending a great deal of time with Mr. Darcy. I am sure it is tiring. Why not go take a rest?" Charlotte was beginning to see dark circles under her friend's eyes. She had suspected there was more to the accident than Elizabeth was letting on, but she didn't want to intrude. She knew in due time her best friend would tell her.

"I am as well as can be expected. Mr. Darcy has periods of nearly normal mental health, and at other times he is much worse and almost combative. He seems to have memory problems. This might be a problem because the day before the accident he actually—"

Colonel Fitzwilliam and Mr. Cummings entered the hallway, and Elizabeth stopped speaking to listen to them. This was somewhat frustrating to Charlotte because she knew Elizabeth was about to tell her what had been bothering her since Monday. She stayed to hear what the doctor had to say.

"His memory problems seem to have affected only a few days before the accident. He has good short-term memory, but I am deeply worried by the fact that he retained knowledge this morning only to lose it again when he slept. Let me look back in the journal articles related to his condition, and I will get back to you with more information.

"For the time being," he continued, "I think Miss Elizabeth should spend as much time as she can with the patient. She seems to calm him, and she has a way of convincing him of what has happened better than any of us. I agree that we should limit his visitors, even family members who may insist upon seeing him, until he is more consistent in his behavior and memory. Any kind of stressor could cause setbacks, and we simply cannot risk more. I am going to have to ask you, Miss Elizabeth, to ease his anxieties as much as possible, even if it means leading him to believe he has a chance to win your hand in marriage."

Charlotte gasped and looked at Elizabeth with wide eyes. "Pardon me," she stammered. "I was unaware Mr. Darcy wanted to marry Elizabeth."

Mr. Cummings said, "Yes, and I am afraid to say it, but I believe he is about to propose again. He is asking to speak with you privately, Miss Elizabeth."

Charlotte stared at Elizabeth and mouthed the words, "Again?", but Elizabeth gave her a pleading look to silence her.

"Colonel, do you still think I should avoid answering him? What if this becomes a daily occurrence?"

The colonel looked at the doctor, then back at Elizabeth and said, "I am afraid so. If his past behavior is an indicator of future responses, we simply cannot risk another setback. The doctor and I think that maybe if he does not have such an emotional response right before he sleeps, then he might start retaining memory. In other words, we might not have to convince him every time he wakes up that he had an accident and his foot is broken. I am sorry to say it, but if you are careful and avoid a definite refusal, we might see improvement. I am sure that is what we all want."

Elizabeth felt the heat rise in her face. She didn't like being manipulated into doing anything. "Colonel, I hope you have no doubt that I want him to improve. I was simply asking if your thoughts had changed since he woke up."

"Pardon me, Miss Elizabeth, I meant no harm and certainly did not mean to offend. Of course I know you want him to improve." He would have to be careful not to use his battlefield tactics with her. She was smart enough to see through his games and would not put up with it.

Elizabeth took a deep breath and tried to calm herself. "Forgive me too. It has been a stressful two days and from the looks of it, we will not see relief for some time. I am just trying to gather my courage and am trying to figure out what I will say when he proposes—again. I have been told my emotions are an open book, so to willfully deceive Mr. Darcy may very well be outside my capabilities. I am sure you understand."

Mr. Cummings replied, "I believe you will carry a greater burden than any of us, and I want to offer my sincere apologies. However, what needs to be done cannot be changed, and I have no doubt you can do this. Think of him as a young child who has been awfully good and is asking for a treat right before dinner. He deserves the treat, but you know it is not the right time."

Elizabeth had young cousins, and she could imagine such a scenario happening. The problem was that she was still angry at Darcy for interfering with Jane and Bingley. He wasn't a child who had been awfully good; he was a meddling, conceited, pompous man who didn't deserve her acceptance. Delaying or telling him "not before dinner" wouldn't change that. "So, you are saying he deserves to marry me and I should just tell him 'not now'? Do I not have any say in my future?"

Madeline spoke up. "Might I offer a suggestion? I gather that you are upset with him about something. Let us make him work a little at winning your hand. You are a jewel indeed, and he knows it.

Unfortunately, he also thinks he is quite the catch, and he is someone who has never been refused anything in his life. There is more than a little pride on his part. But if you can look past his assumption that you will accept him, and make him work for your hand, then somewhere along the line he will either decide you are too difficult to catch, or he will change his ways and rise to meet your expectations. Are either of these two options acceptable to you?"

"So, you are saying that if I keep delaying my answer, he will either give up, or change into someone I can accept?" Madeline nodded. "I doubt the latter because I know my own mind . . . but unfortunately, I also know Mr. Darcy, and he will not give up easily. I do not see either as viable outcomes, but I do see your point. Even if he never remembers what happened Monday, eventually one of these outcomes will occur."

They all turned their heads as they heard Mr. Darcy calling from the sitting room, asking if he had been forgotten.

Colonel Fitzwilliam bowed slightly. "I believe it is your time, Miss Elizabeth."

*****

"Ah, Miss Elizabeth, do sit down. Are you ill? Shall I ring for tea?" Darcy asked.

Elizabeth forced a smile to come to her lips. "I am well, thank you. And how are you? Is the pain terribly bad?"

"It is tolerable. I must admit I am not accustomed to sitting down when a lady is standing. Do you mind sitting down? There is something I wish to discuss with you."

Elizabeth groaned inwardly. It appeared he really was going to propose again. "Certainly." She carefully sat down on the chair near his knees and not the one by his head. He looked at the empty chair and motioned for her to move seats. *So, he thinks he can dictate where I sit?*

She pushed her unkind feelings aside and tried to look at it like her father would. Her father had taught her several things, one of which was to see the humor in things. It is where most of her impertinence came from. She decided she would try to look for the things that were funny, which meant forgetting about the two previous proposals. Nothing could be funny about them. She appeased him and moved chairs.

"I want to thank you for reading to me. It appears you have done quite a bit for me that I cannot remember. I wish there were some way to repay you."

Here it comes; he is going to offer all of Pemberley. "I am not expecting anything in return."

"But I am not accustomed to being in someone's debt. In fact, it is a rare thing indeed."

Elizabeth smiled, noticing his slightly disheveled hair and two days' stubble on his face. She knew that under normal circumstances, he would never appear in such a state of undress. His valet, Abbott, had come to shave and clean him while he was sleeping and, therefore, was sent away again. She laughed inside at the contrast between his present state and his regular appearance, clean and well-put-together.

She tried to remember what was the last thing he had said. "I doubt you have ever been in someone's debt before. I doubt you let anyone do anything for you at all." Then she remembered she should be less confrontational. "You have been without parents for so long. You are used to being self-sufficient."

"It is true. My mother died very suddenly, and I have been without her for a long time now. But although my father is dead, I am not entirely bereft of him. He passed very slowly and wrote several tomes of advice for me."

"I can imagine he advised you on a great many things." *Maybe he just wanted to talk. Maybe he is not going to propose.*

"One area of advice I am planning to follow with exactness." Darcy gave her a smile that showed dimples on each side of his face making him look quite ruggedly handsome.

She raised her eyebrow in a saucy way. "Oh? I imagine you follow your father's advice with exactness in many areas, but what, pray tell, are you referring to? Managing Pemberley? Guardianship of your young sister?"

"Marriage."

Oops. Fell into that one. She tried not to laugh at herself for her naivety. "I imagine that advice on that topic may be difficult to follow with exactness. There are a great many variables that one must consider."

"True. Are you interested to know what kind of advice he gave me on the most important decision of my life?"

Not really, not if it means you will make an offer to me. I wonder if the late Mr. Darcy ever gave you advice on proposing with sensitivity and without the expectation of an acceptance. "I believe it matters little what I want because it seems from your excited posture that you intend to tell me anyway."

"Indeed I do, Miss Elizabeth. He told me to pick someone who will always make me think. Someone who will challenge me, question me . . . someone who has a will of her own."

If you only knew what my will was. "A woman like that should not be too hard to find. I am sure you know many thoughtful ladies who are well-educated on a number of subjects."

"Educated, yes; intelligent, no. But I did find someone. In the most unlikely of places."

This is becoming awkward. What does he expect me to say? She remembered to look for the humor. "Are you asking me to guess, or are you awaiting my congratulations?" *Please do not make me guess.*

"Both, I suppose. I will give you a hint. I have seen her in many different settings."

"I imagine an intelligent lady can live anywhere. I assume you found her outside your circle of friends if, as you say, it was in an unlikely place. Considering you are eight and twenty and not married, I assume this is a recent acquaintance."

"Not too recent. I have known her for several months. However, we were separated for most of that time. You have no idea who this wonderful lady is?"

You have no idea how well I do! "If you are making me guess, then I shall ask, is it Caroline Bingley?" A surprising look of disgust came over his face.

"Of course not. She agrees with me even if I change my position! A woman like that could never satisfy me. No, my father also told me to find someone who will make me laugh." He softened his look. "Miss Bingley does not make me laugh, but *you* do."

Here it comes. "I am sure there are plenty of ladies who do."

His smile got wider. "Perhaps, but both intelligence and humor in one woman is a rare find. I shall not delay any further. You are everything my father wanted for me. You alone have stood out among all of the husband-hunting ladies of the *ton*. You stir feelings of curiosity and intrigue like no one else. Will you consent to be my wife?"

"Sir, your father seemed to be a wise man. I am sure he would advise you to give serious thought before declaring yourself to a lady. One never knows how an intelligent and humorous woman might reply to such a question."

He looked perplexed for a moment. "But I *have* thought about it. For months I have struggled, but all in vain. I have had my share of society, and now I want you!"

"What you want and what you may receive are still unclear, as I have not given you my answer."

He smiled. "I stand corrected. I should have known a witty, intelligent lady would want some time to consider such an offer. By all means. But I expect an answer at some point. I have informed Colonel

Fitzwilliam of my plans to propose, and if you have any concerns, I am sure he would be happy to tell you all my dastardly deeds as a young boy. I will warn you that I was under his influence then!" Mr. Darcy seemed pleased with himself.

"You can be sure," Elizabeth said cheekily, "that the colonel will have many opportunities to express his opinions on that subject. I will take into consideration all that you have offered. And considering that we have spent these last fifteen minutes alone, I wonder if he is making assumptions of his own. Perhaps we should invite him back in now?"

"One more question first," Darcy said with a grin.

"You may ask, but I may not answer," she said teasingly. She felt relieved that she had made it through his third proposal without verbally flogging him. He even seemed pleased with himself. She wondered if he was pleased only because he still assumed a favorable response.

"Will you read to me every day? I fear my sources of entertainment are limited."

"If you wish it."

"Oh, I do. You can be assured of that. Oh, by the way, you look beautiful with your hair down."

Elizabeth reached up and, sure enough, the two pins she had thrown in her hair early that morning had come undone, and she looked just as disheveled as he did. *Perhaps I should be seeing the humor in myself as well.*

CHAPTER 5

The evening was spent in much the same way as the morning. Elizabeth and the colonel dined with Mr. Darcy while Madeline took a stroll in the gardens. Conversation was prevalent, not only because of the colonel's natural wit, but because Darcy, for some reason, seemed to have a lot to say. It was as though a sudden surge of energy was passing through him. Instead of barely smiling at an amusement, he laughed. Instead of silently raising his eyebrow at an interesting comment, he responded easily in a friendly manner. It was unusual behavior, and both Elizabeth and Colonel Fitzwilliam noticed the change.

The colonel assumed it was due to Darcy's conversation with Elizabeth, and he thought it must have gone very well. He remembered the subtle nod Elizabeth gave him when he entered the room, confirming that Darcy really had proposed again.

Elizabeth, on the other hand, assumed the changed behavior was of an entirely different nature. She too attributed it to the proposal, but in her mind, Darcy was more open and confident because he assumed she would accept. It irked her more than she cared to admit, and once again, she wished she didn't have to play such games with him. Instead of speaking truthfully to Darcy as a friend, she was feigning interest and encouraging him to court her.

Yes, courting, that was what Darcy was doing. He was trying to impress her with his *joie de vivre*. Coming from someone naturally so reserved, it should have been very amusing, but she was too upset to enjoy it. Deep down he was still the same interfering and prideful

Darcy she had known all along, and she was in no mood for amusement.

So, he thinks that he will not be refused? He thinks any woman would accept his suit? He is convinced that no matter how he proposes, whether with veiled insults or guessing games, he will get an affirmative answer? If he only knew my true feelings. No amount of courting will change my opinion of him. An hour's pleasant conversation cannot change the fact that when it comes to my sister's happiness, he is no different than his meddling, overbearing aunt.

Thinking of Jane reminded her that she still needed to read his letter. She decided it was time to end the charade for the evening and stood to excuse herself. "I am afraid I am behind on several correspondences. Would you mind if I retire early? Besides, Mr. Darcy, you have been rubbing your leg for quite some time. Perhaps it would be wise to take some pain medication and get some rest."

Darcy looked embarrassed. "Was it that evident? It throbs a great deal, and my head is not any better. I was afraid to ask, because I did not want to appear rude, but pain medication does sound heavenly."

"Then, I will see you in the morning." She didn't quite know how she felt about reading Darcy's letter. One thing she knew: the letter couldn't be good. Nevertheless, she owed it to him and to herself to read it. In a way, she felt responsible for his accident. If he hadn't felt the need to deliver the letter in such weather, then the horse wouldn't have gotten spooked. She took a few steps up the stairs before being stopped by her cousin.

Mr. Collins was seriously displeased. "Miss Bennet, I might warn you that you have a duty to your family to behave appropriately, and spending so much time with Mr. Darcy when he is so ill is a dangerous endeavor. Obviously, your regret in refusing my proposal is prompting you to spend excessive amounts of time with him in hopes of receiving another proposal while he is in a weakened state. But you must know that you have no chance to win Mr. Darcy's hand.

"I am sure he has not looked twice in your direction," Mr. Collins cautioned. "He only wishes you would leave him be! You may have refused the only offer of marriage you will get when you refused me, and your obvious regret in doing so is influencing your behavior now. Your choices in the past have branded you, and there is nothing you can do about it now. You must accept that I am with Charlotte now; I am sorry to tell you that I have made her happier than a gorilla with bananas."

Elizabeth laughed out loud, noisier than she intended. Mr. Collins thought she was pining over him! He assumed because she had refused him, she would always be a spinster! Little did he know! She had done a masterful job of not laughing until he described himself as a gorilla! Flashes of his hairy chest and slimy, balding head overpowered her resolve.

Doing her best to present a straight face, she nodded. "Yes, sir. I take your meaning quite literally. Thank you." She pushed past him and wiped her face with her handkerchief, retreating to her room as quickly as possible. A neat pile of newly-laundered handkerchiefs was waiting on her bed. She exchanged her sodden one for a new one and breathed in the smell of fresh linen. Between Mr. Collins's assaults and her tears over Mr. Darcy, it was remarkable how many handkerchiefs she went through each day. Thank goodness Charlotte's servants were so quick with these things.

What nerve Mr. Collins had to trap her on the stairs and give her yet another sermon about her behavior! At least it was almost over. She was planning to depart on Monday, which meant there was less than a week left of enduring his spittle and sermons. A post-chaise was sounding lovelier each day. After all, Mr. Darcy would only be able to propose so many times in five days.

She moved the handkerchiefs aside and sat down on the bed. She was tired, but she promised herself she would read the letter. She had tucked it under her book that morning, out of view of the servants and everyone else. She pulled it out and examined the warped, dirty, ink-smeared letter. It was two pages long, and he seemed to have written quite small. Apparently, he had a lot to say.

Did she really want to read this? Did she really want to discover what he so desperately wanted her to know? No. She stood up and paced a little. Why can't men hear the word "no" and accept it? First, Mr. Collins with his awful proposal, and then, Mr. Darcy! What is so wrong about a lady who refuses to marry except for love? She recalled Mr. Collins's horrible proposal when he first asked for a private meeting with her. She had begged her mother and Jane not to leave, which he interpreted as a sign of modesty.

"You would have fallen short of amiability in my eyes if you were not so modest. Your modesty does you justice. But let me continue with why I feel the need to find a wife."

"No, sir, I beg of you. Do not—"

"First, a clergyman must set the example of sacred matrimony in his parish. Since he is looked upon with the upmost respect and honor, he must wed. His example of matrimony will encourage those less fortunate to desire the same situation for their own lives rather than settle for unseemly behavior. Second, I can think of no better way to secure my happiness than to marry a lady such as yourself, regardless of your being raised in the country."

"Mr. Collins, I implore you to stop—"

"I will not stop, no matter how generous you are with your humility. For I have seen these last two weeks your wonderful qualities, and your modesty only convinces me all the more of your suitability. You should know that I singled you out nearly from the beginning as my future bride and have grown only fonder as I spent time with you. Without pausing for breath, he continued, "But I must return to my reasons for marrying. Third—perhaps I should have mentioned this first, for it is the most important reason I have in offering my hand to you—it is the particular advice and counsel of the noble Lady Catherine de Bourgh that I find a suitable wife that will do me the honor of

attending to her ladyship's needs. Only a week before I left Kent, she summoned me to her grand estate, Rosings Park, and she kindly said to me . . . do you know what she said to me?"

Elizabeth groaned. "No, but it does not matter what she said, because I cannot—"

"She said, 'Mr. Collins, you are a man of one and thirty and must find a wife! Any clergyman of mine must be married.' Can you believe her ladyship's condescension in seeing to my needs? She is most generous. When we are married, we will dine there at least once a week, and I suspect even more regularly once she sees what a wonderful bride I have chosen."

"Sir, please stop. I have not answered you, and in truth, you have not even asked! I cannot be your wife. I am sure of it!"

"Oh dear, you are quite correct!" Mr. Collins got down on one knee. "I have yet to ask the most important question a man can ask. Will you marry me and serve and protect as a most loyal wife should?"

"No, sir, I cannot. I will not. Now get up off the floor this instant!"

Mr. Collins paused, and shifted his weight, but remained on one knee before her. "You can see why I chose to pick from my lovely cousins at Longbourn instead of from my own neighborhood. When your father dies, and from the looks of his health, it may not be long, I will inherit Longbourn and you will once again be living in the same house you grew up in!

"I pride myself on my own condescension, for I have always admitted my own faults and rarely see any in others. I flatter myself, however, to have noticed your attentions toward me. When you handed me the potatoes at dinner the other day, your hand grazed mine, and it was like providence! I knew from that moment on that nothing could keep me from having you."

She couldn't help but lace her next comments with sarcasm. "Sir, I have not given you my consent. I, in fact, am grateful to be held in such esteem by one so closely attached to Lady Catherine de Bourgh, but I insist I am in earnest. I cannot marry you."

"I am not so unlearned as to not know when a lady is seeking encouragement. Your refusal is not unusual for a young lady who secretly means to accept a man when he applies again, and in fact, I suspect I may be refused two or three more times before you agree."

Two or three times? She had refused him at least five times now! Elizabeth was ready to spit right back at him. She was grateful he was now on his knees, and therefore his spittle had gravity working in her favor. "It is quite extraordinary to assume that any lady would refuse a man she hopes to obtain once, let alone twice, or even three times. But even if such ladies exist, I am not one of those ladies. I am perfectly serious in my refusal. For I know that you could not make me happy, and I would be the last person in the world who could make you or Lady Catherine de Bourgh happy!"

"Lady Catherine de Bourgh would not be anything but pleased in my choice of brides. Why would you ever say such a thing?" However, as he said the words, doubt showed on his face.

"No matter what praise you can give of me to her, eventually she will see me as I am, and I doubt she will be pleased to know that I have a strong will and do not cower to noble women who think too much of themselves. I fail to see the delicacy in your opinions about the health of my family, but even being homeless would in no way prompt me to accept your hand. Good day."

As she walked away she heard him say, "When I speak of this with you the next time, I hope to receive a more favorable answer. I am not calling you cruel, for I understand the custom of refusing the man you intend to accept, but I might warn you that you must think about your duty to family, and that you might never receive such a proposal from another."

It was all she could do to not slam the door behind her as she raced out of the house toward Oakham Mount.

Looking back at the disaster of her proposal from Mr. Collins, she had to admit that all three proposals from Mr. Darcy compared quite favorably. Mr. Darcy had been prideful, but not ignorant of the fact that she did have a choice. He had offended her family, her station, and her lack of fortune in at least two of the proposals, but he was not callous in his regard of them. He had shown true emotion in declaring love and admiration, whereas Mr. Collins made no such attempt.

To Mr. Collins, Elizabeth was a logical choice, a convenient choice. To Mr. Darcy, Elizabeth was not some passing whim. He said he had struggled long with his emotions, but in vain. The proposals of the two were quite different.

She finally concluded it was time to read the letter. She opened it and settled herself back against a pillow on the window seat. With a candelabra lighting the room and the soft sound of raindrops splashing the window pane, she examined the letter. There were parts that she definitely wouldn't be able to read because of the water damage, but for the most part, it was legible. She closed her eyes one last time and willed herself to read it. Her apprehension made her hands shake and her heart beat faster. She opened her eyes and willed them to look at the page.

Miss Elizabeth Bennet,

Be not alarmed, madam, on reading this letter, nor apprehensive about it being a repetition or renewal of my previous proposal, which seemed so disgusting to you. I write only to clarify the two issues you lay at my feet. Although I admit I was shocked to hear your refusal, it was the reasons for the refusal that I find myself most alarmed by. For, if given proper perspective and clarification, neither will have much merit once I have explained them.

Or so he says! She suppressed the urge to groan. *So, it will be one of those letters; he wants to enlighten me about how wrong I am.* She continued reading.

> *The effort it has taken to disclose the following is great indeed, and I pray that you will heed my words with an open mind, for it is not easy for me to share such personal feelings. You must pardon the freedom I take in writing to you in this way, for I find my mind can do little else but be frank and honest with you. It would do neither of us justice—not me for staying up and writing this missive, nor you for accepting it—if you do not read with an open mind. For me, this letter is of more importance than any I have written thus far in my life. I can only say one more thing before I reach the purpose of the letter. It is that . . .*

The words smeared at that point and Elizabeth tried to figure out what was the one more thing he so desperately wanted her to know. She sighed. So far, he was presumptive, assuming she would accept the letter. Yes, she had accepted it—but he shouldn't have assumed she would! Also, he had declared that her two reasons for refusing him could be explained away. She could not imagine anything that would suddenly change her mind on those points, but she had to admit he had her attention. She read on.

> *You accuse me of interfering with your dear sister, Miss Jane Bennet, and my friend, Mr. Bingley. Of this you are correct, but to help you understand why I did it, you need to know something: I sincerely doubted*

her affection. You undoubtedly are a reliable source of knowledge when it comes to your eldest sister, and I must defer to your judgment. You know her much better than I do. If you say that Miss Bennet's heart truly was touched, then my knowledge and opinion on the matter of her heart has no foundation. But until you revealed this knowledge to me, I could only go on what I witnessed of her behavior.

I had not been in Hertfordshire long before I saw that Bingley showed a preference for Miss Bennet. I had seen him numerous times display this type of infatuation, and I had little concern because never in the past had a lady ensured his good opinion longer than a few weeks. It was not until the Netherfield Ball that I had any apprehension about a serious attachment. Like I said, he had taken a fancy to a number of ladies in the past, and when a new one would come along, his interest in the last dwindled.

But when I had the honor of dancing with you, and Sir William joyously reveled in the nuptial rumors circulating, my eyes were opened to the fact that marriage was not only hoped for, but expected between the two! I then began to watch Miss Bennet for any expression of her true feelings. I studied her closely that night. Her manners were kind, open, and engaging. Her cheerful nature was evident toward my friend, but I concluded that there was no element of particular regard for him.

This perspective I now know from your revelation to be false, but at the time, I saw no real attachment to Bingley. Bingley is an honorable man and would have married her if that was the expectation. However, I do not think it right for a man *to marry a woman who does not love him. He is too good of a person to find himself in a forced marriage. I admit I knew well of his growing love and admiration for her, but . . .*

Again it was smeared.

. . . and so I find that is the only reason I interfered. For without mutual love, how can a marriage bring happiness? I can imagine they would get along nicely at first, but soon tire of each other and live separate, unfulfilled lives. I did not want that for my friend. Mr. Bingley is the best friend anyone could ask for. I was trying to help him, but I see now, with your revelation of your sister's true heart, that I was wrong to have interfered.

I do not know what I can do about this situation. Not only did I convince him to leave Netherfield, but I also withheld information that Miss Bennet was in London all those months. I am ashamed to admit these things, for such actions are beneath me, and I despise deceit of any form. I should have let him, as an adult, make his own decisions.

I am afraid the next thing I must say may pain you, and I apologize in advance. If it was simply the neutrality of Miss Bennet's feelings, then perhaps I may have not interfered. But there was more cause for concern. The ball revealed further the total lack of propriety so frequently and uniformly portrayed by your family. I speak specifically of your younger sisters, your mother, and at times, your father. I know what I say pains you, and I do not intend to offend. Neither

you nor Miss Bennet have anything to censure. In fact,
you should both be praised for your dispositions.

Elizabeth fumed. *He doesn't mean to offend? How could he not with those words!* She put the letter down. She wanted no more of it. The rain had let up so she stood and opened the window. The fresh late-evening air was helpful and the deep purples and blues that the night cast upon the gardens calmed her. She could see the shapes of the manicured hedges and perfectly trimmed trees reflecting the faint light that shone through the storm clouds. Lady Catherine demanded perfection for the grounds around Rosings and the parsonage. If only the problems in life could be trimmed and pruned into symmetry like that.

What a strange thought to have, Elizabeth mused. She had always wanted to stand out, to be different, and to be unique. Rosings's unnatural austerity held no true beauty for her. Elizabeth usually enjoyed the challenges life brought, even vexing ones, like Mr. Darcy.

Her thoughts turned back to Jane and the unfinished letter. So many emotions were running through her mind. She knew Jane was shy. Charlotte had even counseled her on the matter; she had warned her that Jane needed to be more affectionate with Bingley. Elizabeth had not shared Charlotte's opinion and did not pass on that advice to Jane. So, could he be right?

She let out a groan. If Mr. Darcy believed as he said he did, then she and Jane were partly to blame. Elizabeth pushed those forgiving emotions down deep. Jane was still miserable, and she was not ready to overlook Darcy's part in it. She groaned again. She knew she had to keep reading. She had gotten this far in the letter and simply had to continue. She sat back down on the window seat and proceeded to read.

Nevertheless, Bingley is too kind of a man to see these things. Please take my apologies to heart and know that deep down, my purpose was not to harm either party, but instead to . . .

Why does it always smear the most important parts? She read on, trying to make out the next paragraph, which was badly smeared as well.

. . . Of this, you can be sure . . . for never would I have interfered if I had believed . . . was the case. Now I see that I am wrong. Please forgive me. I will attempt to right my wrong by . . . as soon as possible.

Now, to the other offence you accused me of. I do not know the exact offences of which I am accused by George Wickham, but perhaps if I reveal a few experiences, it might alter your perspective on the man. George Wickham was the son of a very respectable man, the steward of my late father. Thus, George and I grew up very close, and he was like a brother to me.

However, there has always been a darker side to Wickham. There was never a time in our childhood when I was disciplined for poor behavior that Wickham was not involved. He, of course, could talk himself out of punishment, whereas I did not have the skill to do so.

Blind to his negative influence on me, we remained friends many years. It was not until I left for Cambridge and became close to several others that I began to see his true self. He followed me to Cambridge one year later, at the expense and generosity of my father, where he revealed himself as the flagrant rake that he is. I was witness to his scheming, womanizing ways, ranging from servants to married women. We naturally grew apart, for I could no longer respect him.

It was not until my dear late father passed that I again heard from him. By this time, he had left university and was gambling heavily. My father had loved him like a son. He had paid for a gentleman's education, and yet Wickham threw away the opportunity. Regardless, my father had left him a living at Kympton in his will. From my previous description of the lifestyle Wickham had chosen for himself, I am sure you can imagine what I felt about him taking vows and serving in the church.

As grace would have it, Wickham came to me and stated he did not want to take orders and wanted instead monetary compensation of three thousand pounds to replace the living bequeathed in my father's will.

I was more than willing to agree to his terms. I have the papers that were written up and signed in front of my solicitor to prove this to be true. My cousin, Colonel Fitzwilliam, can also validate the truth of the matter since he was an executor of the will. I plead with you to appeal to his knowledge if you have any remaining doubts.

Of the exact offences that Wickham has laid at my door, I admit I am entirely ignorant. However, knowing his smooth talking ways, I imagine they were half-truths laced with a good helping of charm. I know him too well to imagine that he told you the truth, and I know you too well to imagine you accepted blatant, outrageous lies. But I am certain that you are too wise

not to see through his false goodness when offered the
truth in its entirety. I do implore you to once again
speak with . . .

Smeared. Elizabeth was pretty sure it said Colonel Fitzwilliam again. The letter had become somewhat intriguing, but she was amazed to see half a page remained. What more could there be to say? Wasn't telling her of Wickham's lies and womanizing enough? How could she have believed Wickham?

Mr. Darcy had said that Colonel Fitzwilliam could verify all of the above, but she knew, after reading this letter, that speaking to the colonel was not necessary. If Darcy were guilty of any misdeed, he would never have offered a respectable man like the colonel as a witness; he would only do so to prove his innocence. *No! I am not ready to forgive Mr. Darcy!* But in her heart, she already knew Darcy had written the truth. She returned her focus to the rest of the letter.

. . . Unfortunately my dealings with Wickham did not
end with settling the living. Twice, I was solicited for
money to pay off his debts of both honor and
otherwise. Out of pity, I helped him the first time; but
when he approached me a second time, I think you can
hardly blame me for refusing to assist. He then
contacted me a third time, and stated he had changed
his mind, and was ready to serve in the church, and
demanded the living back. I, of course, refused him. I
did not hear from him until two years later when he
entered my life in a devious and cruel way.

What I am going to disclose is so deeply
painful that I have told no one of it, except Colonel
Fitzwilliam. I had to tell him because the incident
involved my young sister, Georgiana, in whom he and I
share guardianship. Last year, I employed a Mrs.

Younge as a companion for my sister. Georgiana got along nicely with her. I even congratulated myself in finding someone so fitting for a girl of fifteen. I was sorely wrong.

A few months into her employment, Mrs. Younge suggested a trip to Ramsgate so Georgiana could further her studies and get some fresh sea air. I found out later that Wickham went to Ramsgate as well, undoubtedly by design, for he had a prior acquaintance with Mrs. Younge.

Georgiana's trusting nature and affectionate heart, combined with the help of the scheming Mrs. Younge, led to a renewing of old friendships from growing up together. Mr. Wickham recommended himself to her, and with the help and encouragement of Mrs. Younge, convinced Georgiana that she was in love, and she consented to an elopement. She was but fifteen, an excuse I have used to ease her guilt of the situation. Mr. Wickham, however, knew very well what he was doing.

I am grateful I unexpectedly joined them the day before the intended elopement, for Georgiana confided in me and revealed the plan. Even now, just thinking about what nearly happened has stirred feelings that I cannot easily repress. I informed Mr. Wickham that he would receive none of Georgiana's thirty-thousand-pound dowry in marrying her. That was enough incentive for him to leave, and to dismiss Georgiana entirely with no remorse for how he hurt her by doing so. Undoubtedly, the dowry was all that Wickham cared about, and my dear sister has not been the same since.

One might ask why he would go to such great lengths to hurt me, for if he had succeeded in ruining Georgiana, his revenge would have been complete indeed. His reasons for doing such things I cannot know. If this narrative, as honest as I could be in writing it, does not clear up any half-truths he may have told you, I fear nothing will. He is the lowest of scoundrels and I should have . . .

More smears? Should have what? If only she could read all of what it said. She took a deep breath. How could Wickham's easy manners conceal his true nature so well? She thought of the pretty words he spoke that were indeed flattering, even leading her into believing that he was developing feelings for her.

She then was reminded of an incident with a girl named Mary King, a young lady whom he hadn't even looked at twice until her uncle died and left her a handsome ten-thousand-pound dowry. All of this seemed to fit well into Darcy's account of his character. Was it not just last week that her sister, Lydia, wrote and informed her that Miss King's hand was refused to Wickham? Did Miss King's parents suspect his mercenary ways? She quickly returned to the letter to read the last paragraph.

This, madam, is a faithful narrative of every event and dealing I have had with George Wickham. If you do not believe his accusations against me to be false, I pray that you will at least acquit me of cruelty toward the man. I am sure you are not the first, nor the last, to be imposed upon by his easy manners. As I said at the ball, his manners make it easy for him to make friends, but whether or not he is able to keep them is another story. Nevertheless, I have done all I

*can do to help you understand the truth behind my
actions.*

*What you choose to do with this information
now is entirely up to you, but I encourage you to
appeal to the testimony of Colonel Fitzwilliam if my
word is not enough. Perhaps in consulting him, you
can protect yourself from any more of Mr. Wickham's
deceits. I would wish no harm to come to you.*

I will only add, God bless you.

Fitzwilliam Darcy

Elizabeth wanted to scream! The last thirty minutes she felt
like she had been emotionally assaulted. One minute, she seemed to
know what to think, and the next, was a blur—just like the view from
the rain-splattered window where she sat. She was riddled with such
guilt and anger and pity and sorrow and, finally, remorse that she felt
whipped. If the things Mr. Darcy said were indeed accurate, and she
could sense that she was already accepting that they were, then it
meant that she was wrong. Elizabeth did not like to be wrong, and
truth be told, it did not happen often. However, when it did happen,
she was humble enough to admit it.

She quickly read through the letter again. The second time
through was no less emotionally trying than the first. Darcy started out
very arrogant and presumptive in his addresses to her, which justified
some of her anger toward him. He assumed that what he had to say
would change her mind. But she had greatly misjudged him. All this
while, she had perceived that he was interfering, overbearing, and
controlling toward the amiable and mild-tempered Bingley. In fact, his
explanation showed that he valued the friendship enough to protect
Bingley from the unhappiness of a loveless marriage.

She wondered about this for a moment. In the finest circles, love was a rare element in a marriage. More often than not, marriages were arranged for financial reasons and social status; love was rarely involved. Could Mr. Darcy be a romantic? Could he wish for a loving marriage not only for his friend but himself as well?

She thought back to his original proposal, how he had professed his admiration and love for her. He really did care for her. Why else would a man offer to a woman who was so far beneath him financially and socially?

No, no, no, no! All this time she had been sure of one thing! She was sure that Mr. Darcy only offered marriage to get what he wanted, and at the moment he wanted her. She had felt she had a right to feel indignation because she was not a prize to be won! But looking at his proposals from the perspective that he was a romantic changed things. Yes, he wanted her, and probably felt like he deserved her simply because he had never been refused anything in his life. But did he really love her? She had never really considered that he actually loved her.

How could he love her? Ever since the Meryton Assembly, Elizabeth had almost gone out of her way to show him she did not desire his good opinion. She had argued every point he made. She had teased him as best she could.

Oh, dear Lord! Did he take all that opposition as flirting? Had she been flirting? She had never been trying to make him love her! He had scorned her at that assembly, and her pride was hurt momentarily, but then instead of truly scorning him back, she had played with him like he was a toy on a string. She had such decided, distasteful opinions of him that she hadn't taken the time to evaluate the real purpose of her behavior.

She tried to be honest with herself. Was her pride so hurt that she wanted to show him just exactly what he was missing when he refused to dance with her? Did she intend to show him just how tempting she really was? Did she behave differently with him than any other man? Was she different with Bingley? With Wickham?

She groaned with the realization that she did indeed behave differently with Mr. Darcy. She was so prideful that she had crossed society's carefully created rules and treated him differently than any other man she knew. To Bingley, she was cordial, happy, and polite. To Wickham, she accepted his kind compliments graciously and humbly.

But with Mr. Darcy, she had argued and quarreled. She debated every issue she could with him. She had not behaved as a proper lady should. She had tried to prove her superiority to him in every dialogue. She was reminded of the time Miss Bingley asked her to take a turn about the room. She remembered the conversation well. She had accused him of pride and vanity, right to his face, in front of Miss Bingley. Although Miss Bingley had opened the conversation, it was Elizabeth who broached the suggestion to tease Mr. Darcy.

"Oh no, Mr. Darcy is not a subject to be laughed at," Miss Bingley asserted. "He has a calmness and presence of mind that defy it. For, if we laugh, we will simply expose ourselves."

Elizabeth let out a chuckle. She was baiting him well. "Mr. Darcy is not to be laughed at? That is an uncommon advantage as well as a great loss to me, for I dearly love to laugh."

He put his pen down and looked her directly in the eyes. "Miss Bingley gives credit where none is necessary," he said. "I dare say the wisest of men may be rendered ridiculous by the man who wishes to make life a joke."

"Certainly, Mr. Darcy, but I am not one of them. I hope I never ridicule those who are wise. But in follies and nonsense, I dare say, I take my delight in and find amusement aplenty."

Mr. Darcy smiled slightly and cocked his head. "It has been the study of my life to avoid such weaknesses, those that expose men to laughter or ridicule."

Elizabeth returned the same half-smile and cocked her head in an identical manner and asked, "Such as vanity and pride?"

He raised his eyebrow, obviously sensing the trap. "Yes, vanity is a weakness indeed," he said. "But pride, where there is true superiority of mind, will always be under good regulation." He leaned back into his chair, showing how confident he felt in his superiority of mind.

She turned her head to hide the giggle, but that didn't stop Miss Bingley from stepping in. "Pray, what is the result of your examination of Mr. Darcy?" she asked, flashing her most charming smile at him.

Elizabeth collected herself and turned back to Mr. Darcy. "He owns without disguise that he has no defect."

His smile faded slightly as he deliberated her words. "I made no such claim," he insisted. "I have faults enough. My temper I dare not vouch for, for it is too unyielding. I also cannot forget the follies or offenses against myself so easily as others. My good opinion once lost, is lost forever."

"That is a failing indeed! But I cannot laugh at that. I see you are a man who is safe from me."

She thought she heard him murmur, "I dare say I am not," but when she looked back at him, he had already returned to his letter.

Oh, why did she delight in baiting him so? And did he really say, "I dare say I am not"? If so, was he admitting his weakness for her company as far back as when Jane was sick at Netherfield? Has he really had feelings toward her that long?

She was quite fatigued with the mental examination of the letter, her actions, his intentions, and every other poorly held belief that she had had of him. Was he really a devoted and loyal friend, rather than a meddling, pompous man? Was he the victim of a smooth-talking Wickham rather than the perpetrator? Her mind was very confused. She walked to her bed and collapsed, her weary head welcoming the soft pillow, and willed herself to think no more on it tonight. This decision did not stop her from holding the letter close to her as she fell asleep.

*****

Elizabeth was awakened by loud knocking on her door. Her tired eyes were trying to evaluate what was happening. The sun was still low, earlier than her normal waking time. The knocking came again, followed by her cousin's voice, shouting through the door.

"Cousin Elizabeth! It is decided! You will stay another six weeks!"

What was he talking about? And why was he so energetic this early in the morning? She crawled out of bed and realized she had slept in her clothes. She walked her foggy mind and body over to the door and opened it. Mr. Collins, who must have been too excited to wait until he was fully dressed, was shaking a letter so forcefully that the hair exposed in his open shirt shook and swayed with each movement. *Ugh! Must I witness his chest rug this early in the morning?* She swallowed and forced her eyes away from the vacillating hair. "To what do you refer, Mr. Collins?"

"I just received a letter from my humble benefactress, Lady Catherine de Bourgh, and as you well know, there is none wiser than she, for her very opinion heralds respect and stimulates in all those who know her a great desire to please. Her mind is so sharp for her age, not that I am saying her age is past the prime of life, for I cannot see any fault at all in one as noble as she.

"But I digress," he continued. "I mean to tell you she has arranged it all! You need not worry about a post-chaise on Monday! For she has made it quite clear that she will condescend to personally deliver you to Longbourn in six weeks' time herself, her very self! Do you realize what this means?"

Elizabeth was so fully saturated by his saliva and overcome by his enthusiasm, that she could not yet comprehend his words. Why was her mind so tired? What was he saying about six weeks? "I do not understand your meaning. Hold on a minute." She hadn't realized she was still gripping Mr. Darcy's letter in her hand and nearly wiped her brow with it. She turned back to her dressing table, put down Mr. Darcy's letter, and grabbed a fresh handkerchief.

While keeping her distance, she asked a second time, "What exactly are you referring to? Lady Catherine has offered to take me home? But not until six weeks from now? This will not do. I have lingered long enough and have a great many things to do back at home. I cannot stay."

Mr. Collins stepped into the room and grabbed Elizabeth by the shoulders. "Yes! You must!" he insisted. "Mr. Darcy's life and well-being depend upon it!"

Elizabeth felt one large splatter on her left eye, and she shook off his hairy grip and stepped back in disgust. Could he at least keep his distance before showering her with such nonsense, let alone his saliva? "I will not! And I beg of you to keep your distance."

"I see you are dressed. That is good. Her ladyship desires tea with you as soon as possible. She will explain everything! Oh, I am so pleased to offer this service to her . . . and her nephew, of course. She said it was the one thing she desires from me, and I shall give you to her, I shall!" With that he turned and left Elizabeth to clean and dry herself.

*****

"Good Lord, Darcy! We cannot keep having this same argument!"

Elizabeth recognized the conversation immediately and went into the room. "Good morning, Mr. Darcy. I see you are having your morning argument with your cousin. May I participate? I dearly love to debate, and it seems I have once again missed a most entertaining one."

Darcy looked at her confused. "Miss Elizabeth, how good to see you. I appreciate you coming, but I must tell you that now is not a good time. I do desire to be in your company, but I have pressing matters to attend to. Perhaps you could return later? What do you mean 'my morning argument'?"

"Unfortunately, Mr. Darcy, I am fully aware of your pressing matters. As we have said the last two days, you now have limitations in accomplishing those pressing matters. Might I suggest you take a moment to evaluate the state of your foot and detect for yourself what exactly the limitation might be? Trust me. Just look at your foot."

Madeline moved slightly away from the foot and removed the blanket. Mr. Darcy's face showed surprise, then confusion.

"I do not understand," he said quietly.

Elizabeth chuckled. "I think we are seeing a pattern of behavior, and I have a plan that might make each morning a little easier for us all. Each morning you wake up needing to be reminded of what happened to you and your foot. Each morning you are agitated and upset until I enter the room. Each day you calm a great deal when I read to you. Does any of this sound familiar?"

Mr. Darcy said, "No, I am afraid not. I really have no idea what you are all referring to." She noticed he was not nearly as angry as the other mornings. He continued, "You really read to me?"

"Yes, sir. And I plan on doing it again if you will just do as the nurse and Colonel Fitzwilliam have suggested. Now, when I get back, I will tell you my plan, and we shall see how well it works. Do you need something for the pain?"

Darcy looked dumbfounded. His frustration and confusion was evident. "First, tell me why I seem to be at a loss, yet all of you know what is going on."

"That is part of my plan. Now, I am going to go ring for breakfast, and we can eat together. Would you like that?"

"Indeed."

Elizabeth let out a frustrated sigh and walked out. She found Charlotte just outside the door. "Good morning, Charlotte. How are you?"

"I am well, but the more important question is how are you? You look as if you did not sleep well. Come, let us talk in my parlor." Elizabeth followed her into the parlor and sat down. "I want to apologize for my husband waking you up. He received a note from Lady Catherine at first light, and I am afraid he was too overjoyed to be respectful."

Charlotte continued, "I know he can be . . . interesting, but you must forgive him. I struggled with his nature for some time until I realized that he feels most happy when he can share his opinion. So, I let him express it in all his verbose ways, and then he settles down and leaves. I know you do not understand what it is like, but I am not so ignorant to believe that mine is the only marriage with difficulties. You, on the other hand, will have little to complain about when you are married to Mr. Darcy."

"Charlotte! How can you say such a thing! I have no intention of marrying Mr. Darcy!"

Surprised, Charlotte stammered, "But I thought he proposed!" Then reading Elizabeth's stubborn expression she said, "Ah, so I see you did not accept him. May I ask why? I judged you poorly at first when you refused Mr. Collins, but I accepted your reasons. However, Mr. Darcy is a match that cannot be improved upon. How can you refuse such an offer?"

"I know you would think so, but we are different, you and I. We both want happiness, but for you happiness comes from feeling secure and having a home of your own. For me, well, I want to be deeply in love, and I do not love Mr. Darcy."

"Not yet."

"I do not take your meaning."

"I mean, Mr. Darcy is a decent and kind man. Do you not see that?"

Elizabeth remembered all her feelings while reading the letter the night before. She needed someone with a fresh perspective. "I will not answer you that, but there is something that I just now decided I need your help with. Mr. Darcy proposed on Monday, and the morning of his accident he gave me a letter. I wish to hear your views on the contents of the letter. I value your level head and rational mind, and that is exactly what I need at the moment. But first, let me give you a little background information."

Elizabeth explained the details of Mr. Darcy's interference with Jane and Bingley, and then filled in the parts about Wickham that Charlotte didn't already know. She gave a truthful description of the terrible proposal as well, and was blatantly honest about her angry refusal and Mr. Darcy's reaction. "I only tell you these things so that you can have all the necessary knowledge at your disposal to help me make sense of it all."

"I will do what I can. Are you sure you want me to read it? It feels inappropriate for me to read a private letter from Mr. Darcy."

"Now that you know about the letter, I am very confident that is exactly what I desire. If I were home, I would talk this over with Jane, but I cannot, and it is very troubling. I cannot stop the whirlwind of emotions. I have had such an onslaught of feelings, and I do not know what to do with them. I need you. I need your insight. You are not one who runs away with your feelings. You act, rather than react. In fact, I will bring you the letter this very moment."

Elizabeth leaned in and kissed Charlotte on the cheek. She felt a wave of relief come over her about this decision. On her way up to her room, she notified the kitchen to prepare breakfast trays.

In addition to the letter, she retrieved three things. She needed paper, pen, and ink.

*****

"So, will you try my plan?" Elizabeth asked. Darcy hesitated, saying nothing.

Colonel Fitzwilliam sighed. "Come, Darcy, surely you see the benefit of her plan!"

Madeline tried to encourage him as well. "I think it is an ingenious plan, and I cannot believe I did not think of it earlier."

All three watched Mr. Darcy curiously. He was behaving very oddly. "So, you think that if we write a letter detailing what I am supposed to remember and have me sign it . . . then have me read it first thing every morning . . . you think that I will not react the way you say I have; which, according to you, has been somewhat emotional and irrational."

Colonel Fitzwilliam nodded. "Yes. Until we figured out what could calm you," and motioning subtly to Elizabeth, he continued, "we had a terrible time convincing you of the accident and your injuries." He couldn't help but chuckle at seeing Darcy flush red at his subtle hint about Elizabeth's influence.

They had been trying to convince him to follow this plan for at least fifteen minutes, but so far without success. By now, Elizabeth had learned the power of her influence, and so she petitioned once again. "Can we just try it? I do not know if it will work, but it would be so much easier on all of us if we did not have to repeat the same crisis every time you wake up." She knew voicing her personal preference was the key to getting him to agree, so she ventured, "I know I would like to try it."

He eyed Elizabeth carefully, then the colonel, then Madeline. "Very well. Obviously, I am vastly out-numbered in this argument. If you think the idea shows merit, I am willing to try it. I trust you all. Well, Madeline, I have not known you very long, but since these two fine people seem to trust you, I trust you too. I must trust that you are trying to help. But I am afraid that I will be a poor scribe sitting in this position. Miss Elizabeth, would you write down what you think I need to know? And then, I will sign it."

"Certainly. Colonel Fitzwilliam? Can I speak to you for a moment?" Colonel Fitzwilliam walked to the desk and leaned over to Elizabeth. She lowered her voice and whispered, "It might be a good idea to include in the missive that he has proposed, and that I have not given him my answer yet. We saw how well that worked yesterday."

"Let me think on that. Perhaps just keep it to the accident and injuries and his limitations. We can always add that later if he proves to be more emotionally stable. Have you noticed he seems to be a little different this morning? I mean, normally when you come in and become involved he is totally altered and compliant, but this morning we have had to negotiate and persuade him to even try out your plan. What do you think the cause of it is?"

"I do not know," she replied. "I did notice that he was hesitant. Perhaps he is beginning to remember my refusals?" She was surprised that her next thought was, *I hope not.*

"Do you think it is another setback? If so, what was the catalyst this time?" Although speaking to Elizabeth, he was eyeing Darcy suspiciously. Darcy was watching them closely and leaning forward, as if to try to hear what they were saying.

Elizabeth sighed. "I do not know. We are doing everything the doctor says. You do not think I should . . . no . . . of course not."

Colonel Fitzwilliam turned his head back and saw a blushing Elizabeth. He arched his eyebrow quizzically. "Should what?"

She fidgeted and stole a glance at Mr. Darcy. "I just wondered if you thought I should accept him . . . that is, until he gets his memory back. I cannot believe I suggested such a thing. It would do no one any good to lie to him. I mean, what if he gets his memory back and is under the impression that I changed my mind?"

Colonel Fitzwilliam struggled not to smile. "Have you changed your mind?"

"Of course not!" Elizabeth said a little too quickly and too loudly.

Mr. Darcy had obviously overheard Elizabeth and asked, "Of course not what? What are you speaking of?"

"Nothing, Cousin. Miss Elizabeth was just putting me in my place. You know as well as I do how strongly her opinions are held. I was just checking on one particular opinion, and it appears I am still wrong."

He grinned back at Darcy, but didn't dare look to see what Elizabeth was doing. He didn't want to play games with her, but sometime soon he would need to address her reasons for refusing his cousin. He had his suspicions, but he needed to hear her reasons from her. Once her exact thoughts were known, he could figure out a method of attack. And not for the first time he thought, *and this accident may very well provide the opportunity to change an opinion as decided as Elizabeth's.*

"Well, I have found even if you know you are right, Miss Elizabeth always has something challenging to say that makes you question your own position." Darcy then smiled for the first time that morning, and all three in the room noticed it. "It is one of the things I love about her. I mean . . . I appreciate about her." His face turned red, and he was suddenly very interested in the chaise's detailed embroidery.

*****

"So, what do you think? Are you ready to sign your reminder letter?" Elizabeth asked.

"I admit I am more than a little embarrassed that I respond that way each morning when . . . well, when I need to use the chamber pot. And all this time you have been witness to this behavior? You have not . . . you have not helped me, have you?"

This time it was Elizabeth's turn to be embarrassed. "Certainly not." The colonel was right about this morning. Usually he wasn't so self-conscious around her. There was something bothering him. "I am sure neither one of us would have appreciated that level of assistance. I was happy to have been useful at the time of the accident, and later when you needed someone to read to you, but there was never anything improper between us."

She was suddenly reminded of how she had admired his handsome chest and nearly dropped the quill in her hand. She saw him notice the fumble and tried to reassure him. "Nothing that was not absolutely necessary. Is that what has been bothering you, sir? I assure you propriety has been maintained, besides the occasional time when we are left alone like we are now."

Darcy reached out and placed his hand on her trembling arm. "You need not worry about being alone with me. Before I sign this, might I ask your assistance in writing one more letter? There is a particular letter that I have wanted, no needed, to write for a long time."

Elizabeth was happy to have a task to do while Madeline refreshed herself and Colonel Fitzwilliam updated his aunt. *Perhaps this will take up all of the time and he will not propose after all*, she hoped. "I would love to help you." She headed to the desk, and sat down. "Whom should I address it to?"

Darcy's voice trembled a little as he said, "Let us skip that part, so that the anonymity might be maintained. Let us just start with 'Dear Madam'."

She wrote as neatly as possible and then looked up at him. "And then?"

He hesitated for a moment, and then with a surge of pressured speech he said, "I have long admired you and your beauty. My heart struggles to keep at a steady pace when I am near you, but I fear it is much worse when I am not. If my heart could speak, it would tell you that you are the most unique lady of my acquaintance. All these years I have struggled to define what I desire in a wife, but it was all in vain until I met you."

Elizabeth's pen remained frozen after "Dear Madam". *So much for time running out*, she thought. It was obvious what was happening. She turned back around to Mr. Darcy. "I am not sure I should be the one to help you with this kind of letter. Perhaps we should wait until the colonel comes back?"

"No. You know he loves a good laugh, and I need someone who can feel the words I am saying. Go on. Write. Do you need me to repeat it?"

She shook her head. She finished writing his sentiments and then said, "Done. Now what?"

"It was not until I heard your laugh or experienced the intriguing sparkle in your eyes that I knew that all the years looking at the finest ladies of the *ton* did little to prepare me for the depth of my feelings for you."

She wrote as fast as she could while he continued.

"At first glance, one would assume I had all but given up on love. But your sweet smile encourages me every time. I admit love seemed impossible at first; now, I feel I am impossible without your love. I cannot imagine life without you by my side, teasing me, discussing essential items of our daily lives, and telling me how wrong I am. Never have I been more happy to be wrong than when your opinions are shared. I need you to know how ardently I love and admire you."

He paused to let her catch up. When she stopped writing, he continued, "There is little hope for a fool in love. My heart fell in love without my consent, or even my knowledge of the matter. God knows I have struggled to repress my feelings. One would look on our match as unwise, however to leave a heart exposed and raw from starvation would surely be even more unwise."

"Sir, perhaps we should not mention how unwise the match is. It may make the lady feel offended."

"But it is true. Our match will not be looked on favorably, that is until they get to know the lady. Then, I will have to fight off the *ton* with a stick. Go ahead and write it." He again waited until she turned and finished writing. Then, he continued, "Although I do not look forward to weaving our families together, living at Pemberley will help."

Elizabeth interrupted again. "Do you have something to say about this lady's family? Are they unfit?" She knew she was getting angry but couldn't help herself.

He looked uncomfortable. "It is just that they tend to be somewhat unrestrained in their behavior. Not many in my circle would appreciate their version of acceptable—"

"Might I remind you that her family is the very reason she is who she is? Her father and mother raised her. Her siblings influenced her to be who she is, and if you love her as much as you profess, then you can only congratulate them on doing such a fine job. A love letter, as this obviously is, should not belittle her family in any way."

Elizabeth continued, "I am just speaking from experience. I would not appreciate hearing such censure of my own family. I love them. And if you expect this lady to love you back, I suggest you avoid making derogatory statements about her station in life or her family." She was proud she had expressed herself so calmly, for she did not feel calm.

"Hmm, perhaps you are right."

"I am."

Darcy smiled, showing his dimples. "Well, I do not usually like being wrong, but what else would a lady like to hear or not hear?"

Seeing him smile back so warmly made her relax. She hadn't thought her correction would have been so easily accepted. "It is not my letter, Mr. Darcy." An even larger grin formed on his face and she thought, *Well, at least not yet.* They sat in silence for a moment just looking at each other.

She turned back around and picked up the pen again and dipped it in the ink. She needed to look at this differently. Here was a man who has tried and tried to properly propose, but he has just not gotten it right. Although he was getting better at expressing himself, his proposals left much to be desired. She couldn't help wanting to laugh at his behavior. Here he was, trying so hard to dictate a love letter, a letter to her, and he thought he was being sly and secretive. She let out a giggle.

"What is so funny?"

She tried to hide her laughter. "It is just my handwriting is obviously feminine, and I am afraid your intended lady will be quite confused when she receives it."

"But I intend on signing it."

She felt lighter already and wanted to play with him a little. "Indeed, but until she sees who it is from, I am afraid the letter might not come across the way you intend."

"You have a point. But in this situation, I assure you she will understand. Let us continue." He waited until she was prepared. "I do not profess any expertise in expressing myself, but our time together leads me to believe that these sentiments will not be much of a surprise."

No, I have to admit you are right. I am no longer surprised. Here it comes.

Darcy cleared his throat. "Miss Elizabeth?"

She turned around. "Yes?"

"I wish to propose to this lady but do not know how best to ask it. How would you like to be proposed to?"

She chuckled because his question could be taken two different ways. She thought she would play with him again. "At the moment, I am content with my life and do not feel the need to secure a husband." She smiled back at him.

He looked confused for a moment, and then a small smile crossed his lips. "I think you mistake my meaning. I was not asking *would* you like to be proposed to. I was asking *in what manner* would you like to be proposed to."

She felt the humor of the situation and let out a laugh. "I know, Mr. Darcy. I was only teasing. But if you are truly asking in what manner I would like to be proposed to, then give me a moment to consider the question. If I disliked the man, then it would not matter how he proposed, for I would not accept him. If I respected the man but did not love him, then his words and sincerity would matter a great deal, but I still would probably not accept him." She paused. She carefully considered her words, for surely the next comment was the answer he was seeking.

"And if you loved the man? What then? What words could he say to make you accept him?"

Elizabeth was pensive for quite a few minutes. She kept opening her mouth to speak her thoughts, but she was so shocked at her own view that it nearly made her stutter. "If I loved the man, then once again it would not matter how he proposed." As soon as she said it, she knew it was true.

"Because you would accept him . . . am I right?"

She nodded. She was speechless. Why did this revelation matter so much? She had considered three scenarios. In the first and the last—whether she disliked the man or loved the man—her answers were the same; it would not matter how he proposed. Then, why was she so critical of Mr. Darcy's proposals?

If I respected the man, but did not love him . . . her words seemed to roll around in her head like a lead weight. Is that how she felt about Mr. Darcy? Did she respect the man yet not love him? Could she now refer to him as a friend? Is that why the method and words he used to propose held so much meaning?

For so many months, she had told herself how much she disliked him. If that were true, then his method of proposing would not have mattered to her in the slightest. She would have turned him down without a second thought, as she had Mr. Collins. If she had disliked him, she would have been merely amused by a poor proposal. But she had not been amused. *His words and sincerity would matter a great deal . . .* Yes, Darcy's words and sincerity had mattered a great deal to her.

"Are you well? You look a little pale." Darcy was looking at her with a sincere look of concern.

"I do not know. Perhaps I need some fresh air. But I cannot leave you until someone returns." She took a deep breath and tried to school her features. Mr. Darcy was beginning to fidget and shift his position again. She needed to collect herself before he got agitated. She tried to pacify him by saying, "No need to worry. I feel better already. The moment has passed. Shall we continue?"

"If you are sure. We can finish this another day."

She knew she was avoiding his eye contact and made a conscious effort to look him in the eye. When she did so, she was struck once again with the realization that she did respect him.

He was a good man. He was intelligent, kind, a good friend, and when he felt comfortable with someone, he made good conversation. His manners, although guarded at times, were remarkable. He had shown himself to be quite the gentleman, and he had a way of dealing with his officious aunt that even the colonel did not have. And in the face of her argumentative and confrontational ways, he shined and rose to the challenge.

She knew more of him since reading his letter last night. Not only was he a good friend, he was a devoted friend who would go to great lengths to see to his friend's happiness. And he had been quite generous to Wickham repeatedly, almost to a fault. His good opinion did matter to her.

Tears threatened at the insides of her eyes, so she turned away and looked back at the desk. After ensuring her voice was strong, she said, "Your memory might not last for another day. Who knows whether tomorrow you will feel the same way about this lady? Perhaps we should finish this letter."

"Miss Elizabeth, finishing the letter is not what matters. I fear I have played on your emotions the last half hour. I can see that you are upset. I am sorry. I do not know what has gotten into me. My emotions are usually tightly reigned in, but I find that is not the case today. I feel a certain level of anxiety, and it is making me do strange things.

"I should have told you earlier. Please forgive me for not being completely honest, but this is your letter. It is for you. I have wanted to express my love and admiration for you so many times, and as providence would have it, I was given the opportunity to do so today. I can see from your slumped shoulders that you are crying. Please, forgive me. I only have one more line to write, and if you would be so kind as to write it for me, well, actually for you, I would appreciate it."

Elizabeth sniffled but didn't turn around. "Proceed. I am ready." She picked up the pen and dipped it in the ink.

"Marry me," he said softly.

CHAPTER 6

"And then he signed both letters, the reminder letter and the proposal letter." Elizabeth felt uncomfortable calling it a love letter even though it obviously was one. "Then he asked to be left alone," she said.

"Was his mood poor? Did you refuse him again?" Colonel Fitzwilliam asked.

"No, he was calm and controlled. He graciously accepted my request for more time to consider his proposal, and then he suddenly said he wanted to be alone. The change was very abrupt."

Darcy's dismissal of Elizabeth worried the colonel deeply. It was not like him—at least not like the Darcy of the last two weeks, the Darcy who was madly in love with Elizabeth. Darcy would seize any opportunity to be with her. "Well, how long has it been? Abbott is here to tend to him. God knows he needs a good shave. Do you think I should send Abbott in or send him back to Rosings? He has been in the same shirt and breeches for three days now."

"I get the impression that something is bothering him, something deep. I wonder if his memories are coming back and he does not know how to interpret them. The doctor said that memories can come back all at once, or come back slowly, or not come back at all. Maybe he is remembering my refusals."

"I hope not; at least, not yet. Well, I, for one, cannot stand to see him in such disarray anymore. Come on, Abbott, it is your moment to shine . . . or make Darcy shine, that is. Oh, Miss Elizabeth, Aunt

Catherine has been waiting for you to call. Apparently she notified Mr. Collins early this morning and you still have not come."

"Yes, I know. I am going to make myself presentable and then walk to Rosings. Thank you. I have an idea of what she desires to speak with me about, and I admit I am not thrilled to approach her."

Colonel Fitzwilliam smiled and patted Elizabeth's arm. "Just keep an open mind. Not all her ideas lack merit."

Elizabeth blushed and looked down at her hands. "So, you know that she intends to convince me to stay another six weeks?"

"Let me put it this way—it was not her idea."

"Then whose idea was it? Mr. Darcy's?" Elizabeth watched Colonel Fitzwilliam closely.

After deliberating for a moment on the benefits and dangers of misleading Elizabeth, he gave an easy smile and said, "What do you think?" It may have been slightly less than truthful, but he could not pass up the opportunity to influence Elizabeth. If she thought Mr. Darcy had suggested it, she might be flattered. Women like to be flattered. If she felt flattered, then she might examine her feelings toward the man. If she did, then she might examine the kind of man he is; only good would come of that. He still felt bad, but it was for her own sake.

He could see that Darcy was right about her. She was amazing, and they belonged together. Darcy needed someone who would challenge him and keep him humble, yet make him laugh. Darcy had experienced so much heartache early in his life. First the death of his mother, then his father, and then the responsibility of caring for his young sister, not to mention running Pemberley. Taking on tenants and an estate of that size when he was just three and twenty had taken its toll on him. Yes, Colonel Fitzwilliam could ask for forgiveness later, but for now, letting her believe it was Mr. Darcy's idea served his purposes perfectly.

"I see. Well, there is little to do but go to her now," Elizabeth sighed. "I might be some time before I return, so take your time with him." Colonel Fitzwilliam turned to signal Abbott, who was waiting across the hall, keeping a respectable distance while the two of them talked. "I will leave you to do what you need to without my assistance; God knows he has had enough help from me," she teased with a smile. Hearing the mirth in her voice, the colonel looked back and gave her a smile in return.

Now she was forced to turn her thoughts toward Rosings. She considered going upstairs to freshen up but decided against it. She grabbed her shawl and wrapped it around her shoulders. In her mind, it didn't matter whether or not she was presentable for Lady Catherine. She might as well get it over with.

The sun was out, and it was a beautiful day for a walk. She felt the absence in her daily routine acutely. She wanted to explore and stretch her legs a little before being manipulated by Lady Catherine. However, she knew if she delayed any longer she would not only be dealing with an officious woman, she would be dealing with an officious, irate woman. She pressed on and walked straight to Rosings.

Just as she approached the grand manor, she realized that she had left her love letter—no, her proposal letter—on the desk at the parsonage. She grumbled at herself for being so careless. She had told the colonel about the letter, but she didn't especially want him to read it. And who knows who else might read it. But it was too late to turn back now.

After being escorted by the butler into the music room, she waited patiently for what was about to come. Colonel Fitzwilliam had said to keep an open mind, but all she could think about was how much she wanted to go home. She thought of Jane and her father and all the books she had left behind. She thought of Oakham Mount and the paths where her feet led her mind into blissful rationality. Oh, how she needed a long walk to clear her mind!

"Do stop pacing on my rug, Miss Bennet. I pride myself on my choices of décor, and that one was imported from France, I will have you know. It is one of a kind, made especially for me. I will not have you destroy it with your shuffling feet."

Well, if you are trying to convince me to stay with that kind of flattery, you will be very disappointed. "Yes, Lady Catherine," she smiled.

Elizabeth waited while Lady Catherine dismissed the servant with orders for tea and refreshments. She watched as the overbearing woman took her place of power at the center of the room and then motioned with her hand where she desired Elizabeth to sit. Elizabeth smiled, but sat down where she was told. The seating arrangement was not the battle she wished to fight today.

"I suspect that you desire to thank me for my offer," Lady Catherine said, looking down her nose.

"No, ma'am."

Surprise rose in every crevice of the wrinkled face. "I see you are up to your impertinent ways again. Of course you are grateful. How could you not be? I imagine your father will be quite impressed that I offered such a thing."

"My father is impressed with a number of things, but he does not mind letting me travel by post, I assure you."

"He may have felt that way before I wrote to him and told him of your new plans, but now that you have a safe and reliable method of travel, I would think that he will prefer it immensely."

They were interrupted temporarily by the arrival of their refreshments, and Elizabeth's stomach growled quietly. She could see that the raspberry muffins and chocolate cream puffs that she loved so much were on the tray, and there were enough to feed five people! Suddenly she was very grateful to be at Rosings.

The last few days, and most of the last few weeks for that matter, had been filled with nearly inedible food that Elizabeth had often forced herself to eat. *Poor Mrs. Wilkinson! If only she had a lick of talent in the kitchen.* She reached for one of the chocolate cream puffs. Maybe she could stall this argument until all the pastries were eaten. "You wrote to my father?"

"Of course I did! What else would a most loyal aunt do but ensure the health of her favorite nephew? I sent it by express yesterday and just received the return letter a moment ago. So, it is all arranged. He, of course, did not argue with me. No one ever does, except you." Lady Catherine poured the tea and handed Elizabeth a cup, who took it greedily.

The tea was heavenly. It had just a hint of lemon and milk, like the tea she made at home but so much better. Such a delicious concoction could never be obtained at the parsonage. Elizabeth was delighted to indulge her senses.

She reached for another chocolate cream puff, and the cream leaked out onto her finger. *Too bad I cannot just lick it off.* She instead used her napkin and bemoaned the precious cream. She placed the rest of the cream puff on her tongue, feeling the smooth, sweet icing graze her teeth as she bit into it. She had to take a bigger bite than intended to encase the cream threatening to escape, but she didn't mind. She didn't intend to do much talking with these delightful treats in front of her. She tried not to moan in pleasure, but a small one escaped her mouth. To hide the moan, she thought she should probably say something. "I will do whatever Mr. Darcy needs of me."

"Good. Then it is all settled."

Elizabeth was shocked back from staring at a raspberry muffin. "What? What did you say?"

"Personally, I am a little shocked that you so readily agreed, but I do know what is best. Perhaps you are beginning to see that."

She contemplated delaying the correction until she got one of those muffins onto her plate, but it was not in her nature. "No, Lady Catherine. I meant I will do what Mr. Darcy needs of me while I am here, but I cannot stay another six weeks." She took a moment to evaluate Lady Catherine's response while enjoying another long drink of her tea. The expected displeasure came quickly enough but not so quickly that Elizabeth couldn't reach for a muffin and take a bite first.

"I dare say you shall! I am under strict doctor's orders!"

Elizabeth coughed on the muffin. "Doctor's orders? It was not Mr. Darcy who suggested it?"

"Why would he do something like that? No, indeed he did not. Darcy would never request your presence when he is to be engaged to my daughter. As soon as he is well, it will be settled. The doctor came straight over yesterday and insisted that you stay six more weeks. He said you were talented and showed marked abilities in handling my nephew's specific needs, and that he had never seen such influence for good. Coming from that man, it is a commendation indeed, and I agreed with him, despite the fact that I so despise him." Lady Catherine eyed Elizabeth suspiciously, picked up a cream puff, and tried to daintily nibble on it.

Elizabeth's stomach was too happy for her to make sense of what Lady Catherine was saying. Why did Colonel Fitzwilliam say it had been Mr. Darcy's idea? Or had he? She couldn't remember the conversation now with the delicacies before her. She took another bite of muffin and felt the small tart fruit, still warm from the oven, mash against her tongue and cheeks. It was beyond anything she could have hoped for. The sugar crystals sprinkled on the top crust counteracted the tartness perfectly. She took another bite ravenously and then tried to calm herself.

She had to keep her wits about her because if Lady Catherine offered her another muffin right now, she would do anything. The pleasure in her mouth was so intense that without realizing it, she relaxed and slouched a little into the back of the chair.

"So, you see, it is the express medical counsel that you maintain the interaction you have had with my nephew until he is well. At that time, I shall be happy to do you the service of transporting you to Longbourn myself. And do sit up! You will drop crumbs all over! This behavior is exactly what I would expect from a lady raised with no governess."

Elizabeth sat up but only to grab another chocolate cream puff. She promptly put its entirety in her mouth and gave a slightly wicked smile. *How are these manners for you?* But even her extremely blissful taste buds couldn't stop her from saying, "Lady Catherine, I assure you I do nothing more than anyone else would do. I do not know why he responds so well to me."

"Exactly my point. No one really knows what will work with head injuries. So, whatever you are doing, keep doing it. Whatever you are saying, keep saying it . . . for six more weeks."

She swallowed the last bit of cream puff, finished the last of her tea, and put her cup down. Should she ask for more tea or forge on into the battle? At the moment, her senses were overwhelmed. Her taste buds had a certain level of control over her that she couldn't quite explain. All she knew was that she desperately wanted another muffin, and she was ready to do anything to get it.

"If I stay, and I have not agreed to do so, mind you," Elizabeth replied, "I would wish for something in return." She picked up her tea cup and gestured her desire for more. What was wrong with her? Why was she negotiating? Why couldn't she think past a warm raspberry muffin and more tea?

Lady Catherine slowly smiled. "It seems you have been won over by my cook's talent. I rarely get to compliment her on her usefulness. Now, hold your cup steady." She poured the hot liquid into the cup. She then pushed the refreshment platter closer to Elizabeth. "If there is anything you need, just ask. My cook is used to special requests, and I am happy to loan her to you in exchange for your services."

Was it really over? Had she really just accepted to stay at the parsonage in exchange for a few baked treats? She eyed the last muffin jealously. Without fully being aware of what she was doing, she snatched it up and took a bite. Then she realized that in doing so, she had just sealed the deal. They sat in silence for a minute while she finished it.

At one point, it looked like there had been too many refreshments; now, there was not enough, for she had just sold six weeks of her time for a few cream puffs and muffins. *And impressively perfect tea, do not forget.* She giggled. *It very well might be worth it.* She savored the full cup she held possessively in her hands.

*****

Charlotte was in the garden when a beautiful carriage pulled up to the parsonage. She didn't recognize it but knew it must be someone important. She brushed her hands off on her apron and put down her basket of clippings. She watched as a young lady with strikingly blonde hair was handed out of the carriage by the footman, followed by an older woman. There was something about the delicate, yet precise, mannerisms that reminded her of Mr. Darcy. She started making her way toward the two women when she realized who they were. "You must be Miss Georgiana Darcy!"

Georgiana blushed and looked down at her hands. It was not easy being well known to people by name but not by face. What was worse was when people knew her, or at least knew of her, yet she had no idea who they were!

She gathered her strength. The gardening woman obviously was not preparing to give her terrible news, which meant that her brother must be alive. Her purpose in coming was forcibly guiding her to speak. "Is he well? I do apologize for sounding rude, but I have not slept or thought of anything else. Has he survived?"

"Yes, dear! He is well. He has woken up and is doing splendidly, or so I hear."

"Is he not here? Was he transported to Rosings after all? I was sure that my cousin would stand his ground on following the doctor's orders."

"Oh no, he is here, but I see little of him. I am Mrs. Collins, but please call me Charlotte. My husband is your aunt's rector. We have the privilege and honor to host him during his recovery. But enough about me, I am sure you wish to see your brother. Let me take you to him." She took the young lady's arm and tucked it into the crook of her own, as if they had known each other for years. "Would you mind introducing me to your friend?"

Georgiana was surprised at the kind, friendly manner Mrs. Collins showed her. Tears threatened to well up in her eyes as the stress of the last few days overwhelmed her. It wouldn't have been the first time tears sprung up.

She looked over her shoulder at her companion, Mrs. Annesley, for strength. Sure enough, Mrs. Annesley patted the back of her fingers under her chin and tilted her head up, a gentle reminder to stay strong and keep her chin high. Georgiana smiled back at Charlotte. "This is my companion, Mrs. Annesley." The three women exchanged greetings and headed toward the house.

They stopped just inside the front door. Georgiana watched as Charlotte knocked on the adjoining room's door. The house was small but well furnished. Her aunt must have donated most of the furniture, because her ornate and somewhat expressive taste was written all over the room. From rug to painting, she could see her aunt's influence everywhere.

Her thoughts were once again brought back to the closed door in front of her. Why wasn't someone answering? Had something happened? Did someone leave him alone? Her heart started pounding as hard as ever, and just when she thought she could not take it anymore, the door opened and there stood Abbott.

"Abbott!" Georgiana ran and threw her arms around the valet. Then realizing how inappropriate it was, she stepped back. When she looked at the man, she sensed that something was wrong. "Is he well, Mr. Abbott?"

"Yes, for the most part," Abbott answered. "I was just finishing his shave. That is why it took me so long to answer the door. The colonel is here as well." He stepped back and bid her enter.

The invitation to see her brother and cousin did not need to be offered twice. Georgiana stepped around him and saw her two favorite men. Her brother was using a washcloth to wipe off the rest of the shaving cream, and he was smiling broadly at their cousin. Just then Colonel Fitzwilliam noticed Georgiana. He stood up quickly, took long strides, and embraced her, swinging her around in a full circle.

Mr. Darcy called out, "Georgiana! I did not know you were planning to come. Splendid!"

Georgiana looked to Colonel Fitzwilliam in confusion. "But your letter said for me to come."

"Indeed, sprout. Darcy is just tired. He has had a long day already." Now wasn't the time to remind Darcy that he had already been told Georgiana was coming. Nor was it the time to explain Darcy's memory problems to Georgiana. Georgiana would see the problem soon enough.

The colonel tried to mask his anxiety in front of Georgiana, but he was worried about Darcy. Throughout his bath, Darcy had displayed signs of memory loss again. Twice he had told Richard that he intended to offer marriage to Elizabeth. He seemed to have forgotten that he had dictated a love letter asking her to marry him not more than an hour ago.

At one point, his memory was so poor that Richard had to show him the reminder letter explaining the accident. It seemed to have helped some, and Darcy had once again asked all the typical questions Colonel Fitzwilliam was getting accustomed to answering.

By the time the shave had started, Darcy had appeared to be rational again, but the colonel was still uneasy. Until now, memory loss had only happened when he fell asleep or was given medicine. Today, ever since he had asked Elizabeth to leave him, he was struggling. *Why did he lose his memory of the accident again? Why doesn't he remember everything we explained to him this morning?* That wasn't the usual pattern.

When Abbott had started dressing Darcy, which was a real chore because of the broken leg, Richard had left to discuss what was happening with Madeline. She too had been worried and had come to check on him. She had taken his pulse, which was strong but a little too fast, and administered the doctor's three word memory test, which he had passed. The only thing she could account for was that he hadn't eaten in a while. She was in the kitchen right now, ordering food and refreshments. The colonel hoped she would be back soon.

Georgiana heard someone behind her and turned around. A woman was carrying food, but she didn't look like a servant. Georgiana gave Richard a questioning look.

"Georgiana, let me introduce you to Darcy's nurse, Madeline. Madeline, this is Darcy's sister, Miss Georgiana Darcy."

Madeline was pretty good at making quick judgments about people. From the look of Georgiana's posture, which was erect except for the dipped chin, and from the look of her perfectly executed curtsy, this was a refined, but terribly shy, young lady.

Madeline smiled kindly. She could tell that this girl would need extra care. "Dear girl, you have been through so much these last few days not knowing how your brother is doing." Tears appeared in Georgiana's eyes, and Madeline quickly put down the food and put her arms around her. "There now, as you can see, he has survived and will have a great many things to tell you."

Georgiana's shoulders shook as she let a stranger voice her own thoughts and feelings and comfort her in this way. She let Madeline hold her for a few moments while she tried to regain control. She had seen her brother alive, he was speaking, he recognized her, and he was happy she had come. So much relief rippled through her body all at once, and then a new wave of tears sprung forth, and she sobbed. "I am so sorry. I have just been so

135

worried. We could not travel yesterday because of the wet roads, but we came as fast as we could. I did not even stop at Rosings."

"Are you going to embrace a stranger and leave your invalid brother all alone over here?" Darcy asked smiling.

"Oh dear! You have not even had enough time to say hello yet? Well, go see your brother." Madeline said tenderly.

The incentive was too great to resist, and she rushed over and threw her arms around his neck "Are you well? Do you hurt? Can I get you something?" She pulled away slightly to evaluate his face.

Darcy chuckled. "Did you really think a simple horse accident could do me in? Yes, I am well. Yes, I am in pain. And from the sound of my stomach reacting to that delicious-smelling food, I would say I am hungry."

Madeline picked up the tray of food and brought it over to the table near Mr. Darcy. "Do you want pain medication now or after you eat?"

"After I eat. First, I want to chat with my dear sister." He turned back to Georgiana. "I have so much to tell you, Georgiana!"

Madeline cleared her throat. "Perhaps you can share your news while you eat." She nudged the plate of potatoes and pheasant in front of him. "This was sent from Rosings a moment ago, and if you do not eat it now, you shall be eating it cold."

Darcy did as he was told, balancing the plate on his lap as best as he could. He took a bite of the cheese-and-buttered-herb potatoes and closed his eyes. "This is heavenly," he groaned. "But I feel bad that I am eating all alone. Can we ring for refreshments for the weary travelers?"

Mrs. Collins, who had been standing near the door, spoke up. "I would be happy to. I will order some food at once." Then she turned and left.

They all watched Darcy closely as he enjoyed his meal. Georgiana kept thinking about how her prayers had been answered and that she was witnessing a miracle. Richard was still pondering what could have caused the earlier setback and was very happy to realize that Elizabeth's reminder letter had actually worked. Madeline was quickly organizing the medicine she needed to give him while wondering how much Georgiana knew about Elizabeth and her brother. She didn't have to wait long for an answer.

"Did you get my letter, Georgie, about Miss Elizabeth?"

"Oh yes! I am thrilled that I will have a sister soon. When will I be able to meet her? Or have you not proposed yet? Your letter said you were going to propose, but it arrived just before the colonel's express telling me about the accident."

"No, I have not proposed yet. But it is the first thing I am going to do as soon as I get a chance."

Colonel Fitzwilliam let out a spurt of laughter, which made Madeline giggle, which only brought on more laughter from the colonel. By now, the looks being aimed at him from Darcy and Georgiana were highly entertaining. Georgiana was truly confused. Darcy was giving him the ever-practiced look of disdain. He couldn't help himself and laughed harder. He stood up and walked over to Darcy and patted him on the shoulder. He cleared his throat to speak but found himself laughing again.

"And what is so funny, Richard?" Darcy asked with a frown on his face.

Madeline's giggles stopped immediately but Richard's deep laughter did not. Richard was laughing so hard now that tears were forming in his eyes. He had to wipe at them. It felt so good to laugh after the stress of the last few days. He tried to pull himself together, but it only made him laugh harder. "I am afraid I am not sure what has gotten into me. I cannot seem to get control of myself."

Madeline walked over to Richard, and with a strained, controlled smile, she said, "Perhaps you should get some fresh air, sir." She giggled only briefly before stifling it.

"Indeed, I believe a brisk walk would do me good." Chuckling, he shook his head and left the room.

"Madeline, would you mind leaving us as well? I would like to have a private word with Georgiana. You too, Mrs. Annesley."

As they both left, a servant brought in the refreshments. Georgiana poured the tea and eagerly bit into a scone. She was surprised how dry it was. "Well, eat up, William, or your food will get cold." She put into practice her polite face and hesitantly took another bite of scone. When her mouth and tea had disposed of the undesirable food, she asked about the accident. "Tell me more about your fall. Or did you want to talk about Miss Elizabeth first?"

"Well, to be honest, apparently I dictated a letter to that effect. I believe Richard put it over on the desk. It was written by Miss Elizabeth, and I signed it. It is simply too difficult to write in this position. Go on. Go get it, and read it. I would love to talk to you about it."

Georgiana was grateful that she could put down her dry scone politely, and she went over to the desk. Sure enough, there was a letter written in a clearly feminine hand resting on top. She scooped up the single sheet of paper and started to read.

Dear Madam,

I have long admired you and your beauty. My heart struggles to keep at a steady pace when I am near you, but I fear it is much worse when I am not. If my heart could speak, it would tell you that you are the most unique lady of my acquaintance. All these years I have struggled to define what I desire in a wife, but it was all in vain until I met you.

It was not until I heard your laugh or experienced the intriguing sparkle in your eyes that I knew that all the years looking at the finest ladies of the ton did little to prepare me for the depth of my feelings for you.

At first glance, one would assume I had all but given up on love. But your sweet smile encourages me every time. I admit love seemed impossible at first; now, I feel I am impossible without your love. I cannot imagine life without you by my side, teasing me, discussing essential items of our daily lives, and telling me how wrong I am. Never have I been more happy to be wrong than when your opinions are shared. I need you to know how ardently I love and admire you.

There is little hope for a fool in love. My heart fell in love without my consent, or even my knowledge of the matter. God knows I have struggled to repress my feelings. One would look on our match as unwise, however to leave a heart exposed and raw from starvation would surely be even more unwise.

Although I do not look forward to weaving our families together, living at Pemberley will help. I do not profess any expertise in expressing myself, but our time together leads me to believe that these sentiments will not be much of a surprise.

Marry me.

Fitzwilliam Darcy

Georgiana looked up with tears in her eyes. "It is beautiful, William! I cannot believe you would share such a thing with me. I know we are close, but to share the letter in which you propose is amazing. Thank you for trusting me with this."

Darcy's face looked very perplexed. He quietly reached for the letter and took it out of Georgiana's hand. His eyes scanned the words that echoed his feelings about Elizabeth. Sure enough, there at the bottom was his signature.

"Is there something wrong? You look pale. Why are you sweating? Is it too warm in here?" Darcy just kept reading and rereading the letter in his hand. Georgiana was worried something was really wrong because he still had not said a word. "William? Are you well? Should I get Madeline?"

Finally, Darcy blinked. "Is there perhaps another letter on the desk?"

"I can look." She went to the desk and lifted a book and said, "Yes, there is. It is written in the same hand."

Darcy let out a sigh that came out more like a groan. He rubbed his head with his hands and brushed his hair back. "Leave me, Georgiana. And bring that other letter over here."

"But, Brother, have I done something to displease you?" She watched him fidget, and she handed him the second letter. He shook his head, but she couldn't help the sick feeling she had in her stomach. Her mind ran through the details of the last few minutes. He was excited for her to read the letter, but when she did, he became quiet and dismissive. She suddenly realized that he had never intended for her to read the love letter but instead wanted her to read the second letter.

"I am so sorry. I imagine you are quite embarrassed for me to have read such a personal letter. I should have stopped as soon as I realized that it was a love letter. Please forgive me. I will leave you now, but may I first say one thing? Congratulations! I cannot wait to meet my new sister. I am sure if she is as lovely as you make her sound in the letter, then she and I will get along wonderfully."

Darcy looked up at her, and his eyes tried to focus. "Congratulations?"

"You proposed! I am sure you are the happiest of men now!"

Darcy looked pensive but then a small smile crept along his face, "Indeed. Thank you. I believe you are the first to wish us joy. But

I admit it has not sunk in yet. I still am so shocked that what I have wanted for so long will truly happen. I admit I did not know how I was going to propose . . . I had so many ideas of how to do it . . ."

Georgiana was so pleased to see his mood lighten. She could tell he was fidgeting in a different manner, more from excitement this time. She found it odd. His emotions were vacillating widely, and it was very unlike him. She patted his arm and leaned in and embraced him. She was grateful when he returned it.

"Well, William, a love letter like that is a new and exciting way to propose. Now, she will have something to remember the moment by. You will have to tell me all about it sometime, but I can tell you are tired and need your pain medication. I would love to hear what her face looked like when she transcribed her own love letter! How romantic! It is like something out of the ladies novels I read!"

Darcy squirmed a little. "Indeed. I am sure someday I will tell you all about it. For now though, I think I will take more medicine. Could you get Madeline?"

"Absolutely." Georgiana then left the room and almost ran into Richard and an older, portly gentleman. "Richard! You sly thing! Now I know why you were laughing in there! I cannot believe you did not tell me he proposed and is engaged! Well, he is asking for pain medication. Do you know where Madeline is?"

Richard raised his eyebrow. "Georgiana, this is Mr. Cummings. Mr. Cummings, this is Darcy's sister, Miss Georgiana Darcy. She has just arrived. Georgiana, would you mind telling us what makes you think Mr. Darcy has proposed?"

"It was in the letter! I think he intended me to read a different letter, but I am so glad for the misunderstanding because now I know just how happy they will be. His sweet, romantic words are so amazing!"

"And does he remember that he proposed?" Mr. Cummings asked.

"Of course he does. Besides being in physical pain, he is quite overjoyed. But I must go to Rosings now. I must refresh myself from my travels." Georgiana danced over to Richard and kissed him on the cheek. "It was nice to meet you, Mr. Cummings!"

After she left, the two men quickly entered the room to find a grinning Mr. Darcy.

"Well? Are you going to congratulate me or not?" Mr. Darcy said. "And who is this with you?"

Richard gave Mr. Cummings a knowing look. It appears Georgiana did not pick up on the memory problems. "This is Mr. Cummings."

"Ah, yes, according to the letter intended to spark my memory, you have been instrumental in my care. I thank you."

"It has been my pleasure. Colonel Fitzwilliam has been telling me about your day. I understand you have implemented Miss Elizabeth's idea of a reminder letter. Do you feel that has helped? Are you anxious? Do you have questions about the accident?"

Darcy's grin turned to a frown. "Well? How am I supposed to feel about losing my memory? Am I anxious? Probably not as much as I should be after losing my memory, but that may be because I just got some wonderful news. Doctor, I believe I must ask you if I can celebrate with a little brandy. Well, can I?"

Mr. Cummings cleaned his spectacles. He was hesitant to ask but knew he had to be thorough. "And what might you be celebrating?"

"I am so glad you asked because my cousin here has been as silent as a dead canary in a mine shaft! I am to be married! Miss Elizabeth has accepted my hand!" Darcy slapped his hands down on his lap in excitement.

"Cousin, tell me, what do you remember about proposing to Miss—" Colonel Fitzwilliam was stopped midsentence by the doctor's hand on his arm. He looked at his face and instantly realized someone else entered the room. He followed the doctor's subtle motion and saw Elizabeth standing in the doorway. What had she heard? What should they tell Darcy? Would correcting him cause another setback? Would she go along with the misunderstanding and let Darcy think they were engaged?

He quickly scanned her face and body language to see what she felt. She had a gentle smile and curtsied briefly. She was leaning against the doorframe, almost as if asking to come in. The colonel made a quick decision and vowed he would ask for forgiveness later. He was not happy with how things were going to play out in the next few minutes. One of two things was going to happen: either Elizabeth would be very unhappy with him, and he would have to do a lot of groveling; or Darcy's recovery would deteriorate. He weighed the options, and at the moment, groveling was the preferable outcome.

"May I come in?" Elizabeth asked.

Colonel Fitzwilliam intervened before Darcy spoke. "I understand congratulations are in order, Miss Elizabeth! Darcy here was just telling me about how you accepted his hand! I could not be happier." He made quick strides to her, grabbed both her hands, leaned into her, and whispered, "Forgive me. Somehow he thinks he proposed and you accepted. Please play along."

He pulled back and saw a very surprised look on her face. The surprise turned quickly to indignation and then to anger. She opened her mouth to speak, and Colonel Fitzwilliam squeezed her hands and gave her a pleading look that was met with a piercing glare.

In normal tones, and trying not to grimace, she replied, "Is that so? I believe Mr. Darcy and I were planning not to tell anyone until he was well." While keeping her anger in check, she gave the colonel a look that told all of what she felt. While addressing Mr. Darcy, she still kept her eyes on the colonel, "Is that not so, Mr. Darcy?" She pulled her hands free from the colonel but leaned into him and hissed under her breath, "You are on my list, sir! You just watch and see how well I can play along with this plan that I most certainly did *not* agree to. You are playing with fire, you know. And when one plays with fire, one usually gets burned!"

"What did you say, Cousin, to make my intended turn her wrath on you? I can see from here that you have angered her. I must insist that you treat her with the respect that my future wife deserves."

Elizabeth could see Darcy sit up straighter and square his shoulders in defense of her. If she hadn't been so angry at the colonel, she might have felt flattered that in his dependent state he still felt the need to stand up for her. How did she get stuck in this situation? How could she get herself out of it? She was not going to let the colonel get the upper hand.

She smiled brightly and turned toward Mr. Darcy. "Sir, the colonel was just telling me his deepest thoughts on the engagement. It appears you have won the race for my hand. Another day and he would have proposed to me himself! Can you believe he would admit such a thing? Oh! I probably should not have told you that! Dear me! Where are my manners? I think I am just taken by surprise that I might have received two offers of marriage in just as many days! It is not often that one would receive two chances at felicity!"

Elizabeth took her seat at Darcy's head and put her hand on his. She then turned her glare back to the colonel and raised her eyebrow in defiance.

The colonel didn't skip a beat. "Indeed it is so. Darcy, I admit all your talk about her made me question my own feelings. However, I believe I said to you, Miss Elizabeth, that I would have offered on *behalf* of Darcy, since he is unwell. You mistake me just now for I indeed said that if Darcy hadn't proposed within the day, then I would have done it for him, that is, on behalf of him, not instead of him. I am well aware of his regard for you and would never try to compete for your affections, which I am sure are quite solidly set on Mr. Darcy."

Elizabeth turned a pleasant smile on Mr. Darcy and squeezed his hand. "Indeed it is so. For who could resist a man so kind and gentle and well-read? But I do not think I misheard you, Colonel. I distinctly remember hearing you say he was truly a great man, so much so that you have struggled with feelings of inadequacy, being a second son and all."

Colonel Fitzwilliam glanced quickly at Darcy, who seemed to be getting irritated, or jealous, one of the two. Neither feeling boded well for the colonel. His next remark would have to set the matter to rest once and for all.

"You have hit it on the head, Miss Elizabeth," he began. "For I could never offer marriage to you, no matter how charming your lovely face is, because as you have informed me many times, you come with no fortune. Being a second son, I must marry into wealth. So, it is that you heard incorrectly. I can see how well matched the two of you are. I was only frustrated by seeing how the accident was delaying your union. Congratulations are truly in order! Doctor, is Darcy well enough to have a toast?"

Mr. Cummings tried his best to smile reassuringly at Mr. Darcy. "I do not see why not. Brandy, in moderation, would be appropriate, and I certainly think that this conversation requires a drink for all of us."

CHAPTER 7

Mr. Cummings accepted the offer of brandy, and was surprised to see Elizabeth take a small glass too, which she quickly emptied. He watched the "engaged" couple carefully. He felt badly that Elizabeth was once again in a difficult position, and he had no idea how to remedy it. More than anyone else, she was bearing the brunt of the burden of caring for Mr. Darcy. He wished he could lighten it for her. But at the moment, Elizabeth didn't seem burdened—she seemed happy. She was still resting her hand on Mr. Darcy's; it looked like more than a simple gesture done to pacify a patient. She didn't seem to just be going through the motions or playing a part.

Mr. Cummings and Colonel Fitzwilliam sat quietly in the corner, whispering observations to each other. They couldn't resist eavesdropping on the couple, and Elizabeth didn't seem to mind being overheard. Their conversation was easy and unpressured. She appeared to genuinely enjoy talking with him, despite the fact that she was playing the role of his betrothed against her will. Both Mr. Cummings and the colonel noticed the change in her. The conversation between the two men stopped when they overheard the banter between Elizabeth and Mr. Darcy develop into a more serious dialogue about their future.

Mr. Darcy looked to be very pleased with himself. He said, "Pemberley's land is more rugged than your home in Hertfordshire, but I have no doubt that you will find it to your liking. Oh, how I wish I could have you visit before I bring you home as my wife! Then again, introducing you to the staff as the new mistress will be truly monumental. They all miss having a woman's touch. Of course, Georgiana tries, but she is not out yet, and with my reclusive nature, I admit the staff has had little opportunity to host balls and dinner parties. They will be thrilled to begin doing so again."

He continued, "I imagine that we will create our own traditions once we are married, but there are a few from my youth that I would like to preserve. We always have a large party of family stay with us through the Christmas holidays. It will be very merry to have your family for Christmas and Boxing Day and on into Twelfth Night."

"That would be lovely, but I always sensed that you did not like my family, specifically my mother and younger sisters."

The two gentlemen overhearing the conversation simultaneously stiffened. Given Darcy's volatility, Elizabeth was walking a very tight rope. Bringing up sensitive, emotionally provoking topics was not desirable.

Darcy didn't seem to mind. "I have had some unkind feelings toward them in the past, however, I have reflected on that quite a bit. Take your mother for instance. No, do not worry, I will be kind. I see you square your shoulders, but my opinion is not quite as bad as you may think. Be patient as I try to put words to my thoughts.

"You see, before I proposed, well, before I knew I was in love, I performed my role in society as a bachelor dutifully. I went to the minimum amount of soirées. I accepted invitations to dinners and other events selectively. I learned that among the *ton*, there are all kinds of rules. For example, take the well-known rule that a man must perform as a gentleman to any lady and offer his services, especially when a lady is in need. Unfortunately, there is also an unspoken rule among these so-called gentlemen that certain women are not actually ladies, and therefore their behavior to them will not be scrutinized as intensely."

Elizabeth thought she knew what he was saying. "Like with servants or widows."

"Exactly. Those with less social standing do not demand to be treated as ladies, and society has accepted the fact that the men in higher society are not required to treat them in a gentlemanly manner."

"But you feel differently."

"Indeed. My servants have no fear of me; I would never think about them in that manner."

"But what does this have to do with my mother?"

Darcy reached out his hand and Elizabeth placed her tiny fingers in his. "I learned early on, well before the days of Cambridge, that my status as the heir of Pemberley gave me power. Power to do nearly anything I wanted. If I wanted to be a womanizing rake, well, I could be. If I wanted to drink my life away or gamble ridiculous amounts of money every day, then I could."

"But you have done none of those things. You are moral and kind to all those around you."

"Moral, yes; kind, not necessarily."

Elizabeth squeezed his hand. She wasn't about to let him belittle himself, but she didn't know any more what she thought about his kindness. At one point, she had thought him to be unkind. But ever since reading his letter about Jane and Bingley and Wickham, her thoughts and feelings about the matter had changed. Everything she had once thought about Mr. Darcy had been called into question when she read that letter. She remembered her thoughts when she read it for the first time like it was yesterday . . . or was it yesterday? Her days were so long and full of emotions that she couldn't tell which day it was anymore.

Darcy continued, "But I do not mean to discuss my behavior, I only mean to say that there is a wide range of acceptable behavior. The more wealth, status, or titles a family has, the more lenient the rules. A very wealthy lord or duke can literally do no wrong. He can say what he wishes; he can do what he wishes. And if he does anything improper, it is simply not talked about. Even the gossip columns will keep his secrets.

"It is not uncommon for husbands and wives to live totally separate lives, with mistresses and lovers on both sides. The only time they are together is to perform their public role as a married couple. I have seen them come together to a ball, dance a set, and then separate to opposite corners of the room. I learned quickly that this is not what I wished for in my marriage . . . in our marriage."

"Me neither. I vowed to myself that the only way I would ever accept a man's hand was if I could love and respect him. He would have to value me for who I am, respect me and my opinions, and look at no other." Elizabeth blushed a little. She hadn't intended to be so open with her personal views on marriage. *What does it matter? He won't remember it tomorrow anyway!*

"Thank you. I hope you know that I do value who you are. I do respect your opinions, and I will look at no other. To be honest, I have not looked at anyone else since I met you."

Now it was Elizabeth's turn to say thank you, but if felt awkward to do so. Hadn't he declared himself numerous times? Why was this time any different? She swallowed and squeezed his hand once more. He started drawing circles mindlessly on the back of her hand, which she found very distracting. It sent tingles all the way up to her shoulder, and it was so pleasant a feeling, that she wanted his hands on her arms as well.

She snapped her head up and tried to get a grip on herself and her thoughts. This was Mr. Darcy! And they most certainly were not really engaged! She still had strong objections to him! She realized she had been leaning in toward him, and she righted herself slightly but didn't pull away her hand. She decided she needed to keep him on track. "And what does this have to do with my mother?"

"Well, I observed an interesting behavior among the mothers of eligible single ladies of the *ton*. It is perfectly acceptable to throw one's daughter and her assets at bachelors, as if the lady were up for auction. I could name the dowries and accomplishments of most of the women I have ever danced with, simply because of their mothers. I have to say, a determined mother is a foe indeed. There were many times I was nearly trapped in the parson's mousetrap by a mother, and if it were not for my detection of these somewhat-creative schemes, I would not be in a position to offer for you for I would be a married man.

"Nevertheless, mercenary, matchmaking mothers abound in all ranks and classes, from London's elite society to country towns. It was not until I realized this that I examined my opinion of your mother. You see, she did no more to encourage Miss Bennet and Bingley than many other mothers of the *ton*. I did not judge the mothers of the *ton* who acted so, simply because they were rich and titled. I, however, did not give the same consideration for your mother.

"I realized I had misjudged her. I realized I had been prideful of my own status and wealth. I may not have been living the way many in my class deem acceptable—immorally, that is—but neither did I censure them for doing so. I had altered my moral views enough to think that they were entitled to behave any way they wished, simply because they were wealthy. If your mother had fortune and connections, then I might have excused her actions from the beginning. In fact, her behavior was no different, possibly even better, than many mothers who have sought my fortune for their daughters."

"Better? Sir, do not stretch the truth. I am aware of what my mother is."

"You are wrong. Trust me. The stories I could tell you are not appropriate for a lady's ears. Trust me when I tell you your mother is not nearly as bad as some who have been bred and raised for generations to be refined and cultured."

Elizabeth was taken aback by this revelation of Mr. Darcy's feelings. She was truly moved emotionally. All this time she thought he looked down on her family. She filed this topic away to think more on later. She finally whispered her response, "I trust you." And she did. But why?

She didn't get far in her contemplation of this because Mr. Cummings interrupted the conversation. She had completely forgotten the men were still in the room. At the moment, she was captivated both in body and mind with the intelligent and revealing conversation of Mr. Darcy and those distracting circles he was drawing on her hand!

Mr. Cummings spoke up. "I must be heading home now as dinner will be served soon. I believe if I come to the table one more time in my work clothes, my dear Mrs. Cummings will feed me to the chickens as scraps. But before I go, I would like to have you try on that foot brace, Mr. Darcy. It appears the swelling on your ankle has gone down quite a bit. Colonel, would you mind assisting me in fetching it from my carriage?"

"Absolutely." The colonel knew the doctor didn't really need help, but leaving the "couple" alone for a few more minutes wouldn't hurt.

After they had stepped outside into the dimming light of day, the doctor turned to Colonel Fitzwilliam. "She is amazing. We cannot let her go. I first saw her talents in her quick, clear mind during the accident, but now I see that she is kind and even a little feisty! Did you see her turn that engagement situation back on you! Oh, she was mad! I would love to be a fly on the wall when she gets her hands on you!" At that thought, the colonel's face paled a little, as he wondered what fierce words Elizabeth had in store for him.

Mr. Cummings continued, "I think you were right in there, when you said that she does not know her own feelings. She is tender to him in ways that a mere friend would not be. She accepted the false engagement very quickly and almost seemed happy with it. Did you hear her engage him in conversation as if they had been courting for months? And did you hear her correct him when he quoted Samuel Johnson incorrectly? No, sir, the usual fortune hunter would have let that one slide. We must do all we can to ensure they have as much time together as possible."

Colonel Fitzwilliam smiled mischievously at the energetic speech from the doctor. "Is that a doctor's order?"

They both let out a chuckle. "I will leave that answer up to you. It seems things are progressing nicely. Come, the splint is in the back."

The colonel grabbed the brace, which looked like a giant, cloth-covered boot with boards running up the sides and multiple large fabric ties going down the length. He was surprised at how heavy it was.

He followed the doctor into the sitting room again and found Madeline sitting next to Darcy. She was checking his pulse, and they were laughing together in easy conversation. Elizabeth was standing by the window, with her back toward Darcy, sniffling and trying to hide that she was crying. *What happened? I was only gone a few minutes!* He quickly evaluated Darcy to see what he had missed. Darcy appeared pleased with himself and didn't seem to notice that Elizabeth was upset. The colonel quickly put the boot down by Darcy's foot and walked over to Elizabeth.

He placed his hand on her shoulder. She jumped a little at the touch but did not turn. "What is wrong, Miss Elizabeth? Did something happen?" He handed her his handkerchief.

She quietly took the handkerchief and dabbed at her small tears. She whispered, "He asked if he could kiss me."

Surprise shined on his face, but he collected his thoughts quickly and asked, "Did you let him? I do not mean to pry, but you seem upset."

"I cannot do this anymore! All this dishonesty and deceit! How will placating him now help him recover! I simply cannot play this game anymore. At some point, he is going to start to remember what has happened, and at some point, we will have to tell him the truth!

Do you know how ugly I feel? That man there is a decent man, and we are playing mind games with him!"

"Yes, he is a decent man."

"And he deserves to know the truth. I have not agreed to marry him. But did you ever see him so relaxed and content? He was so open and kind in his words . . ."

"He usually is open and kind with those he trusts."

"That is my point! He trusts us, and we are feeding him falsehoods! And I am not so sure that is the best course of action."

"Let me get this straight. And do correct me if I am wrong. You had a pleasant evening with him. You now see that he is a decent and kind man, and you desperately do not want to hurt him with these lies. So much so, that you let him kiss you—"

"I did not let him kiss me! Not in that way you are thinking. I simply offered my hand." She turned a new shade of red.

It was obvious there was more to the story. "And then?"

The crimson in her cheeks was making her hot, and her gown seemed to have grown too tight around the rib cage. She couldn't breathe. She couldn't see straight. Everything seemed to sway with each blink of her eyes. How could she have crossed the line with Mr. Darcy? How had she been so confused? And for God's sake, how in the world did Colonel Fitzwilliam know something else had happened? "I am not sure I understand you," she lied.

"I am saying, a lady like yourself does not turn scarlet because she offered her hand to be kissed. I am saying there is more to the story. I am saying Mr. Darcy looks very pleased with himself. I am saying you seem a little guilty. I am saying—"

"Stop it! I am not some prisoner of war whom you are interrogating!" She attempted to hold firm in her statement and looked him straight in the eyes. Something in his look told her he would not judge her. His eyes were kind, gentle, and there was an element of something else . . . hope?

"Why do we not take a walk in the gardens? You seem to be in need of some fresh air." Without asking, he took Elizabeth's arm and led her toward the door. He called over his shoulder, "Darcy, Miss Elizabeth wanted to see the sunset. I told her how beautiful it was tonight, and I know she would appreciate it. We will be back shortly."

The colonel held the front door open for her, and she exited into the cool night air. As they were leaving, she caught sight of Mrs. Wilkinson through the kitchen window, who eyed them suspiciously. She had already broken down once in front of Mrs. Wilkinson this week; doing so again was sure to arouse her alarm. *Well,* Elizabeth thought, *I have good reason to cry this time.*

The evening sun truly was breathtaking as it peeked through the grove of trees. There was a natural rise in terrain to the south, which meant, with a little effort, they would have an unobstructed view of the sunset. She already knew that was the path she wanted to take. Her anxiety propelled her feet at a quick pace which the colonel had no problem matching. As they reached the top of the hill a few minutes later, she had already made the decision that she could not shoulder the burden on her own. She would have to tell the colonel.

"Miss Elizabeth, we are free here to discuss whatever you need to at any volume you like."

"I am not one to raise my voice, but I will warn you that mind games and manipulation techniques do not find favor with me. Do not try to weasel the truth out of me. If you have questions, then ask, and I shall answer you honestly."

The colonel eyed her suspiciously. "Well then, I will get straight to the point. Did you let him kiss you?"

"No."

"Did you refuse to let him kiss you?"

"No."

"You said you offered your hand. Did he kiss it?"

"Y . . . yes."

"I see. And that kiss was all that happened?"

"No."

He looked a little confused. "Then the only thing I can surmise is that you kissed him."

"Yes."

"A real kiss?"

"Define real."

"A kiss, Miss Elizabeth, is defined as when lips touch each other in a loving way."

"Then, no."

"No? But you kissed him. Ah, I see. You kissed him on the cheek."

"Yes. There. Now I have said it."

"Actually you said very little, it was I who did all the talking. But give me the podium a little while longer. Let me see if I understand this correctly. When he asked if he could kiss you, you politely offered your hand . . . he kissed it . . . and then, what? You felt the need to lean over and kiss him on the cheek?"

She started pacing. She wrung her hands over and over again. "I have never had my hand kissed that way before. He did something to me. He made my heart thump hard three times in my chest each time he kissed it. The look in his eyes was so endearing and gentle and almost boyish. It was all I could do not to let my knees collapse. I do not know what happened, but then I leaned over and put my other hand on his cheek. Then he pulled me gently toward him, and I kissed his cheek. It was a simple peck on the cheek, but Mr. Darcy smiled wider than I have ever seen him smile. That is when I knew I had done something wrong. I should not have let my emotions control my actions. I honestly do not know quite what I was thinking. I mean, we are supposed to be helping reorient him to reality, and I just allowed him to hope for a future that is not real."

The colonel reached for Elizabeth's elbow and turned her back around. He paused, wondering how he could make her understand. Pointing to the west he asked, "Have you ever noticed how beautiful sunsets are after a storm?" She shook her head. "When the grey clouds part above the setting sun, you get a true rainbow of colors. The light bounces off the storm clouds, accenting the fact that the hard part has passed and a new beginning is coming.

"You have had your stormy weather with Darcy. Do you see what I am trying to say, Miss Elizabeth? I do not know exactly what happened between you, but I know that you did not favor him when he first proposed. Perhaps these storms have left scars on the landscape.

"But storms provide several things Mother Earth cannot live without. Storms prune the landscape. Whatever is too weak to survive—a tree that is not well-rooted, or a river bank without plant growth—is washed away and deposited where it is needed, bringing fresh minerals and energy to that new area.

"And storms provide rain, or the tears of life. Where rain is, there will be new life. Without a storm's moisture, there can be no growth. Without growth, our lives would wither away and be meaningless. So you see, those tears you shed are proof that you are growing. And every storm brings a promise: after the storm comes a rainbow or a parting of the clouds at the least. That promise is one that is very important. A storm does not last forever.

"Perhaps what I am saying is that you may have had problems with Darcy in the past, but I think that storm is passing. In fact, I am sure of it. I think you already see the truth of what I am saying. Your hard feelings for Darcy are being pruned away. And those tears streaming down your face are only evidence of the potential for growth and healing. And those feelings you are feeling is the parting of the clouds, reminding you that things do not have to stay the way they were.

"There is great hope in the ever-challenging foe of change. It is important to have the storms. They bring growth and new life. But this storm does not have to last forever. Open your eyes, look, there is a break in the clouds. The sun will shine again. That is the promise of the storm."

Elizabeth wiped at her eyes. She had been watching the sunset while listening very closely to the colonel. "But I do not love him. I should not have kissed him."

"If that is the case, then I agree with you, you should not have kissed him. But love comes in all forms. The beginning may just be an element of respect. Do you at least respect Darcy?" She nodded. "Do you see how honest and loyal he is?" She nodded. "Do you see the depth and solid nature of his character?" She nodded. "What more is there?"

Finally, Elizabeth turned to the colonel. "Love! The kind of love that makes you want to be with him at all times. The kind of love that burns like a fever when he touches you. The kind of love that makes you blind to all his imperfections. The kind of love that can never be reproduced or deflected. That is the kind of love I want in my marriage. And I do not love Mr. Darcy like that."

"Perhaps not yet. Give it some time."

"No, you do not understand. I do not want to love him like that. I am not ready to love him like that. I want to be ready for it when it happens, but more than anything, I want that kind of love to be mutual. I am not sure Mr. Darcy's infatuation with me qualifies as the kind of love I am looking for."

Colonel Fitzwilliam laughed out loud. He put his fist up to his mouth and stifled it. "Forgive me. I believe we differ in opinions on that matter. I have never seen a man more deeply in love or more persistent in his pursuit." He let out another laugh. "I would say his love for you cannot be reproduced, except multiple times a day, every day. Would you not say that is a little persistent? Consistent? Resistant to deflection? No, you are wrong, Miss Elizabeth. Darcy's love for you is much deeper than an infatuation. You are simply unbalanced in your understanding of it."

In as deep a voice as she could muster and mimicking Darcy, she said, "Unbalanced? You could say that!" Elizabeth laughed at her own joke, which made the colonel laugh as well.

"Come, the sun has set and Darcy will get suspicious if we do not return soon. You already planted the seed of jealousy by implying I was going to offer marriage to you."

"Well, you deserved it. You have quite a list of offences being created against you. For example, when you told me Mr. Darcy wanted me to stay for the next six weeks . . ."

"Oh no, I only asked you what you thought. It was you who came up with that reasoning. I simply did not correct you."

"Humph! Mind games! Let me remind you, I do not like mind games."

"I am beginning to see that. Oh, and by the way, I will be sure to explain the situation to Georgiana. I believe her ignorance about his memory problems is what caused the crisis tonight. I do appreciate you playing along for Darcy's sake. I did not get a chance to tell you that he lost his memory during his bath, and we have already used the reminder letter effectively. It worked, Miss Elizabeth, it really worked." The colonel offered his arm, as now it was dark, and she was likely to take a wrong step.

Elizabeth took the offered arm. "Are you saying his memory suddenly just disappeared? I thought we had determined that it was sleep or medicine that caused his memory problems."

"I had thought so too, but apparently it can happen anytime. He was physically exerting himself more than he has in the last few days. Maybe that was what caused it."

"Well, I was hoping to see improvement, but this seems like another setback."

"Perhaps, but it was quickly remedied by your kiss. I am sure that kind of excitement burns a memory deep in his soul."

Elizabeth slapped his arm. "No teasing! I feel bad enough as it is!"

"Storms, Miss Elizabeth, storms."

*****

Darcy had his leg and brace propped high up on pillows when the two came back inside. "While you were out, I found William Wordsworth's book of poems on the table. I found something that I think you would like."

Colonel Fitzwilliam chuckled. "You know I do not enjoy poetry like you do. I acknowledge a few good ones now and then, but I simply cannot read a whole book of them!"

Darcy shot his cousin a look to silence him. "I was speaking to Miss Elizabeth." Elizabeth walked over and took her place in the chair at his head and smiled at him. Darcy continued, "Now that we are engaged, may I call you Elizabeth? You may call me William."

Elizabeth looked over at Colonel Fitzwilliam who shrugged. She looked to Mr. Cummings who gave a silent nod of the head. She looked to Madeline, and there was a reassuring smile on her face. She turned back to Darcy. "I would be honored, William. Now tell me about the poem."

"He is speaking about where we came from and why we are on earth, but I am interpreting it much differently. I have read it many times. Here, let me read it to you."

Our birth is but a sleep and a forgetting:
The Soul that rises with us, our life's Star,
Hath had elsewhere its setting.
And cometh from afar:
Not in entire forgetfulness,
And not in utter nakedness,
But trailing clouds of glory do we come
From God, who is our home:
Heaven lies about us in our infancy![3]

Darcy smiled and continued, "I thought it was profound in my situation. Here I am, entirely forgetful, as if I were just born. It makes me feel exposed, 'in utter nakedness' like the poem says. But somehow, somehow, I have found heaven with you."

"That is very profound. Are you always such a deep thinker or only when you hit your head?" Elizabeth teased.

"Now, Elizabeth, you jest. I just find it interesting that I have read that poem numerous times before, and now it means something new! It just proves how persisting in the things that you enjoy brings further enjoyment.

"For me," he continued, "with my memory problems, I find more than ever the sense of a new beginning. I cannot describe it exactly, but all day I had a sense of anxiety and foreboding that did not make sense. I tried to shake it, but until I was reminded of our engagement, it would not abate! Now look at me! Even with the pain and the heaviness of the splint, I have not felt this light in months! You have no idea how happy you have made me. Now I know why newly engaged men say they are the happiest of men. For truly, that is what I am!"

Elizabeth smiled at him and wondered what exactly Madeline had given him for the pain because he was nearly giddy. "And did you get your pain medication?"

"Yes, but only half a dose. Why?"

"I am just concerned for your comfort, William." Darcy reached for her hand and clasped it in both of his. He gave it the gentlest squeeze and looked at her affectionately.

The look gave her goose bumps and made her heart flutter slightly. Why she had this physical reaction she did not know. It made her uncomfortable, but in a pleasant way. She tried to remember what Colonel Fitzwilliam had said. Storms offer promises. He also said they

---

[3] "Ode: Intimations of Immortality from Recollections of Early Childhood", William Wordsworth

have a way of pruning that which was not strong enough. Could she forgive him for interfering with Jane and Bingley? Could she absolve him of guilt? Where these the things the colonel was talking about when he said that storms prune away what is not strong enough?

*****

The next morning Elizabeth was excited to see how Mr. Darcy was doing. Last night's dinner had been very good, and she suspected that Mrs. Wilkinson had received help, but she didn't dare try to confirm it. For the first time in five weeks, she had eaten a meal at the parsonage and felt full afterwards. She noticed that Mr. Darcy had eaten all of his food as well and had even asked for more. She would have to send a note to Lady Catherine thanking her for the food. She decided to write it before she went to see Mr. Darcy; knowing how the last few days have been, there would be little time for herself.

She quickly penned the note and dusted the ink before folding the letter. It dawned on her that the house was very quiet. There was no yelling downstairs. There was no noise at all. She slipped on her boots and crept down the hall. She didn't want to wake Mr. Collins and ruin her appetite. Luckily, she made it past his door and down the stairs without a sound.

She grabbed her shawl and leaned her ear toward the sitting room door and confirmed that Mr. Darcy was indeed not awake yet. *Thank goodness! I might be able to squeeze in a brisk walk before he wakes!* She didn't hesitate to leave immediately, being as quiet as possible.

She realized why it had been so quiet in the house: the sun was just cresting over the east. She had felt rested enough to wake and get moving before anyone else awoke. It was still very early. She smiled at herself. She felt some sort of freedom overcome her as she walked, and she broke into a run. She picked up her skirts and skipped and twirled and jumped over things in her way. Her heart was lighter than it had been for almost a week!

She didn't really hate staying at the Hunsford Parsonage. She had rather enjoyed her visit. If she were to go home in three days, as originally planned, she could imagine feeling quite disappointed. Of course, she wouldn't miss Mr. Collins or his sermons on her behavior. Nor would she miss the terrible food, but she had grown to really love Mrs. Wilkinson. She made a mental note to ask Mrs. Wilkinson if she could write to her from Longbourn. She would miss the beech grove and the path that wound by the gazebo. She would miss the trees near the parsonage. She would even miss the stream and hearing its gentle, comforting sound that always played in the background. She would definitely miss Charlotte.

She wondered where all these thoughts were coming from since she wasn't leaving for another six weeks. She let out a little laugh at herself, remembering how her stomach did not stand a chance at resisting Lady Catherine once she tasted those treats. She still wasn't quite sure she had actually agreed to stay six weeks, but nevertheless, that was the end result. She let her thoughts continue as she danced around in the early morning air. She would miss Lady Catherine's officious ways because they offered much to laugh at. She would miss the colonel and his kind words and friendship. She would miss . . .

Suddenly she stopped walking. There was something else she would miss. Now it was all making a little more sense. She would miss their walks. She already did miss their walks. It wasn't so much the beech grove, or the gazebo, or the river, or the trees . . . it was him. She would miss him. She felt her heart stop momentarily as she came to this conclusion. Why would she miss Mr. Darcy?

*****

The butler looked at her suspiciously. Elizabeth tried to explain, "I know it is too early to call. I just wanted to drop this note off to Lady Catherine. There is no need to disturb her. I was out walking and thought I would deliver it myself."

"Is it about Mr. Darcy?" the butler asked. "I am to deliver information about him immediately, day or night."

"No, not really. I mean, he is mentioned, but—"

"Please come in, Miss Bennet. I am sure she would like to read the note immediately."

"Oh no, I do not want to make it sound urgent. It is really just a thank you letter." She watched as he held open the door and motioned for her to come in. "Very well, but I am sure she does not wish to see me this early."

The butler walked her to the morning room and asked if there was anything she needed.

Elizabeth thought maybe she should ask for that heavenly tea but shook her head instead. "No, thank you." And with that, the butler closed the door behind him, and she sat down. She had been in the morning room only once before, during a brief tour with Sir William Lucas and Maria when they first arrived in Kent. Although a little over-decorated, it was a nice room.

She could see why it was called the morning room since it offered a beautiful view of the eastern horizon. The view beckoned her, and she stood to look out the window. From here, she could see the manicured drive that held miniature trees, perfectly shaped in a neat row. She could see the pink and gray cobblestone path that graced the front entrance and could see a servant sweeping it assiduously.

She wondered why she was let in at all and whether she would just as quickly be sent out again, for it was far too early to call on someone, especially someone as grand as Lady Catherine. She walked over to the bookshelf and noticed a wide variety of books. She saw one that interested her, titled *Plants and Flowers of Northern England*. She opened it and was amazed by page after page of beautiful, detailed botanical illustrations. She noticed that there were penciled notes in the margins: "does not do well with excessive water, plant in rocky soil bed"; "yellow flowers stay blooming well into July, accent with bluebells"; and "this variety has strong fragrance, but does not bloom as long as its parent hybrid".

It must have been owned by a master gardener, and she found herself entranced in it. She began to search for these markings as if they held some deep meaning to her. They were written in masculine handwriting. She found it odd that Lady Catherine would have a book about northern England's plants and flowers. She kept flipping the pages and became engrossed in the little notes made throughout. She felt like she had secrets in her hand that any gardener would want to have. She did not realize how much time had passed.

"I see you have found Mr. Darcy's book on Derbyshire's plants and flowers," Lady Catherine said.

Startled out of her private moment reading the mind of this master gardener, Elizabeth asked, "This is Mr. Darcy's book?"

"The late Mr. Darcy. He took great pride in his gardens at Pemberley. As do I here at Rosings. I find one can never know too much about the grounds one keeps. Trusting the gardeners to know what will grow and do well in each environment is not always a safe assumption. One must help them to make the decisions, even daily decisions, which affect the look and feel of one's estate."

Lady Catherine must have risen early as well as she was already immaculately dressed and groomed. Not a hair was out of place on her feathery head. This morning's ornate hairstyle included some sort of bird; the wing opened over her left ear, and the beak stuck out straight past her nose. Elizabeth didn't trust herself to speak, or she might just giggle at Lady Catherine's pretension.

"The late Mr. Darcy knew I shared a fondness for gardening and left it to me in his will. Unfortunately, the book does me little good since the differences in climate between Kent and Derbyshire are so great."

"Then why do you not give it to Mr. Darcy? Is he aware that you have it? I imagine a treasure like this, with his father's personal notes, would be very valuable to him."

"Mr. Darcy does not know what he wants. I know what Mr. Darcy wants."

Elizabeth's hair on the back of her neck stood up slightly. "You mean about the engagement to your daughter."

"That, and a great deal more." Lady Catherine began taking slow, deliberate steps toward Elizabeth. "The colonel returned late last night and did not give me an update for the day. Please sit down. I have ordered breakfast and tea. I assume you have been out walking again unescorted. I have told Mr. Collins many times not to let you do that, but I see you have found a way to get around him." Lady Catherine reached the end of her path and now stood face to face with Elizabeth. "Do you always go out walking at dawn and make calls to ladies of consequence at ridiculously early hours?"

The sound of breakfast at Rosings was music to her ears, but she would keep her wits about her this time. "No, Lady Catherine. I only wished to give you my gratitude in the form of a note. A note that you could read at your leisure. A note that I specifically told the butler not to disturb you with. If you had not given your butler such strict instructions, then we would not be here at such an early hour."

Lady Catherine sat down and then leaned back in her chair and smiled. "You know, I never told you so, but I like you. You have just enough impertinence to keep one on one's toes. I imagine your ability to say exactly what you are thinking comes in handy while dealing with Darcy's limitations now."

Elizabeth wasn't sure where she was going with this. "Thank you, I think. I am not sure if that was a compliment or a veiled barb."

"See, that is exactly what I am talking about. No one can doubt what you are thinking because your expression shows the truth of what you say."

"I have been told that several times. That is why I sometimes struggle to perform my designated role with Mr. Darcy."

"And what role is that?"

"I mean in dealing with his memory problems. I find it hard to placate him and help keep his anxiety down. Often I am forced to hide the truth from him to avoid setbacks."

Breakfast arrived and trays were set up in front of each lady. The servants brought in mountains of food. Elizabeth noticed cinnamon-and-sugar-powdered rolls, perfectly cooked eggs, at least ten slices of bacon, and some sort of steaming hot, puffy, buttery dish that was falling as it cooled. She didn't know what to eat first. "What is that puffy dish?"

"German pancakes. It is a recipe that my French cook found on her tour last year. I try to keep my staff well-educated, so I sent her on a two-week tour of Europe to learn new methods and new foods. This is one of my favorites. Here, let me get you a piece. You dust it with powdered sugar and maple syrup. It is truly a delight."

Elizabeth watched the butter still boiling on the top of the German pancake and was awed at the speed in which the staff must have delivered such a perfectly executed array of food. "Do you always eat this well this early in the morning?"

"Only when I have special visitors. I am an early riser, so they were prepared for me, and it did not take long for them to add to the food. I waited a few minutes before attending to you so that the food would be ready in time. You must try it."

Lady Catherine handed Elizabeth the steaming, fluffy, buttery pancake. Elizabeth did as she was instructed and sprinkled the pancake with powdered sugar and poured a bit of syrup on it as well. Her fork could cut it easily, and she noticed that it was not bready like a pancake, but rather egg-based. She glanced up at Lady Catherine, who was waiting patiently for her to try it.

She put a bite in her mouth and felt the sweetness engulf her senses. The German pancake was indeed egg-based but was fluffy with a bit of crunchy crust, which delighted her mouth in ways she didn't know possible. She closed her eyes briefly to take in the sensation and combination of flavors. When she opened her eyes, Lady Catherine was grinning at her and seemed very pleased with Elizabeth's response.

"Now, tell me more about Mr. Darcy's memory problems."

She shoveled in another bite and tried not to swallow it whole before she answered. "The doctor says as long as we do not remind him of painful memories, his memory should come back. We thought we had an understanding of why he keeps losing his memory." She quickly took another bite and chewed slowly this time. The smell of the bacon was overwhelming, and she reached for two slices.

"Yes, Richard was going to tell me about that. Here, try this cinnamon bread." She sliced off a piece and handed it to Elizabeth. "Why do you not finish telling me about it? What was your theory for the loss of memory?"

Elizabeth asked for some tea and bit into the crunchy, yet chewy, bacon. There was something about bacon dipped in maple syrup that was heavenly. She looked up with a full mouth to find her cup was being offered back to her. She took it and tried to say thank you, but her mouth was full. She swallowed hard and tried to talk. She asked, "Do you mean besides the head injury?"

"Of course. He has memory problems because of the head injury."

"Yes, every morning he has to be reminded of the accident. So, our theory was that he was losing his memory every time he fell asleep. Then, once, he lost it after we gave him the pain medication. So, we thought that was the reason for his forgetfulness. Sleep and medication."

Lady Catherine sliced a piece of cinnamon bread and placed it on her own plate. "But he has lost his memory at other times?"

"Yes, just yesterday. I was not there, but during his bath, he reverted back to forgetting about the accident and had to be shown the reminder letter."

"Reminder letter?"

Elizabeth was getting frustrated that she was having to talk so much during this fine meal. All she really wanted to do was eat more of that hot German pancake. She could tell it was cooling right in front of her. "I suppose Colonel Fitzwilliam did not get a chance to tell you about the letter since we wrote it just yesterday. It is an explanation of the accident and his injuries, and it details the limitations placed on him by the doctor. It also tells him who Nurse Madeline is so he knows why a strange woman is taking care of him. Since she is not a part of his previous memories, he does not know her at all."

"She helps him do things like use the chamber pot."

She had already taken a bite and murmured her confirmation.

"And this reminder letter helps him? Helps him to remember?" Lady Catherine continued.

Elizabeth swallowed but didn't look up from her plate as she cut another piece of the quickly cooling delights in front of her. "No, it does not help him remember. His memory is perfect up until two days before the accident, but he cannot remember anything from day to day. So, it does not really help him remember, because he is not gaining his memory back when he reads it. The letter simply explains what happened, so we do not have to go through the same crisis every morning as he becomes totally undone with the confusion."

Lady Catherine sipped her tea and smiled slightly. "The letter helps though? The confusion improves after reading it?"

"Yes, it appears so. Colonel Fitzwilliam witnessed its affect and stated it worked." Elizabeth couldn't quite understand why Lady Catherine was asking so many questions and not eating. She drank her perfectly made tea and looked up to sheepishly ask for more. Then she saw the smile on Lady Catherine's face. It was broad, and she was attempting to hide it with her tea cup, but something about it made

Elizabeth lose her appetite. Lady Catherine put her cup down and filled Elizabeth's.

Elizabeth realized that Lady Catherine was smirking. Her eyes were lifted at the corners, and she had a cat-like look on her face. Something was wrong. Elizabeth evaluated why she would be smiling when all they had been doing was discussing Mr. Darcy and his memory problems. There should not be anything but concern in her face. Yes, something was wrong. She put down her fork and knife and took the napkin off her lap. Lady Catherine handed her teacup back full.

The door opened and Colonel Fitzwilliam walked in quickly, still buttoning his waistcoat. "Miss Elizabeth! I was just on my way to the parsonage! Would you mind escorting me?"

Lady Catherine turned to her nephew, "Richard! You are up early! You are not even going to greet me? Come and sit and have breakfast. I will ring for—"

"No, thank you. Miss Elizabeth, I see you are ready." He walked over and offered his arm.

Elizabeth recognized the look Colonel Fitzwilliam was giving her. She had seen it the night before when he wanted her to play along with the engagement. His eyes pleaded for her to trust him. He placed a gentle hand on her elbow to help her up, and she appeased him. His grip got firmer as he pulled her toward the door. She turned back to look at Lady Catherine, who was once again smiling like a cat with a mouse. She tried to give a curtsy, but it was hindered dramatically by the fact that Colonel Fitzwilliam was nearly dragging her out the door.

They were out the door and nearly running to the parsonage. When they made a turn and were hidden from Rosings's view, Colonel Fitzwilliam quickly stopped and turned to face her. "What did you tell her? What does she know?"

His grip on her elbow was so tight it was hurting. She pulled away and he dropped it. He ran his fingers through his hair. She felt like she was in trouble for something but had no idea what. "I do not take your meaning," she said.

"I am sorry for grabbing your elbow. Forgive me. I have tried very hard to limit what my aunt knows about Darcy. What does she know? What did you tell her? Does she know about his memory problems?"

"I had no idea she did not already know!" Elizabeth whispered.

The colonel swore under his breath. "Excuse me. That was not appropriate for a lady's ears. You must tell me everything. What did you tell her?"

Elizabeth tried to retell the conversation as best she could. As she told him what had been said, she saw Colonel Fitzwilliam get more and more upset. He began pacing but continued to listen intently. She finished explaining about how Lady Catherine had knowledge of the reminder letter and of its success. "And then you came in and dragged me out of the room. That is all that was said."

Colonel Fitzwilliam stopped pacing. "I am afraid that is enough."

CHAPTER 8

"But I do not understand, Colonel. Why do you want to limit Lady Catherine's information about Mr. Darcy? I assumed you had been telling her about his condition all along."

Colonel Fitzwilliam took a deep breath. "This will not be easy to explain, considering she is my aunt, but the fact is I do not trust her. For one, she conceded too quickly to my request that she stay away. For another, she smiled, and that is not like her. I do not know; maybe I am being unreasonable. Surely she would not do anything to hurt her favorite nephew, right?"

"I do not know her that well, sir. I imagine that since she wants him to marry Miss Anne de Bourgh, she would only want to help. What makes you so suspicious?"

"It is my gut." He put a firm fist in the center of his abdomen. "Right here. It is telling me that she has a plan and we need to be prepared. It is telling me that she is not as heartbroken about his accident as she should be. It is telling me that I should fear her. Something is coming. Her willingness to keep you here, and her ignorance of how Darcy feels about you—it is going to turn out badly. The Aunt Catherine I know would never have complied with the doctor's wishes: a doctor, I might add, with whom she has a long, terrible history; a doctor whom she avoids at all cost . . . literally."

Elizabeth looked confused. "Why would she avoid Mr. Cummings?"

"I heard some gossip once when I was stealing a snack from the kitchen at Rosings. About ten years ago, when Anne was seventeen, something happened. Anne had been sick off and on for about five years by then, but she had been on a good stretch of health for several months. She was even being allowed outside again, undoubtedly due to my uncle's insistence. He was always an advocate for Anne. I myself witnessed many arguments between my aunt and uncle about Anne's health over the years, but my uncle always had the upper hand. He knew something about my aunt that always kept her in check. I never knew what it was, but it must have been quite significant to keep a woman like my aunt in line. I often wondered what it was.

"Ah, but I digress. You asked about Mr. Cummings. Well, the gossip from the kitchen said that there was an enormous fight ten years ago between my aunt and uncle about whether or not Anne should come out and make her curtsy. Obviously my uncle thought she was healthy enough to do it, and my aunt felt otherwise. The argument got heated, and suddenly my uncle collapsed, gripping his chest. He became weak and very ill—barely conscious, in fact. For two days my aunt did nothing.

"When he finally had enough strength to pen a letter, he summoned the doctor without her knowledge. When Mr. Cummings arrived, expecting to be let in, my aunt said it was all handled and there was no need for a doctor. Then the butler made a bold move, and instead of showing the doctor out the door he took him to see my uncle. The doctor was shocked and very worried about the patient. He prescribed an elixir to steady his heart rate.

"According to the kitchen staff, my aunt came in and found the doctor examining her husband and said she would not pay for his services as they had not been requested. Mr. Cummings tried to explain that the patient needed this new medicine every day, twice a day, for the rest of his life, or he would die. My aunt then changed her mind and promised to be diligent in administering the medicine and graciously allowed Mr. Cummings to finish the examination.

"Two days later the doctor came back. The patient was worse, so he asked if the medicine had been given as prescribed. My aunt told him it was too expensive and that he should prescribe something less expensive, like laudanum. Can you believe she had the gall to tell the doctor what to prescribe? The doctor and my aunt got into a very heated exchange that was heard by everyone in the household. Eventually my aunt had two footmen escort him out the front doors.

"Two days after that, my uncle died, the butler was dismissed, and Anne never made her curtsy before the queen. My aunt won everything she wanted through deceit—by promising to administer the medicine and then breaking her word."

Elizabeth sat down on a bench and put her head in her hands. She tried to take deep breaths as she carefully considered the colonel's story. Lady Catherine was responsible for the death of her own husband. She had refused to call the doctor and then refused to administer the prescribed medicine.

Elizabeth looked up at the colonel and asked, "So, you think it is suspicious that she did not put up a fight to keep the doctor away? Because Mr. Cummings knows this about her?"

He nodded. "I am afraid her allowing him to attend to Mr. Darcy surpasses my expectations of her behavior. I do not think she wants Darcy to die. I am just worried. She is so used to controlling every aspect of everyone's lives. I would expect her to insist on controlling Darcy's convalescence. She should be fighting us on every issue. She should not have agreed to stay away. She should not be content with the vague updates I am giving her. She should not have agreed with the doctor about trying to keep you here.

"Do you not see?" he continued. "Something is wrong! It is not like her to sit back as a passive observer. She has to have a hand in everything. I just do not trust her. But I cannot find my way into her devilish mind to figure out what she is planning. So, I tried to limit her information until I could understand her strategy . . . but now she knows everything."

"Thanks to me and my appetite."

"Pardon me, your what?"

"It is the food at Rosings. And the tea. It does something to me. When she presents such wonderful-smelling, tasty treats in front of me, I simply cannot help myself. It is like a drug. I get one taste of it, and I melt in her hands. That is how she got me to agree to stay for six more weeks."

"I do not understand. Are you saying she is putting something in the food?"

Elizabeth laughed. "Should I? After the story you just told me, I wonder if she would!"

"I would not put it past her. But I am serious."

"As am I! I cannot stand Mrs. Wilkinson's food, and I have had nearly six weeks of it. As soon as I see food or tea from Rosings, my stomach takes over and it is all I can think about."

The colonel evaluated her a moment. She did look a little thinner than when he first met her two weeks ago. "Is the food really that bad? I admit the tea has been merely tolerable, but I have had worse on the battlefield. If it is so bad, why do the Collinses keep her?"

"I suppose Mrs. Wilkinson is like family. Personally, I have grown very close to her. She is a dear friend. I have the utmost respect and admiration for her. I would never dream of complaining about her food to the Collinses for fear they might dismiss her. I must admit my mother always said I had a refined preference for food. So to be honest, the food very well may be acceptable to most people, but unfortunately not to me. She tries so hard though."

"Try or not, if she cannot excel at the job, she should seek other employment."

"Oh, do not take this out on Mrs. Wilkinson. I think we are in agreement about two things. One, we should watch Lady Catherine very closely. Two, I should not be eating at Rosings anymore." She let out a spirited laugh and stood up.

"Agreed," the colonel replied. "I will do my part, and you do yours. Now, let me escort you properly to see how Darcy is doing." He offered his arm to her, and she readily took it.

*****

Darcy was awake by the time they got there. Madeline was hurrying around the room when they entered, and she looked very relieved to see them.

"Darcy, my man! How are you this morning?" The colonel took long strides over to him and slapped him on the shoulder. "You look terrible. Did you just wake up?"

Darcy rubbed his head. "Indeed, but for the life of me I cannot figure out why I am at the parsonage."

"Ah! And you probably want to know why your head hurts, as well!"

Darcy looked surprised. "Indeed. Did I drink too much? I cannot explain it, but I am foggy in my brain. I keep thinking I am in some sort of dream."

Elizabeth knew exactly the moment Darcy noticed her because he sat up straighter and a small smile graced his lips. She acknowledged his smile and said, "Good morning, Mr. Darcy."

"What a pleasant surprise, Elizabeth! How are you this morning?" He started moving his legs off the chaise in an obvious attempt to stand and greet her, but she rushed over to his side.

"Oh, do not get up on my account. Here, let me get you something I think will help with that foggy mind." She made sure he was settled back on the chaise before she turned to the writing desk. She shuffled papers and realized once again that her love letter was still there. She quickly folded it and tucked it into her dress. *Will I ever learn? A thing like this cannot be left lying around!*

She found the reminder letter and brought it over to him. "This, sir, is something you had me write to help explain why your

177

head hurts. If you would just take a moment to read it, I think it will explain a great deal." She handed it to him and stepped back, watching him as he read.

It was several minutes before he reached the last page. Everyone was waiting for his response, but instead of giving one, he simply started over and read it again. Madeline stepped out to refresh herself, but both the colonel and Elizabeth stood by in anticipation. When he finally reached the last page again, he looked up, and took a good, long look at his right foot, rotating it one way and then the other, grimacing when he rotated it inward.

"Do you have questions?" Elizabeth asked hesitantly.

"Yes. When can I go home?"

The two onlookers chuckled slightly because they were expecting a much different response. The colonel spoke up first. "I am afraid you have about five more weeks of this. The doctor says not to move you until you can bear weight on it. It was a pretty bad break. How does the splint feel?"

"Tolerable. It only hurts when I move it. It is quite heavy, though. I take it that this accident was recent. The letter said it happened Tuesday. What day is it today?"

"Friday, sir," Elizabeth replied. "May I just commend you on taking this all so well? This is the best morning you have had so far."

"Thank you, Elizabeth. Where is this Madeline? Was she the woman who was in here running around? I am afraid I was ordering her like a servant. I should apologize. From the sound of this letter I should apologize for a great deal. It seems I have been somewhat . . ."

"Irrational?" Colonel Fitzwilliam suggested.

"Emotional?" Elizabeth added.

"No." Darcy said. "I have been—"

"Confused?" Elizabeth proposed.

"Aggressive?" Colonel Fitzwilliam offered.

"Persistent and determined?" Elizabeth teased. Her eyes lit up at seeing how well the letter was working. It was resolving the morning crisis without any intervention.

Darcy took a look at the two in front of him. A small smile crept along his face. "I take it I have been all of the above?"

The three of them laughed, and Elizabeth felt the warmth of his gaze on her, and she suddenly blushed. His eyes were saying something to her. Did he remember any of it? Was it simply the letter that seemed to make things go smoother? Or did he still think they were engaged?

She reviewed his reaction to the letter and the news, and she was confident that he still had memory problems. But something was nagging the back of her mind. There was some minor detail she was missing. What was it? She shook her head, trying to dispel the unsettling suspicion that something was different this morning. She couldn't help but ask him, "Mr. Darcy? May I ask if any of this seems familiar? Did the letter remind you of anything that has happened? Anything at all?"

Darcy genuinely looked surprised at the question. He shook his head and said, "No, not at all. I had to read it twice to retain all that was in the letter. I still cannot believe what happened. You all have been so helpful. I am so grateful to be alive."

Colonel Fitzwilliam smiled and looked at Elizabeth. "Well, one thing that Miss Elizabeth did not put in the letter was how she was the one who saved your life. Her quick mind stayed rational during a time when many women would have fainted. She did not put it in the letter, because she did not want to boast, but I would say she is the reason you are alive."

Darcy's eyes were locked on Elizabeth's. His deep, penetrating gaze was intense and thoughtful. Elizabeth looked away shyly and said, "It was not necessary to remind him of such facts, Colonel Fitzwilliam."

Darcy's gaze was not leaving Elizabeth's face. "No, I believe that kind of information is vital. I am sure it will help me a great deal. Would you mind telling me about it, Elizabeth?"

That was it! He had called her by her Christian name! He had done it earlier too! She narrowed her eyes at him suspiciously. "Indeed, I will tell you, but I am afraid my telling of the story will not be as animated and grandiose as it would be if your cousin told the story. Why do I not leave you two so you can do your morning ritual while I will check on your breakfast?"

"Very well, but I would still like to hear the story from you."

"Certainly, if that is your wish. Colonel Fitzwilliam? Do you have a moment?"

The colonel followed Elizabeth out of the room, and Elizabeth closed the door behind them. He looked at her expression and wondered what was wrong. He waited patiently while she wrung her hands, tucked stray hairs behind her ear, and took several deep breaths. "I can see you are disturbed. Out with it! What is nagging you?"

"He called me Elizabeth."

"And the problem with that being . . . because it is improper? Miss Elizabeth, he hit his head. Not all of the rules of society are in place yet. For one, you two have had many private conversations without chaperones as well as the fact that—"

"Colonel, today is the first day he has done that. Do you not see? He must remember last night's conversation when he asked if he could call me Elizabeth. He must think we are engaged!"

The colonel considered this for a moment. "I do not think you are right. I think it is something entirely different. If I may, I might divulge a story to you about Deborah."

"Who?"

"Deborah. She was the only woman I have ever met whom I considered making an offer for. I sought out her company and unofficially courted her for several months. She had only a small dowry, and I admit I dragged my feet several times in asking permission to court her. Then I left for the next battle and never saw her again. I heard she married and moved to Scotland."

"What does she have to do with Mr. Darcy?" Elizabeth asked.

"Well, it was not long into my fascination with her that I started thinking of her by her given name. I dreamed of calling her Deborah. I wished to call her Deborah. I had to catch myself all the time, and there were several times that I almost slipped. It was my familiarity with her in my mind that made me want to call her Deborah, not the fact that she ever gave me permission, which of course she did not."

"Truly? I mean, you really do not think he remembers asking if he could call me Elizabeth? It is pretty obvious that he does not remember the accident or his injuries, but maybe he remembers bits of yesterday."

"I definitely think he does not remember any of it. But if you would like, I will ask him not to use your Christian name."

Elizabeth thought about it a moment and then had a better idea. "Perhaps you could correct him once while I am gone and see how he responds. If he seems embarrassed, then I will agree that it is the familiarity in his own mind. But if he is confused, then we will know he has some memory of last night's conversation."

"You know you are asking me to play mind games." He grinned at her.

"Yes, but not with me. My only rule is no mind games with me! You may use any battlefield tactic you desire to get him to remember or admit to remembering, but we have to know if he is making progress! We have to know if he still thinks we are engaged!"

*****

The rest of the morning went smoothly. When Richard corrected Darcy as Elizabeth requested, Darcy was terribly embarrassed. Darcy then divulged to his cousin that he wanted to propose to Elizabeth, thus fully absolving Richard of any fears that Darcy remembered anything of the last four days. He later related Darcy's response exactly to Elizabeth.

"Miss Elizabeth, he was mortified that he had slipped in front of me. He most definitely did not mean to use your Christian name. I do not think he even realizes that he did so in your presence. And I am fully confident that he does not remember last night. In his mind, he has not proposed yet, but I am afraid he has already asked me to arrange a private conversation with you."

He smiled and continued, "I have to abide by his wishes, Miss Elizabeth. You should have seen the excitement in his eyes as he told me how he had made up his mind, how you were everything he wanted, how he could not stand letting another day go by without professing his love for you."

"Colonel, spare me the details of his professed love. I have seen the look on his face, I have seen the spark in his eyes, and I have most definitely seen the dimpled smile he gets when he is expressing his love for me. Believe me when I say I know how it will go. It may not be the exact same words—in fact, he seems to be improving—but the proposal will be the same. I will steel myself for it and give him my usual answer."

"Or . . ."

Elizabeth threw her hands up. "Or what! Or I could accept Mr. Darcy's proposal? Colonel, might I remind you that he does not need to be told lies? There are certain things that he simply cannot make right in his current state."

"Storms. It is simply storms." And with that he grabbed his hat and left the vestibule, leaving a shocked and frustrated Elizabeth staring after him with her mouth agape.

A servant had witnessed the last of the argument. Embarrassed, Elizabeth quickly grabbed the tea tray from her, gave a weak smile, and then walked into the room to have her ever-so-necessary, daily private audience with Mr. Darcy. Madeline must have been talking to Darcy about something pleasant because both of them were smiling. As soon as Madeline heard Elizabeth come in, she gathered her things, nodded conspiratorially to Darcy, and out the door she went. Was this ever going to get easier? Couldn't she simply add to the reminder letter that he had already proposed? *Today started out so beautifully.*

"Today started out so beautifully, did it not, Miss Elizabeth? Too bad it looks like a storm is coming."

Elizabeth was startled to hear her exact thoughts verbalized. Had she spoken them out loud? "Yes, Mr. Darcy. I took advantage of the weather and walked at dawn."

"I remember that you take great delight in your walks."

"Yes. It seems your memory before the accident, for the most part, is entirely intact."

"I hope I never disturbed you on your walks."

"No, sir, you did not. I found them enjoyable, although we really did not talk much."

"You do not think so? Hmmm . . . I remember our conversations and your company on the walks to be very enjoyable."

Elizabeth noticed Darcy's piercing eyes penetrating deep into her. What was she supposed to say? She tried to be as honest as possible. "At the time I did not realize how enjoyable they were. Since your accident, I have come to realize I rather miss our unexpected encounters." She hoped she wasn't being too forward, but a little encouragement to get the expected daily proposal out of the way would not hurt.

"I had thought those unexpected encounters would be enough to express my sentiments." Darcy smiled warmly and affectionately. "Miss Elizabeth?"

"Yes?" *Here it is.*

"There is something I must confess. Those unexpected encounters were not so unexpected for me. I would wake early and search you out just for the chance to walk by your side. It was the highlight of my day."

Darcy readjusted himself on the chaise and Elizabeth stood to help him. She tucked a pillow behind his back, and adjusted the elevated, broken foot. "Is that more comfortable?" She stood at the chaise by his head and waited for his reply. Instead of speaking he reached for her hand and ever so gently kissed the back of it. The warmth of his kiss sent vibrations all the way into her chest, and the heat it created made her cheeks go warm. Instead of dropping her hand he held it close to his chest. She could feel his heartbeat through his clothes, and it was oddly moving. It was steady, but comforting. She blushed deeper and had to look away from his deep brown eyes.

"I want to thank you for all you have done, as well as what you are currently doing for me. I cannot tell you what it means to have you here with me during this difficult time. I cannot imagine anyone I would rather have by my side."

She found her voice after a moment. "Thank you, sir."

"But I might confess something more if you do not mind. I am a very selfish creature and must admit I do not want anyone else at my side for the rest of my life. I want you, Elizabeth, to love, to hold, to cherish, and to grow old with. I want to be able to repay the service you have offered so graciously to me, and the only way I know how to do that is to offer you my heart. Indeed, I need not offer it because it has claimed residence with you for many months. I know now that it cannot survive without your love in return. Please tell me you will marry me. Please tell me that I do not have to wait any longer looking at your blushing face for a reply."

"You mistake my blush, sir."

Darcy looked quizzically at her. "How so?"

"I find that I am not accustomed to having a man hold my hand next to his heart, and I am feeling a little overwhelmed. May I have it back?" She tried to make it sound like she was teasing him, but in all reality she did want it back, and soon, or she was going to have to catch her fall. He seemed reluctant to let it go, but he did release it, and she quickly found a chair. She knew she was breathing fast, and she really needed to calm herself.

Minutes flew by like they were seconds, and the whole while Mr. Darcy just looked at her, his eyes going from her hair, to her lips, and to her restless hands in her lap. Several times she opened her mouth to speak, but the words wouldn't come. She blushed and looked down at her lap. After what felt like hours, Elizabeth whispered, "Sir, I apologize. I am not ready to give you an answer."

Darcy finally looked away. "I have asked you before, have I not?"

She glanced up at him, so startled that she gasped. "You remember?"

He slowly shook his head. "No, but your reaction just confirmed it. I take it we are not engaged or that piece of information would be in the reminder letter."

Her heart ached to explain. "Please, let me explain."

"You refused me. What other reason could there be?" His voice was weak and cracked at the end.

"Yes, but for two reasons that you have clarified for me already. You explained yourself in a letter that you wrote me. Indeed the reason for your accident was because you were trying to give me the letter."

"You accepted a letter from a suitor you had refused?" She nodded. "Why?" He glanced up to look at her briefly.

She didn't know how to explain it. "It was raining very hard. I had so many things I needed to say to you, and I was a coward and did not say them, but I am going to say them now. I must. I know you do not remember my refusal, and I am glad of that, for I was unkind. I fear my words were harsh and my manner unguarded. I said so many things that cannot be taken back now, but perhaps your memory problems are a blessing for the time being because I am afraid you were quite distressed. How could you not be after I said such awful things?"

His gaze was fixed on her. "Certainly you have no need to apologize. I ascertain that whatever you called me, I must have deserved it."

"No, William. You did not. I must apologize, or I will forever relive that day and wish I had. Please give me a moment more before you ask to never see me again."

"What did you call me?"

Elizabeth hesitated. "I called you ungentlemanly and said you had a selfish disdain for others. I also said—"

"No, not then . . . just now. You called me William."

"I did?"

"Yes, I am certain of it."

A new blush filled her cheeks, and she felt the warmth all the way to her ears. "I apologize, sir."

"No, do not apologize. It was wonderful. I . . . . I suppose I rather liked it. Have you called me William this whole time?"

"No." Elizabeth knew she was getting into dangerous ground because he was asking questions that would show that they had lied to him multiple times, and she tried to school her features to not betray the falsehoods that lingered like a hangman's noose. She didn't chance glancing up at him either. She knew she was no good at bending the truth. Every person who ever knew her told her she was an open book, ready to be read by anyone who wanted to know what she was thinking. She let out the breath that she didn't realize that she had been holding.

Darcy whispered to her, "I did not mind in the slightest, I promise. I wish I could explain how it felt, but it was most certainly not unpleasant. Please look at me." He sat forward and reached his hand up to her chin and lifted it. "There. Now I see those eyes that captured my heart."

Tears started forming in her eyes, and she could not hold them back. "I am sorry, Mr. Darcy. I have to tell you how sorry I am for refusing you in such a manner. It has been an enormous burden to carry ever since I did so, and I am so sorry. I have never spoken to anyone with such fervor and anger. You must understand that I wish I could have that moment to do over again." She bowed her head once again and reached for her handkerchief and dried her eyes. His hand dropped her chin but only enough to take the handkerchief and wipe the corner of her eye where a remaining tear was threatening to fall.

"So, do you regret refusing me?" His voice was soft and smooth to Elizabeth's ears.

"No. Well, yes, no. Definitely no."

"Yes, no? I do not understand your meaning."

She took a deep breath and stood up and started pacing. "I stand by my refusal, at least for half the reasons. The other half you explained in your letter, and I understand now that I misjudged you terribly. But although I stand by my refusal, I very much regret refusing you in such an insulting way. As I said earlier, I was not kind. I could have been much more . . . well, to use your words at the time, I could have been more civil."

"Miss Elizabeth, I am beginning to wonder what I did to make you so, how did you put it . . . insulting? Could I read the letter I wrote you? It might help me understand what you are saying. And to be honest, I would love to know why you refused me."

"I think that is a fair request. Give me a moment and I will go get it." She wiped her eyes one more time and smoothed her skirts.

She hurried out the door and nearly ran into the colonel. "Oh! Excuse me! I will be right back. Do not go in. Not yet. We are not finished. Do not look at me like that! I am well!" But her tears betrayed her once again. "Really, I am well. But give me some more time with him."

Colonel Fitzwilliam smiled and nodded. "What are you doing in there?"

Elizabeth sniffled and through her tears gave him a quirky grin. "Pruning." She turned and left him wondering what she meant, but she knew he was smart enough to figure it out. She ran upstairs to her room and looked for her letter. Not until she did a thorough search did she remember that she had given it to Charlotte. She ran down the stairs in the most unladylike fashion; again nearly running into the colonel. "Have you seen Mrs. Collins? I need her immediately."

"I believe she is putting away the gardening tools before the storm arrives. Can I help you?"

"No, thank you. I am well. Do not be discouraged."

She went out the front door and saw Charlotte loading the tools into the wheelbarrow. "Charlotte! I need that letter I gave you."

Charlotte looked concerned but dropped the tools and hurried into the house. Elizabeth followed close behind her, nearly stepping on her heels. Charlotte led her into her chambers upstairs, and the letter was handed over. Elizabeth grabbed it, but Charlotte held it tight, not releasing it immediately. "Lizzy, you have a lot to be thankful for."

"I know, but I cannot talk now." The letter was released, and Elizabeth hurried down the stairs, short of breath, and for a third time almost ran into the colonel. He seemed to have stepped right into her path this time. She gave him her most impatient look. "If you will please move your person, sir. Mr. Darcy is waiting for me."

"I see. And you are anxious to get back to him and his proposal?" The grin was broad and hid nothing of the humor he was feeling.

Elizabeth rolled her eyes and pushed him aside. She then entered the sitting room, and turned to close the door only to see Richard's smiling face behind it. She slammed the door in his face and heard loud laughter from the other side.

Mr. Darcy asked, "Are you well, Miss Elizabeth? You seem breathless."

His kind, gentle tones calmed her heart enough to help her turn around. "Indeed, I was only running to get the letter, sir." She walked over to him and handed him the dirty, warped pages. She saw him look at them with intrigued, curious eyes as he glanced over them and then looked to her for an explanation. "I dropped it in the rain. I apologize. You should be able to read most of it."

Darcy's face looked pensive, and then he gave a weak smile to Elizabeth. She saw him take a deep breath and start reading. They sat there for what seemed like hours, with her watching his every facial expression. It seemed to be a cycle of concern, pain, anger, fear, and, every once in a while, humor. She started tapping her foot unconsciously, and when he looked up from the pages to look at where the sound was coming from, she stopped immediately and put her hands on her knees to calm them. *What is taking so long?* Finally, he looked up and folded the sheets back together in a very methodical manner. He was being painstakingly slow just to irritate her; she knew it.

"I think I see why you refused me. I gather that you heard about my advice to Bingley and that Wickham had some colorful stories to tell you." She nodded. "And how did you hear about Bingley?"

"From Colonel Fitzwilliam, sir."

"I see. Although I still do not remember the actual proposal or your refusal, I am quite familiar with these two problems addressed in this letter. And if they are the reasons for your refusal, I would like to clarify any questions you might have that I may not have addressed in the letter."

She tried to stay calm, but thunder clashed outside very loudly, and she jumped at the sound. "I just need to know if what you said in the letter was true. Did you really think Jane unfeeling toward Mr. Bingley?"

He nodded and placed the folded letter on his lap. "Indeed. I saw a kind, considerate lady who would be obedient to her mother's

189

wishes. I truly felt she would marry Bingley if your mother insisted upon it, but not because she loved him; instead, because she could tolerate him. Quoting from your mother that night at the Netherfield Ball, 'He is a fine catch', and she would be a fool not to accept him. But as you can see from my letter, I admit that I was wrong."

She huffed in response. "So, admitting you were wrong is the best you can do?" She paused and closed her eyes and bowed her head. She looked up at him and said, "Pardon me, I did not mean to speak so frankly. I do not know what has come over me and my nerves. I did not mean to offend you again."

"You are correct, though. And if you will once again be my scribe, I will write to Bingley this instant and tell him all, with your permission of course."

"I cannot disclose Jane's current feelings. It would be a betrayal."

"Hmmm . . . Well then, perhaps you could tell me if his returning to Netherfield would be generally acceptable to the neighborhood, speaking in general terms that is."

"In general, Bingley was well liked, and the neighbors would welcome him back, but he must make his intentions very clear. The neighborhood may doubt his preference for the area after all these months away. Perhaps there is another neighborhood he enjoys visiting now."

Darcy smiled and let out a chuckle. "I cannot speak to Bingley's preference for the entire neighborhood of Hertfordshire. But without betraying any confidence, I can safely vouch for the fact that he still thinks a great deal about one particular estate there."

Elizabeth felt her heart lighten momentarily, and she let herself smile a little. "Well then, perhaps we should mention that the neighborhood has some fine opportunities that he has yet to fully appreciate."

"Indeed. I shall say that very thing."

Elizabeth leaned forward and put her hand in his and whispered, "Thank you." She let her isolated tears drop on the pages in his lap.

*****

There was a knock at the sitting room door. Mr. Darcy had just finished dictating his letter to Bingley, and Elizabeth handed it to him to sign. They both looked at the door as it slowly opened.

Colonel Fitzwilliam peeked his head in and with a grin said, "May I disturb the two of you yet? It has been nearly two hours. You must be in need of refreshment."

"I would love some, Cousin." Darcy carefully penned his name at the bottom of the letter and then asked Elizabeth, "Would you see that this gets mailed immediately?" He smiled at her kindly.

Elizabeth tucked the letter into her dress and curtsied. She lifted the tea tray from the table and offered, "I will bring this cold tea back to the kitchen and get some fresh tea and refreshments." Then she left the Colonel and Darcy alone. Her heart had not been this light in some time. It was even lighter than it had been during her morning walk.

She went directly into the kitchen and didn't even knock. She found Mrs. Wilkinson drying her hands on her apron and sitting with her was Madeline, sipping tea. "Madeline! I see you are even smarter than I thought! You found the best company to spend your time with."

"Yes, Mrs. Wilkinson has been very helpful these last few days. It is not my house, and I find when I am not attending Mr. Darcy, there is no real place for me to go. So, I found myself in the kitchen once, and I admit I retreat to it frequently now. Mrs. Wilkinson seems to be quite invested in Mr. Darcy's care."

Mrs. Wilkinson laughed. "I admit I am an old gossip, but you, Elizabeth, have not spoken to me for two days, and I needed an update about Mr. Darcy, not to mention I admit I needed some diversion from Mrs. Marquis."

"And who is Mrs. Marquis?" Elizabeth asked.

"The French cook from Rosings. I guess they had one to spare and sent her to help in my kitchen . . . *my* kitchen!" She said that last little bit in a huff. Then she turned to Elizabeth and smiled and leaned in to kiss her cheek. "Do not worry about me; I am not offended in the slightest. If anything, I appreciate the help. I have learned a lot in two days' time. For example, did you know that you should pound meat with a cleaver before you cook it? Oh! And I have never used so much salt before! And did you know that cooking something slowly traps the juices inside and makes for a much better gravy?"

Elizabeth had been worried about how Mrs. Wilkinson would feel about help in the kitchen. "If she is so helpful, why do you need diversion?"

"For one, she rearranged all my pots and pans, and then she reorganized my pantry. When she was done with that, she went to my spices and put them in alphabetical order. If I did not know better, I would say she has lost her wits entirely. She keeps muttering under her breath in her fancy French accent, 'I cannot werk in zeese conditions!'"

Elizabeth laughed and Madeline spoke up, "She seems to do all the planning of the menus too. What was she going to have you prepare for tonight's dinner?"

"Strawberry tarts. She gave me the recipe and spent an entire hour reviewing how to make it. It was as though she thought I could not read! Of course I can follow a recipe!"

Elizabeth grinned and tried not to laugh. "Well then, let us get started. I would love to learn how to make strawberry tarts."

For the next half hour, all three ladies washed strawberries, measured sugar and flour, and whipped the cream. It was the most enjoyable time Elizabeth had spent with Madeline. She really came alive when not "on duty". Madeline had an infectious laugh that sent all three ladies into fits of laughter over everything that was said. The tarts were placed in the oven, and then a servant came in and curtsied to Elizabeth.

"Excuse me, Miss Elizabeth, but the gentlemen sent me to fetch you. They want to know if you are bringing the tea."

"Oh dear! I forgot! Tell them I will bring it in right away." She turned to Mrs. Wilkinson and explained, "I meant to bring in tea but got sidetracked making the tarts."

"Do not worry, dear. I will make fresh tea and have it brought into you. In fact, I am now an expert at making tea. According to Mrs. Marquis, this new brand is better with lemon and milk."

Elizabeth hugged Mrs. Wilkinson. "Sounds perfect. Thank you."

Madeline followed her into the sitting room where they found two very lively gentlemen laughing. When the ladies came in, the colonel stood and bowed. Darcy tipped his head, and his eyes landed on Elizabeth. She felt warm under his gaze. She curtsied politely and took her usual seat next to Darcy.

Madeline asked him, "How are you feeling, sir? You seem to be in good spirits."

"For the most part I am." He glanced at Elizabeth and continued, "My head hurts, but my foot is much better unless I move it or the colonel, here, bumps into it."

"It was an accident, Darcy!"

"I know, Richard. I was just teasing. You forget I have spent a great deal of time with Miss Elizabeth, and her wit must be influencing me."

Madeline looked curiously at Darcy. "Do you need any pain medication?"

"Will it make me sleepy?"

"Yes, it probably will."

"Will it make me forget what has happened today?"

"It has in the past."

"Then absolutely not. I can handle the headache and the pain in my foot."

"Very well, sir." Madeline sat down and picked up her needlework.

Tea was brought in, and the rest of the afternoon was spent enjoying each other's company. They talked about many things, but nothing as deep as the letter, the proposal, the refusal, or the memory problems. It seemed like those topics were not allowed. Immediately before dinner, Darcy started squirming and readjusting his position a little.

Colonel Fitzwilliam asked, "Darcy, man, what is wrong with you? You look like you have ants in your pants."

Darcy cheeks flushed slightly, and he glanced at Madeline, who looked up at him.

Madeline stood up and asked Elizabeth to go fetch some of those strawberry tarts they had made. Elizabeth stood and tried to read what Madeline was really telling her. Madeline made a gesture for her to go away. She understood that Madeline was asking her to leave the room, and it suddenly dawned on her that Darcy must have needs that Elizabeth couldn't be a part of.

"I might be a while," Elizabeth said. "I will have to sneak them out of the kitchen, but do not worry, I am better than any thief in London. I shall return with strawberry tarts in fifteen minutes." She said the last part of the sentence almost as a question to which Madeline nodded. It appears fifteen minutes should be enough time to do what needed to be done. Elizabeth decided she and Madeline needed a code word to communicate these things; she felt a little embarrassed for not figuring out what was happening sooner.

She exited the room and closed the door behind her. There was a footman at the door, speaking with Mrs. Collins, and he handed her a book and left. Charlotte turned toward Elizabeth and smiled. "I am supposed to give you this book to give to Mr. Darcy. Apparently Lady Catherine says Mr. Darcy would appreciate it."

It was the late Mr. Darcy's gardening book! Elizabeth took it in her hands and looked at it with confusion. Why would Lady Catherine give up a book that she seemed determined to hold on to? "Thank you, Charlotte. He will be very happy to have it."

"Is now a good time to discuss that letter?"

Elizabeth smiled. "Indeed it is. I apologize for ignoring you these last few days. It has been quite the emotional whirlwind. I do not know if I can handle this level of excitement for five more weeks."

"If not, you could go home with my sister as planned."

She wasn't sure why she felt such strong feelings, but she voiced them to Charlotte: "No, I really do think I would rather be here."

"Does this have anything to do with Mr. Darcy and his proposal?"

"Proposals. Plural."

"Did he propose again?"

"Yes. It is getting difficult to keep track, but I think we are going on five or six times now."

Charlotte led her into her private parlor and pulled two chairs close together. "Five or six times? And each time you have refused him? Lizzy! What is going on in that witless mind of yours?"

Elizabeth looked away from Charlotte. How could she explain something she didn't fully understand herself? "I already told you of my previous impressions of Mr. Darcy. And you know he called on me every day at the parsonage before the accident. Apparently he was trying to court me. I had no idea he loved me."

"Did he really say he loved you?"

"Yes, 'ardently', as he put it."

"But you do not believe him?"

"Actually, I am beginning to see that he truly does care for me."

"Well then, you always wanted to marry for love, now you can. Why refuse him?"

"I want to love him too."

Charlotte looked at her quizzically. "Tell me more about how you feel about him."

"Well, he is much altered since the accident, and it is not just the memory problems. He is kinder. He smiles at me, and it makes me flush beet red when I see those dimples. He seems to have kinder views about my mother as well."

"Your mother?"

"I know you have gotten accustomed to her behavior and her ever-fragile nerves, but it was very clear that Mr. Darcy could not stand her and thought very ill of her. Mr. Darcy tries very hard not to show his emotions and thoughts, but he is more easily read than he thinks. He admitted to me that he had unkind feelings toward her, so I know I was right. But apparently he wishes to marry me against his better judgment and against his character, regardless of whom I am related to!"

"So, he loves you no matter who you are, or how you were raised? Lizzy, I simply do not see your logic! To have a man devoted to you in such a way is nearly a miracle! How can you pass up this opportunity?"

"I told you. I want to love him like that too."

"Do you love him? Even just a little?"

"I do not know. My feelings have changed recently and so dramatically that I am very confused. I have come to the conclusion that everything I ever thought about Mr. Darcy was wrong. He is not as prideful as I once thought. And he certainly is more amiable than I first thought. What I judged as disdain in social situations was his discomfort and shyness. He has even been somewhat charming, perhaps more than a little charming. I rather like our conversations of late."

"Then what are you waiting for?"

"I guess I will feel it when the time is right. I will know somehow that I should accept him, and hopefully it will not be too late."

"You think one day you will just know."

"Yes. I think I know my heart well enough to know if I am in love."

Charlotte tried not to laugh. "Well, Lizzy, maybe you are right. But I just want to add one more thing. When the time comes and you do know it is right—when you feel that your heart is telling you it is love—do not hesitate. A man like Mr. Darcy is hard to come by, and I would secure him as soon as you 'know'."

"I will. Charlotte, I promise you I will. I just hope I will know my own heart when the time comes."

CHAPTER 9

The next week passed very much like Friday. Every morning Darcy would be directed to the reminder letter, and every morning he would calmly ask a few questions after reading it. He seemed to take it well, and his emotional volatility improved each day. He was in good spirits and only took the pain medication at night. In fact, he soon stated his head didn't hurt anymore.

Every day without fail, and as soon as possible, Darcy would ask for a private audience with Elizabeth. And without fail, he would profess his love and ask for her hand in marriage. Elizabeth became more and more uncomfortable with these proposals, but she couldn't decide why. Was it because they seemed to improve each time? Was it because he was becoming more charming and less offensive in declaring himself? Was it because he didn't seem to expect an acceptance? She concluded that it was because of all these reasons. He was changing. He certainly was not the Mr. Darcy she had known before the accident. He slipped and called her Elizabeth only once, but she didn't correct him; she merely raised her eyebrow, and he flushed with embarrassment.

Each evening she recorded the day's proposal in her journal, which she had begun keeping after the third proposal. She had documented what she remembered from the first three and kept up with it after that. The sixth proposal was kind and gentle. The seventh was sweet and generous in his praise of her. The eighth was humble and from the heart.

She found herself both dreading and anticipating each proposal. She would report how it went to Madeline, whom she found to be a great confidant. However, she held back from disclosing full details to Colonel Fitzwilliam as he teased Darcy mercilessly whenever he could. But he seemed to have stopped teasing Elizabeth and didn't pressure her about her feelings for Mr. Darcy. That was different as well.

Despite the teasing, the two gentlemen had a special bond that grew each day. The colonel always seemed to know when Darcy wanted to be left alone with Elizabeth, and Madeline seemed to disappear at the same time. Elizabeth thought it was probably because they knew Darcy was anxious to propose, so they coordinated their disappearances at the same time to ensure him an opportunity to do so.

Georgiana was careful not to cause any stress during her visits. However, in the back of her mind she kept wondering about Elizabeth and her brother. If William had dictated that love letter, then why were they not engaged? Richard had instructed her to keep their aunt away from the parsonage and to not divulge any details about William's condition. She played along with the story that Madeline, Elizabeth, and Richard were the only ones allowed to see him. She tried to escape Rosings daily, but she had to be careful under her aunt's watchful eye. As suggested by Colonel Fitzwilliam, she would inform her aunt she was going for a walk, or visiting the shops in town, or mailing a letter . . . and never admitted she was seeing her brother. She didn't understand all the secrecy, but she trusted the colonel and did exactly as she was told.

The Collinses saw Maria Lucas off on Monday as planned, leaving Elizabeth and Mr. Darcy as the only guests of the house. Mr. Collins kept his distance and stayed busy with his duties. He seemed to ignore Elizabeth all together. She didn't miss him, his hair, or his spittle in the slightest.

The ninth and tenth proposals were done somewhat clumsily because Darcy attempted to be funny. They certainly made Elizabeth laugh, but they did not change her mind.

The eleventh proposal was entirely different from all the others. He didn't praise her or profess his love. He simply asked her if she could ever see herself marrying a man like him. She, of course, deflected the question, but he persisted and insisted on an answer. She argued that such a question was entirely impertinent, but he pressed her to answer it anyway. Finally she nodded that she had spent much time considering it.

This, of course, made Darcy smile and press her further for clarification. He asked her, "Do you think about marrying me or a man like me?" She told him she did not feel comfortable answering such a bold question, but she knew her blush gave her away.

He seemed content to drop the subject after that, and they read Wordsworth together for several hours. They started playing a game with each other. One would begin to quote a poem, while the other would try to finish it first. That led to further games. Darcy would begin to recite a poem, and Elizabeth would race him by trying to find it in the book before he finished. Elizabeth lost most of the time, but there were a few times he seemed to conveniently "forget" the next line, which offered her a little more time for her search.

Soon ten days had passed since the accident, and the doctor came to evaluate the patient. Darcy asked to speak with him alone. After their private conversation, the doctor invited the colonel to join them. He then asked that Madeline come in as well. Elizabeth and Georgiana were left outside the sitting room door, quietly waiting for a report. Georgiana broke the silence first.

"Miss Elizabeth?" Georgiana asked.

"Please, call me Elizabeth or Lizzy."

"Only if you call me Georgiana or Georgie."

"Certainly. What is it, Georgiana?"

"I was just wondering. The letter William gave you, do you still have it?"

Elizabeth didn't know which letter she was asking about. "Yes. Which one?"

"I did not know there was more than one. I am speaking of the love letter. The one where he proposed."

Elizabeth frowned. "I did not know you knew about that letter," she said.

Georgiana blushed slightly. "Yes, he accidently had me read it the night I arrived. It was beautiful."

"Yes, I still have it."

"Did you like it?" she asked shyly.

"Well, it certainly started off flattering."

"You did not like it?"

"One usually does not belittle the family of the one you are asking to marry you."

"I see. So, is that why you refused him? Is that why you keep refusing him? Is he making the same mistake as in the letter?"

"At first I was upset because of the offensive nature and manner that he used. But that was only a minor part of my reason for refusal. And yes, he seems to have stopped making that mistake."

"If he has stopped making that mistake, why are you refusing him now?"

Elizabeth looked away. She found she was at a loss for words. Should she be honest with Georgiana? There really was no other option. It was not in her nature to deceive. "Georgiana, I do not know why I keep refusing him now. Please do not ask me to explain my answer; I do not know if I can."

Georgiana smiled and patted Elizabeth's arm. "I will not ask then. Let us just keep this between us. I admit I myself have done things and felt emotions that are hard to explain. I expect your feelings are complicated and have a great deal of history behind them. But I do feel I need to say one more thing."

Elizabeth looked at her and returned her kind smile. "Go ahead."

"I would very much like to have you as my sister."

*****

A few minutes later, Mr. Cummings, Madeline, and Colonel Fitzwilliam came out laughing. All three pairs of eyes were on Elizabeth. Mr. Cummings smiled at her and shook his head and bowed to her. He started putting on his outerwear, and Elizabeth began to panic, worried that he was going to leave without giving her an update. For some reason, she felt very left out. After all, she had invested a great deal of time in the care of Mr. Darcy. Shouldn't she be told what the doctor said? She took a bold step and stood in front of the doctor with her hands on her hips and asked, "And how is Mr. Darcy?"

The doctor chuckled again and took off his spectacles and started to clean them. When he placed them back on his face, he put his hand on her shoulder and said, "I would say he is better than I have seen him thus far. Excuse me, I must be going."

Elizabeth watched as the doctor left, closing the door behind him. *What was that? Why was he so vague? And why was he chuckling so?* She turned to Colonel Fitzwilliam and asked, "What did he mean?"

"I do not see his comment as unclear. He stated Darcy is doing better than ever. I do not think he had any hidden meaning. Come, Darcy is wanting to visit with us all."

Elizabeth frowned; it all seemed so suspicious! She knew she would not be the best company at the moment. She needed to think about everything Georgiana had said. She decided to go straight to the writing desk and write a letter to Jane. She had just received a letter from Jane that morning informing her that there were rumors that Charles Bingley was returning to Netherfield.

Dearest Jane,

I am so glad to hear that our neighbor is to return. Your letter was written rather ill, making me think that you wrote it in haste, for you did not mention how you felt about the news. Are you anticipating seeing him? Do you think he will pay a call on you?

I have much to tell you, but I have come to the conclusion that I only wish to share my news of Kent when we are together—that way I can hug you and cry with you. I do not mean to be secretive; it is simply that some things are better shared face to face when one can immediately answer questions. For now, I will simply tell you a little more about Mr. Darcy's recovery.

This morning he woke up with a mild headache again, but the wound on his head is nearly healed. I doubt he will even have a scar. Madeline has been dressing it with a cream every day. The foot only causes pain when he moves it, and it is much better than before. Yesterday Madeline even let him sit up and put his feet on the floor for over an hour. Even so, we still have to convince him every morning not to put any weight on it. The doctor thinks it will be at least four more weeks before he can stand. But it is remarkable how much he has improved in the ten days since the accident.

I know what you really want to know is whether or not he has his memory back. The truth of it is he does not. He reads the reminder letter daily, and he seems to have no memory of all that has happened since two days before the accident. I think there is *some improvement in his demeanor, however. After he reads the letter, he nods and accepts the contents now with little question.*

You asked if he is still proposing. Indeed he is. I have started keeping a journal of the proposals. We are now on the twelfth attempt. Just this morning, he told me that he prays for me. He prays that I will accept his hand. It was really sweet, and I had the strangest feeling. I cannot describe it. It was as if he knew something I did not know. For a moment, I wondered if he had some spark of memory, but when I asked him if he was well, he simply said, "Never better", and then continued with the proposal.

He then disclosed how far back he was drawn to me. Apparently my eyes caught his attention at the Meryton Assembly! Are you not surprised? That same assembly where he danced only with Miss Bingley and Mrs. Hurst? Yes, more importantly, the same assembly where he said, "She is tolerable, but not handsome enough to tempt me". So, my impertinent self simply had to ask him about that comment. I know you will lecture me for it, but I had to.

He remembered it well and said he always wondered if I had heard him. He did explain himself, however. Do you remember my last letter telling you about Mr. Wickham and his sister, Georgiana? Well, Mr. Darcy had only rescued her a few months prior to coming to Netherfield, and he was still very worried about her. He had just received a letter from her that was weighing heavily on his mind. His gloomy mood kept him from asking me to dance, but he admitted he watched me all night long.

After his explanation and apology, he took my hand and kissed it ever so gently and then said, "For many months now, I have considered you to be the handsomest woman of my acquaintance." Dear Lord, Jane! I nearly fainted! I have never imagined or received such a compliment! You, I know, have heard of your beauty for all the years of your life, but I have always developed my mind because I felt that was all I had. The look in his eyes when he said it sent shivers up my spine, and I knew he was in earnest. I have never felt so self-conscious. I had on my least favorite dress, the pale blue one with the lace on the bodice that was always a little plain on me. My curls were ever so unruly and had already fallen out of my lazily made bun. But never had I felt more beautiful.

Oh Jane, I do not know what has come over me! How can one express the change of heart in a mere letter? I long to see your face and hold your hand and tell you all the things I do not have time to write. For now, I leave you with all my love.

Your dearest sister,

Elizabeth

She dusted the ink and folded the letter. She took a deep breath and, for a moment, really missed her favorite sister. She wanted to talk to her by candlelight while they brushed each other's hair. She wanted to see her beautiful face and tell her that Bingley still loved her! But she could not. Not for another four weeks. She contemplated writing another letter to her Aunt Gardiner, but before she could begin, she heard quite the ruckus outside the sitting room door. There was only one woman whose voice was that loud, and she felt warning shudders go up and down her spine. Colonel Fitzwilliam stood up behind her, and the room went silent.

Lady Catherine entered, draped in a brown fur, and following closely behind her was the sweaty Mr. Collins, whose hair had plastered itself in an unnatural way, leaving a bump in the center that needed desperately to be combed down. Elizabeth stood and curtsied. Lady Catherine looked down her nose at her and turned away from Elizabeth.

Darcy broke the silence. "Aunt Catherine, how good of you to come. Please sit down. We can order tea."

"I do not come on a social call, Fitzwilliam. I am here to give you some light reading." She snapped her fingers, and Mr. Collins shuffled to her side and handed her several stacks of papers. She perused them momentarily and then said, "It pains me to do this, but something must be done."

Colonel Fitzwilliam eyed her suspiciously and glanced at Elizabeth and then back to Darcy. "Aunt Catherine, what have you done? And what does this have to do with Darcy?"

The hair on the back of Elizabeth's neck stood on end. Was this the scheme Colonel Fitzwilliam had been so worried about?

Lady Catherine gave a sly smile. "Richard, you may leave now. I no longer have need of you in this conversation."

Darcy tensed and obviously sensed something too. "Richard will stay."

"Very well, but there is little you or he can do about it now." She took determined steps toward Darcy and handed him the papers. "I assume your head injury still allows you to read and understand the significance of these papers."

Darcy took the papers, and Colonel Fitzwilliam quickly knelt beside Darcy and read over his shoulder. Elizabeth watched both their faces turn concerned, then irritated, and then angry. Both their chests were rising and falling with great depth and rate. Elizabeth felt like maybe she should leave, but something told her she needed to stay. She wanted to stay.

What was in the papers? And who were the papers from? Why were the gentlemen so disturbed? She glanced at Lady Catherine, and saw that her eyes were fixed on Elizabeth, looking her up and down haughtily. Elizabeth recognized that judgmental look, and she stood taller and raised her chin in defiance. Lady Catherine only smirked and turned her glare back to her two nephews, who were sweating now.

Page after page was read and placed on Darcy's lap. Minutes sped by as Elizabeth silently watched the two gentlemen, and her curiosity was nearly leaping out of her chest. Was the colonel right? Did Lady Catherine have a plan? What was it? And why were the two gentlemen so angry? What could Lady Catherine possibly do to elicit such a response?

The silence was broken when a servant announced an arrival. "Mr. Matthews for Lady Catherine."

"Ah, Mr. Matthews, your timing is perfect. It appears my nephews are reading the last page."

"I would have been here sooner, but I stopped by Rosings first and was directed here by the butler," Mr. Matthews said.

Elizabeth wondered who Mr. Matthews was. He was tall and lean but had a big nose that he wiped with his handkerchief. He was quite young, maybe one and twenty, and he was somewhat handsome, but he wore his hair quite short, almost as if it had been shaved off a month ago. He walked slightly slumped-over, and there was something in his eyes that spoke of distrust. Elizabeth shuddered. He carried with him a small doctor's bag, and it rattled when he placed it on the ground.

Darcy cleared his throat. "Richard, would you please help me to stand?"

"You cannot bear weight yet, Darcy."

"Then you stand on my bad side and hold me up. I do not think I can address these papers from her solicitor unless I am standing." Darcy was already moving his feet off the chaise, and the colonel moved to his right and helped Darcy to stand up.

Elizabeth went to Darcy's other side and helped balance him. Mr. Darcy looked down at Elizabeth and whispered a quiet thank you, and then he stood as tall as he could. Elizabeth could tell he was unsteady on his feet and that he was shaking slightly.

Darcy took a deep breath and said, "So, you think me unfit to manage Pemberley? So, you think that Anne has the strength to take on my care as my wife? You think I have lost the mental capacity to raise Georgiana unless I am married? To Anne, of all people? So, you think that Mr. Cummings, who has at least forty years' experience as a medical doctor now needs to be undermined by a second opinion from this man behind you who is younger than I am? A man who has no knowledge of my injury, and no manly pride to stand up to you?

"I ask you, Aunt Catherine, how long did it take you to find someone to cower to your desires? How long did it take you to create this plan of yours? Had I even awakened before you were scheming to force me to marry your daughter? Had you grieved in any way before you attempted to take away everything in my life I hold dear?"

"Now, Fitzwilliam, you know I am quite disturbed over your injury and current limitations. But you must admit that having to read a reminder letter every morning in order to start your day does not demonstrate the mental strength and fortitude necessary to be master of an estate. If you have to be told every morning which tenants are cheating you, which crops were planted, and what your steward's name is . . . It simply will not work. I am afraid you need a wife. And as you can see from the papers, Anne will do perfectly. She is a part of your old memories. You trust her, and you were going to propose! A stableman heard you tell Richard about your plans to propose. So you may not remember, but you love my dear Anne."

Colonel Fitzwilliam countered, "He most certainly was going to propose to someone, but it was not Anne. Do you know something, Aunt Catherine? I really should not be shocked! You would threaten to declare him incompetent unless he marries Anne? Is this your plan? Is this doctor, Mr. Matthews, supposed to find him incompetent?"

Mr. Matthews spoke up, "I intend to do a thorough exam and give my most honest, expert opinion—"

Lady Catherine hushed him.

Darcy smiled and addressed Mr. Matthews, "Whatever the price she has offered for your services I will triple it, no quadruple it, if you turn and leave right now."

Lady Catherine grabbed Mr. Matthews's arm. "Do not let him get to you. Your opinion is valuable, and you are not one to be bought and sold, are you?"

He bowed his head and said, "No, ma'am," and then stepped back behind Lady Catherine.

Elizabeth felt Darcy shaking further, and she offered more support. He placed his arm around her shoulders to steady himself. She could feel his weight shift slightly, and she stepped closer. He smelled of soap and sandalwood. The warmth of his arm around her shoulders was distracting, but she tried to stay focused. Now was not the time to be carried away with the realization that she was very nearly in Mr. Darcy's arms. Now was not the time to feel goose bumps up and down her arm, as she had her arm wrapped around his back, making her feel so warm and comfortable. She scooted a little closer, and held a little tighter.

This was a man whom she used to care little for, but being in his arms made her understand a few things. She wanted to have him hold her. She wanted him to lean on her when he needed it. She wanted to be there for him. Always. Memory problems or not, she knew it now.

She wanted to let her heart speak all it was feeling. She wanted to accept his proposals, but was it too late now? Was Lady

Catherine really going to take everything from her at the very moment she realized what was most important? Would she lose the only man she knew she would ever love to his sickly cousin, Anne, because of a conniving, officious, overbearing, demeaning woman? She felt so much anger surge through her that she too began to shake.

Mr. Darcy looked down at Elizabeth, obviously noticing her trembling. He whispered, "Are you well, Elizabeth?"

Lady Catherine overheard them. "Elizabeth? Did you just call her Elizabeth? Since when do you address her so informally?"

Elizabeth stood taller, and she felt Darcy lean away from her, but she held him tightly. "I gave him permission when I accepted his hand in marriage." Every pair of eyes went to her, including Mr. Darcy's, and she looked up at him and smiled. The look in his eyes was everything she had been waiting for. He loved her. And she loved him. She knew it now. She had been right when she talked to Charlotte; she would know it when the time was right. And the time was right.

Mr. Collins screeched out a loud gasp and came bounding toward her. "Get out! Get out of my house this instant! How dare you claim an alliance with Mr. Darcy! I do not want you here another quarter of an hour. I will pack your things for you this instant!"

Darcy flinched slightly but yelled back, "Step back, man! Keep your mouth from spewing its contents onto me and my Elizabeth. And do not address my betrothed in such a manner! You heard her! We are engaged, and I will have you know I can still hold a pistol at dawn to defend her, even with a broken foot!" Mr. Collins stepped back and trembled with fury. "Now, Aunt Catherine, I believe the papers from your solicitor said I needed a wife. It did not specify who should be my wife. As you can see, I have one, or will have one as soon as I can walk down the aisle and declare my love for all who desire to hear it."

Everyone was waiting for Lady Catherine to speak. She took slow, deliberate steps toward Elizabeth. With a finger she jabbed at Elizabeth's chest. "You! You! You harlot! You and your arts and allurements! To prey on a man weakened by injury! To claim an alliance to one of the greatest men in all of England!"

Colonel Fitzwilliam spoke up, "Madeline, would you please come stand by Darcy?" The accusations and verbal assault continued from Lady Catherine to Elizabeth while Madeline took his place. Once he was assured that Darcy was stable, he tried to position himself between Elizabeth and his aunt. "Aunt Catherine," he said, "it is you who has preyed on Darcy in his injured state. It is you who has claimed an alliance to him that will never be. I have been witness to Miss Elizabeth's so-called arts and allurements, and I assure you, she held Darcy's heart well before the accident. It is she who your stableman overheard us speaking of. Darcy proposed to Elizabeth nearly two weeks ago, before the accident."

Lady Catherine glared at Elizabeth, and she was so close that the fur was inches from Elizabeth's face, but Elizabeth held her ground. "It is true, Lady Catherine. He did propose to me before the accident."

"This is not to be borne! This is inconceivable!"

Elizabeth felt stronger than ever. She felt Mr. Darcy give her shoulder a slight squeeze, and she decided now was as good a time as any to stand up to Lady Catherine. "What is not to be borne? That your nephew could wish for a wife who was healthy enough to produce an heir? Or that his heart fell for me?"

"I have every objection to you and you know it! Who are you? What do you have to offer my nephew other than your obvious attempts to seduce him?"

"Aunt Catherine!" Darcy and Colonel Fitzwilliam bellowed at the same time.

Elizabeth was not going to be spoken to that way. "I seem to have a great deal to offer Mr. Darcy. Even in his confused state he wishes for nothing else but to be married to me. To use his words from two days ago, his 'very happiness' resides with me."

212

"I demand to know how you trapped him into believing you mean something to him! And Darcy! Are the shades of Pemberley to be thus polluted? I insist on being satisfied! How can a mere country miss, with no connections, no fortune, and no social status, trap you? And when in such a confused state! It is impossible!" she screeched.

Elizabeth smiled back at her with all the confidence of the world. "If your ladyship has declared it impossible, why then is your fur shaking in fear? Why does the look of terror fill your eyes?"

"Darcy, you must end this infatuation and think of Georgiana! Think about what a connection to Miss Bennet would do to Georgiana's marriage prospects! You owe it to your family! Your duty calls for reformation! It is not too late to change your mind. Anne is strong. She will make a good wife."

Darcy then smiled. "I never had any intention of marring Anne; nor she me. And, if I read your papers from your solicitor correctly, I need a wife, or you shall take away all I have. And, since I have made my choice, I suggest you leave. I am sorry that I shall never call you Mother, but from the behavior and actions you have displayed just now, I doubt I shall ever call you Aunt again. It is despicable what you have done. You should be ashamed of yourself! Since I cannot leave at the moment, I ask that you leave immediately!"

Colonel Fitzwilliam took Aunt Catherine's arm, which she directly shook off. "Let me be rightly understood, Miss Bennet. This match, to which you have the presumption to aspire, will never take place. No! Never! Mark my words!" She turned on her heels and stomped out of the room with Mr. Collins and Mr. Matthews close behind.

They all stood there and watched them leave. The door was slammed closed, and the room became very silent. Elizabeth heard Mr. Darcy let out his breath and felt him relax a little, but then she felt him slipping. "Colonel, help us!" The colonel swiftly eased Darcy down to the chaise. She quickly tried to assess him alongside Madeline. "Are you well, William?" She was kneeling by his side now, and with her hand she brushed back a stray curl near his eyes.

He reached up to her hand and took it in both of his. "I am well. You have accepted my hand. Finally! And not a moment too soon!"

Colonel Fitzwilliam cleared his throat.

Elizabeth looked up at the colonel, who looked a little sheepish, and his eyes gave it away. His eyes were warning Mr. Darcy of something. She looked at Mr. Darcy, who was turning a little red in the face. It suddenly hit her. "Finally? Did you just say finally?" Neither man said anything, but they exchanged desperate looks between the two of them. "You remember? All this time you remembered?"

Darcy tried to meet her eyes, but the look in them said war was about to break out. How could he explain that he would do anything to win her hand? "Not exactly," he hesitated.

A million thoughts ran through her mind. *"Not exactly?" So, he does remember!* She suddenly needed some private time with Mr. Darcy; she needed answers now. It did not matter that she had just battled Lady Catherine. It did not matter that she had just accepted his hand.

She stood up and put her hands on her hips. And without turning, she said to Georgiana, who had been sitting silently all this time, "Georgiana? Would you mind leaving us for a moment? I am afraid there are a few things that your brother and I need to discuss. And Madeline, I suggest you go retreat to the kitchen, because your services are not required for the next half hour. Colonel Fitzwilliam? I tire of your presence. I would leave if I were you."

She didn't take her eyes off Mr. Darcy or her hands off her hips, but she could hear when the last of them had left and closed the door. She stared at him, and his face was so guilt-ridden it was painful to watch. "Please explain. What does 'not exactly' mean?" She started tapping her foot impatiently.

"I truly do not remember the first proposal, or the refusal afterwards."

"But you do remember the others?"

"Richard said I proposed several times. But yes, I remember some of them."

"What do you remember? When did you . . . oh! How could you? How could you deceive me like this? All this time you knew I kept refusing you but you kept asking?"

"Technically, you never refused me. You always asked for more time or promised to answer me later."

"Do not deflect the question! What do you remember?"

"I remember everything since last Friday, when you let me read the letter that I gave you the day of the accident. At first everything was foggy, but reading that letter was very helpful. I realized how desperately I wanted to marry you."

Elizabeth was furious! "Are you telling me you have been deceiving me for a whole week? And you thought you could trick me into accepting you?"

"No. Not at all. I knew you needed more time, that is all, and I was right."

"No, sir, you are not right. A marriage cannot start with deceit! It will only fail! We have no engagement!" She turned and started for the door.

"Elizabeth, please do not walk away! I cannot come after you! My foot is broken!"

"Now you remember that your foot is broken? And do not call me Elizabeth!" she yelled.

"I apologize, Miss Elizabeth. Please. Come sit down for a moment, and we can talk about this," he pleaded.

She stopped with her hand on the doorknob. Her voice was weak and cracked as she murmured, "I trusted you."

"You can still trust me. Everything we have built is true. I am exactly the same man. I am the same man that I dare say you fell in love with."

Elizabeth felt the insides of her eyes tingling, and she knew she would start crying any minute. She was glad she had her back to him. All this time he knew? He remembered the last seven proposals? All this time he had been planning his next one? What did this mean? Who else knew about his memory coming back? "Did the colonel know you remembered?"

"He suspected it for some time now, but it was not until this afternoon when Mr. Cummings came that I divulged the fact that I remember everything since that day you let me read the letter. You have to believe me, I meant every word. I love you, Eliz . . . Miss Elizabeth. You do not know how hard it has been to see the love shine in your eyes every day and have you not accept me. You do not know how hard I have tried to show you the real me—the me who would do anything and give anything to have you by my side day in and day out. You do not know how hard it is to be trapped on this chaise when I so desperately, with every fiber of my being, want to go over there right now and comfort you.

"I see you are crying. I feel miserable for causing it, but please, do not ignore the love you feel for me. I see it in your eyes every time you look at me. I see it in your pain that you feel. I have hurt you, and I regret doing so, but you must come back and talk with me. Do not leave me. I have never felt so helpless in my entire life! If you do not come over here, so help me, I will come to you."

Elizabeth heard movement behind her and turned around, and through tears, she could barely make out that Mr. Darcy was trying to stand up on his own. She hurried over to him and pushed her hands down on his shoulders, easing him back on the chaise. He looked up at her gratefully which made her even angrier. "Trying to get up will only injure you further, and I am not inclined at present to offer my services a second time."

Darcy took her hands off his shoulders and kissed them tenderly. He turned them over and kissed the inside of each palm. He squeezed them and brought them up to his face and caressed them to his cheeks. He looked deep into her eyes and tried to express all he felt. "Please, Elizabeth, sit down."

She didn't know what possessed her to do it. It could have been her weak knees, or the lightheadedness from her heart pounding so fast, or that deep, penetrating look in his eyes, but she sat down in her usual chair.

Darcy had to do this right. He had to get it right this time. "I am a fool. A fool in love. A fool in love with a woman who has just learned the truth of her own heart. A heart that is so pure and kind that she never suspected my feelings until I made a disaster of a proposal. A proposal that I have been trying to remedy for the last week. Well, I suppose it has been longer than that, but I only remember the last week.

"Please forgive my haughty, expectant, prideful nature. I do not deserve you. You are everything I want but nothing I deserve. I am a man who was brought up on good principles but was raised to value things that no longer matter to me. My wealth, my connections, Pemberley, my family—none of it will matter if I cannot share it with you. You are everything to me. I never knew I was blind until the day my eyes were opened and I saw your expressive, brown eyes flash with delight at the assembly! Now my eyes are forever changed. I know now that you offer me vision, vision for a truly happy future. A happy future with you, and only you.

"I admit I did everything to avoid you in Hertfordshire, but at the same time I could do nothing but be drawn to you. You have a power over me that can never be remedied. Your smile, your impertinence, your raised eyebrow, your verbal challenges . . . all of these things are so engrained in my heart that I simply changed the day I met you. You made me a better man. I want to be the man I know I can be, and with you as my wife, I know I will be. Before you, I was nothing. I was a man in search of something he knew not what. If you must accuse me of something, then accuse me of loving you so wholeheartedly that I would ride in the rain and present myself to you—a woman who had so heatedly refused me—to give you a letter. And if you must, accuse me of being too persistent.

"I love you, dearest Elizabeth. With every fiber of my being, I love you. Please, I beg of you to marry me. You are my other half, my better half. You have made me whole. I cannot survive without you now. I have learned to value your opinion over any other. I have not looked and cannot look at any other woman for the rest of my life. I do not know how many times I have actually proposed, but I will not give up, I will persist. I will fight for you until I have not breath left in me to speak the words. Marry me."

She had watched him give his speech through tearful, painful eyes. He was still holding both her hands tenderly. She did not know what to think. She cleared her throat and whispered, "Thirteen."

Darcy was confused. "Pardon me?"

"You have proposed thirteen times."

"And how many times do I need to propose before you will make me the happiest of men?"

She took her hands away from his and pulled out her handkerchief and dabbed at her eyes. She then put the handkerchief away and carefully placed her hand on his cheek. "You swear you will look at no other?" He nodded. "You swear you love me?"

"Most ardently."

"Then the answer is thirteen." She leaned in and kissed his cheek for the second time.

*****

He pulled her tearful face into him and embraced her so tenderly and gently, relishing every moment and every part of him that was in contact with her. He laced his fingers in her loosened hair and whispered in her ear, "Dearest Elizabeth, thank you for believing in me. After all the absurd, irrational, and irresponsible things I have said and done, thank you. I will forever be in your debt." He pulled her face away from him enough to look in her eyes.

There was that look again. That deep, penetrating look that seemed to melt her heart. She felt a curl come loose from her bun and he was quick to grab it and twirl it in his fingers. He tucked it behind her ear and then leaned in to kiss her. Her heart started pounding. He was moving so slowly, but his intentions were clear: he was going to kiss her.

Suddenly the door burst open and Colonel Fitzwilliam called out, "Do not mean to interrupt, Miss Elizabeth, but your things are heading out the front door."

She stood up. "What?"

"Mr. Collins is standing firm in the fact that he wants you out of this house. He packed your things himself, and I had to wrestle him to get these two letters from him. I believe they are your two letters from Mr. Darcy." He handed her the letters.

Charlotte came rushing in and said, "I am so sorry, Lizzy! I tried to stop him, but he insists you leave this moment."

Elizabeth said, "But it is nearly dark! Where am I supposed to go?"

Mrs. Wilkinson came barging in, took off her apron, and threw it on the sitting room floor. "She is coming home with me."

Mr. Collins came in and said, "She most certainly will not! Mrs. Wilkinson, if you leave, you will have no position in my kitchen! Miss Bennet will have no tie to my household!"

Mrs. Wilkinson picked up her apron and turned to Mr. Collins. She very deliberately grabbed his hand and placed the apron in it. "Then I resign! I hated that hot kitchen anyway! Come, Elizabeth, before your saliva-spewing cousin drenches me with his rebuttal."

"What did you call me?"

"You heard me, you hairy buffoon! And close that dumb mouth of yours!" Mrs. Wilkinson grabbed Elizabeth's hand and started pulling her toward the door.

*****

"Oh, Mrs. Wilkinson . . ." Elizabeth sighed.

"Betty."

"I always wondered what your name was. What am I going to do? What are you and your family going to do?"

"Do not worry about me. My husband and I have been very frugal and saved every farthing I got from my service with the Collinses. We live meagerly, but we can survive on his income from the shop. I am glad to be free from that stove and having to cook all day. I would much rather do something unproductive with my time, like knit or embroider screens or write letters or cut perfectly good flowers just to decorate my home."

"You are mocking the life of a gentleman's daughter," Elizabeth laughed.

Mrs. Wilkinson was glad to see Elizabeth smile. "Indeed. But no more talk about me. Would you like to stay for a while or would you like to go home immediately?"

"I assume home would be the best choice. What is Mr. Darcy going to do? Now that Mr. Collins knows, I am sure he is not welcome there, and he has cut all ties with his aunt so he certainly is not welcome there . . . and he is not supposed to be moved for at least four more weeks." The wagon was rolling to a stop in front of a small cottage that looked cozy and well cared for.

"I am afraid we do not have footmen. How are you at lugging your trunks?"

"I am a regular pack mule." They unloaded all her belongings and entered the small cottage, and she found two children running to greet their mother.

"Elizabeth, this is Frank, he is ten, and just younger than him is Rebecca, she is six, and that little creature over there sitting too close to the fire is Jacob, he is one." She had her arms full of Elizabeth's belongings but quickly put them down and hugged them all lovingly. She picked up Jacob and spoke to him like he was grown and chastised him for playing too close to the fire. "And you, Frank, should know better than to let him play that close."

"Yes, Mamma," Frank said with his head bowed.

"Frank, this is Miss Elizabeth. Now bow like I taught you." He bowed a perfectly executed bow.

Elizabeth curtsied and saw that Frank blushed. "Master Frank, it is a pleasure to meet you."

Rebecca squealed, "My turn! My turn!" and showed off her curtsy.

Elizabeth leaned over and said, "That would have been good enough to do in front of the queen, Miss Wilkinson." Rebecca beamed she was so proud. Mrs. Wilkinson shooed the oldest two away to play.

"I am afraid I do not have a spare room, but I will have Rebecca sleep with us, and you can have her bed. It is not much, but it will be better than a chaise."

"Poor Mr. Darcy! He has been sleeping on a chaise for ten days! No wonder he still takes the pain medication at night." She took a deep breath. So much had happened in the last hour. She felt dizzy. She would have to take a moment to gather her thoughts later, but for now, she was a guest in Betty's home. She turned her thoughts back to the conversation at hand. "Who watches the children while you are at work?"

"The two oldest are in school, and the youngest goes to a neighbor until Frank comes home. I do not have the money to pay the neighbor, but we exchange services. My husband, Charles, works in a milliner's shop and gives her a discount and brings her things that were damaged in shipping and cannot be sold. It is not the ideal situation, but it works. He will be home soon since today was a short day, and he can take us to purchase your fare for the ride home."

"Thank you, Betty."

"No, thank you! I am so glad I do not have to serve that ridiculous Mr. Collins anymore!"

*****

"I came as fast as I could, Colonel. What is the problem?" Mr. Cummings said.

"Darcy insists he leave this house."

"He wants to go to Rosings?"

"No, he wants to go to Hertfordshire. Miss Elizabeth accepted his hand and has been evicted by Mr. Collins." The colonel explained all that happened this afternoon, including his aunt's attempts to force Darcy to marry Anne.

"Well, it has been a busy afternoon here." Mr. Cummings entered the sitting room to find Darcy sitting up with his feet on the floor. "It looks like you are feeling better."

"I am sure my cousin informed you of what I desire. I cannot stay here, and Rosings is out of the question. I want nothing to do with those people, and I am sure they are scheming some other ridiculous plan. I want to leave no later than Monday, hopefully tomorrow."

"I take it by your determined look that you have a plan," Mr. Cummings said.

Darcy then explained that the boot immobilized his foot quite well, and the only trick would be to get him in and out of the carriage. With enough footmen, his cousin, and his valet, Abbott, he could make it into the carriage without problems. He had two of his personal carriages here in Kent because Georgiana had brought one, so he would have plenty of room to elevate and cushion the foot during the carriage ride. They would take it slow, half-speed if needed; Darcy knew he could do it.

222

Mr. Cummings said, "Well, now seems like the right time to offer you a device that I own. It is a chair with wheels on it. That way you can move about the room and, if careful, you can even go outside. I did not want to give it to you just yet because that would make it look like you could be transferred to Rosings, and we all agreed you did not want that to happen. But since you are determined to leave, and most likely will be asked to leave by Mr. Collins shortly, I suggest we make plans to move you tomorrow."

"Truly? I was prepared to negotiate, beg, bribe, or do whatever was necessary to get you to agree. I cannot sit on this chaise any longer!"

Colonel Fitzwilliam smiled. "I am getting tired of this place as well! When can we depart?"

Darcy replied, "First, I believe I need to write a letter and offer my carriage to a certain someone."

The colonel grinned, and Mr. Cummings chuckled and said, "Well, at least I know you will be traveling in good hands. She will ensure your compliance. Oh, and congratulations, for real this time."

Darcy looked confused, "What do you mean 'this time'?"

Colonel Fitzwilliam laughed deeply and said, "It is not the first time we have celebrated your engagement to Miss Elizabeth! But that is a story for another day."

CHAPTER 10

The knock on the door at this hour was very curious. Mr. Charles Wilkinson unlocked it and opened cautiously. A tall gentleman smiled at him in the rain.

"Good evening. My name is Colonel Fitzwilliam. Is this the Wilkinson residence?"

Upon hearing the familiar voice, Elizabeth jumped up from her chair and ran to the door. "Come in, Colonel Fitzwilliam! Do not just stand there in the rain!" He stepped in and took off his hat. "How is Mr. Darcy?" she asked.

"Better than ever. He wanted me to personally deliver this to you." He handed her a letter and heard a murmured thank-you. She retreated to the corner where she read the missive.

Colonel Fitzwilliam then warmly greeted Mrs. Wilkinson and complimented her on the bold move of quitting her employment, his effusive praise bringing a blush to her cheeks.

Mrs. Wilkinson replied, "I did not give it a single thought. I have wanted to be free from Mr. Collins for some time now. I admit when I heard Lady Catherine at the door, I seemed to find duties near the sitting room door, and I heard most of what went on."

"And I am sure Miss Elizabeth filled you in on the rest."

"Of course. What is to be done about Mr. Darcy? Where will he go?"

Elizabeth looked up from her letter and answered Mrs. Wilkinson's question, "He is going to Hertfordshire. Mr. Bingley's last letter said he would be there Sunday."

Colonel Fitzwilliam explained further, "The plan is to leave tomorrow morning, and once at Longbourn, Darcy will ask Miss Elizabeth's father for permission to marry her. Then we will go to Netherfield, Bingley's leased estate, arriving only a day before Bingley. Darcy is confident that Netherfield will be prepared enough to receive Darcy, Georgiana, and I. Of course, if for some reason Netherfield is not ready to receive us . . ." He looked over to Elizabeth.

Elizabeth smiled and finished his sentence, "Then all I have to do is tell my mother I am engaged to a man worth ten thousand a year, and she will put my sisters out in the barn to accommodate you at Longbourn! This will work! But what does Mr. Cummings think about moving him so soon?"

"He admits it is not ideal, but Darcy is determined, and I am afraid we all know how determined he can be. His persistence in obtaining all that he desires is unprecedented." They all laughed and giggled over that. "So, our carriages will come by around ten in the morning. It sounds like the rain has let up a bit, and I should probably head back before it worsens."

"Thank you, Colonel. Please send him my deepest regards," Elizabeth said with a faint blush that she hoped was not noticeable in the candlelight.

"It is interesting how quickly storms come and go. Just miraculous! Do you not agree, Miss Elizabeth?"

"Indeed," she replied with a smile.

Mr. Wilkinson closed the door and eyed Elizabeth with a look of perplexity. "Was that comment about the storms supposed to mean something?"

*****

The night was long, and sleep did not come quickly. Darcy wondered if he should have proposed differently. What made her finally accept him? He wondered if he had been right to play along with the memory loss. He remembered her tearful words, "I trusted you," and that bothered him deeply. He wondered if she had accepted him only to save him from his aunt. He wondered a lot of things.

When the clock struck two, he whispered for Madeline. Perhaps some pain medication would help the throbbing in his foot. When she didn't answer, he tried once again to simply be grateful Elizabeth had accepted him. They had a lot to discuss, but he prayed that she truly loved him like he loved her. With these thoughts, he reviewed every interaction between them since his memory had returned. It took a great deal of time, but every look, every word, every touch was replayed in his mind, until he fell into a dream-filled sleep.

*****

Elizabeth repacked her trunks; everything had been thrown in hastily by her cousin, so it took some time, but even that did not make her sleepy. She realized she still had the late Mr. Darcy's book on northern England's plants and flowers. She carefully put the book back in the trunk and climbed into bed.

A battle raged in her mind and heart. One part of her was relieved that his memory was back. She had been so worried! Another part of her was angry that he had misled her, making her believe his memory was still gone while he kept proposing. Of course, this led her to think about the many different proposals and how they had changed and improved over the last ten days. She also replayed their embrace and the moment when she thought she would get her first kiss.

After exhaustedly reviewing all of the events of the day, she began to fear for the future. She feared what her father would say when Mr. Darcy asked for permission to marry her. She had told her father about Mr. Darcy's memory problems, and Lady Catherine had told him Elizabeth was caring for Mr. Darcy, but her father had no knowledge of Mr. Darcy's regard. He knew nothing about the first proposal, let alone the twelve that followed. How would he react when he learned everything that had happened? He would undoubtedly find it all endlessly humorous. She could imagine him toying with Mr. Darcy; she feared her father would laugh at him.

And what would her mother say? She had always hated the man! *But I am sure she will be very polite to him when she remembers he is worth ten thousand a year!* She smiled. She knew that when she shared her feelings about him, her mother's attitude would change.

What were her feelings now? She knew she loved him, but when did this occur? How long had she desired his good opinion? Her thoughts reviewed all their time together since the accident, and little by little she could see how her feelings had changed, ever so slightly, from the very moment of his first proposal. She had been touched by the emotion he showed that night; that was when she first questioned her opinions of the man. He had a way of looking at her that melted her heart. If he had never made his feelings known to her, she would have always interpreted that deep, penetrating gaze as selfish disdain rather than thoughtful admiration. How could she have not seen his regard all that time in Hertfordshire? It still amazed her.

She rolled over in bed, and the clock struck two. She wondered what he was doing at that moment. She imagined him sleeping restfully, with stray curls covering his eyes. She imagined holding his hand and reading Wordsworth to him as he lay like that. Suddenly she was tired. She had spent many hours reviewing her feelings and thoughts, but imagining holding his hand was the one thought that calmed her enough to let her mind drift quietly to sleep.

*****

Ten in the morning came and went, and Elizabeth rechecked her trunks. The rain had stopped just before she fell asleep last night, so she knew it was not the weather that delayed him. She wondered if

228

Lady Catherine had somehow stopped him from leaving as planned. She wondered if getting him into the carriage was even possible. She wondered if he had changed his mind.

"He will come, darling. Why do you not read for a moment? The colonel will send word if their plans change," Mrs. Wilkinson assured her.

"Is it that obvious? I am terribly nervous."

"If I did not know better, I would say you were anxious to see your betrothed."

"I am. I have a great deal on my mind. But enough about me— what about you? Will you seek other employment? Do you have any other skills besides cooking?"

She chuckled. "So, now you are calling me skilled in the kitchen? Goodness girl! I think you might be the one who hit her head!" The comment worked exactly as Mrs. Wilkinson had hoped; a small smile graced Elizabeth's face, and her eyes lit up.

"Oh, you are definitely skilled. I think you really know how to kill a meal."

"You do know I do not do the actual slaughtering, correct?"

"Yes. So, you may take my meaning any way you desire." Elizabeth let out her first laugh that morning. The clock struck eleven, and her laugh dwindled.

Mrs. Wilkinson tried again to distract her. "I make a very good lady's maid. I did that for two years for a young lady. But when she married, she did not wish to take me with her, and, to be honest, I did not want to go with her; my husband had just proposed and there was no position for him on the new estate."

"Truly? You fixed the young lady's hair and helped her dress?"

"Indeed. I liked that position much better than being a cook. I was rather good at it too. I like to think that I had a hand in helping her attract her husband."

"I can see you being a very fine lady's maid. So, will you look for a position as a lady's maid again?"

"We shall see. My youngest is a handful." The sound of a carriage out front was finally heard, and Elizabeth jumped up to look out the window.

"It is them! Both carriages are here! He came!" She couldn't describe the relief she felt. She took in her first unguarded breath in over an hour and turned back to Mrs. Wilkinson. "Betty, you must promise to write to me! I have come to value your friendship so much!" Mrs. Wilkinson nodded with tears in her eyes. Elizabeth gave her a quick hug and then opened the door and watched as Colonel Fitzwilliam stepped out of the carriage. He stopped and said something she could not make out to someone in the carriage. Footmen appeared in front of her, and she directed them to her trunks. She could not wait any longer; her feet propelled her to the first carriage in hope of getting a glimpse of him.

Colonel Fitzwilliam bowed. "Miss Elizabeth, forgive our tardiness. We were delayed in leaving."

"Was there a problem getting him in the carriage?"

"Indeed, it was more challenging than we imagined. He is weak and offered little help," he teased. "He was also very loath to leave Mr. Collins before receiving one last spit bath." The worry on Elizabeth's face turned into a sweet smile with that comment.

She heard Mr. Darcy's voice from inside. "Do not let him tell you lies, Miss Elizabeth. Lady Catherine was the time-consuming obstacle."

The colonel smiled and continued, "Perhaps you and Mr. Darcy can discuss it on the way to Hertfordshire. Madeline will be riding with you in case he needs anything, and I will be riding with Georgiana and Mrs. Annesley in the other carriage. May I?" And he offered her a hand into the carriage.

Mr. Darcy was in the far corner, and his leg was propped up on the seat in front of him with several blankets and, of course, the large splint. Madeline was sitting next to his foot, with her hand on the splint, stabilizing it. She looked around and realized the only seat available was right next to Mr. Darcy. She must have looked surprised, because Darcy felt the need to explain.

"If you would feel more comfortable riding with Georgiana, I understand."

Elizabeth shook her head. "No, this shall be fine." She took her seat next to him, and she muttered a thank-you as he handed her an extra blanket. She looked to Madeline, who was reading a book with a sly smile on her face. It was Elizabeth's book. But somehow Elizabeth felt that the Shakespearean comedy, *Much Ado about Nothing*, was not the reason for the grin. "I see you found my book," Elizabeth said.

Madeline grinned wider but didn't take her eyes off the pages. "Yes, you left it in the sitting room. I assume you do not mind me reading it on the way to Hertfordshire. I find I get quite engrossed in a book. I do not notice what is being said around me or even what is happening. I am afraid you two are on your own for conversation. I hope this does not seem rude."

Darcy cleared his throat and said, "I am sure if I need you, I will have to go to great lengths to get your attention, correct, Madeline?"

"Indeed. I cannot vouch for my attentiveness in the carriage today; I am in a very captivating part of the play. Now if you will excuse me, I simply must get to my favorite part before we arrive."

They felt the driver climb up to his position, and seconds later the carriage departed. After several minutes of silence, both Elizabeth and Mr. Darcy let out a simultaneous sigh. Elizabeth looked at Darcy and caught his eyes watching her. They both laughed quietly.

"Did you sleep well?" he asked.

"Not terribly well. It took some time to actually fall asleep."

"For me as well. Was anything in particular troubling you?"

Elizabeth paused. "I found myself reviewing the last several days looking for any evidence that you had your memory back."

Darcy looked surprised. He wasn't prepared for the topic to be brought up so soon. She was more upset than he realized. "I suppose I should apologize again. It was deceitful to have hidden my improvements."

"Yes, it was. I am sure you had your reasons."

"I believe you are aware of my reasons, Miss Elizabeth."

She felt a little anxiety and anger rise into her throat. "And would those reasons be to sneakily court me? Or to play on my sympathies for your condition? Or to secure my hand through manipulation? Because I, for one, do not appreciate mind games."

"Yes, my cousin warned me about that. It was none of the above. I did not mean to trap you or confuse you. I only wanted to spend more time with you so you could see who I really am."

She knew if she wasn't careful, her tongue would get her into trouble. But the warning came too late as words began quickly flowing from her tight lips. "And who are you? Are you a prideful, aloof man who speaks little? Or are you a kind, thoughtful, well-read gentleman who knows how to pull the heartstrings of unsuspecting young ladies?" Elizabeth didn't know why she was snapping at him so forcefully. She glanced at his face and saw a slightly pained expression. She softened her tone and reached out for his hand. "Or perhaps you are a charming, loyal, persistent man in search of the one thing his heart most desires."

Darcy squeezed her hand. "I admit I have been prideful. But aloof? I have been called brooding, but aloof?"

She let out a small giggle. "I agree with brooding."

"I only brood when I am uncomfortable in my surroundings."

"And are you brooding now, sir?"

"Definitely not. I am quite comfortable." He caressed her hand and then brought it up to his lips and kissed it through the glove.

She had to look away as the warmth on her hand ran up her arm straight to her face; she suddenly felt quite flushed. All her anxiety and fears from the night before seemed to dissolve with that tender kiss. She knew at that moment that she held no ill feelings about his faked memory problems. She had him now, and that was all that mattered. She left her hand in his, and they rode in silence for some time. The carriage rocked and bounced with the road. Although she had some embroidery in her reticule, at the moment, she did not intend to take back her hand. She watched the trees pass by one after another. She rested her head on the back of the carriage and took a deep breath. "I am sorry too."

"Excuse me?" Darcy said.

"I am sorry too. You were not the only one who was deceitful."

"Whatever do you mean?" Darcy squeezed her hand gently.

"I mean I should have told you from the very beginning that I had refused you. Maybe you would have gotten your memory back sooner. I tried to convince Colonel Fitzwilliam, Madeline, and Mr. Cummings—"

"Stop, Elizabeth. Stop."

She looked at him confused. "Stop what?"

"Do not analyze and revisit the past. Can we simply move forward to a future that can hold only happiness?" His leg bumped against hers, and he stiffened slightly at the sensation. Never before had he sat so close to a lady in such confined quarters. And never had he felt the need to simultaneously pull away out of propriety and yet scoot closer to feel her warmth. He daringly leaned nearer, close enough for their shoulders to touch. Suddenly, Madeline coughed.

They both straightened and looked at Madeline, who seemed to have no expression at all on her face. "Perhaps we can continue this conversation at another time," Elizabeth laughed.

✶✶✶✶✶

The next two hours were spent with quiet murmurs between the two. True to her word, Madeline was oblivious to their conversation. Both Elizabeth and Mr. Darcy seemed to have forgotten the stress of yesterday, and they talked amicably. They talked about all sorts of things. They talked about how they felt about each other, they talked about their different perspectives on how their relationship had grown, and they also talked about their future hopes for the marriage.

After a quick stop for lunch, Elizabeth began to notice some tension in his voice, although his words were still kind and engaging. He grimaced every now and again when the carriage jostled or bumped. She could see him stiffen after an especially hard rut, and several moments passed before he fully relaxed again.

"Are you in pain, Mr. Darcy?" Elizabeth asked.

Madeline, who had been so engrossed in her book, looked up immediately. She had been trying to give them as much privacy as possible, but she heard Elizabeth's words loud and clear. "Mr. Darcy? Are you well?"

"I admit I am uncomfortable, but I have made it the last three hours. It is not three hours more until we arrive in Hertfordshire. I should be fine."

Madeline's years of experience rose into action, quickly assessing the patient. His skin was pale, small beads of sweat dotted his brow, and his face was fighting a grimace. He sat protectively, leaning against the carriage with his back stiff, and his right arm was braced against the carriage window. She did not need to be told what to do. She rummaged through her bag and pulled out the pain medication.

Shaking his head, he said, "Truly, I can make it. That medication does more than take the pain away; it puts me to sleep . . . and alters my mind a little. I do not wish to sleep right now."

Elizabeth's experience guided her as well; she knew he was in pain and that he was avoiding the medication because he was enjoying their time together. She also knew that she had a great deal of power in convincing him to do what was needed. He was not as emotional and irrational now as he had been in those first few days, but he was still the same man inside. He would do anything to spend more time with her.

She chose her address carefully. "William?" she said quietly. She soon saw his soft eyes turn to her, and the smile she knew would be there did indeed appear. "Take the medicine. If you need to sleep, sleep. I will be here when you wake." He looked at her in obvious debate. She contemplated doing what she had wanted to do since seeing his handsome chest on the day of the accident. But would it be proper? Would he think ill of her? She saw him start to shake his head, and she knew she had to act quickly. She placed her palm on his chest and was surprised at how firm it was. For a moment she left it there, and she could feel his chest rise and fall rapidly. She repeated, "Take the medicine."

He reached up to her hand on his chest and held it there. With the increase in pressure she could feel the heat rising into her gloved hand, and she could feel his heartbeat. He kept eye contact, and she heard him whisper his consent. It was a beautiful moment. He realized then that she truly cared for him. Although little was said between the two, volumes were spoken merely by that gesture of her tiny hand on his chest.

The medicine was administered, and moments later he started to relax. He tilted his head toward her and drowsily stared at her beautiful face. He was dreamlike, and he felt so many things. He felt gratitude for winning her hand—*her* hand.

He realized he was still holding her hand, and he looked down at it. It was so tiny. He wondered what it would feel like to hold her gloveless hand. The thought somehow felt familiar. Had he held it before? How could he have forgotten? Now he was more determined than ever. He wanted very much to hold her bare hand. He took off his own glove, which seemed quite determined to stay on. The medicine was working, he could tell, but his curiosity was stronger than the drugs. What would her fingers feel like in his?

He reached for her hand and started pulling at her glove. Little by little he inched it off each finger. He looked at it in complete amazement as if he had never seen a female hand before. He remembered watching her hands dance on the keys of the pianoforte at Rosings when Elizabeth had told him he needed to practice his communication skills. Remembering what had been said at the time, he whispered aloud, "Neither of us perform to strangers." His voice was slurred, more evidence that the medicine was working. He couldn't even feel his foot anymore.

Elizabeth watched a drowsy Mr. Darcy take off her glove, and although entirely improper, she allowed him. They were engaged after all. And to be honest, it was a very thrilling sensation. It made her heart race, and she felt something stir deep inside her. She had the sudden urge to turn her head to him and kiss him. But he was mumbling strange things. His head was bobbing with the most minor bumps of the carriage, and she knew he was nearly asleep. She watched him lower the hand he had been so engrossed in, as if it suddenly had become too heavy to hold up, and he looked at her. His eyes were glossy and the eyelids heavy. "You can sleep now, William," she said. And with that permission, he closed his eyes, and his heavy head landed right on her shoulder.

She looked over at Madeline with startled eyes. Madeline had a small smirk on her face but did not acknowledge that a man's head was now resting on Elizabeth's shoulder. She simply read Elizabeth's book with even greater concentration. Elizabeth whispered, "How much did you give him?"

Madeline put her book down. "Are you accusing me of drugging him?"

"Well, look at him! He will be mortified if he wakes up and realizes what he is doing!"

"I do not think he will remember. What a pity. But you will remember it, so I suggest you enjoy it while it lasts."

"And you call me impertinent!" Elizabeth heard a soft laugh from Madeline and saw her smile.

Madeline was right though. Elizabeth did enjoy it. His warm breath was right at her neck, sending shivers up and down her spine, causing her heart to beat wildly in her chest. She had never been this close to a man nor felt such strong emotions surge through her. An overwhelming desire to kiss him rose again, and for a moment she felt a bit too warm.

She repositioned herself so she could look down at his face. He had a peaceful look, yet somehow he still had dimples. Was he smiling in his sleep? Elizabeth glanced at Madeline, who had resumed reading. She then brushed a curl away from his eyes. She took a moment to inhale his masculine scent and closed her eyes, trying to imprint that smell into her memory forever. It wasn't long before she fell asleep too, a consequence of being awake until after two in the morning.

*****

"Elizabeth!" Madeline whispered. "Elizabeth!" When that didn't work, she gave her a gentle kick. The two of them still had their hands entwined and their heads leaning together. Both were fast asleep. Madeline could tell they had turned off the main road, and she could only assume the winding path was the entrance to Longbourn. Sure enough, a small estate was visible through a break in the trees, and the carriages were slowing. She tried one more time with a slightly less gentle kick, but it wasn't Elizabeth who woke; it was Mr. Darcy.

"Ouch! Why did you kick me?" he asked, lifting his head off Elizabeth's shoulder. He looked around and suddenly realized the proximity of Elizabeth, still asleep against his side. He also recognized the shrill voice of Mrs. Bennet coming at them from only a few yards away. He gave Elizabeth's hand a firm squeeze and said, "Elizabeth, we are here." He was still a little foggy and drowsy from the medicine.

Elizabeth woke and heard her mother's high-pitched voice proclaiming their arrival. She straightened and released Mr. Darcy's hand. She looked to him and gave him a small smile. "Are you ready for this?"

"I think I have been ready for this for months."

She looked out the carriage window as it was slowing and saw her entire family lined up ready to greet them. Theirs was the first carriage; Georgiana's was the second. It finally stopped, and her father opened the door and looked inside. His curiosity about the seating arrangement was evident on his face, but miraculously he didn't comment.

"Welcome home. I have not had a moment's peace since you left." He helped her out of the carriage and then reached in for Madeline and assisted her. "I assume you have a plan on how to exit the carriage, Mr. Darcy, or have you forgotten already?"

Elizabeth groaned. "Papa, be nice. Mr. Darcy no longer has memory problems. I told you that in the express last night."

"He seemed to have forgotten that a gentleman does not sit next to an unmarried lady on a long carriage ride."

Madeline quickly spoke up. "I needed to sit across from him to stabilize the foot, sir. It was the only option at the time." Mr. Bennet raised his eyebrow at the woman.

Elizabeth was then greeted by the members of the other carriage, and she began introductions to her family. When she introduced the colonel, Lydia and Kitty squealed and giggled. She realized she had neglected to warn him about her sisters' love of a man in uniform. She then introduced Georgiana, who gave the smallest curtsy but was quite flushed in the face. She then introduced Mrs. Annesley and, finally, Nurse Madeline. She introduced each member of her family to the travelers.

Colonel Fitzwilliam smiled politely and bowed to each of the ladies. "It is a pleasure. I have heard much of Miss Elizabeth's sisters—you especially, Miss Bennet. I would offer to escort you in, but duty calls, and I must assist Mr. Darcy out of the carriage and into this wheeled contraption. If any of you would like some entertainment, simply stay and watch us get a lame man out of a carriage."

Lydia and Kitty giggled again. Lydia fluttered her eyelashes and asked, "Will you be lifting him, Colonel Fitzwilliam?"

Elizabeth sighed, took both sisters by the arm, and escorted them inside the house. "I am sure Mr. Darcy would appreciate some privacy. Georgiana, come in and refresh yourself with tea." Elizabeth glanced back to make sure Georgiana and her companion were following; she also looked over her shoulder to watch as Colonel Fitzwilliam and Madeline climbed into Mr. Darcy's carriage.

After twenty minutes of sipping tea, Elizabeth couldn't stand it any longer; she made her excuses and escaped to her father's study. She found her father there, staring out the window, laughing at the team of people helping Mr. Darcy out of the carriage.

"Ah, Lizzy! I do not think I have ever seen a gentleman scoot on his bottom before. You just missed it. I am not sure how many more people can fit into that carriage or huddle around the door, but apparently Mr. Darcy has made it safely to the ground."

Elizabeth saw Mr. Darcy standing on one foot, being pivoted around in order to sit in the wheeled contraption, and, sure enough, his coattails separated to reveal a dirty, dusty backside. Elizabeth giggled, and her father looked down at her.

"Is there something I should know, Elizabeth? You mentioned he wanted to speak to me. I cannot imagine what about. I hardly know the man. I am sure we did not exchange more than a few greetings when he was in Hertfordshire. I was quite shocked when Lady Catherine de Bourgh wrote me and expressed her desire for you to stay longer to take care of him. You, however, did not feel the need to tell me he was in Kent at all until after the accident. I wonder, why all the secrecy?" He grinned at his favorite daughter.

"I suspect he will make his purpose known shortly. They are wheeling him in now. Excuse me." She wondered if she should have explained further. Perhaps it would make it easier on Mr. Darcy. She turned back around. "Papa? He is important to me. Be nice."

"I suspected that, poppet. But I must admit I have never been asked permission for my daughter's hand, and I am not entirely sure I am prepared. I might slip up a few times. I might even call him the wrong name to see if he remembers his own name or has the gall to correct me. A man who cannot remember one day to the next wishes to marry my daughter! You cannot deny me what could potentially be the greatest amusement of my lifetime."

"I told you, he does remember. There are still a few things he has forgotten, but he has retained everything in the last week. Now, I am going to say this one last time: be nice."

*****

"Mr. Darcy, are you sure you do not want some tea before we speak? Do you still like tea?" Mr. Bennet asked.

"Papa!"

"I was only referring to the fact that he may want something stronger! What do you accuse me of, Lizzy?" he said with a grin.

Mr. Darcy sat up straighter and addressed Mr. Bennet. "I do enjoy a bit of brandy. That much I remember." And he flashed a smile at Elizabeth, reassuring her he would be just fine.

"Well, then! Let me push you into my study, and we can have a little private meeting. Lizzy, if you wish to know what is said, feel free to find me later; I may be the only one who will recall the conversation."

Elizabeth narrowed her eyes at her father. She warned him one more time, "Papa, please."

"I know, I know. Come, Mr. Darcy. I hope you are not afraid of some imported French brandy."

"It is my favorite." He looked over his shoulder and gave Elizabeth a confident smile and hoped his own fears didn't show on his face.

Mr. Bennet pushed him directly in front of a large desk and took his time collecting the brandy and glasses. He removed the lid of the decanter and poured a healthy amount for each of them. Holding up one glass, he took a moment to observe the color. He then eyed Mr. Darcy and evaluated him. The man in front of him looked a little nervous, but confident. Perhaps a little too confident. *This will be amusing*, he thought. He handed the man his drink, walked behind him, and stood to look out the window. He sipped the brandy and felt the warmth fill his chest. Minutes ticked by, and yet neither one said anything. Mr. Bennet could be patient.

Darcy cleared his throat. "I can be patient too."

Mr. Bennet smiled out the window. "From what I understand, you have been quite the patient, as in the one who was the invalid. The man who needed to be cared for. The man who—"

"Yes, indeed, I was a patient man, but that will not last for long. I came to discuss Elizabeth."

Mr. Bennet turned and looked at Mr. Darcy and smiled. "Elizabeth?" he asked. "And you are on such familiar terms, are you? She did not inform me of any such relationship. Am I to assume you are having delusions as well as memory problems?"

"Sir, I see where Miss Elizabeth gets her wit, but I am in earnest and ask for your permission to marry her. I have asked her, multiple times in fact, and she has finally accepted my suit. I seek your consent."

"Consent to what?"

"To marry your daughter."

"Which one?"

"Miss Elizabeth."

"Oh, just checking. You never know with head injuries."

"Sir, do your best. I can spar with you and will not falter."

"What day is it?"

"Excuse me?"

"You heard me. Or did you forget the question already?"

"It is Saturday."

"And who are you?"

"Fitzwilliam Darcy of Pemberley."

"Well, that was an easy one. Who is the king?"

"That idiot."

Mr. Bennet laughed out loud and slapped his thigh. "Indeed! You truly do have your memory intact!"

Mr. Darcy relaxed a bit as he saw that Mr. Bennet had no intention of refusing him. He had already endured enough refusals for a lifetime, and he didn't need any more obstacles. He finally drank a bit of his brandy and appreciated the aroma and the smooth way it went down. "I admit if you refuse me, it will not be the first refusal, not the second, or even the seventh. I can assure you Elizabeth has certainly kept me on my toes."

"Not literally. I mean, you cannot walk. Forgive my dry humor. So you have proposed more than once?"

Mr. Darcy answered, "Thirteen times."

Mr. Bennet let out a hearty laugh. "Tell me of these multiple proposals. I would very much like to hear about them."

Mr. Darcy leaned back and told Mr. Bennet what Elizabeth had told him about the original proposal and refusal. Then he told him about the letter that he wrote to refute Elizabeth's accusations.

"But you do not remember the proposal or the letter? It seems every time you give a detail, you say 'she said I did this,' or 'she said I did that'."

"My memory fails me from two days before the awful first proposal until four days after the accident—approximately a week. But everything before and since then I can recall perfectly."

Mr. Bennet looked thoughtful. "I enjoy a good story, especially one where my Lizzy refuses a perfectly good suitor. Continue."

Mr. Darcy then explained the most recent proposals as best as he could remember them. He knew Mr. Bennet wanted to be entertained, so he carefully detailed the ridiculously vague answers Elizabeth gave him. He explained about continuing to use the reminder letter after his memory returned and deceiving them all so he could keep proposing, hoping she would eventually say yes.

He explained that the colonel suspected a change immediately. Richard could soon tell that he recalled what was happening from one day to the next, but he never said anything. He explained that Madeline caught him slipping up a few times and quickly guessed the truth, but during that whole week, Elizabeth did not suspect a thing. He then told him of his aunt's threatening letter from her solicitor. He detailed how Elizabeth boldly stood up to her and accepted his hand, proclaiming her commitment in front of everyone.

Mr. Bennet poured more brandy for the two of them. "So, my Lizzy held her ground with that pompous Lady Catherine de Bourgh? Judging by the praise of the obsequious Mr. Collins, she seems fearful indeed."

"Elizabeth was wonderful. And my aunt *is* someone to fear. I am afraid she will make the introduction of Elizabeth into the finest circles a little more difficult. You see, all this time my aunt had her heart set on me marrying her only daughter, Anne. That was the goal in the threats from her solicitor. She did not take into account the fact that any wife would meet the demands. And I was fortunate enough to have Elizabeth save my life for the second time. My aunt was not happy."

"Yes, my Lizzy does make an impression; one that apparently can stand the test of your memory problems."

"Indeed. Am I to assume then that I have your consent?"

"How long do you think we have before she comes barging in to 'save your life' again?" he asked with a wry grin.

"You may be a better judge of that than I."

And almost on cue, there was a knock on the door that Mr. Bennet recognized. "Welcome to the family. Although I must warn you, my wife and youngest daughters can be difficult to bear. Perhaps you might want to forget you know them after all."

"Yes, my memory problems might come in handy."

The knock was heard again, and Mr. Bennet called out, "Come in, Lizzy!"

CHAPTER 11

"Do not fret, poppet. I only sparred with him a few times. And unless you told him about my political views on the king, he passed any test I could give him. Congratulations, Lizzy. I could not have parted with you to anyone less worthy," Mr. Bennet said with a smile.

"Your political views?" Elizabeth asked with concern. She was sure she had never discussed her father's eccentric political views with Mr. Darcy.

"It was nothing. Maybe he can tell you about it later. You two may have a moment alone since I am confident he cannot do much to you from a chair. Rejoin us when you are ready. I, for one, intend to create my own entertainment. Wish me luck. I am about to announce to your mother that she has a daughter engaged to be married. Now, watch and see whose mental capacities are intact! Ha! What fun I am having today!" Mr. Bennet leaned in and gave his smiling daughter a kiss on the forehead. Then he shook Mr. Darcy's hand and left, closing the door behind him.

Elizabeth turned to Mr. Darcy, whose dimples were being displayed at their finest. He was so handsome sitting there. His strong, broad shoulders were very attractive. He reached a hand over to her, and she readily took it. "My father trusts that you will be a gentleman. But that grin on your face makes me a little curious as to what you have in mind."

"Come." He motioned to his lap.

Her eyebrow raised in challenge. Did he think she was so easily won over? "Now, Mr. Darcy, a lady does not sit on a gentleman's lap."

"But perhaps this lady does." He grinned at her and opened his other arm. "Do I not even get to embrace my betrothed? Do you not have pity on a man who is bound to a chair?"

"Perhaps that would be appropriate. And since you cannot stand, I suppose I must come to you." She smiled at him slyly.

"My thoughts exactly," he said with his grin broadening.

He pulled her into him, and she sat gingerly on his left leg, attempting not to put any weight on the right. His masculine, clean, sandalwood scent was intoxicating, and she wrapped her arm around his neck, leaning her head into his, making their foreheads touch. She could feel his breath on her lips and cheeks. She could feel his chest rise and fall more rapidly than usual; she knew hers was. He wrapped his arms around her waist and gave her a gentle squeeze.

He turned his head slightly and put his mouth by her ear. "Elizabeth, dearest Elizabeth, you have saved me in every way possible," he whispered.

She had already been flushed from the contact and his gentle touch, but his words and breath at her ear sent a wave of delight throughout her whole body. It reminded her of being in the carriage, and she was overcome with a great desire to kiss him. Her heart was pounding, and she could feel his hands move up from her waist to her hair, and he gently, caressingly, pulled her head away from him for a moment. She could see his dark eyes gazing at her, questioning, searching for something.

What is he waiting for? Permission to kiss me? Is not sitting on his lap a clear message? Moments passed with their eyes locked on each other until she realized he was waiting for exactly that: permission. She gave him a slight smile, which grew in size until she raised her eyebrow in preparation to say something witty when all of the sudden his lips caressed hers, once, then twice. But the third time could not be called a caress. It was full of energy and a passion that shocked her.

She clung to him, letting his lips take hers in every way imaginable. She pulled in a much-needed breath of air but only enough to engage once again in this newfound delight. Their lips moved gracefully together, making her heart dance in her chest. His hands pressed her face to his as if she was his very breath, as if he could not survive without her, and she knew she could never again go another day without him. He was gentle but persistent with his ministrations. *Is this what I have been missing by refusing him? Good Lord! I shall never refuse him a thing again!*

They heard her mother screech on the other side of the door with a desperate call for her smelling salts. They both knew their moment was over. Mr. Darcy released her lips hesitantly and then went in for one last kiss. Elizabeth sat up and blushed becomingly. He touched her rosy cheek and whispered, "You know that blush is quite becoming."

She looked at him curiously. "Yes, I have heard that before."

"From whom?"

"From you. I believe it was right before proposal number two."

"Indeed? Well, I have been accused of knowing the desires of my heart and being consistent."

"Is that another way to say persistent?"

Footsteps were heard outside the door, and Elizabeth jumped up off Mr. Darcy's lap and smoothed her skirts. The door opened, and her mother was waving her handkerchief and swaying dramatically from side to side. She clung to the door with the other hand for support.

"My dear Lizzy, is it true? Mr. Darcy has proposed?"

Elizabeth smiled and said, "Yes, Mamma. We are to be married." Mr. Darcy took her hand and kissed it tenderly on the top, and then he turned it over and kissed the fleshy part of the wrist, sending a fresh blush to her face. *He did that on purpose! Right in front of my mother! I shall prevail!* She boldly leaned down and put a hand on his face and leaned in and kissed his lips tenderly once. She watched him flush red as well, and she smiled mischievously back at him. *How is that for impertinence, Mr. Darcy?* "Mamma, now I must marry him! For I have been compromised! Is it not so, Mr. Darcy?"

He tried to gain some semblance of control over himself. The moment before Mrs. Bennet's intrusion was still fresh in his mind, and to see her tease him so was overwhelming. *Drat! If I could just stand and take her in my arms!* She gave him a look, and he realized that he hadn't answered her yet. "Indeed. I must marry you, for no man would want you after a kiss like that," he said with the same mischief in his eyes. His words did exactly what he had hoped; her mouth popped open in shock. He heard Mrs. Bennet inhale deeply and then figured he had better explain. He squeezed her hand and said, "Except me."

Mrs. Bennet let out an enormous sigh and swayed back and forth until Jane came and led her out of the room.

"Come," Jane said, "you must sit down, Mamma. You should probably eat something as well. You know how you get those headaches when the flutterings in your chest come." Jane flashed a smile and managed a wink at Elizabeth as she led their mother out of the room. There was much to discuss it seemed.

Mr. Bennet had witnessed the kiss his daughter bestowed upon Mr. Darcy, and he was more than a little shocked. If he was not prepared to have a man ask for her hand, he certainly was not prepared to see her kiss him so casually in front of him. He came up behind Mr. Darcy's chair and leaned down and whispered in his ear, "Perhaps I trusted in your limitations a little too much."

Darcy tilted his head back and not so quietly said, "A determined man knows his limitations but finds a way to make them his strengths, sir."

Mr. Bennet looked at his favorite daughter and firmly pressed his hands on Mr. Darcy's shoulders. "Let us just keep our strengths to ourselves until you can properly escort my daughter down the aisle. I know your foot is broken, but let us keep our hands from deflecting to Rome, shall we? Or Russia?"

Mr. Darcy was indeed confused. "I do not take your meaning."

Elizabeth blushed and slapped her father's arm. "Papa!"

Mr. Bennet smiled at his creative warning and ignored his daughter's plea for silence on the matter. "We do not want any roamin' hands or rushin' fingers, do we?"

Mr. Darcy recognized the play on words and turned beet red, and he bowed his head and said, "No, sir. All English from here on."

"Good. From the color of your ears, I see I have made my point."

*****

The colonel had ridden to Netherfield, and it was indeed ready to receive their party. This created mixed emotions for Mr. Darcy. If he chose to go to Netherfield, he would not have to endure the "flutterings, and tremblings, and the poor nerves" of Mrs. Bennet, whose attitude toward him had changed quite dramatically in the past hour. He now was treated with excessive respect, and he had to deflect ridiculous compliments that rivaled Miss Bingley's. Also, if he stayed at Longbourn, it seemed he would be watched very closely by Mr. Bennet; he did feel a little sheepish for kissing Elizabeth like that. These were the reasons he did not want to stay at Longbourn.

But, if he did stay at Longbourn, he would see his Elizabeth daily and have plenty of time in her presence. They couldn't possibly be chaperoned *all* the time, and he would probably be able to steal a few kisses here and there. These were the reasons he wanted to stay at Longbourn.

Netherfield was much bigger and could house the whole party, as well as the servants, quite comfortably. It would also provide refuge from the two youngest Bennets, who did not seem much improved since the autumn. He knew Bingley's sisters were not going to be there, which was another advantage to staying at Netherfield. These were the reasons Netherfield was the better option.

The main problem with Netherfield was that Elizabeth would not be there. Even if Georgiana invited her for tea and dinner every day, Elizabeth would still have to go home each evening. He was very grateful to have his sister with him—otherwise he would have no real method of extending an invitation to Elizabeth. The invitation would most likely be extended to Miss Bennet, for Bingley's sake, and they would all enjoy a very pleasant visit, no doubt, but it would just be a visit. He would miss her so much every time she left.

Simply put, if he stayed at Netherfield, he would see less of Elizabeth and that was almost reason enough to stay at Longbourn. He struggled with these thoughts, and his mind was quite preoccupied at dinner. Mrs. Bennet's voice interrupted his deep thoughts.

"Mr. Darcy, I do say, you look quite well for having taken such a spill as Lizzy described in her letters. Are you in much pain now? You had the most dreadful scowl on your face just now."

"No, ma'am. My foot is only painful at night or when a storm is coming. I apologize for being distracted. I was just deep in thought."

Mrs. Bennet said, "I do hope my Lizzy has not caused you grief. She delights in vexing me. Oh! But I am sure that she has long outgrown that phase. She will be a most loyal and loving wife— spirited, perhaps, but loyal."

Colonel Fitzwilliam nearly choked on his wine. "Pardon me. It is just that Mrs. Bennet's words rung familiar with me for a moment. Darcy, did they ring familiar to you?" He looked at Darcy, who stared back at him in confusion. "Do you not have a horse that is spirited and loyal? One that was hard to break?"

Darcy shook his head and said, "Forgive my cousin; he seems to have lost his mind more recently than I did." Laughter erupted for several minutes from the entire dinner table, and the party enjoyed a few more jabs in mock of Darcy's memory problems.

When the jollity started to die down, Colonel Fitzwilliam tried again. "Well, I will not bore you with the details," he said, "but Darcy has a love for spirited horses. Very recently he acquired a horse that was somewhat difficult to tame. She was quite spirited, and I am not entirely sure Darcy accomplished his task in breaking her, but he did seem to earn her loyalty." He then glanced at Elizabeth and Darcy followed his eyes.

Something was familiar. Spirited? Loyal? Horses? Suddenly he was hit with a flash of thought about darkened skies and the feeling of wild wind in his hair. He shook his head a little and looked up at Colonel Fitzwilliam. Was he remembering something? Another flash of his horse refusing alfalfa whipped through his head. It was like seeing glimpses of something he had seen before. He blinked several times and caught the eyes of his cousin, who had a very satisfied grin on his face.

Dinner was finished, and the men left to have drinks in the study, leaving the ladies to talk privately. Elizabeth gave Jane a warning look, effectively preventing her from asking about Mr. Darcy just yet. Instead they chatted about the journey and Elizabeth's stay in Kent.

"So, Mrs. Wilkinson must have been quite a good friend to you while you were there." Jane remarked. "I still cannot believe she resigned her employment for you!"

"I can. She is very loyal to those she respects, and she certainly did not respect Mr. Collins. I feel bad for Charlotte, however, because now she has the task of finding a replacement."

Jane paused. "Well, perhaps it is not my place to say," she shyly said, "but I have no doubt that Lady Catherine will help her with that duty."

Elizabeth laughed. "You are correct. I have no doubt she will have a hand in it."

"Was she really that bad?"

"Yes. She is the type of person who enjoys making others feel small. She needs to feel important and simply being mistress of Rosings is not important enough. Not even being married to Sir Lewis was enough. She sees people as pawns that she can use to obtain more power. To be honest, I believe that was the real reason she wanted Mr. Darcy to marry her daughter, Anne; she wants to control Pemberley as well."

"And now that responsibility will be yours," Jane said quietly. "How do you feel about it? I remember Miss Bingley talking about how grand Pemberley is. I would feel quite nervous to take on such an estate as that." She was touching on topics that she knew Elizabeth would prefer to discuss in private, but at the moment everyone else was occupied. Lydia was arguing loudly with Kitty, and Mrs. Bennet was scolding Kitty. Georgiana was talking with Mrs. Annesley while Mary was quietly reading.

"I am not one to shy away from responsibility. And I certainly will not be scared off by a place I have never seen! I am sure I will have plenty of help for the first few years. How different could it be? I imagine there will be more rooms, more tenants to visit, and more dinner parties than we have here, but if Mamma can run Longbourn with a little help from Hill, I am sure I can handle Pemberley." Elizabeth swallowed her fear and tried to sound as confident as possible.

Jane realized she had said too much. She reached her out hand and gave Elizabeth's arm a squeeze. "I have every confidence in you. I did not mean to imply anything other than that."

Elizabeth felt all the love and concern in Jane's touch, but giant tears sprung up in her eyes anyway. She tried to blink them away. The stress of the last two weeks—the first horrid proposal, the accident, her worry for Mr. Darcy, Lady Catherine, her eviction from the parsonage, and the long journey—suddenly it all caught up to her. She hid her eyes but not before Georgiana noticed her discomposure.

It would not do to lose herself in front of Georgiana. She excused herself and caught a glimpse of Jane mouthing the words "I am sorry".

As she headed toward the stairs, she met Colonel Fitzwilliam wheeling Mr. Darcy into the sitting room, and although she did her best not to make eye contact, she could feel Darcy's gaze on her. She would surely be asked about it, but for now she needed to retreat to her room for a moment. She knew her face was easily read and she needed a few minutes to regain composure. Surely Mr. Darcy could handle her family without her.

Mr. Darcy did indeed notice the tears in Elizabeth's averted eyes. How could he not? As he watched her hurry up the stairs, he wished again that his foot was not broken because even propriety would not hold him back from comforting her. All this time, she had stayed strong. She had endured countless hours of stress, and he knew his condition and his proposals had only added to her difficulties. He could not recall any moment when she had faltered, and yet now she was hurting. Now, after they had finally found peace between them, she was left to cry on her own. It was eating him alive to be stranded in a chair.

After watching Elizabeth go upstairs, the colonel wheeled Darcy into the sitting room. Darcy awaited Elizabeth's return while distractedly trying to maintain the minimum level of sociality with the other Bennets. He checked his watch frequently. The longer she was gone, the more his concern grew. Fifteen minutes passed. Surely Jane knew what had happened. How could he ask her about it without being too obvious?

"Darcy, what do you think?" Colonel Fitzwilliam asked quietly.

He was so preoccupied with Elizabeth's emotional state that he did not hear what his cousin had said. "I apologize. I was not attending you. What did you ask?"

"It would probably be a good idea to start loading you into the carriage and get you settled at Netherfield. It is well past dark and—"

"Yes, yes, I know," he whispered. "Just a moment longer. I do not want to miss saying goodbye to Elizabeth."

Darcy's brooding nature was drumming up all sorts of offenses he must have committed, everything from sitting next to her in the carriage to kissing her so passionately. He rubbed his head with his fingers, trying to massage away the tension and the headache that was building. He hadn't taken any pain medication for his foot since the carriage ride, and it ached tremendously. The colonel caught his eyes, and, without a word, he stood and walked behind Darcy's chair and took ahold of the handles.

"It appears Darcy has had a big day. I must insist he retire to Netherfield," the colonel said.

Mrs. Bennet seemed to have noticed for the first time that Elizabeth had left the room. "Where is Lizzy? Jane, go and get Lizzy. She must say goodbye to her betrothed like a good girl."

"Yes, Mamma." Jane gave a small smile to Mr. Darcy, whose relief showed in his face all too well. Jane stopped by Darcy and leaned into him and whispered, "I have no doubt she wishes to say goodbye."

Darcy smiled in return. *Oh, how comforting those words were!* Whatever was bothering Elizabeth, it was not because of him. He turned a pleading look to the colonel, who sighed and resigned himself to waiting a little longer. Darcy gave him a look of gratitude and watched his cousin nod and start taking his leave of the Bennets. Darcy saw him pay especial attention to Kitty and Lydia, who had been fawning over him all night, asking for stories of the battlefield. He would have to thank him for giving him this moment, for surely his cousin was giving unnecessarily lengthy farewells. Richard was a good man to do this for him. He checked his watch one more time but was caught in the act by the very woman on his mind.

"I suspect you are needing to rest, Mr. Darcy. Forgive me for abandoning you for a few minutes. It does appear that you have survived without me," Elizabeth said quietly to him.

He turned around and saw her. Her beauty was astounding. Her eyes were bright, although a bit red and glossy, but she had a sincere smile on her lips. Those lips. How he would love to take her in his arms once again and give her a proper goodbye.

He had spent so much time with her over the last eleven days at the parsonage. Moments apart had flown by quickly because he had known that they would be reunited soon, being under the same roof, but not this time. He could not be sure when he would see those expressive eyes again. Her eyes spoke volumes. She would miss him too; he could see it in her face. She dreaded saying goodbye too. He suddenly had a thought. "Miss Elizabeth, since we seem to have done a thorough study of Wordsworth, does your father have any other books I might read until we meet again? I am afraid Netherfield's library is quite limited."

She smiled brightly at him. "Certainly. I will take you there, and you can pick out a book yourself." Turning to address her father, she said, "Papa, Mr. Darcy needs to borrow a book from your library. Do you mind if I assist him?"

Mr. Bennet was not as unobservant as he appeared. He knew very well what they were doing. It was blatantly obvious that they wanted a private moment to say goodbye. "I would not recommend *Julius Caesar*; you know how those Romans are." He saw them both blush slightly at his hidden warning, but he nodded and watched them roll away.

Once in the library, Mr. Darcy reached back and took her hands in his, pulling her in front of the chair. She knelt down beside him, and he saw the hurt she was trying to hide. "What is wrong?" he gently asked.

"It is nothing. You do not need to rescue me. I am well."

"But you do not seem well, Elizabeth. And you rescued me once, perhaps it is my turn. Please tell me what is troubling you."

She sighed. "I am sorry to have worried you. I simply got overwhelmed thinking about how fast my life has changed. It feels like

I have lived a year's worth of experiences in just the last two weeks. I admit I will miss my old life here when we are married. I will miss Longbourn and my sisters and my parents . . . But it is more than that. I am sure I will be very happy at Pemberley, but I never even seen it. And soon I will be mistress of it."

"Well, we agree on one point: I am also sure you will be very happy there. Elizabeth, it is just a house, like any other house. Together we will make it our home. You will see. And Pemberley has functioned quite well without a mistress for a very long time; I am confident it will survive a little while longer until you feel up to the task." He paused. Elizabeth smiled but made no reply. "What can I do, Elizabeth? How can I help? I may not be able to carry you off into the sunset, yet, but I can kiss your tears away."

She smiled and looked into his caring, kind, loving eyes. "I would like that very much."

And so he did. He pulled her face to his lips and placed numerous kisses on her eyes, her brows, and eventually, after many minutes, he found his way to her lips, where he placed one sweet, tender, chaste kiss. "Goodnight, my love."

*****

Darcy had been loaded into the carriage and Colonel Fitzwilliam gave Georgiana the cue that it was time to depart. Georgiana was no simpleton. She knew her role in getting Elizabeth to Netherfield. As she bid the Bennets farewell, she immediately invited Elizabeth and Jane for tea the next day. The invitation was kindly accepted. She saw the relief in Elizabeth's eyes, and on impulse she quickly embraced her. "My brother and I will look forward to seeing you. What time should I send the carriage for you?"

Elizabeth hugged her back warmly. "We should be home from church around ten. Is that too early?"

"Definitely not. I will have practiced my pianoforte for hours by that time."

"Well, save some for me. I have yet to hear your talent. It is a skill I am afraid I lack."

Georgiana looked at her confusedly and said, "But William says you are so accomplished at the pianoforte."

"Thus proving himself to be complimentary but an unreliable source for truth. I shall have to punish him somehow."

"But he is very reliable! He never lies!"

Is that right? Only for seven days in a row about having lost his memory, reflected Elizabeth, but the thought only made her smile. She no longer held ill feelings about his deception. "I am sure you are right. I will see you tomorrow then." Elizabeth watched Colonel Fitzwilliam hand Georgiana into the carriage, and he put his hand to his hat and tipped it slightly before climbing in himself. Elizabeth and Jane watched as the carriages rolled away. Jane took Elizabeth's arm and guided her into the house.

"Come. We have much to discuss," Jane said.

Elizabeth did as she was told. Slowly they climbed the steps to their room, where Jane guided her to the chair in front of the mirror. Without words, Jane took out the pins in Elizabeth's hair and gently shook out the bun. Her hair cascaded down her shoulders, and Jane picked up the brush and started making slow, repetitive strokes through her hair. The gentle pressure on her scalp was so soothing. It had been a long time since they had brushed each other's hair. Elizabeth watched Jane's face, so serene and peaceful. Jane was being very patient. Elizabeth finally let out the breath she didn't realize she had been holding and sighed audibly. "I am well."

"I know, Lizzy. I can see it in your eyes. You are in love." Jane continued brushing.

"And what about you? How do you feel about Mr. Bingley coming back?"

Jane looked thoughtful. "I suppose it will be hard to see him at first. There is no getting around it now. With you engaged to his best friend and needing a chaperone, I will be in his company a great deal. I have resigned myself to accepting whatever he has to offer. I will be delighted if we can be friends, but I am afraid my feelings for the man will show, and he will be uncomfortable in my presence. There, I have said it. I still care for the man very deeply."

Elizabeth reached up and stopped Jane's hand from brushing further. "Then let me tell you a story." They traded positions and Elizabeth brushed Jane's hair and told her all she had learned in Kent. With each stroke, she felt a great burden of secrecy being lifted. "I am so sorry I could not tell you earlier, Jane. It seems Mr. Darcy was under the impression that you did not truly care for Mr. Bingley. He is a most loyal friend and felt the need to protect him."

"Protect him from me?"

"No, from our mother and her matchmaking schemes. Mr. Darcy could see how Mamma had set her eyes on Mr. Bingley as your perfect wealthy match, and he assumed you had similar mercenary designs. He did not recognize what was so obvious to me. You loved Mr. Bingley. You still love him."

Elizabeth looked at Jane in the mirror. Jane's eyes, with the subtlest crease of worry, urged her to proceed with the story. "So, believing you to be indifferent, Mr. Darcy counseled Mr. Bingley to avoid you—to leave Netherfield and not return. Mr. Bingley relied on this counsel a little too much if you ask me. A little backbone and some self-reliance could have saved you two a great deal of unhappiness."

"Are you saying what I think you are saying?" Jane asked timidly.

"I am. Mr. Bingley has been just as unhappy without you as you have been without him. He has one purpose in returning to Netherfield, and that purpose is to see you. He was warned by Mr. Darcy to make his intentions clear this time. I assume Mr. Bingley has learned his lesson and has made the giant leap to follow his heart. He loves you, Jane; I know it! Mr. Darcy could not directly confirm it, but Mr. Bingley's decision to return to Netherfield speaks for itself. I think we will see a much more determined suitor tomorrow."

"Oh, do you think we will really see him tomorrow? We are heading to Netherfield so early; I cannot imagine us still being there when he arrives. He is traveling from London, is he not?"

"I believe so. But, Jane, tell me at once—how do you feel about Mr. Darcy's role in separating you? I had the hardest time forgiving him when I found out. It was my primary reason for refusing him for so long. I could not accept a man who rejoiced in separating my most-beloved sister from the man she loves."

Jane smiled and said, "I do not place blame where it should not lay. As you said before, it was simply friendly counsel—counsel that Mr. Bingley chose to heed instead of believing in my affection. I am much relieved to hear that he still cares for me, but I am not going to let my heart go as quickly as I did last time. The man who left in November . . . well, now he must earn my love, just as Mr. Darcy had to earn yours."

"No, Jane. Do not do what I did." Elizabeth put down the hairbrush and kneeled in front of Jane to look in her eyes. "If you have even the slimmest chance at happiness, you must fight for it. If he truly still loves you, then trust him. Do not hide your affection. I know you are disappointed he did not trust you last autumn, but it is *love*! Love, Jane! Love is worth all the storms and troubles that come with it. I cannot even express how grateful I am to feel such acceptance and devotion from Mr. Darcy. It will be the same for you. Mr. Bingley is made to love you, I know it."

Elizabeth hesitated and glanced away, unsure how to put her other thoughts into words. "You may not like what I have to say next," she continued, "but you know I cannot help but say what I feel. When I read that letter from Mr. Darcy explaining how he did not think your heart had been touched, I knew he was partially right. You show such little emotion. Even now as we talk of your broken heart, you do not cry, you do not flinch, and you do not flush with the anger you must be feeling. You are masterful at hiding how you feel. But you must not."

She looked into Jane's eyes and squeezed her hand gently. "Promise me," Elizabeth said, "that you will not hold back, Jane. Promise me you will love him just as deeply as you can, and promise me that you will show it to him the first opportunity you get!" Jane looked pensive. And then, for a brief moment, Elizabeth saw the love in her eyes. She saw the dear, love-struck sister that she knew months ago. She leaned and kissed her sister's cheek. "Promise me," she whispered.

"I promise. I do not know whether I am excited or scared to see him. My heart feels both right now."

"I know exactly how you feel. Just *show* him how you felt last autumn, and he will be in as much danger of falling in love with you now as he was then. Maybe even more so now that he has seen what it is like to live without you."

"Thank you. It must have been terrible for you—knowing about Mr. Darcy's interference and yet needing to be amiable to him in his time of need."

"Yes, it was at first, but my feelings were pruned, the tears were shed, the clouds parted, and the storm ended . . . just as promised."

Jane looked at her with confusion.

"I am sorry, it is just something the colonel said to me once; I suppose it stuck." They embraced each other and giggled, each so happy for the other to have found a love match. "We always wanted this, Jane. Now it is in reach for both of us! And I, for one, intend to drink a great deal of tea tomorrow, well into the afternoon when a certain someone will arrive. What do you think?"

"I cannot agree with you more."

*****

The carriage arrived just as they returned home from church. And as it turned out, they did not need to drink tea well into the afternoon: Bingley arrived just before luncheon. They had spent the morning in the music room, listening first to Georgiana and then to Elizabeth. Elizabeth had chosen an Italian love song, and she couldn't remember when she had blushed more frequently or consistently; it seemed to permeate every area of her body. Having Mr. Darcy in the room made the words so much more moving and meaningful. She vowed she would never again try to serenade Mr. Darcy in front of others. She felt she had made a complete fool of herself. It did not help when he started singing along with her.

She was reminded of the time she had asked him to sing to her. He had chosen a simple folk song, whereas she had foolishly chosen a love song that made her feel quite exposed. As he sang the male lover's part of the duet, she sang the female lover's part, and try as she might, she could not shake the goose bumps from her arms and neck. His deep, baritone voice made her quiver with a sudden desire to be in his arms and to be kissed as the duet lyrics described. She was beyond embarrassed when Bingley started clapping vigorously in the doorway at the end, thus announcing his arrival.

Elizabeth rose from the bench. "Mr. Bingley!" she cried. "You are here earlier than expected!" She glanced at Jane, who also had risen from her seat. Bingley's eyes scanned the room and then froze on Jane.

The room all waited for him to say something. When he managed to snap out of his distracted state, he answered Elizabeth, "I was able to get an early start," but his eyes remained fixed on Jane. "Miss Bennet, it is an honor to have you in my home. You as well, Miss Elizabeth and Miss Darcy." The last was said as an afterthought, but no one seemed to notice.

He scanned the rest of the room and addressed Darcy, "So, I see you have found a way to be useful! Entertaining ladies is not a habit you once fancied, but I hear congratulations are in order. I am so delighted that you two have found each other, and what a couple you are! Your voices blended so perfectly, and if I knew any Italian I would have said you two were . . . well, I do not know what I would have said. Is it too forward of me, Miss Elizabeth, to remark that you have stolen the most sought-after heart in Derbyshire? And this good man, although undeserving, has won a most-prized possession: a lady's love. Oh dear, I believe I am rambling. Am I rambling? I feel like I am. It must be the journey. Perhaps I should freshen up. Miss Bennet, Miss Elizabeth, will you stay for the noon meal?"

Although he had asked both of them, it was to Jane whom he looked for an answer, and therefore Elizabeth left it up to Jane to answer for the both of them.

Jane blushed and looked briefly at her hands. Then she raised her chin ever so slightly and smiled. "We would be delighted, sir."

Bingley let out a deep breath and smiled widely. "Splendid! If you will excuse me while I change out of my traveling clothes, I assure you I will be back shortly." He stood there a short while and then took determined strides over to Jane. He bowed deeply, right in front of her, and then turned and left, giving Darcy a solid, gentlemanly pat on the shoulder as he exited.

The room was quiet, and everyone seemed to be in limbo, as if the departure of Bingley's vibrant energy left a void that no one else could fill. Elizabeth broke the silence and suggested to Georgiana that fresh tea be ordered. Georgiana left to speak with a maid, and Jane followed her. This left Elizabeth, Darcy, and Colonel Fitzwilliam alone in the music room.

The colonel stood and mumbled something about the stable hand who wanted to speak with him and fled the room as well.

Elizabeth smiled shyly and said, "You sounded wonderful, even better than before."

Darcy smiled back but raised his eyebrow. "When have you heard me sing?"

She slowly sauntered over toward him casually, still a little discomposed from singing a love song with him. "I believe it was just before the third proposal. But I could check my journal to make sure."

"Your journal? You wrote down my proposals?"

"I did. After the third proposal, I wrote down everything I could remember from them. Then I maintained it daily."

"I would very much like to read it . . . for memory recovery purposes, of course."

"Perhaps someday. Thank you for singing for me again."

"I must have been mad to sing for you before I had secured your hand. I do not fancy myself skilled in the art, so please accept my apologies for imposing on you. I can only point out that I was not in my right mind. I usually only sing for Georgiana."

"I know. You told me that at the time." She walked even closer to him.

"What else did I tell you in my deranged state?"

She was in dire need to shake her embarrassment about the song and, as usual, chose the path of humor to calm herself. She raised her eyebrow at him teasingly and said, "That you liked me against your better judgment, against your character, and against your—"

"I did not!" he said cautiously. Had he really said those things to her?

"Indeed you did, sir. That was in the first proposal."

"No wonder you refused me." He had a slightly pained expression in his eyes.

She took the last two steps and kneeled in front of him. "I was right to refuse you then. If I had accepted you with all the feelings and misunderstandings I had about you at the time, I would never feel comfortable doing this." She put her hand in his hair and brushed back his deep brown curls. "Or this." She took his hand, and caressed it against her cheek. And then she leaned over and whispered in his ear, "Or this." She put her hands on his knees and leaned forward toward his eager lips and kissed him.

"I am most sorry for my prideful and insulting words and behavior." He reached up to her face and pressed it to him, letting himself relax into the underserved, but forgiving, kiss. He made sure his lips did their best to remedy whatever damage his harsh words had done in the past. Maybe it was a good thing he did not know how he had offended her. Between lip ministrations, he whispered, "I am so sorry." She hushed him and crawled into his lap, wrapping her arms around his neck, making him move to a new level of love for this woman. She truly was better than he deserved. He truly was a fool in love.

As much as he loved kissing her, he was rightly aware that he needed to set an example for Georgiana, who would be returning soon. He took a moment more and held her tightly against him, feeling the warm, wet moisture from her luscious lips, and daringly he pressed them further, causing her to relax into his attempts to deepen the kiss. He felt her lips part, and he was lost in the passion as their mouths intertwined. She pulled back slightly and looked at him with dark, dazed eyes. He smiled and touched her pink lips with his fingers and said, "If that is what I get when I apologize, then I will gladly do it again."

She smiled at him lovingly. "Perhaps I should make you pay for your sins a little more often."

"They say repentance is good for the soul," he grinned. She smiled back at him teasingly.

"Indeed." She stood up and stepped away just as Georgiana and Jane came in. Following closely behind them was Bingley. The two lovers exchanged a knowing glance and smiled, each remembering the vigorous lip exercise they had shared a moment ago.

The next few hours were spent huddled in three distinct groups. Mr. Bingley did not leave Jane's side, which pleased all interested parties. And Colonel Fitzwilliam and Georgiana felt the need to keep each other company since the third group clearly wanted to speak alone. No one in the room questioned the laughter or giggles coming periodically from Mr. Darcy and Elizabeth, and no one disturbed them.

When the clock struck five, the room held a tangible silence. The Bennet sisters had been at Netherfield for seven hours. Both sisters looked at each other and nodded. It was Jane who spoke first.

"I imagine Mamma is expecting us soon."

Elizabeth knew their mother would let them stay the night if it was up to her—she was probably already scheming on how to make such a plan come to fruition—but they did need to leave. "Papa is probably wondering at the time as well."

Each sister looked at her loved one and stood.

Mr. Bingley called the servant to order the carriage and offered his arm to Jane. She took it and blushed deeply and walked with him to the door. Elizabeth started pushing Mr. Darcy toward the door as well when the colonel offered to take over.

Mr. Darcy let out a little chuckle and offered his arm to Elizabeth. "My lady, do you need assistance?"

She laughed and leaned over slightly and placed her hand on his arm, which was somewhat awkward because his arm was so much lower than hers. "I thank you, sir. I do declare that you have the most gentleman-like manner of all the men of my acquaintance."

Mr. Darcy startled a bit. "What did you say?"

She saw the change in his demeanor, and she tried to explain herself. "I was just teasing you."

"No," he said calmly. "It was the words you used. Something was familiar about them. Say them again."

Elizabeth reviewed her comment, and then awareness graced her features. He must have remembered her terrible accusations at Hunsford. She looked away from him and whispered, "You remember?"

"No, not really. It just sounded familiar. The part where you called me gentlemanly."

She removed her hand from his arm and stood up all the way. "I am afraid that is because I once accused you of less than gentleman-like behavior." She looked up at Colonel Fitzwilliam, who had a kind look upon his face. Up until this point, she had always thought she wanted him to regain his memory. That was the goal, right? Why now was she wishing for his memory to stay gone? She turned away from them and reached for her pelisse. Colonel Fitzwilliam walked over and helped her place it on her shoulders.

He turned his back to Darcy and lowered his voice so only Elizabeth could hear. "Storms, Miss Elizabeth."

Her eyes glossed over, and she blinked back tears. "I think he is remembering my awful refusal—the first one, the one that hurt him terribly. What should I do?"

The colonel had learned a great deal about Elizabeth over the last two weeks. He knew the reasons behind her first refusal. He knew those concerns were resolved now and that Darcy and Elizabeth would be very happy together. But he still did not know why she was so scared. Why did she still not trust Darcy's love for her? It seemed that there was a little more pruning to do. He didn't fancy himself a philosophical gardener, but it seemed time to intervene.

"Miss Elizabeth, I have learned a lot about war. I know less about relationships, but every relationship, just like every battle, has moments where we fail one another. And yet, in the end, it is not about how many lives were lost; it is about how many were saved.

"What does it matter if he remembers?" the colonel asked. "Can you not see the joy the man has now? Can you not see that nothing will make him waver in his devotion? Not anything in your past, not anything in the future—he is yours for the taking. The time for war is past. Declare the victory that is so obvious to everyone else. Now is the time to let the clouds part and see the growth that has come from the storms. It may not be easy to repair the storm damage.

But it is worth it! I think you need to talk to him about that first proposal, but not with fear for what it will do—rather with anticipation for what it can repair."

"I am scared," Elizabeth said. "I am scared that the man I have grown to love will be hurt all over again because of me. How do I go about telling him things that I know will pain him to hear? I do not think I could tell it to him without completely . . ."

"Then do not tell him face to face. Perhaps it is time for him to receive a letter from you. Tell him how you feel now. Tell him how different it is from what you felt then."

"You do not know how I treated him. You do not know the things I said. He will hate me."

He let out a gentle laugh and bowed to her. "I think you might be underestimating his persistence. That look he has in his eyes is unwavering. I saw that same determined look the day he was refused. I saw it in his eyes the morning of the accident when he was determined to give you that letter. I saw it every day when he confided in me his intent to propose. I see it today. The man loves you. He will never let you go now."

Elizabeth sighed and patted his arm. "Thank you," she said. "I will write him a letter. I really should feel more confident in the man; after all, he proposed thirteen times!" She turned back to Mr. Darcy and walked over to him and knelt down at his knees. "Mr. Darcy—"

"Please call me William." Mr. Darcy said with concern in his eyes. He reached up and touched her cheek and searched her eyes, which were still glossy from recent tears. "I am sorry if what I said pained you. But we will have plenty of time to discuss it. Will you come tomorrow?"

"I will, William, I will. Oh, and I have something to give you from your aunt. She gave it to me to give to you. I meant to give it to you earlier, but I suppose I have been quite distracted of late."

"My aunt gave you something? What is it?" Darcy looked to Colonel Fitzwilliam and the cousins exchanged curious looks.

Elizabeth winked at Darcy. "I shall leave that detail a mystery in anticipation for tomorrow."

Darcy took her hand in his and brought it to his lips. He whispered, "I guarantee nothing but seeing you makes me anticipate tomorrow."

CHAPTER 12

The next day was filled with drenching, torrential rain. The Bennet sisters were trapped at home, listening to their mother ramble on about things that they simply did not care about; their thoughts were three miles away at Netherfield. Lace, flowers, wedding trousseaus, and advice on how Jane could secure Mr. Bingley held little interest when the men they wanted to be with were such a short distance away, and yet they were unable to see, touch, or hear them.

On Tuesday, Elizabeth contemplated taking the carriage to Netherfield, rain or not, but was informed the roads were already impassable with mud. She then considered riding on horseback, but her mother wouldn't even hear of it. "On these wet roads, Elizabeth? Your horse would certainly fall, and you would break your neck, no doubt. Then what good would come of you being engaged to a man of ten thousand a year? No, you will wait here until the roads dry."

"Indeed," replied Mr. Bennet tersely. "Who would even contemplate sending her daughter on horseback to Netherfield in the rain? Certainly no one we know."

Mrs. Bennet steeled her eyes at her husband. "It is one thing to ride on horseback when it might possibly rain. It is another thing altogether when the ground is already soaked from two days of storms. Sometimes you can be so ridiculous, Mr. Bennet!"

"Oh yes, I can be quite ridiculous. It must run in the family."

"But I need not ride, Papa," Elizabeth said. "I can walk. It is only three miles. I do not mind getting wet."

"My dear, I know you are anxious, but Harold says the roads are flooded to his knees. I am sincerely worried for your safety. Unless your mother is willing to let you wear breeches and boots, I cannot let you attempt the journey. What do you say, Mrs. Bennet? Shall we see if my clothes will fit her?"

Although disappointed, Elizabeth couldn't help but smile at her mother's aghast look. As Mrs. Bennet began to shriek her reply, Elizabeth retreated to her room. She decided to heed the colonel's suggestion and write to William. The sooner he knew about her horrible accusations and terrible refusal, the sooner they would both be able to move on.

She poured her heart onto the paper, begging his forgiveness. As she wrote, she realized that he had already made amends for his role in the first proposal; he had apologized several times, and each successive proposal had demonstrated his improvement. She had apologized once before, but he didn't remember it. It was time to make her amends.

She had the servant, Harold, set out for Netherfield as soon as the rain started to let up. Unfortunately, the rain and wind returned soon after he left, which only added to her misery. His return from Netherfield took a long time, but she soon learned why. Mr. Darcy had insisted he respond to her letter at once and had made Harold wait while he penned his reply. He had written:

My dearest Elizabeth,

I agree wholeheartedly with you that you must pay for your sins. I shall have to think of a way that is agreeable to both of us.

In the meantime, I have come to the conclusion that it is actually I who should apologize. If you really were as impertinent as your letter claims, I must have provoked you terribly. I am sure I acted unpardonably if I compelled you to declare I was "the last man in the world whom you could ever be prevailed on to marry."

I have learned a thing or two in my many attempts to secure your hand. Nothing I could have said would have changed your opinion so decidedly set against me. It was not until your heart moved, by itself, by your choice, that I finally won your love. But I will not let you ignore the fact that my persistence endured until your heart moved.

I told you once that I prayed for the Lord to change your mind and heart. Each time I prayed, I felt a wave of peace overcome me and I knew he would answer my prayer. I knew I simply had to have faith that things would change. I saw the change in the way you looked at me. Each smile, each blush, and each tender comment inspired me to continue with my efforts. I must admit I saw your love well before you did. Either that or you were aware of my aunt's plans the whole time and wanted to look the heroine.

The man you sent from Longbourn is waiting patiently for me to finish this, and I admit I will delay him a moment longer, for I must tell you how ardently I admire and love you. My heart is so full of longing to see you again, but the weather rules us all, and it does not look like I will get my wish today. I will keep your words close to me and conveniently "forget" what you felt obligated to inform me of concerning that awful first proposal. Truly it does not matter to me if I ever remember the event. Instead I will memorize your kind words of missing me and your sincere attempts to ameliorate my sporadic memories.

However, although I do not remember the event you detailed in your letter, I do remember that we found a most agreeable way for me to pay for my sins. I keenly recall our conclusion that, "Repentance is good for the soul." Therefore, before I absolve you of any ill-doing, I must first see you take the proper steps in the repentance process. I look forward to when our lips can discuss this appropriately so that we can once and for all put that day behind us. Then, and only then, will I truly forgive you. I look forward to that moment.

With all my love,

Fitzwilliam Darcy

Elizabeth, of course, was much relieved and a little embarrassed at his veiled, yet bold, request to kiss her again. His teasing manner was indeed delightful.

She reread all her letters from William that night. The first, and most important, was the letter he gave her the day of the accident. The second, and most cherished, was the love letter in which he proposed. Her well-trained eyes seemed to skip right over the part where he said the match would not be looked upon well. She knew he did not feel that way anymore; therefore, it was no longer distressing to her. The third, although short, was comforting, as it detailed his plans to escort her to Hertfordshire. The fourth, in his light and flirting manner, left her missing him all the more.

When the next day proved to be too wet to travel, she penned a note of her own in response.

Dear William,

I must clarify whether you want me to call you William or Fitzwilliam. You asked me to call you

William, yet you sign your name Fitzwilliam. I only wish to call you what you feel comfortable with.

As for your reference to me paying for my sins, I truly have not the foggiest idea what you could mean. Would you wish for me to see Reverend Anderson? I do not see how he could help my impertinence. If he could, I assure you he would have rid me of it long ago when I slyly snuck the communion bread from the back room to feed the ducks; he seemed somewhat put out that I lavished my attention on them rather than his sermons.

I do recall, however, the method you used to apologize for your sins. Might I be so bold as to inquire whether you are suggesting I use the same method? Rules of society are so different for gentlemen and ladies. Is there not a different method of repentance required of ladies? Perhaps I should consult an etiquette book on the matter, although somehow I doubt what you allude to could be found in an etiquette book. But truthfully, I would be happy to pay for my sins in the exact manner you paid for yours. I admit that moment has occupied more than a few thoughts during my lonely moments.

I shall never tire of hearing you proclaim how "ardently" you admire and love me. I shall consult my journal and count how many times it has been. I can safely assert that you have proclaimed so in nearly every proposal.

Until tomorrow, I leave you to your penitent heart and recommend that you ponder my words: I love you, William, with all my heart.

Oh, Jane sends her regards to Mr. Bingley. Please pass her sincerest regards onto him.

Elizabeth Bennet

*****

Darcy was staring out the window at the rain on Wednesday when he noticed someone outside. He immediately recognized the man running to the servant entrance of Netherfield through the rain. It had to be another letter from Elizabeth. He waited patiently for the doors to open, and soon he was rewarded. There on the butler's tray was her elegant, feminine handwriting. He offered his thanks to the butler as he claimed it, ignoring the teasing comments from his cousin. Mr. Bingley hovered at his elbow as he opened it.

After he finished reading the missive, he said, "Well, Bingley, Longbourn misses us. I am to send Miss Bennet's sincerest regards on to you."

"Truly? She really sent her regards?"

"Indeed she did, and if you so desire, I will pass on your response in my reply. If you would be so kind as to push me over to the desk, I will begin immediately." Bingley did just that, and while Darcy wrote, Bingley paced, rehearsing his message to Miss Bennet.

My dearest Elizabeth,

Hearing my name, any name, from your lips is a knee-weakening moment for me. Fortunately for my pride, each time you have called me William, I have already been sitting down. Had it been otherwise, we may both have been in danger of further injury.

And do not play coy with me, you minx. By now you should know that ladies are held to much higher standards than gentlemen. These standards, aimed at preserving the reputation of the lady, provide only further evidence that ladies are held in higher regard. If there ever comes a time in society when a man no longer offers his services to assist a lady into a carriage or bows appropriately to acknowledge his respect, it will be a sad day.

So, my point, darling, is that if you insist on me paying for my sins appropriately, society dictates you pay an even higher price for yours. I must insist that you repent profusely . . . and not with Reverend Anderson. I am sure he would not appreciate the particular form of repentance I am referring to.

Bingley has finally stopped pacing and wishes for me to assure you that Miss Bennet is most welcome at Netherfield any day she would like. He states that, at the moment, he can think of no better way to spend his time than getting reacquainted with her. I believe he wishes to say more but cannot think of an adequate mode of expression. I will interject the following on his behalf: he is a lovesick puppy. Send her my regards as well.

We have not had any time to discuss when you wish to marry. I, of course, would prefer to wait until I am actually able to walk. Since my foot is expected to be fully healed in a little over three weeks, my vote is to have the bans read now. If this is too soon, I will understand.

Sincerely,

William Darcy

*****

When poor Harold finally returned from Netherfield Wednesday evening, it was already dark. Elizabeth thanked Hill for the letter and retreated to her room. She read eagerly, giggling, and then quickly found Jane and told her all that Bingley had said. She even told her what William had interjected. As predicted, Jane blushed and asked that Elizabeth give Bingley a response from her, but she knew not what to say. While Jane deliberated, Elizabeth wrote:

Mon petite chou (My little cabbage),

> *You did say I could call you anything I wanted. I suspect that your knees did not go weak at that. You should know by now that giving me such leeway will only cause you heartache, or at the least, a headache.*
> *So, I must conclude that I do indeed need to repent. But if I am not to seek the Reverend Anderson, then who can assist me? Oh, very well, I cannot claim I do not know of what you speak. I, too, wish to hold you again. I promise Reverend Anderson will never be party to such ministrations; his old heart may not be able to take it. Yours, on the other hand, would do well under such strain.*
> *As to when we should marry, I do not care whether you can walk, but I do see the wisdom of waiting until you are able to get in and out of a carriage without the assistance of five men. It would be a very crowded honeymoon. And for your valet's sake, let us refrain from having you enter or exit a carriage unless absolutely necessary until you can walk again; I am sure he did not appreciate your dirty, dusty breeches after returning from Longbourn. If only you*

could hear my laughter as I wrote that! I wish I could have witnessed your face as you read it.

This rain is most frustrating. Every morning I wake with hopes of seeing you, and every morning I am forced to wait. It never seems to let up, and I fear the roads will be unsafe for a while yet. Until then, I will simply await your letters.

Please inform Mr. Bingley that Jane feels as if the long months apart are now fading memories, and she looks forward to being able to renew their acquaintance.

Since you felt the need to interject something, I must also. She is in much need of additional encouragement. His kindness on Sunday was indeed felt, but I believe she is not in the mood for long, drawn-out conversations. I believe she wants to see him just as badly as I want to see you. Now, if she knew I said such a thing, I am afraid she would blush so deeply that her hair would turn red and Bingley would no longer recognize her.

Perhaps tomorrow we will be able to discuss wedding plans. I would be delighted to have the banns read now. I do not know where you desire to marry, perhaps Pemberley, but I would very much like my sister Jane to stand up with me. She is planning to visit my aunt and uncle Gardiner in London in June. We could marry either in the Meryton church in five weeks or in London at the end of June, if you like.

I miss you terribly. I feel like I won a prize and then had it taken from me and put out of reach on a high shelf to simply admire from afar.

With my deepest regards,

Yours,

Elizabeth

She sealed the letter and went to find Harold. When she found him in the kitchen eating dinner, she smiled and asked, "Would you mind delivering this tomorrow morning?"

"As long as you don't expect me to go out again tonight, miss," he chuckled. "A man must eat and sleep sometime!" His impertinence was not lost on Elizabeth, but she found she didn't mind.

*****

The next morning during breakfast, Bingley jumped up and cried, "Someone is here! I believe you have another letter, Darcy!" He bolted toward the front door and returned immediately. He handed the letter to Darcy and stood impatiently nearby.

Colonel Fitzwilliam laughed. "Darcy, do read quickly," he said. "I do not think Bingley can stand it much longer."

Darcy looked up at the expectant face of his best friend. "Do you wish to know if Miss Bennet has any words for you, or do you wish to read a private letter from my betrothed? If the latter, then I will refuse you such an opportunity. If the former, then step back, and let me enjoy the moment."

"I am terribly sorry. Of course. If only I could write to Miss Bennet myself!" Bingley stepped away and ran his fingers through his hair.

The colonel smiled at the two men in front of him. They were besotted through and through. Neither one of them had a lick of sense anymore. It was always "Elizabeth this" or "Miss Bennet that". But he especially pitied Bingley. He had come to Netherfield specifically to court Miss Bennet, and all his plans of love had been thwarted by the rain. Of the two suitors, Bingley stood to lose the most. The colonel decided to help him out.

"You know, Bingley," he began, "if you were to write down your feelings for Miss Bennet, it might make you less anxious. I have heard it is rather cathartic to express oneself on paper. Of course, one would have to be rather careful to make sure such a letter was not accidently folded into Darcy's next letter to Miss Elizabeth. He is so distracted of late, and, well, anything could happen. I warn you to be very deliberate about where you place such a note."

Bingley's eyes brightened. "What an interesting suggestion, Colonel," he said. "Perhaps a very expressive, heartfelt letter would do me good."

"I imagine so," Colonel Fitzwilliam replied. He watched Darcy chuckle and laugh at his letter, and Bingley sat down at the writing desk, leaning over the paper in serious deliberation. *If only love could strike me as it has struck these two good men.*

*****

The fifth day of rain was especially disheartening. Elizabeth paced in her father's library. "Must it rain so much?"

Mr. Bennet recognized how trapped his favorite daughter felt. "I suppose you could move somewhere else, but it is England after all, and it is springtime. What were you expecting? I am sure as soon as it lets up, you shall see Mr. Darcy again. That is, unless he has forgotten the engagement."

"Oh, Papa, will you always tease him about his memory?"

"You know, I used to have a daughter who laughed at my jokes. Either she has already left me or my jokes have lost their humor. Since I favor my own jokes, I will assume that your mind is otherwise engaged. No pun intended." He gave her a quirky smile, seeing that she too realized what poor company she was being.

"I am sorry, Papa. It just feels strange to be away from him. Did you ever feel that way about Mamma?" Elizabeth slumped down into the leather chair and let her head fall against the back.

Mr. Bennet wasn't good at deep, thought-provoking conversation. He knew it was one of his weaknesses as a father, but with five daughters and a silly wife, how could one manage taking anything seriously?

"Poppet," he began, "you know how I feel about your mother. I need not discuss it with you. I might add that I just witnessed Harold walk past the window. . . and if I am correct . . ." They listened as the servant's door opened and Harold called out to Hill that he had another message for Elizabeth. "Yes, there it is. I believe you have news from Netherfield. Would you still like to discuss my relationship with your mother, or shall I save that delightful conversation for another day?" Mr. Bennet looked at his daughter. She was sitting straight up in anticipation, staring at the door of his study, and apparently hadn't heard anything he had said.

Mr. Bennet sighed, and they waited in silence. When a knock was heard at the study door, Elizabeth jumped up and answered it.

"Miss Elizabeth, you have a letter," said Mrs. Hill.

"Thank you," Elizabeth replied. She started opening the letter right then and there but then thought better of it. "Papa, I will not bother you anymore. Thank you." Walking out of the room, she found a quiet place to read her letter. It was several pages this time, and she felt her excitement building.

Dear Miss Bennet,

What? Why was he being so formal? She read a few lines and quickly surmised the letter was not intended for her. She flipped to the next page and saw Mr. Darcy's familiar hand.

Dearest Elizabeth,

Another day of rain means another day of sitting thinking about you. I think about your lovely brown curls and how I have yet to comb my fingers through them. I think about your delicate hands and how it felt to hold them during our ride in the carriage from Kent. Yes, I do remember that, although vaguely. I think of your engaging, captivating eyes and the expressions that dance on your face. I think of many things, most of which I dare not write in the event that someone besides you were to read this. But I miss you terribly.

As for the dirty, dusty breeches comment, there are two things you must know. First, when I read it, I was not in the least bit embarrassed, rather flattered that you took the opportunity to look at my backside. I hope it met with your approval. The second thing is to let you know that when the colonel heard me laugh so loudly, he insisted I reveal the source of such jovial entertainment. He too enjoyed your comments and laughed heartily.

Now, do not worry, I have not read to him any other part of the letters you have written to me. I only shared that little section with him. I confess this to you now to show you that I can laugh at myself, and, more importantly, in hopes that I might have reason to ask for your forgiveness again. Since we have concluded that forgiveness is a noble virtue, one which we both earnestly seek, I am now eager to find an excuse to beg your forgiveness. I am afraid that ever since I experienced the merits of being forgiven, there is little left for me to think about. I do not even have a book to distract me, because we forgot to look for one when we went to your father's study.

I think a wedding in Meryton's church would be wonderful. I hope five weeks is enough time for your mother to organize such an event because I doubt I will be able to wait a day longer. In fact, let us set the exact date. What do you say to June 13? If I am correct, that is a Wednesday. After the wedding breakfast, we could travel to a small estate of mine that I frequently use on my travels to London. From there we could leave Thursday for the rest of the ride to Pemberley. I do not think there is a better time to see Pemberley than late spring, unless it is early autumn, mid-summer, or late winter; but then again, I am a little biased.

I also thought you would enjoy celebrating our anniversary on the thirteenth, a date you might find meaningful. Some say the number thirteen is an unlucky number, but I have found it to be very lucky, even miraculous. I have been meaning to ask you, what was it that I finally said in proposal number thirteen that made you change your mind?

How I love you so! I must apologize to Miss Bennet, for Bingley has nothing for me to report to her in my letter. I must also apologize for wasting ink and paper, for somehow my letter has grown to several pages, yet I only remember writing one. Perhaps you could ask Miss Bennet to review the contents and see for herself how I could have written such a long letter. Please inform her that everyone at Netherfield sends their good wishes. And if she desires to send any good wishes in reply, I would be happy to distribute them. I pray tomorrow that the clouds will part and that we can be reunited.

Sincerely, your most devoted admirer,

282

William

Elizabeth laughed at the letter in her hands. Their attempts at matchmaking Mr. Bingley and Jane were worse than her mother's! And that was saying something! She stood and went to find Jane. She had a delivery to make on behalf of Mr. Bingley.

*****

Friday at Netherfield was spent in anticipation of a response from the Bennet sisters.

Darcy requested some entertainment after luncheon, and Georgiana was relieved to do something other than work on her lessons. Mrs. Annesley was kind but insisted that she maintain her studies.

Georgiana also managed to escape long enough to talk with her brother that afternoon. She was so relieved that he really did have his memory back, most of it at least, and the joy in his eyes was greater than she had ever seen. It lit up his whole face. He expressed how proud he was of her. They even discussed Mr. Wickham and the incident at Ramsgate, a topic that they had always avoided. Now, he said, she was ready to be told everything. After a deep breath, Darcy explained every detail of his dealings with Wickham.

Hours later, Georgiana was still pondering what her brother had told her. She shuddered to imagine the things Darcy had described. It was hard to believe any man capable of such actions, let alone someone she had once walked with arm in arm. It made her feel melancholy. She was staring out into the stormy sunset with such thoughts when she saw a rider come up to the front gates.

"Who could that be at this hour?" she asked.

Both Bingley and Darcy perked up. Bingley rose and went to the front door and returned with a letter in hand. "Well, Darcy! We, I mean you, have a letter from Miss Elizabeth." He took long strides and handed his friend the letter. He peered over his shoulder, waiting for him to open it.

Calmly holding the letter, Darcy said, "Georgiana, would you mind playing the pianoforte again for us? Something soothing and calming, perhaps. Why do you not take a seat, Bingley? And then I will share what Elizabeth has to say."

Bingley knew it was a subtle warning, but he couldn't help himself. Was there a letter in there for him? Or did Miss Bennet think him too bold? "I would indeed like something relaxing to listen to. I will push you over to the chaise, Darcy, so you and I can enjoy the music together."

Georgiana nodded and walked over to the pianoforte. William had received many letters over the last few days, and she had seen him reread them frequently. She loved to see his initial reaction as he read one for the first time. Bingley helped him to stand and Darcy pivoted from the wheeled chair to the chaise. Madeline stood to assist but was not needed. It seemed William was doing so well these last few days that she was not needed much of the time. She propped his foot up on a pillow. William uttered his appreciation, and she nodded and sat back down. Georgiana placed her hands on the keys and began the concerto, all the while watching her brother.

Darcy opened the letter and was pleased to see a second, sealed envelope with feminine handwriting that stated, "Netherfield". He smiled, took pity on Bingley, and said casually, "Bingley, there is a note for Netherfield in my letter. I assume that it is meant for you." He hardly had a chance to finish his sentence before the letter was snatched from his hand.

Bingley looked down at the letter he was holding and smiled. "I have not the faintest idea what this could be."

Darcy chuckled, along with Colonel Fitzwilliam. Then he focused on his letter from Elizabeth. He slowly read each word as the music played.

Dear William,

I shall have to return to calling you William since you made no comment about me calling you "mon petite chou". I can only infer that you were deeply offended, so I offer you my most sincere apologies and will ask for your forgiveness as soon as possible— tomorrow, if we are lucky.

As you can see, Jane did have some comments about the length of your letter, which she felt obliged to share with the party at Netherfield. I assume whatever kept her blushing and smiling all day was explained in her comments. I feel secure in knowing that her words will find their way to those who desire to read them.

My father wishes to send his approval of June 13. My mother, on the other hand, will not stop asking why it must be on a Wednesday. Did you not know that weddings must be done on Saturdays? I am being well educated on how a wedding should and should not be done, and my mother has a great deal to do with any frustrated sentiments in this letter.

In fact, I think she is considering turning me out completely and sending me to Netherfield tomorrow and Jane too. For once, I see her logic. I do not know if she is gaining more sense, or if I am losing mine, but we are beginning to think alike.

I must state that rain or not, I intend to see you tomorrow, so I suggest you start praying for sun. I do not know what has come over me! I feel like a wild animal that has been caged! My only respite has been your letters, and I thank you so kindly for them. I admit I now know most of them by heart.

I will attempt to be in a better mood, but would it be too much to ask to have a little relief from the pouring rain? I just need one day with you, and then I will be able to endure Mother Nature's continual spring deluge. And who came up with the name "Mother Nature"? Why must all things that vex me be mothers?

Forgive me. I am in a foul mood. My mother is ready to send us on horseback to Netherfield in this weather, heedless of the risk, but I see I already mentioned her desires to do so above. Now I seem to be repeating myself. Not only does my mother want to make sure I am a "good little soon-to-be-wife", but she thinks she has the power to see to it that Mr. Bingley and Jane have a future as well. If she only knew what you and I have been up to! At least seeing Jane happy has brought a smile to my face. Thank you for your efforts on their behalf.

I wish to defer answering your question regarding why your thirteenth proposal finally changed my mind until we can speak in person. I do have a ready answer, one that if you truly had all of your memory back would not surprise you. Can I be any more secretive? We shall see.

Do not worry too much over this letter; I admit I am not in the best of moods. But then again, storms do end with a promise. (Read that last line to Colonel Fitzwilliam. He will enjoy that. He might even have a parable or two to relate.) I hope the clouds part soon.

If they do, you might see me walk to Netherfield, and you will once again be shocked at my appearance, for I will have six inches of mud on my petticoat! It will be a familiar scene I am afraid to admit.

I shall close this depressing missive and send it to you with my deepest love,

Elizabeth

Mr. Darcy looked up and caught Georgiana's watchful, concerned eyes. He must have shown his concern at Elizabeth's frustrations and the tone of her letter. He gave her a reassuring smile. He looked over to Bingley, who was staring off absentmindedly with the biggest grin on his face. At least his letter was good.

If only he could ride to Longbourn and help improve her spirits. But how could he get there with a broken foot? He once again felt an overwhelming frustration that he was confined to a chair. If he had two good feet, he would have found a way to Longbourn. He would have swum through the mud, if necessary. As it was, he could only hope the roads would be better tomorrow. Colonel Fitzwilliam's voice broke his concentration.

"I believe I no longer hear rain. Could it be? Has it stopped?"

Darcy tried to sit up straighter and see out the window, but he was too far away. Bingley, however, bolted up out of his dazed, contented state and dashed to the window.

"It has stopped! And I see the moon!" Bingley said.

Colonel Fitzwilliam smiled. "Thank goodness! Now I will not be forced to spend another day with two grown men moping around the house, plotting to somehow use their fortunes or connections to alter the weather. Let us all hope that the clouds and rain stay away because I do not think Georgiana and I can endure seeing you two lament about your ladies at Longbourn anymore. I think I will retire early with a glass of brandy. Will you gentlemen join me?

And so they did. They discussed everything, and yet nothing, while sipping the amber liquid. The fire died down, and all three men knew it was time to retire. Bingley made an observation that all three were keenly aware of: the rain indeed had stopped.

*****

It was early Saturday afternoon, and the skies were sunny. Elizabeth and Jane received a note inviting them to Netherfield and they planned to depart as soon as the roads were passable. They each took turns looking at the road and reporting its condition, and it seemed their wait was almost over.

Each sister was wrapped up in her own, similar thoughts, when there was an unwelcome visitor at the door. Elizabeth recognized the shrill, commanding voice immediately. Her mouth tightened and her brows knitted together. Jane noticed something was amiss and looked inquisitively at her. Elizabeth whispered, "You are about to meet Lady Catherine de Bourgh."

"What is she doing here?" Jane said with a very worried look on her face.

"I assume it is to carry out her threat that, 'this match, to which you have the presumption to aspire, will never take place,'" Elizabeth said, imitating Lady Catherine's nasal voice with all the impertinence she could muster. She tried to sound like she was not afraid of the woman, but in truth, Elizabeth was shaking, and her palms had become damp. *She cannot take William away from me, no matter what she attempts!* But she felt far from reassured. Elizabeth stood up and faced the entrance as the very lady herself was being shown in.

Jane stood and stepped back to the side. She carefully watched her sister for signs of discomfort and tried to think of a way to help.

Lady Catherine pushed her way into the room, followed by Mr. Collins and another gentleman Elizabeth did not recognize. Elizabeth had just opened her mouth to welcome them when she was interrupted.

"Miss Bennet, you can be at no loss to understand the reason for my treacherous journey here on such difficult roads."

Elizabeth answered her, "The title Miss Bennet is rightfully claimed by my eldest sister, Jane. But you are mistaken, madam. I cannot account for the honor of seeing you here."

"Impertinent girl! You knew whom I was addressing! You ought not to trifle with me. However rude and insincere you feel the right to be, you shall not find me so. I come with alarming news that you, Miss Elizabeth Bennet, must account for. I speak with all sincerity and frankness and demand to know at once whether or not it is true!"

Elizabeth still hadn't heard any alarming news, and she was at a loss to guess what subject Lady Catherine was referring to. Her engagement to Mr. Darcy was over a week old; it was hardly news now, even if Lady Catherine considered it alarming. "I must ask that you be clearer in your declaration, your ladyship, for I do not take your meaning."

"You claim you know nothing of why I am here? You see no error in your behavior? Am I to assume that you feel the right to steal from me?"

"Steal from you? Lady Catherine, I assure you I know nothing of what you speak."

She smiled in a mischievous way and spoke to the man Elizabeth did not recognize. "She denies it. But we shall see about that scandalous falsehood." Turning back to Elizabeth, she said, "I want my book back. Mr. Collins saw it in your possession when you left, a full week after you were to give it to my nephew. Now what do you say? Did you or did you not admire it and its contents?"

"If you are referring to the late Mr. Darcy's book on flowers and plants of northern England, then I declare you are correct that I admired it. You, however, are quite mistaken if you are under the impression that I desired it for myself. I only wished—"

Lady Catherine interrupted her and raised her voice to new octaves. "Then you admit that you still have it in your possession?"

Elizabeth felt flushed in her face and saw Jane slip out the servant's door. *Why would she leave me to face this alone?* Elizabeth stood as tall as she could. "Mr. Collins did indeed see it among my possessions. He very haphazardly threw it in my trunks with the rest of my belongings. He can claim no caution with how he turned me out that night. If I had been afforded even ten minutes to pack my own things," she said, "I would have had time to place the book in Mr. Darcy's hands."

Lady Catherine laughed menacingly. "Oh, I see! You wish to deflect blame from yourself onto a man of the cloth, your host! You would have us believe that this is somehow Mr. Collins' fault? You admit to two weeks' worth of possession of the said object, but now claim that if given a mere ten minutes, you would have given the book to Darcy. I think not! What reason could you have that made you hold onto it for a full week's time? The book is not yours!"

"Madam, I assure you I am well aware the book is not mine. And I might correct you when you repeatedly say that I stole from you. Indeed I did not. The book was given to me to give to Mr. Darcy. It is no longer yours to stake a claim on."

"Then you have stolen from my nephew! A most-prized family heirloom! Is this not evidence enough of your mercenary ways? First, you aspire to marry my nephew—you, a country girl, with no fortune, connections, or dowry—and then you steal from him before the marriage has even taken place? What else have you taken? Perhaps we need to conduct a thorough search of your room!"

Lady Catherine turned once again and spoke to the man who still had not been introduced. "Is that not what you came here to do? She has all but admitted to having the book in her possession! I suggest you do your job as magistrate, and seize the property she has stolen."

The man stepped forward. "I would like to ask you a few questions, miss," he said.

Elizabeth was beyond furious. "Excuse me, but I am under no obligation to answer any of your questions! You force your way into my home, accuse me of crimes that I have not committed, and now you wish to question me? Did you really believe the rants of a bitter, old woman so readily?" Lady Catherine scoffed.

The man said, "My name is Sir Reginald Williams. I am the magistrate in Kent. I traveled fifty miles to discuss the incident that may or may not have taken place in my jurisdiction. I am a fair man. I listen to all parties. Now, do you have this book in your possession?"

Lady Catherine screeched, "Of course she has it! Of course she denies it! Do you imagine that someone immoral enough to steal from me would simply tell you whether or not she still possessed the stolen item? This is not to be borne! You must search her belongings!"

Elizabeth said nothing. She did indeed have the book. She evaluated the three visitors before her. Mr. Collins was looking at her with unabashed hatred—which was now a mutual feeling between them—and his tongue was hanging out in a dumb-dog-like expression. Lady Catherine feigned serious displeasure but Elizabeth could see her hidden smile and pompous confidence. Sir Reginald seemed kind and had said he was a fair man. Would he listen to her explanation? Would simply having the book in her possession be enough proof to arrest her?

She faltered momentarily in her answer. "Perhaps we should consult Mr. Darcy. Since it is his book, and your ladyship has agreed that you gave it to him, I suggest we defer this conversation until he is present."

Lady Catherine scoffed again. "And let him watch his betrothed be arrested right before his eyes?" she sneered. "Have you no heart?"

"I am afraid that accusation would only rightfully apply to the titled woman who stands scoffing in front of me. It is you who cannot feel joy when your nephew finds his own happiness. It is you who busies yourself with vile and conniving schemes."

Elizabeth continued, "Do you really think that I would withhold something that would bring my future husband joy? You say it is of great worth, and I assure you it is. But it was not until I suggested you give it to him that you even considered such a notion. First, you accused me of stealing it from you, now you say that you actually gave it to my betrothed. Do you expect me to cower to your demands? I must ask all of you to leave this very moment."

Lady Catherine bellowed, "Tell me at once, do you or do you not have the book?"

Elizabeth heard the front door open and then saw the very reassuring sight of Colonel Fitzwilliam entering the room. He stood a whole head taller than everyone else.

Colonel Fitzwilliam breathlessly asked, "What can I do for you, Aunt Catherine?"

"Nothing, Richard. I am here to see justice for a crime that Miss Elizabeth Bennet has committed."

"Yes, Miss Bennet's note mentioned the book, and I came immediately to clarify a few things." He stretched out his hand to Sir Reginald. "I am Colonel Richard Fitzwilliam, the least favorite nephew of this lady. And you are?"

"Sir Reginald Williams, Colonel. I am the local magistrate in Kent. Miss Elizabeth Bennet will not answer whether or not she has the book in her possession. Perhaps you could assist us in gaining her cooperation."

The colonel smiled and gave a wink to Elizabeth and then stepped between her and the three travelers. He answered Sir

Reginald with a serious look on his face. "Of course she still has the book! Darcy is fully aware she has the book. I do not see the problem."

Elizabeth wasn't sure where the colonel was going with this line of speaking, but when Sir Reginald asked her to confirm if this was correct, she nodded.

Sir Reginald looked disgusted for a moment. Repeating himself he asked, "Mr. Darcy is aware you have it?"

Colonel answered for her, "Of course he is! And he has no reason to doubt that she will return it. I personally overheard them discussing it six days ago. He has been aware of it being in her possession for at least that long, possibly even longer."

Elizabeth watched with relief as Colonel Fitzwilliam gallantly defused the situation. "If you need his witness," he continued, "Darcy is on his way here and can clarify everything. He has a broken foot and getting in and out of a carriage is a little tricky, but my word as a colonel should be good enough."

Sir Reginald turned to Lady Catherine. "Madam, it seems that there has been no crime committed. Certainly the word of your nephew is good enough for me. Now, if you will excuse me, I have fifty miles of bad road to travel and hours to contemplate your obstinacy in accusing a fine lady of such an act. I shall be leaving now." He turned to Elizabeth and bowed. "Miss Elizabeth, forgive me for intruding on your afternoon in such a manner. I assure you Lady Catherine de Bourgh will not trespass on your hospitality one moment longer. Is that not correct, your ladyship?"

Elizabeth had watched in delight as Lady Catherine's face became more and more heated during Sir Reginald's address. But when Sir Reginald suggested Lady Catherine leave, Elizabeth thought she would see the lady's eyes bug out. She tried not to smile.

Lady Catherine spoke to her nephew. "Richard, I cannot believe you have turned on your own family! Your father will hear about this!"

The colonel replied, "I hope he does, and would you mind telling him the wedding will be here in Meryton on June 13? He will be pleased to know that Darcy has found a woman worthy of his sister's only son. I am sure my father will insist on being introduced to the lady who has caught the heart of the most eligible bachelor in northern England!

"I shall write today to inform him of the love match. It is a pity that so many of us marry for money. It is a pity that so many of us who have money have so much to lose. Ah, I think I hear the carriage now. Aunt Catherine, would you like to stay and hear what Darcy has on his mind? I understand he knows a little about your own love match, a match that I understand was—"

"Enough!" Lady Catherine shrieked. "Do not speak of what you do not know!"

Elizabeth was suddenly very curious. "Do tell me of the love match of this fine lady, Colonel Fitzwilliam. I find myself quite interested in love stories of late." Lady Catherine shot her a look that could have killed, but Elizabeth just laughed. "Do tell me! I am exceedingly intrigued from my head to my toes!"

The woman lowered her voice, "Richard . . . I warn you. You have a duty, a sense of loyalty that Darcy never had. Do not speak of things you know nothing about."

The colonel took a seat and crossed one leg over the other and smiled. "Miss Elizabeth, it happened a long time ago—"

Lady Catherine turned around and called to Mr. Collins, who faithfully followed her out the front door. Sir Reginald bowed again and followed after them. The colonel let out a deep chuckle and then stood up. "I am terribly sorry for my aunt's behavior. What book were they talking about?"

Elizabeth released all her tension into one giant, unladylike burst of laughter that could have rivaled the undignified snorts of her sister, Lydia. When she recovered, she said, "Colonel, now I must know this story of Lady Catherine, and why it made her turn and pivot as if you had poked her with a branding iron!"

He chuckled again. "I have no idea!" he said. "Darcy simply instructed me to threaten to tell the story of her own love match from long ago. He did not have time to expand on it, so I was quite shocked that the little he did give me was enough to make her leave! I have never before been so curious to hear juicy gossip from my cousin! And I assure you, I *will* hear it!"

CHAPTER 13

Elizabeth laughed so hard her sides hurt. "So, you had no idea what book Lady Catherine was ranting about?"

Colonel Fitzwilliam smiled widely, shaking his head. "No. But I have learned to piece clues together pretty quickly. It is a useful skill on the battlefield; a soldier can never be too observant. All I knew was what I overheard you telling Darcy the day before the rain started. You said my aunt gave you something to give to him.

"Then, when Jane's note arrived at Netherfield informing us that Aunt Catherine was here, demanding something about a book of his . . . well, I just pieced two and two together. I confiscated your servant's already-saddled horse and raced here as fast as I could, hoping to be of some use. I am afraid I left your man quite stranded."

"Yes, and from the looks of your calves, the roads are quite muddy still," Elizabeth laughed again.

Colonel Fitzwilliam stood up immediately. "Dear Lord! I am filthy! I did not mean to get mud on your chair. Mrs. Bennet will be furious with me!"

"Do not worry," assured Elizabeth. "I believe the heroics of your actions will spare you her displeasure on that point. Thank you, by the way." Elizabeth smiled back at Colonel Fitzwilliam, who nodded his acceptance of her gratitude, and then she said in a much more serious tone, "Is he really on his way here?"

Colonel Fitzwilliam tried to mask his face. "Of whom do you speak?"

She blushed brightly. "Mr. Darcy."

He chuckled, "I know, Miss Elizabeth. I just like to see the look in your eyes when you say his name. You know, I saw that look weeks ago, immediately after the accident. During that first day when he was unconscious and no one could get you to leave his side, I knew, even then, that you had stronger feelings for him than you realized.

"But to answer your question, yes, he is on his way. Bingley too. I imagine they will be here in another ten minutes. Now, we must come up with a plan of attack. We must find out the story behind Aunt Catherine's love match. I guarantee it was not her marriage to Sir Lewis de Bourgh."

Elizabeth stepped into the hall to order tea and refreshments to be ready in ten minutes, and then she returned to the colonel. "I do have a strong desire to hear the story that left her quivering in her boots! What are you thinking?"

The colonel chuckled. "I may be good at manipulating the enemy, but Darcy is a stone wall. I have never had much luck with him. I was hoping you had a secret tool you could use to—how shall we put this—*persuade* him into telling us all he knows."

"I can think of a few secret tools, but none of them involve you hearing the story."

"And is that how you pay me back for rescuing you from that horrid relative of mine?"

"Perhaps I might be able to get him to speak. I will do my best." And then as an afterthought, she smirked and added, "He has a lot to atone for." She laughed at her little joke that only Mr. Darcy would understand.

Colonel Fitzwilliam gave her a curious grin but shook off his desire to pursue that last comment. It was obviously something that she did not intend to share. He watched her look outside as they sat in silence for a spell.

A few minutes later, Jane came in and went straight to Elizabeth. "I am so sorry I left you alone with her!" she said. "I could tell she was here to make trouble. The only thing I could think of was to go get help! Luckily, Harold had the horse saddled, and I sent him with the note as fast as he could ride. After that I tried to find Papa. If anyone could stand up to Lady Catherine, it would be him. "

Elizabeth took Jane's hands in hers. "I understand now. Thank you so much. You did the right thing. But I am told that we will be having more desirable visitors in a few minutes. Would you help me change into my rose-colored dress?"

The colonel rolled his eyes. "I feel for you ladies who cannot see that a mere dress is hardly noticeable to a man who is in love. I doubt he will notice what you are wearing."

Elizabeth raised her eyebrow and said, "Do you doubt my methods of extracting information, Colonel?" Awareness graced his features, and she giggled as she left the room.

"Well, I admit I have never tried that method on an enemy," he mumbled under his breath.

*****

The colonel stood there for several minutes, unsure if he should sit down in his muddy pants, wait for Darcy to arrive, or return his horse to the stranded servant at Netherfield. After a few minutes, he heard the carriage out front, and he found his choice was made for him. Darcy and Bingley had arrived, bringing him a new set of clothes and returning the stranded servant as well.

The colonel went out to meet the carriage and passed Bingley, who was making a beeline to the front door with a look of determination on his face. He chuckled at Bingley's impatience. When he turned back to help Darcy out of the carriage, his cousin had already descended to the ground.

"Darcy, man! Look at you! Mr. Cummings would be very proud! I am trying not to laugh at your hopping skills, but I admit they are better than your scooting skills. Careful now, no putting weight on your foot."

Darcy pivoted and sat in the chair. "Yes, I know, Richard. But I have cheated a little, touching my toes down a few times, and the foot seems to tolerate it well." The colonel gave him a disapproving look.

"Richard, it has been nearly three weeks of not using it. It is hard to imagine that I will be ready to walk down the aisle next month unless I start practicing. Besides, I have Madeline's permission to begin applying very slight pressure. She has been doing stretching exercises without the splint, and it feels good to move it again. She flexes and rotates it ever so gently. The woman has a great touch."

The colonel started wheeling Darcy over the cobblestone drive and into the house. He grumbled under his breath, "Yes, you are getting touched by quite a few ladies lately."

Darcy felt for Richard. They had shared a long talk one day during the rainstorms about Richard's marriage prospects. Richard had always been a smooth talker; he was a ladies' man, an ever-confident charmer, and an evasive bachelor. But Richard had confided his regrets that day.

Seeing how happy Darcy was with a woman who loved him just as deeply as he loved her made Richard question his own marriage criteria. As a second son, it was no secret that Richard had to marry into wealth. He often used it as an excuse to avoid women in whom he was not interested. He declared confidently that a marriage of financial convenience was necessary and thereby felt safe to flirt and enjoy any lady's company.

But now he was reevaluating his priorities. He wanted what Darcy had and what they hoped Bingley very soon would have. He wanted a woman with whom he could create a real foundation for a happy life. They had spent several hours discussing various ladies and the unique qualities that appealed to Richard.

Darcy had given only one piece of counsel: "Do not let society's rules and restrictions limit your opportunities. In other words, duty be damned." Richard had been thoughtful and stood and looked out the window for the longest time before he responded.

"It worked for you. Perhaps I shall someday see love in a woman's eyes like Miss Elizabeth's love for you." That night, Darcy had been overcome with gratitude for Elizabeth. Without her, he would still be as sad and alone as he had always been; he had never realized how lonely he was until he met her.

Light, feminine laughter awakened Darcy out of his thoughts from a few nights ago. He looked up at the source and, sure enough, his heart stopped. There, descending the stairs was the lady who had changed every facet of his life: heart, body, and soul. She had her hair in the most attractive, elegant, braided bun, leaving long, brown, cascading curls both on the sides of her rosy cheeks and at the nape of her neck. The dress he had only seen once before, and it had a more-than-flattering neckline; he was ashamed to admit it, but his eyes immediately noticed how nicely it accented her curves. He took a deep breath in response to her beauty, but he was overwhelmed. It had been six very long days without seeing her, and she could not have been more welcoming.

Her bright eyes flashed flirtatious, loving, and yes, intimate looks full of longing. She had missed him. It was always easy to read Elizabeth's expressions, but he was acutely attuned to them at the moment. He smiled up at her, and reached his hand out to her even though she was still a few feet away from him. She elegantly curtsied before offering her hand, and she gave him a wink.

That wink was what did it. Up until that moment, he was overwhelmed with her presence, but now, now he was beyond reason. He needed to hold her. He needed to tell her how much he had missed her. He kissed her hand, and then looked in her eyes and smiled. He prayed that they would find a way to properly welcome each other, and it wasn't just a figure of speech—he truly prayed that he could get her alone. He admitted that praying to the Lord Almighty for a few stolen kisses was not the most respectful of prayers, but he prayed it nonetheless.

"Mr. Darcy, welcome back to Longbourn. I do not believe you have seen the gardens in spring. May I show you the buds and blooms before we have tea?"

Thank you, Lord! I swear my prayers will have more wholesome intentions from now on! He leaned forward and whispered with a sly grin on his face, "I would love to see your buds and blooms." Shock at such a daring comment registered on her face, but she did not blush. Instead she raised an eyebrow at him in her saucy manner, and he leaned back, basking in her beauty again.

How could he have possibly won her hand? How could he possibly deserve such a woman? How could he possibly have found true love when he did not even know he was looking for it? As she pushed him out to the back gardens, he bowed his head and silently gave a short, respectful prayer of gratitude.

And then, as soon as they were out of sight, he took her in his arms and held her close. He could smell the lavender in her hair. She sat there on his lap, cuddled, for many minutes. He rubbed her back and played with the curls at the nape of her neck. She arched her neck up to him, and she nestled her face into his neck, sending shivers and goose bumps throughout his body.

He suddenly was struck with the realization that her father could come across them at any moment. He had promised to keep his hands to himself. He did not want to jeopardize any future opportunities to be alone with her. He cleared his throat and let out a sigh. "Elizabeth, I am afraid your father—"

"—is helping a tenant fix a fence. And I am sure Mamma has not finished spreading the good news of our engagement. She was so frustrated she could not go out because of the rain. And since Mary, Lydia, and Kitty were anxious to see Aunt Phillips, that just leaves Jane and I at home. And since Bingley accompanied you here, I doubt that they will come looking for us."

"And what about Colonel Fitzwilliam? Are we really going to desert him so quickly?"

"Ah, but he and I came to an agreement. He has agreed to let me torture the truth out of you in any way I deem necessary."

"The truth?"

"Yes. It seems you have vital information about Lady Catherine and her love match. It was quite effective in making her desist from her scheme to have me arrested."

"I see. So, how exactly are you going to torture me?" he asked grinning.

She could hear his smile and looked up to see the dimples she loved so much. She reached her fingers up and touched his cheeks. "Hmmm, I have my ways. I could do this," she said and ran her fingers through his dark curls. "Or I could do this," she whispered and kissed the corner of his chin under his ear.

"I do not fold easily, my dear."

"Are you saying I should stop? Is there no hope?" she said teasingly, as she adjusted his cravat and managed to run her palms across his upper chest.

He closed his eyes and moaned slightly. "I do have my weaknesses," he whispered, savoring the sensation of having her touch him. And suddenly her lips were on his. His body responded on instinct and pulled her to him, devouring her lips and face with his own.

*****

Mr. Darcy did come to his senses. He could kiss her forever like that. He could, as she put it, atone for the sins of his aunt, until the sun went down. Even though they weren't technically his sins, he didn't argue the point; he was happy to apologize to such an extent that one would call his repentance efforts entirely thorough. They did have a few good laughs between kisses when she told him of the crisis that had occurred. She was lively in her mockery of Aunt Catherine's efforts to trap her in supposed thievery. She was especially descriptive about how the colonel's threats to disclose the story of her love match had affected his aunt's countenance.

Finally, Mr. Darcy conceded, "Elizabeth, you have successfully knocked down any resistance I might have had. I am butter in your hands. Let us go inside. No doubt my cousin is feeling awfully lonely with Bingley and your sister, who are probably so engrossed in each other that they have completely forgotten his presence. I owe him a great deal, and this story will make up for all his trouble. In fact, even though he has been so attentive during my recovery, I am confident this story will more than repay my debt."

She gave him one last kiss and removed her arms from around his neck and stood up. "Very well," she smiled. She pushed him into the house where they did indeed find Colonel Fitzwilliam sitting separate from the courting pair, quietly reading a book. Jane and Bingley were huddled close, her hand in his. Elizabeth was thrilled to see such a tender moment between her sister and Bingley. *It will not be long until he proposes.*

Mr. Darcy cleared his throat, effectively gaining the attention of those in the room. "I have been told that if I do not cooperate, I shall be left a lone man in an empty church on June 13. To avoid that fate, I will reveal a story that might just curl your toes."

He paused for dramatic affect before continuing. Elizabeth sat next to him and held his hand. "I first learned of this story from my mother when I was twelve, the week before she died. She called me to her room, where she sat pale and weak. I remember feeling as if she had some great wisdom to bestow on me, and I memorized every word she said.

"As you know, my mother was the younger sister of Aunt Catherine. And as Aunt Catherine never tired of telling everyone, my mother wanted me to marry her daughter, Anne. Supposedly they had planned the match since our infancy. My mother disclosed to me that day that she, in fact, did not want me to marry Anne and never had.

"When I asked her why, she started to cough excessively, and it took her several minutes to calm herself. My mother then revealed that her sister Catherine was not who she seemed to be. This news, of course, was both surprising and intriguing because even at the young age of twelve, I knew Aunt Catherine was a fearsome woman.

"My mother told me her parents had been unable to have children for many years, which left the estate without an heir. My grandfather, unfortunately, spent time with other women, including a young servant girl who was merely fourteen. As you can probably guess, the girl became with child, and my grandmother, already shamed that she could not produce an heir, resorted to hiding the girl in the country and faking a pregnancy of her own. The plan was to adopt the girl's child as their own.

"My grandmother did just that, and Catherine was born. Three years later my grandmother finally conceived your father, Richard, and two years later, my mother. My grandparents were thrilled that there now was a true heir, and their preference was sadly shown. Catherine was nothing but a child at the time, but she could tell she was different. She tried to regain her parents' affection, but it did little good. This, of course, led her to behave in more and more eccentric ways because it seemed that was the only way Catherine would get any attention from her parents.

"When Catherine was twelve, her parents told her of her true parentage without disclosing the identity of her birth mother. They sent her to school, where she was left alone to work through the emotional shock. My mother was seven at the time and remembers Catherine coming home from school for holidays. On one such holiday, my mother found Catherine in the barn kissing a stableman who was much older than her. She ran and told my grandparents.

"Catherine was again sent off to school. This time she was not allowed to return until the following year. When she did return, she was rude and cold to my mother. She would tease her, pulling her hair and hiding her dolls, all the while playing the role of the dutiful daughter in front of their parents. However, her antics were noticed, and she was sent back to school. Catherine's birthday came and went without any acknowledgement.

"When summer came, Catherine begged her parents to let her come home for the summer. By now my mother was nearly ten years old, and she noticed the strained relationship between her parents and her oldest sister. Catherine, however, had learned to hold her chin up high.

"At the end of that summer, Catherine announced to her parents that she was in love with the stable hand and they wanted to marry. Grandfather was furious and, of course, refused to allow such a thing to occur. Here is where the story gets good. Apparently, to make matters worse, the stable hand was the brother of her birth mother—her uncle—but Grandfather never told her that."

Gasps erupted from the room, but Darcy continued, "Catherine was sent back to school and wrote home daily about how she loved this man, begging Grandfather to let her marry him. After a few months, she wrote home to tell him that she was pregnant and now she *must* be allowed to marry him. Grandfather took her out of school and brought her home. He finally disclosed to Catherine the identity of her birth mother. He told her that the man she loved, and had been intimate with, was truly her uncle.

"Catherine was indeed pregnant, and was sent off to a quiet country estate to have her baby. When the baby was born, Grandfather found a decent home for it, and Catherine came back home. Instead of being sent off to school again, she was assigned a companion and private tutors. In her parents' eyes, Catherine was to be watched closely and could not be trusted.

"Catherine reformed her ways and never was anything but proper and obedient. Her parents began to trust her again. Enough time had passed uneventfully that it was clear the pregnancy had gone undiscovered. They had thwarted a public disgrace.

"So, Catherine made her curtsy in front of the queen and went to every ball and soiree imaginable for four years. Finally, Sir Lewis de Bourgh showed interest in Catherine. Grandfather arranged the marriage. One week before the wedding was to occur, Catherine visited home one last time. She was found to have reunited with her lover and uncle—the very week before her wedding!

"Grandfather was furious and thought the only way to teach her a lesson was to tell her betrothed of her true parentage and her hidden pregnancy, as well as her most recent indiscretions. Our uncle, Sir Lewis, took the news hard, but instead of breaking the engagement, he said he still wanted to marry Catherine. A few months into the marriage, Catherine was pregnant again but lost the baby. It was many years before she conceived again. Sir Lewis had given up hope for an heir, and they no longer shared a bedroom.

"One spring, after visiting her parents for Christmas, Catherine announced that she was pregnant again. Sir Lewis, of course, knew the baby was not his, but he accepted the child anyway. Yes, I can see from the looks on your faces that you gather my meaning. Catherine was unfaithful to her husband over the Christmas visit, once again with the stable hand, her uncle. Anne's true father is also her great-uncle.

"Sir Lewis told my mother the whole story when Catherine started spreading rumors that my mother and Catherine had planned for Anne and me to marry. He did not want Anne to marry her cousin after having such a close relationship to her biological father. He always felt Anne's poor health was a result of her biological parentage. So, while he was alive, Sir Lewis was always able to keep Catherine from exerting too much control over Anne because he knew these secrets about his wife's past and the identity of Anne's true father.

"Unfortunately, our uncle died suddenly, and from what I was told by my father, quite suspiciously as well. A dismissed butler paid a visit to my uncle, your father, Richard, and confirmed that our aunt was really the cause of her husband's death. She would not give him some medication that the doctor had prescribed, and he died."

Having finished his tale, Darcy leaned back against the chair and looked at all the dumbfounded looks on all their faces. The room was entirely too silent. He let out a chuckle. "Good Lord! It was not a ghost story! Now I find it rather amusing, myself, but I imagine my face looked much like all of yours when I first heard it." He looked over at Elizabeth, who had tears in her eyes.

Elizabeth quietly said, "It is such a sad story. No wonder Lady Catherine is so heartless. She was never loved by her parents!"

"And to realize," Jane whispered, "that her heart belonged to someone she could never have!"

Colonel Fitzwilliam scoffed, "Yes, but it did not stop her from returning time and time again to be with her uncle! That is not right! How could she do such a thing? I shudder to think of it!"

Bingley only shook his head.

"So," Darcy finished, "now you know the deep, dark secrets of Aunt Catherine, and what I have held in confidence all these years. I do not even think that Anne knows, although I should probably tell her so that she has the power to exert some control over her life. I feel for Anne sometimes; my aunt has sheltered her and coddled her for her whole life. But at least I know that Aunt Catherine treasures her and loves her. After all, she is the love child of that stable hand she so dearly loved."

Elizabeth then had a sudden spark of memory and asked, "William, you never did tell me about why you were late the day we left Kent. How did she delay you?"

Darcy laughed. "It was everything but nothing. Aunt Catherine insisted she check my trunks herself because she did not trust the servants to pack my things, even though Abbott has been doing it for years. Then she insisted that I say goodbye to Anne, and that delayed us for a quarter of an hour. Then she made us wait for a basket of food from Rosings, which took another quarter of an hour, and then when it came, she decided that the food was not to her liking and sent it back.

"After an hour of strange demands and requests, she gave up and let us go. To be honest, I think she was feeling bad that she had tried to force me into marrying Anne. It was her way of trying to apologize without admitting she was wrong."

The colonel laughed and slapped his leg. "Darcy, are you still delusional?" he said. "This is Aunt Catherine we are talking about! I do not think she has a lick of remorse in her body. Did the story you just told leave you any doubt?"

"Perhaps you are right. She did seem to act very oddly however."

Elizabeth said, "I think I may know the real purpose of all those efforts to delay you. She wanted to search your belongings for that book! No wonder she knew I had not given it to you! All those other things she did were to mask her real purpose. And it worked.

"You, sir, were searched! I must agree with Colonel Fitzwilliam and say that she felt no remorse. Certainly her behavior today was indicative of her scheming ways. She was looking for an excuse to break our engagement, and that was the last option she had, or at least I hope so. It was not pleasant going head to head with her all alone, and I pray I never shall again."

Darcy smiled and squeezed her hand and said, "Yes, dear, and I believe I have apologized profusely for my relation's behavior already." He gave her a knowing look that made her blush deeply.

The conversation went on for several more minutes with everyone expressing how they felt about the actions and history of Lady Catherine. The Bennets trickled home, and the gentlemen were invited to stay for dinner, which, of course, they accepted.

*****

Bingley proposed two days later, and Jane was thrilled. Mr. Bennet did not sport with Bingley as he had with Darcy, which was a great relief to Bingley. Mrs. Bennet was beyond reason and could not stop repeating, "Two daughters married! And to such fine, wealthy men!" Darcy and Elizabeth were more than pleased with the outcome of their matchmaking efforts, but they were even more ecstatic when Jane and Bingley approached them about sharing a wedding day. Both couples could not have been more pleased to share such a blessed day with their favorite sister and best friend.

And so a daily routine was created. For the next several weeks, either the gentlemen visited Longbourn or the ladies were invited to Netherfield, the latter being the preference of both couples. The weather complied, and they spent every day together. Both parties conveniently found ways to offer the other couple a few moments alone each day. Bingley and Jane used the time to discuss important decisions and steal a few chaste kisses; Elizabeth and Darcy found ways to argue with each other, thus forcing them to seek for forgiveness from each other—a favorite moment for both of them.

Elizabeth would push Darcy around the gardens and find a secluded place to climb up on his lap, wrap her arms around his neck, and run her fingers through his hair, which she found he especially liked. Darcy discovered that, even in the presence of others, he could drive her mad by caressing her hand and drawing circles on them with his fingers. There were a few moments where one or the other had to reign in their kisses, but as promised to her father, Darcy kept his hands from deflecting to Rome or Russia—a feat that was more difficult at some moments than others.

Darcy made time to spend with Mr. Bennet; he found his future father-in-law quite entertaining, and, in so doing, he learned a little more about what made Elizabeth so unique. He didn't mind the jabs and jokes about his memory, which he still had not completely regained.

The first few days after the accident were still a blur. Occasionally he asked Elizabeth about that time. She kept saying he should read her journal, but she never actually offered it to him. He sensed that she was not ready to share her thoughts from that time. He concluded she still felt bad about the manner of her refusals, so he resigned himself to the memory gap and tried not to push her for details.

Madeline massaged his foot every day. She would flex the muscles, point his toes, and carefully rotate the ankle. Most days he had no pain. It only ached when it was going to rain; he became quite accurate in predicting meteorological events. Madeline encouraged him to put a little weight on it several times a day, just until it began to hurt. According to Mr. Cummings's estimation, he had just two more days before he could put his full weight on it. He stopped wearing the splint altogether and tolerated putting on his boots as long as Abbott did it slowly. All the progress was encouraging.

On the first of June, Darcy decided he'd had enough of the wheeled chair. After Abbott put on his boots, he asked Madeline to stand him up on both his feet.

"Lean mostly on the left," Madeline cautioned, "until we can see how you tolerate the pressure. Good. Now slowly rock back and forth from left to right. Good. How does that feel?"

"It feels tight, but it is not painful."

She kneeled down and adjusted the angle of the foot. "There. Now try to place all your weight on the right foot."

"It actually feels good to use it." Darcy started to lift his left foot off the ground and put his hand on the wall to balance himself. He grinned from ear to ear. "I think I am finally able to walk. Shall we try?"

Madeline stood and placed her arm under his right arm and said, "Flexing your foot while walking may be tricky, since it is so stiff, but you can take a few steps."

The pressure and tightness increased as he pushed off to step forward. His calves felt tight as well, like they were on the verge of a spasm. "I feel it, but it is still not painful. Let us go all the way across the room." Madeline led him across the room, and he felt her studious eyes evaluating him. "I am well. Indeed, I am well." Madeline cautiously let go of his arm and let him take a few steps without her. His grin widened.

"Try gently bouncing a little to stretch out the muscles."

He did as he was instructed and could feel a slight twinge of pain shoot up his leg. "Well, that hurt a little. But otherwise, I think I can walk."

"I would take it easy for the next few days. Only walk for short periods, and do not go too far away from somewhere that offers a place to sit. It will fatigue easily. And I would stay away from stairs for a little while."

"What about horses?" he grinned.

"No, definitely not yet. The task of stepping into the stirrups would be too much right now. Keep pushing its flexibility until you feel it stretch. Release it as soon as you feel pain. Let pain be your guide."

Darcy felt like a new man. Finally he could embrace Elizabeth like a man instead of holding her on his lap. Finally he would be able to look down into her eyes. He was thrilled. It had been nearly six full weeks, and very long ones at that. He was overcome with gratitude that he had survived such an accident with little problems afterwards. He could feel his excitement building.

He carefully turned around, walked back to Madeline and took her hand, bowing over it and bestowing a kiss on it briefly. "Thank you! Thank you so much for your help. You have been so knowledgeable and patient. But those are not your only strengths. You are thoughtful, kind, generous, and have a certain spark about you that captivates people. No wonder you and Elizabeth got along so well from the beginning. How can I ever repay you?"

Madeline blushed and then blushed harder when she realized she had blushed. It wasn't like her to be so self-conscious. She could usually do her job and fulfill the tasks required of her without becoming attached, but this patient seemed to have found a special place in her heart—not romantically, just sentimentally. To see Elizabeth fall in love with him in front of her eyes had been a priceless opportunity. To witness such a miraculous recovery was wonderful. To feel like she was a part of a family again was emotionally moving, and she could feel her eyes tear up.

Mr. Darcy offered her his handkerchief and asked again, "How can I repay you? I do not know how you feel about Derbyshire, but the doctor there is new and could use an experienced nurse. I wrote to him about you two weeks ago, and he has responded that he indeed has a need for experienced help. I know Elizabeth would like it if you came with us to Pemberley. There is an elderly widow living on the estate who often misplaces her things or wanders out into the dark at night; she could use someone to help her.

"I do not want to pressure you into something you do not want to do," he continued, "but please say you will come. I know Elizabeth and I will eventually have children, and we will need a good nurse."

"Thank you, sir, but you do not need to feel obligated to help me," Madeline smiled. She sighed and then continued, "I too will feel the loss of Elizabeth's friendship. I feel so blessed to have been a part of such a love affair as yours has been. It has truly been wonderful to watch. It certainly made me hopeful that there really are good men who, although quite stubborn, will offer their hearts to the right women and treat them like the precious commodities they are."

"Did you just call me stubborn?"

"Perhaps a better word is persistent," she smiled.

"Persistent, I like. I can be persistent. But I am in earnest in offering you a place at Pemberley. Please consider it. Mr. Jacobson has several patients who could use your help. May I ask where you normally live?"

"I do not have a family, sir. I live where I am needed."

"Then please come to Pemberley. Be part of our family," Darcy said. "We need you. What can I say to persuade you?"

"Well," Madeline said, "after hearing Wordsworth's poems for so many weeks, I admit I have a great desire to see the North."

"Wonderful! I shall write to him immediately. But please stay until the wedding. Without you, it may not have occurred."

"Certainly. I would not miss it for anything."

*****

Elizabeth gasped, "Truly? You can walk now? Oh, William!" She picked up her skirts and ran into his outstretched arms. She could smell his clean-shaven face and neck, and she felt his arms encircle her lovingly. She laid her head on his chest, and he rested his chin on the top of her head.

"From that response, I assume you thought my foot would never heal." She pulled away slightly to look up to him, but he held her closer. "Just let me hold you. I have wanted to embrace you like this for so long. I cannot put into words how I feel at the moment. You are everything to me, Elizabeth. I do not know how I could have survived without you." He wrapped his arms tighter around her and smelled her hair. He felt his heart pound hard in his chest, and he whispered out loud his prayer of thanks.

"Dear Lord, I pray that if you ever put me in harm's way again, that I will have Elizabeth to see me through it. I pray that you will protect her from my prideful nature and help her to see how valuable she is to me. Help her to know that the love I have for her can never be measured, for it is infinite. Help her to never stop challenging me to be a better man than I was, better than I am now, and better than I ever hoped I could be. Help her to know how desperately I need her in my life.

"I promise, Lord, that I will go through anything, any trial, as long as I have Elizabeth by my side. Help me to stay humble and to always be observant of her needs. Forgive me for loving her more than life itself. Forgive me for having no greater priority than Elizabeth.

"I pray, Lord, that you guide my words and actions so that I will always be there for her. Our hearts have melded into one great whole, and I am afraid that neither one of us could possibly survive without the other. I am so grateful that I have finally won her hand and have a lifetime to be with her. And lastly, I pray that I will always be this persistent, for I have learned how valuable a trait it is." He felt her giggle against his chest and he smiled as well.

She looked up at his dimpled cheeks and said, "I do not know a more stubborn man. What kind of a prayer is that?"

"Not stubborn, persistent. And it is about time you admit that my persistence paid off." He leaned down and kissed her forehead, then brushed his cheek against it tenderly, feeling her soft skin on his face.

"Am I to assume you feel it was your persistence that made me change my mind?"

He pulled away slightly and grinned, "Was it not?"

She shook her head. "I did promise to tell you what you said in your thirteenth proposal that finally made me accept you."

"Indeed you did. Shall we sit on that bench, and you can enlighten me? I do want to know the best methods to use to change your mind. I am sure there will come a time when I will need to persuade you to do something else.

"For example, I may have to convince you to stop looking at me that way, or you shall be kissed beyond coherent reasoning, no matter who is watching us. Or, I may need to persuade you to let your hair down, and let me run my fingers through it the way you run your

315

fingers through mine so expertly. Or, I may need to alter your belief in my exceptional self-control. Or, perhaps I will someday need to—"

"Enough already!" she laughed. "I take your meaning. I will do my best at explaining my reasoning in accepting your thirteenth proposal." She led him to the bench, and they sat down; she noticed he walked stiffly, but he did not seem to be in pain. They sat together; he placed his arm around her shoulders as she leaned into him. They stayed like that for several silent, precious moments. She then sat up and very methodically started unpinning her hair. She saw his eyes track her fingers as lock by lock fell past her shoulders. His eyes went dark, and he sighed.

"You look beautiful with your hair down."

"Yes, I have heard that before."

"Should I be jealous? What man has seen you with your hair down and told you that you were beautiful?"

"I do not think it is possible for you to be jealous of this man." She let out a little giggle.

He arched his eyebrow up at her. "Then I am assuming this man was me?" She nodded. "When did I see you with your hair down? Surely I would remember such a sight."

"I believe it was right after your third proposal. It was the first day you woke up, and it had been a very emotionally trying day. I had not taken the time to properly pin my hair that morning, and I had not even noticed that it had fallen out. You had that same dreamy look in your eyes."

He raised his hands up toward her head. "May I?" he asked. She smiled warmly at him, and he took that as permission. He started at the bottom and wound the lower curls around his fingers, feeling the silkiness in his hands. He lifted the ends up to his face to smell, closing his eyes as he brushed her hair across his face. He then dropped the ends and carefully placed his hands on either side of her head, slowly moving his fingers through the chocolate-colored curls.

She smiled at him again. He continued running his hands through her hair over and over again. Each time he came to the ends, he went right back up to the top and repeated the motion. It was so soft and silky in his fingers. It intrigued him and stimulated him in such a way that he was mesmerized. He was completely distracted and did not notice that she had closed her eyes until she tilted her head and leaned into him.

He had never felt such intimacy with her, and his lips came down firmly on hers. He kissed her, and ran his fingers through her hair, which made the kisses all the more enjoyable. He deepened the kiss, feeling her relax under his hands. He grasped her shoulders and brought her to him, clinging to her like he had never clung to her before. Their lips were in unison, every movement he made, she responded to. Every urge she pressured him with, he appeased her. It was a long and wonderful kiss, one that felt new, yet familiar, at the same time.

He felt his heart give way under her ministrations, and he knew there was no other person in the world that could make him as happy as he was at the moment. *Only twelve more days and I can love every part of her!* His hands returned to her hair, and grasped her head once again to create a stronger connection. His body was on fire, and her breathlessness was not lost to him; it only urged him on. He continued with the kiss as if it was the last he would have for many days. He did not want to stop. He could not stop. Having his hands in her hair was so overwhelming. He was shocked at the lack of self-control he felt.

Elizabeth realized her breathing was so fast that she was afraid she might faint. They had kissed many times before, sometimes for even longer, but not like this. She burned deep inside herself and wondered how in the world she was going to make it twelve more days. *Twelve more days!* If she didn't know her lips were quite preoccupied, she would have thought she had spoken those words aloud, for surely she heard them.

"Twelve more days," a rather disturbed Mr. Bennet repeated, clearing his throat loudly. He watched as the two jumped apart and released their grip on each other. He took a deep breath and saw both of their sheepish, flushed faces stare up at him. He stepped forward and stood directly in front of them. He opened his mouth to speak and then was struck dumb. *These poor, love-struck kids*, he thought. He was happy for them; he really was. He just wanted them to maintain propriety a little longer, but from what he witnessed, they would be hard-pressed to behave for twelve more days. He saw them both look down at their hands, embarrassed, and he sighed again.

"All I am going to say . . . no . . . from the looks on your faces, I do not need to say anything at all. I expect to see you inside soon." He raised his hand, waving a surrendering, dismissive gesture, and then turned and left. Setting boundaries was not his strength either. He would have to start working on his weaknesses.

The breathless couple watched as Mr. Bennet walked away shaking his head in laughter. Mr. Darcy watched as Elizabeth started pinning her hair. He leaned into her and said, "I am sorry. I do not know what came over me."

"I think I communicated my willingness effectively, so there is no need to apologize. But I do suggest we continue where we left off."

"I do not think your father would appreciate that."

She giggled, "Not the kisses! I mean I was going to tell you why I finally accepted your thirteenth proposal!"

He smiled back at her. "Of course. How could I have become so distracted? Do tell me; was it when I called myself a fool in love?"

"No, you did that in the fourth proposal as well. I have proof in a letter."

"I wrote you a letter?"

"Are you going to keep asking questions, or are you going to allow me to tell you what finally swayed me?"

"Very well, but first explain the letter. I am deeply curious. I proposed in a letter?"

She sighed, "Yes. After I wrote the reminder letter and showed it to you to sign, you asked me to write another letter for you. It was a love letter. You thought you were very sly in addressing it 'Dear Madam', but I knew it was for me. And yes, you really did call yourself a fool in love. Does that satisfy you, or do I need to expand upon the letter?"

"Do I get to read this proposal sometime? I would dearly love to see how I proposed." She put her hands on her hips impatiently. "Sorry, I will be quiet now. Proceed."

"The letter is part of my answer to your question. While dictating this love letter you stopped suddenly and asked me how I would like to be proposed to. I gave it some thought, and then I replied that if the man was someone that I did not like, it would not matter how the man proposed because I would not accept him. I told you that if I respected the man but did not love him, the method and words used to propose would matter a great deal, but I would still refuse him.

"I was shocked at my own answer because I had already had three proposals from you, and my emotional reactions to them were extreme, as I have told you. I suddenly realized that my feelings for you were not what I had thought all along. You see, I thought I truly disliked you. If that were the case, then the words you used to propose would not have mattered to me. But your words did matter; they did affect me. So, I was nearly struck dumb with the realization that I did respect you and that your words did matter, and that is why I had reacted so strongly to your poor attempts to win my hand." He opened his mouth to ask a question, but she put her finger on his lips and shushed him. "I know your next question, for you asked it then too. You want to know how I would like to be proposed to if I truly loved the man, am I correct?"

"Yes."

"My answer to you then and now, and ultimately the reason why I accepted your thirteenth proposal, is the same. If I really loved the man, it also would not matter how he proposed because I would accept him no matter what words or methods he used. So you see, the multiple proposals may have been flattering, and they certainly improved over time, but even the most charming proposal could not have made me accept your hand until I realized that I loved you. Only then could I accept your proposals, regardless of what you said. Indeed, no one could have changed my mind once I knew you were the one I wanted to be with, no matter how rude and offensive your proposal was.

"William, I love you. I am thrilled to know that we will always be together. On the day of the accident, a part of me willed you to live. I needed you then without even knowing it. You said in your thirteenth proposal that I am your better half. You are my better half too. I am so lucky to have earned your love and admiration."

He could not help himself, with his soon-to-be-father-in-law watching or not, he needed to hold her. He pulled her up onto his lap and whispered in her ear, "I will love you forever and always." He kissed her hair and whispered, "I am not sure what I like better, having you on my lap or hugging you standing up. I shall have to do plenty of both." He heard her confirmation and agreement. He continued because he had so much to say. "I love you so much. I have not spent a single day since I met you without thinking about you. Tell me, when did you start loving me? You admitted that for at least the first three proposals you simply respected me but did not love me. When did it change?"

She reached up and placed a hand on his cheek. Then she gave him a soft kiss on his lips. "I cannot fix on the hour, or the spot, or the look . . . No, I take that back, I do know the look. It was your deep, penetrating gaze, the one that makes my heart race. I once misinterpreted it, but now I know it means so much more than any amount of words could express. But, I cannot tell you the hour, or the spot, or the words which laid the foundation for my love; I was in the middle before I knew that I had begun."

EPILOGUE

"I cannot believe tomorrow will be Christmas, Betty! My first Christmas with William!" Elizabeth said cheerfully. "What did you get Mr. Wilkinson?"

"Oh, nothing special. Nothing like what you are giving your husband."

Elizabeth sat down at the mirror and let Betty's hands work their magic. Her curls began to tame almost instantly. As she watched Betty in the mirror, Elizabeth remembered when she had asked William if she could pick her own lady's maid.

"*Do you have someone in mind?*" *he asked.*

"*I think so. She has a family of her own, so I do not know if she is willing. But we get along splendidly, she is a hard worker, and she has experience as a lady's maid.*"

William said, "Then I do not see the problem."

"*Well, it is a little complicated. Her husband would need a position as well. I was hoping you might know of a shop in Lambton that could use a clerk. He has worked in a milliner's shop for several years, and I hear he does a fine job.*"

"*The tailor in Lambton was looking for help a few months back. Perhaps I could inquire if the position still exists.*"

"*Would you do that for me?*"

"*I would do anything for you, Elizabeth. Have I not proven that already?*"

Remembering his kind words brought a smile to her face. She saw it reflected in the mirror and was once again so happy that Mrs. Wilkinson and her family had agreed to come to Pemberley. She looked up at Betty and asked, "Have I told you lately how glad I am that you are here?"

Betty stopped brushing and smiled back at Elizabeth in the mirror. "Yes, Mrs. Darcy, every day. Now let us get you ready so you can dazzle your husband all over again." She saw small tears of gratitude forming in Elizabeth's eyes. "No, no, no! If you cry, you will make your eyes red and puffy and ruin all my hard work. A strange way to show your gratitude!" Betty teased. Elizabeth wiped her eyes dry and giggled.

Mrs. Wilkinson put the finishing touches on her hair and continued, "You know how protective I am of my perfect results. I worked for years in that kitchen without success, but I am determined to maintain my flawless record as your lady's maid. So, when will you tell him?"

Elizabeth smiled widely and said, "I plan on doing it tomorrow morning. He will make a wonderful father."

"I have seen him take prodigious care of his wife, so I have no doubt of that."

Betty lifted a gown over her head and helped her into it. Elizabeth continued, "Hiding it from him has been the hardest thing I have ever done! I am not good at keeping secrets."

"True," Betty replied. "You are usually easy to read, but you have gotten better since we first met. Do not mistake my meaning: anyone who knows you well enough need not ask what you are thinking because your eyes and face still speak for you. But you are better now at restraining your tongue."

"Do you dare accuse me of losing my impertinence? Mr. Darcy loves that about me!" she teased.

"He also loves to have a wife at the breakfast table with him. Now let me get these last buttons so you can be on your way. You have guests today; it is your duty to be there to greet them."

"Well then, I suppose I must go," she smiled. "It is convenient that the mistress of Pemberley has such delightful, delicious duties."

Betty finished the buttons and looked at Elizabeth with a smile. "There. Now you look like the mistress of Pemberley. And a very fine one you are. I know how hard you have worked, dear. You have really risen to the challenge."

Elizabeth gave Betty her best smile and hugged her. "Thank you," she said as her eyes started to well up again.

"No, no time for that!" Betty giggled. "Hurry along. I think they have already started."

Elizabeth waved goodbye and ventured out of her chambers to the dining room. Most of her guests were already there. "Excuse me for being tardy. I am so glad you did not wait for me." She kissed Darcy on the cheek and smiled at everyone in the room.

"Good morning, Elizabeth," Richard said. He had his arm around his wife, Deborah, and she was looking at him as if he had hung the moon. A month after Elizabeth and William's wedding, they had returned from their honeymoon tour of the Lake District to find a very agitated Colonel Fitzwilliam at Pemberley. She remembered well the conversation that followed.

"I did not realize you would be returning today! What good luck!" said the colonel. Elizabeth was surprised; his words were jovial, but his voice was tight with concern and he seemed distracted. "I just arrived yesterday. I am on my way to Scotland," he continued.

Darcy noticed the change in demeanor as well. "Military duties?"

"No, it is of entirely different matter. You could say it is personal."

William's brows furrowed. "Whatever is the matter, Richard? Are you unwell?" he asked. Richard shook his head. "Would you like to join me in my study for a glass of brandy?"

"I would indeed like some brandy, but I do not require privacy. Elizabeth already is familiar with my problem."

Elizabeth was even more surprised. She could not remember ever having seen the colonel so rattled. She followed them into the study, where she heard the most exciting news since Jane and Bingley's engagement.

"Deborah is not married," the colonel said. He ran his fingers through his hair and continued, "She is widowed."

Elizabeth gasped.

Her husband looked confused. "Who is Deborah?" He poured some brandy and offered the colonel a glass.

Richard took the glass and smiled thoughtfully. "She is the only lady I have ever wanted to marry," he said. "You met her once at the Fredrick's ball on New Year's Eve many years ago, too long ago for you to even remember."

"Was she the redhead you could not take your eyes off? Miss . . . Hopper?"

"Miss Harper. Now it is Mrs. Samuelson. She married four years ago but was widowed last year."

Elizabeth asked excitedly, "Then, have you seen her? Is she well?" Her husband looked at her quizzically, wondering why she understood the significance of the conversation while he did not.

Colonel Fitzwilliam sighed. He ran his fingers through his hair again and then straightened his waistcoat. "I am on my way. That was my purpose in coming north. I do not know whether to feel anxious or elated. Cousin, she has no fortune, and her connections are few, but you counseled me once to not worry about what society dictates. I am going after her. If she will have me, I shall not delay my offer of marriage. As you once put it so succinctly, 'Duty be damned!' I am going after the only woman I ever loved, and there is not a thing anyone can do or say to stop me."

Darcy grinned and stole a glance at his wife before asking, "Then why are you sipping brandy in my study? If you truly plan on winning her heart, go, man! Did you learn nothing from my efforts to win Elizabeth's hand? Time is of the essence."

"You are right! I should leave this instant!" He put down his drink and bowed to Elizabeth. "I only hope my tenacity is as strong as

Darcy's. If he was able to win your hand after that awful first proposal, surely I can charm my way back into Deborah's good graces."

Elizabeth leaned over and embraced Richard. *"I am so happy for you,"* she said. *"But we prefer to call William persistent."*

"Is that so? Well, his persistence certainly paid off. I shall write as soon as I have news."

"We will impatiently await word from you. Go find Deborah," Darcy said slapping him on the shoulder.

Colonel Fitzwilliam looked at Elizabeth and said, *"Elizabeth, do you remember our talk about storms?"*

"Yes, I do."

"Do you remember describing the love you wanted in your marriage?"

"Yes. I wanted the kind of love that makes you want to be with someone at all times. The kind of love that burns like a fever when they touch you. The kind of love that makes you blind to all their imperfections. The kind of love that can never be reproduced or deflected."

"Very good. Your memory is spot on. I know because I wrote it down that night. As soon as I heard Deborah was widowed, I remembered your words; I realized that the love I have for her can never be reproduced or deflected. I knew I had to find her. In fact, I must find her right now. Excuse me." The colonel then left in a hurry.

Less than three weeks later Richard wrote informing them that Deborah had accepted his proposal. The wedding took place in late August at Pemberley. The Darcys were delighted to host such a happy event.

Watching the newlyweds look at each other and brush hands whenever they could brought a smile to Elizabeth's face. William's voice startled her out of the thoughts.

"And what are you grinning about, my dear?"

She leaned in and whispered, "I am so thrilled that Richard found a woman who loves him. I was just thinking about that day he told us he was going to find her."

Darcy looked at the happy couple. "Yes, he was quite determined. Now look at him. He has someone who looks at him the way I look at you." He put his hand on her waist and pulled her into him and kissed her. A few people in the room cleared their throats loudly.

Georgiana laughed and said, "My apologies, ladies and gentlemen. My brother and his wife have no shame. They do it all the time. It is best to get used to it."

The butler came in and announced, "Mr. and Mrs. Jacobson are here. Shall I show them in?"

Darcy answered, "Yes, Reynolds, show them in."

Another set of newlyweds came in with rosy cheeks from the cold and arms full of packages. Elizabeth quickly walked across the room and took the packages and put them on the table. "Madeline! I am so glad you could come! How was the ride over?"

"It was a little slick from last night's storm, but it was still manageable. And how are you?"

Elizabeth knew she was asking about the pregnancy. Only Betty, Madeline, and Madeline's husband, Mr. Jacobson, knew her good news, so Elizabeth made her reply as discreet as possible. "I had a touch of a stomach ailment a while ago, but it is much better now. However, I am sleeping a great deal more than I used to. I am told fatigue is fairly common in cases such as mine."

Then she slyly looked around the room. When she saw that no one but Mr. Jacobson and Madeline were listening, she whispered, "I felt the quickening a few days ago, and it took all my willpower to not jump out of my chair and tell William!"

Madeline smiled and leaned in to kiss her on the cheek, "Well, dear, middle of May it is! Congratulations! I hope to be blessed with such a malady myself, but we have only been married for three weeks, so I believe I will have to spend some time in anticipation."

Richard's loud voice interrupted, "So, this is the famous Mr. Jacobson, the doctor of Lambton! And, of course, Madeline, or should I call you Mrs. Jacobson?"

"Colonel, you have always called me Madeline, and I would not have it any other way. Let me introduce you to my husband. Colonel Fitzwilliam, this is Doctor Frank Jacobson. Frank, this is Colonel Richard Fitzwilliam, Mr. Darcy's cousin I told you about."

Mr. Jacobson reached out and shook Richard's hand. "It is a pleasure to meet you."

Richard grinned and asked, "So, which one of you will tell me how you two ended up married?"

Madeline laughed and said, "It was not a love story like the Darcys, but it was a love story nonetheless. I came here to assist him in his work. He introduced me to the chronically ill patients whom he treated on his rounds. The moment he asked me my opinion on how to treat a patient's arthritis, I knew he was the most humble man I had ever met. Here he was a doctor, had been to university, yet he was asking me for *my* opinion! I admired him from the beginning, but it took him four months to notice me in that way."

Dr. Jacobson flushed red and smiled. "You know that is not true," he replied. "I was just afraid to risk our nurse-doctor relationship—it was working so well. The truth is I was besotted with Madeline the moment we were introduced and found any opportunity to employ her help. I am ashamed to admit that the patients she took care of got a great deal of attention from me. I visited them much more often than any others."

Elizabeth watched them exchange loving glances and stepped in as hostess. "Come in and break your fast. Madeline, you know the Bingleys, but I believe your husband has not met them. Let me introduce you."

*****

That evening, after Georgiana's special Christmas Eve musical medley, Darcy entreated Elizabeth to play. She sat down and flipped through her music for several minutes, trying to decide what to perform. She could sense rather than see that her husband was right behind her. With no pianoforte to accompany him, he started to sing the Italian love song they had sung together at Netherfield. He placed his hand on her shoulder, and she felt the warmth radiate through her. At that exact moment her baby fluttered inside her, and her heart started to race. She looked up at him. Upon seeing him singing so intimately, she blushed.

She placed her hands on the keys and picked up playing where he was singing. When it came time for her to sing, she was already moved with so much gratitude for having the love of such a man that her voice shook with a little too much vibrato. She took another breath and continued to sing about stolen kisses in the moonlight and a lover whose arms ached to hold her true love. William went around to the front of the pianoforte and leaned over, resting his arms on the instrument, and continued singing, all the while looking at her with longing and admiration. She knew that look. And it affected her like it always had.

The rest of the evening was full of laughter, and everyone was excited for the next morning. When it came time to retire, William offered his arm and said, "Mrs. Darcy, may I show you to your room?"

"Hmmm, I know that look in your eyes."

He grinned widely, showing his dimples.

"And I know that smile too."

"You know, I have always wondered something. Why did you agree to the deception? I mean, you are the most honest person I know, yet you allowed Madeline, Richard, and Mr. Cummings to convince you to play along with the proposals. Would it not have been easier to write in the reminder letter that I had already proposed? It would have spared you many days of my minimally charming, perhaps awkward, and very possibly disastrous proposals day after day."

"Not all of them were disastrous, William. A few were entertaining."

"Really? Well, I am glad to hear it," he said. He paused before continuing. "But why did you not just tell me I had already proposed?"

"It was Madeline who convinced me to play along. She told me that if you kept proposing, eventually one of two things would happen. Either you would give up—"

"That never would have happened."

"I know."

"Or?"

"Or you would turn into a man whom I wanted to accept."

"Madeline is wise beyond her years. So, since I did not give up, am I to assume I turned into a man you wanted to accept?"

"You never really changed. I think I did most of the changing. When I realized how badly I had misjudged you, my eyes were opened to the man you really were. I saw a kind, loving, loyal, and wonderful man who was everything I wanted in my husband." They reached her door, and he led her into the room. She had dismissed Betty early in the day, so she could spend it with her family, which left her alone with her husband.

They took their time helping each other out of their garments, but it was no chore, for each enjoyed the other's caresses and loving touches. They dressed in their night clothes, then he brought her over to the chair, and she curled up onto his lap like they had done so many times while his foot was broken. He rubbed her back and played with her curls while she snuggled up into his neck, one hand resting on his exposed chest. It was a pastime that they seemed to do every night, one that they both treasured. When he could tell she had fallen asleep, he picked her up and tucked her into their bed. He kissed her forehead and whispered, "Goodnight, my love."

*****

"Merry Christmas, William!" Elizabeth was almost giddy to give her husband his presents. He moaned and rolled over in bed, but his eyes remained closed. "Hmmm, what must I do to awaken my husband? Is not celebrating our first Christmas enough enticement to wake him?"

She could see he was holding back a smile; his adorable dimples were threatening to expose themselves. She climbed under the covers and slid her hands up his chest onto his neck, and she ran her fingers through his hair in the same manner she had perfected. As expected, he moaned, and a broad, dimpled smile graced his handsome features.

She leaned down intending to kiss him once, but large, masculine arms captured her, and his lips made it quite clear that he was awake. She relaxed into his embrace and let their lips do the communicating for a moment, but her excitement was too strong. She pulled away and squirmed out of his arms. She grabbed the two packages and placed them on his chest.

He most definitely was not finished. He brushed the packages off and pounced on her, trapping her beneath him, her arms pinned at her sides. "Who dares wake me from my slumber?" he growled. He leaned down and kissed her again, but she continued to giggle, making it very difficult to continue. He let her hands go and sat up, basking in her beauty. Even in the early morning hours, with her hair spread out on the pillow in disarray, she was the most amazing sight to see.

"Do you not want to know what your presents are? After all, it is our first Christmas together."

"Can we not wait to open presents downstairs with our guests? I do not want to open all my presents now and have nothing for later."

"Oh, these two are special. They are for your eyes only. I have other, more appropriate, presents for you to open in front of our guests." She picked up the presents and handed the larger one to him. "This one first."

"I will open this only if you let me give you your present early as well."

She squealed with delight. "Wonderful! Now open it!"

He felt it with his hands and tried to guess what it was. "A book?"

"No."

"It feels like a book."

"Oh, just open it!" She giggled again in anticipation.

He untied the string and set it aside and then started unwrapping it. He looked at it in confusion and then looked up at her. "A journal?"

She nodded and said, "More specifically, *my* journal for all of last year." She saw his eyes brighten, and that deep, penetrating look came into his eyes.

"Is this the journal you kept in Hunsford? Where you wrote down the proposals?"

"Yes, darling. I decided it was time for you to read for yourself. It will be simpler than trying to mischievously manipulate the information from me."

"Right. Mind games. You do not like them," he murmured. He looked down at the journal again and then back up at her. "Thank you, Elizabeth. My gift to you is a trip to Bath with Jane and Bingley next month—" Elizabeth squealed in excitement! "—but now I feel bad at seeing how much more thoughtful your present is."

Darcy continued his thanks, "I cannot wait to read this! I am excited to learn what your thoughts were then; although I am somewhat nervous to hear how beastly I was." He traced his fingers along her jawline and leaned down and kissed her tender flesh above the collarbone. She let out a slight sigh, but once again she pushed him away. He looked at her and asked, "What now? Can I not simply enjoy my wife on Christmas morning?"

331

She rolled over and picked up the other present. She squirmed back and handed it to him. He released his powerful, penetrating gaze and looked down at the second present on his lap. He sighed, obviously realizing that his desires would not be met until he opened it.

She watched his face for his reaction as he opened it. Confusion, shock, awareness . . . and yes! There it was! Excitement!

He looked up at her, "Is it . . ."

"Yes."

"Really?"

"Yes, dear."

"Truly?"

"Indeed."

"No . . ."

"Yes!"

"You are . . . ?"

"Yes!"

"When?"

"May."

He threw the crocheted booties off to the side and embraced her as if it were the moment she had first agreed to marry him. He gently placed his hand on her lower abdomen and smoothed out the gown to lay flat against her skin. Sure enough there was a slight swelling; he was shocked he hadn't noticed it before. How many times had he admired her body over the last six months? How many times in the last few weeks had he made love to her and not noticed the fullness of her breasts?

"Are you happy, William? Would you like a baby?"

"I could not be happier. I thought the day I married you would be the happiest day of my life, but now I have this feeling that I cannot describe. I am to be a father? I am so shocked! So soon? We have only been married for six and a half months! Oh, this is wonderful! I cannot wait to tell Richard! Oh! And Bingley! He and I had bets on who would become a father first!" Suddenly it hit him like a giant ocean wave . . . *a father*?

Elizabeth saw a look of fear suddenly cross his face. "What is it, William?"

"I am going to be a father! And you are going to be a mother!"

"Yes, that is usually how it works in marriage. What is wrong?"

"How in the world am I going to be a father? What if I say the wrong thing? What if I do it wrong? I want to be a good father . . ."

"Darling, one thing I have learned about you is that if you want something badly enough, you will find a way to achieve it."

He could tell where she was going with this. It was a frequent route of teasing, so he played his part. "Are you calling me stubborn?"

"No, dear, I am calling you persistent."

"Ah, yes, the term persistent is so much more flattering. It is much better than obstinate, or tenacious, or tireless."

"Or headstrong, or pig-headed, or determined . . ."

"I know, I know. When I am a man with a mission, I cannot be dissuaded."

She leaned in and kissed him passionately, and he responded in kind, leaving her entirely breathless. He once again moved his lips to her collarbone. She tried to speak, but her words came out in a whisper, "It is one of the things I love most about you. If you had not been so persistent, I may never have known such joy."

He murmured something into her neck that she knew from experience meant the time for talking was over.

THE END

If you enjoyed *Pride and Persistence*, please read other books by Jeanna Ellsworth

Mr. Darcy's Promise, published July 2013

To Refine Like Silver, publication planned for November 2014

Praise for *Mr. Darcy's Promise*

"This is a superbly written, highly romantic (while staying completely clean), funny and clever exploration of an alternative path for the classic story of Pride and Prejudice which is so loved all around the world."—Sophie Andrews, Laughing with Lizzie

" . . . I found this to be a memorable, endearing, and poignant variation."— Meredith Esparza, Austenesque Reviews

"Not only was it lighthearted in places, fun, serious, upsetting and very touching, it told a great story with meaning. It made me think, laugh and cry."—Janet Taylor, More Agreeably Engaged

"Mr. Darcy's Promise is a charming novel about a promise that is made to be broken and being patient when it comes to matters of the heart."—Anna Horner, Indie Jane

"The all time best P&P variation I have read. Characters were more true to Austen's interpretation than other stories. The book was very chaste but still tantalizing leaving certain events to your imagination."—Austen Fan 49

"I loved every second of it!!! A book that I most definitely will read over and over again!" — Elizabeth Willey

About the Author

Jeanna is a mother of three daughters, all of whom are well versed in all things *Pride and Prejudice*. She most definitely would say they are her best friends. She shares her best and worst days with them and they share theirs with her. She also proudly states she is the eighth of thirteen children. When she isn't scrapbooking, quilting, or cooking, she is thoroughly ignoring her house for a few hours at a time in order to read yet another fan fiction novel. Somewhere between being a mom, a sister, a cook, and a best friend, she squeezes in three 12-hour shifts a week as a Registered Nurse in a Neurological ICU. She raises chickens, helps her daughter run a rabbitry, and gardens as much as she can. In all her still-under-forty years, she has never claimed to be as happy as she is now. Out of this mindset came a surge of creativity that simply had to be written down. Since she finished her first book, *Mr. Darcy's Promise*, she has stated several times that she has gained something from it that no one can take away from her: hope for her own Mr. Darcy. More than anything, she hopes to prepare her three best friends to look for their own Mr. Darcy and to settle for nothing less.

31339451R00195

Made in the USA
Lexington, KY
10 April 2014